Poor Little Rich Girl

Katie Flynn has lived for man… -west.
A compulsive wr… s and
articles and man… dcast
on Radio Merseys… pool
series after hearin… bers
about life in the ci… ieth
century. She also v…

Praise for Katie Flynn

'Arrow's best and biggest saga author. She's good.'
Bookseller

'If you pick up a Katie Flynn book it's going to be a wrench to put down'
Holyhead & Anglesey Mail

'A heartwarming story of love and loss'
Woman's Weekly

'One of the best Liverpool writers'
Liverpool Echo

'Katie Flynn has the gift that Catherine Cookson had of bringing the period and the characters to life'
Caernarfon & Denbigh Herald

Also by Katie Flynn

A Liverpool Lass
The Girl from Penny Lane
Liverpool Taffy
The Mersey Girls
Strawberry Fields
Rainbow's End
Rose of Tralee
No Silver Spoon
Polly's Angel
The Girl from Seaforth Sands
The Liverpool Rose
The Bad Penny
Down Daisy Street
A Kiss and a Promise
Two Penn'orth of Sky
A Long and Lonely Road
The Cuckoo Child
Darkest Before Dawn
Orphans of the Storm
Little Girl Lost
Beyond the Blue Hills
Forgotten Dreams
Sunshine and Shadows
Such Sweet Sorrow
A Mother's Hope
In Time for Christmas

Katie Flynn

Poor Little Rich Girl

arrow books

20

Arrow Books
20 Vauxhall Bridge Road
London SW1V 2SA

Arrow Books is part of the Penguin Random House group of companies whose addresses can be found at global.penguinrandomhouse.com

Penguin
Random House
UK

First published by William Heinemann in 2002
First published in paperback by Arrow Books in 2002

www.penguin.co.uk

A CIP catalogue record for this book is available from the British Library.

Typeset by Palimpsest Book Production Ltd., Falkirk, UK

Penguin Random House is committed to a sustainable future for our business, our readers and our planet. This book is made from Forest Stewardship Council® certified paper.

FSC
www.fsc.org
MIX
Paper from responsible sources
FSC® C018179

Printed and bound in Great Britain by Clays Ltd, Elcograf S.p.A.

For Chris (née Stiffell) and Roy Smith
a very belated wedding present,
wishing you both every happiness

ACKNOWLEDGEMENTS

I am most grateful to Fr. Victor Walter of St Mary's Cathedral, Wrexham for pointing me in the right direction to discover what life was like in India in the 1930s and I am also grateful to Deb Macleod of Pritchard's Bookshops (in Formby and Crosby) for getting me the books I needed most. As usual I am indebted to the staff of the Wrexham Library and the Central Libraries, Liverpool, for all their help.

Prologue

March 1934

Hester Elliott leaned over the rail of the *Pride of India* and reflected that so far, she and young Leonora Hetherington-Smith had been fortunate. This was their first sea voyage and neither of them had felt ill once since leaving Bombay. Life on board ship, what was more, had been interesting enough to alleviate the boredom which might otherwise have attacked them, and, so far as she could judge, homesickness had not troubled them either.

Not, reflected Hester now, that she had a home in India any longer, for she could scarcely count the large house in which Mr Hetherington-Smith held sway. After her father's death some three months previously, Mr Hetherington-Smith had approached Hester, the child of his best friend, and suggested that unless she had other plans, she might move into his house and begin to get to know his small daughter. He had explained that he meant to send Lonnie home to Liverpool in England, to live with an aunt, and he would like Hester to take charge of her.

Hester had known that her father, Trevor Elliott, had meant to accompany his only child to England one day. Her mother, Kia, who had died when Hester was ten, had been anxious that her daughter should return to their home country when she was an adult. 'I am glad that your childhood has been spent in this beautiful country, that you have learned so much of the culture of the land of your birth, which would have been denied you in England, but once you are grown I believe, and so does your father, that life will be better for you if you go Home,' she had said.

Even now, the memory of that long-ago conversation made Hester smile. To be sure, her father was a native of Liverpool and had spent the first twenty-two years of his life in that city, but both she and her mother had been born and raised in India, had known no other home. Yet in common with all Anglo-Indians, they thought of England as 'Home' and indeed, when the heat of summer was at its height, Hester could understand their craving for a cooler, greener land, even though she only knew of it from books and the conversation of others.

The ship had docked at Alexandria after passing through the Suez Canal. Hester had been doubtful whether she should take young Lonnie ashore at a port famed for its vices, but Lonnie had had no such doubts. 'I'm sick of being cooped up in this wretched ship; I will go ashore, I will, I will!' she had announced, glaring at Hester as though the older girl was her most hated enemy. 'I know you are my governess, but you are still a servant and you will do as I say!'

It had been the first serious rift between them, though Lonnie, like most English children brought up by an Indian *ayah*, was both spoiled and arrogant. She was used to getting her own way and never considered the feelings of others and though Hester, at eighteen, was only ten years Lonnie's senior, she was beginning to realise that she would have to put her foot down and take command, or the younger girl would become impossible.

Accordingly, she had decided not to allow Lonnie to accompany the party going ashore at Alexandria and had been surprised, and pleased, at the child's eventual acceptance of her decree. Returning to the ship later that afternoon, however, her pleasure had fled on meeting Lonnie on the quayside with one of the deck hands. Lonnie was eating virulent pink sweets from a greasy paper bag and the boy – for he was little more – carried an armful of mixed fruit and had a delicate, transparent length of material, patterned in blue and green, around his neck.

Hester had borne down upon them full of wrath, only to be disarmed by the boy's saying jovially: 'Little miss here explained that she had missed you when you left the ship, when she lingered to watch the monkey dancing to the barrel-organ. So I said she might come along a-me to the bazaar and we've had a grand afternoon, haven't we, missie?'

Naturally, Hester had said nothing to the boy, apart from thanking him for his kindness to her charge, but as soon as she got Lonnie to herself she had given her a fearful telling-off, warning her that such behaviour would not be tolerated either by herself or by her English aunt.

'You had no right to leave me,' Lonnie had said calmly, cutting across Hester's diatribe long before it was finished. 'If I were to tell my father that you went ashore and left me behind, he would have you whipped and thrown into a snake pit.'

Despite herself, Hester could not help laughing. 'What a little liar you are,' she had said. 'Why, your father would agree that, as your governess, I have every right to punish you when you do wrong.'

'Oh, punish!' Lonnie said airily. They were in the cabin and she took her silver-backed hairbrush off the dressing table, untied her hair ribbon and began to brush her limp, light-brown locks. 'Punishment is giving me extra schoolwork, or making me miss a meal, or not speaking to me for a whole half hour. Not letting me go ashore was wicked and mean, and if you try it again . . .'

All Hester's amusement fled. The child was actually daring to threaten her, yet she could see Lonnie's point in some ways. The voyage was a long one and diversions such as a trip ashore rare enough. The *Pride of India* only made two landfalls, Alexandria being the first, and since there was little she could do about it if Lonnie decided to go off without her she had better devise a form of punishment which meant she could keep her eye on Lonnie at the same time. Thinking back to Mr Hetherington-Smith's instructions, she seemed to remember that he had said she would be in charge of his daughter at all times until they reached Liverpool, when Miss Emmeline Hetherington-Smith would, presumably, share her duties. This obviously meant that, if she wished to go ashore, Lonnie must accompany her.

Having lived all her life in the East, however, Hester knew the value of saving face, knew that she must employ it now if she was ever to get anywhere with Lonnie. Accordingly, she said reprovingly: 'Have you any idea of the dangers which surround one in a foreign port, Leonora? Have you never heard of the white slave trade? Some men would give a good deal of money to add an English girl to their harems, or to be able to boast of an English slave in their servants' quarters. If you were shipped to somewhere like South America, your lot would be miserable indeed and your life short. Did you not think of that when you disobeyed my instructions and went ashore alone?'

'Well, I did, because I'm not a fool,' Lonnie said

scathingly. 'Why do you think I made that silly young man take me to the bazaar? There was a nasty old man on the quayside who kept trying to persuade me to go with him. He said he had six beautiful white ponies and a granddaughter who looked just like me and he said we might ride the ponies and eat sweetmeats and have a wonderful time until the ship sailed.'

At the mention of the old man on the quayside, Hester had actually felt the hair on the back of her neck prickling erect and it seemed as though iced water trickled down her spine. It occurred to her that both she and Lonnie had had a very narrow escape, for how would she have explained to Mr Hetherington-Smith and his sister that she had lost Miss Leonora whilst ashore in Alexandria? So instead of scolding Lonnie any further, she had given her a big hug and assured her charge that she would not leave her again.

That evening, when Lonnie was asleep, Hester had considered her position anew. Her employer had paid her first-class passage on the ship and had told her that though she would be answerable to his sister, it would be himself who would be paying her salary. 'My sister is a good deal older than me and somewhat set in her ways, so I have written to her, explaining that I wish you to continue in my employ until such time as my daughter no longer needs you,' he had said. 'However, I have been forced to practise a small deception to make this acceptable to Miss Hetherington-Smith. In short, my dear Hester, I have told her not only that you are the child of my dearest friend, but that you are twenty-four years old, and are experienced in dealing with small children. I fear that if my sister knew the truth – that you are eighteen and have never before been a governess – she would either persistently interfere with your treatment of Lonnie or dismiss you out of hand.' He had smiled at Hester with real affection and understanding in his rather sad dark eyes. 'So if you wouldn't mind lending your support to this small deception, I should be most grateful, for I love my daughter and would feel a good deal happier knowing that she is in the charge of someone I trust, rather than at the mercy of an English servant who might not take to her.'

Remembering the trust that Mr Hetherington-Smith had placed in her, Hester had tried to persuade Lonnie gently to do as she wished, avoiding direct conflict. When the ship docked in Gibraltar, the two of them had gone ashore with a party of other passengers and Lonnie had behaved beautifully. At Hester's suggestion, she had used some of her own money to buy her aunt a china vase, delicately hand-painted with exotic birds whose brilliant feathers were a source of considerable pleasure to Lonnie.

Hester had helped her to pack the vase in soft blue tissue paper and then to place it in a white cardboard box, and until now had not doubted that it would reach Liverpool in pristine condition. Now, surveying the heaving waves under her nose, Hester noticed for the first time how the sea was losing its blue-green brilliance as they left the Mediterranean behind them and headed out into the Atlantic. She watched the waves beneath her, realising that the gentle surge had become a turbulent grey sea, with white-topped combers coming at the ship from all directions, so that she began to pitch and toss. The gentle breeze of the Mediterranean had given way to a cold and blustery wind. Every now and then, a particularly violent gust whipped a fine spray into her face and she was rather enjoying the experience when she remembered that Lonnie was by herself in the cabin, painting a picture of Gibraltar, complete with the apes which they had visited during their short stay. The child might be frightened by the sudden change in the weather, Hester told herself, hurrying down the nearest companionway.

Entering the cabin, she saw at a glance that Lonnie was in no way perturbed by the violence of the elements, though she had one hand around her water pot. The other wielded her paintbrush, though the movement of the ship was causing a good deal of the paint to fly in unplanned directions, Hester noticed. 'It's a bit rough,' Hester said cheerfully. 'How's the painting coming along? I'd suggest a stroll on deck, but I don't suppose you would fancy a walk in such a wild wind.'

Lonnie looked up and slung her paintbrush down on the floor, then crossed to the small basin in one corner of the cabin and tipped her paint water away. 'I do fancy a walk,' she said, going over to the hanging cupboard and getting down her coat. She began to struggle into it, speaking as she did so. 'Daddy has told me all about English weather, Miss Elliott, so I dare say it will be just like this in Liverpool. He seemed to think we might not like the cold much after India, but I'm sure we'll enjoy it, because being too hot is horrid, isn't it? And Liverpool is so beautiful, with all the parks and art galleries and lovely shops.'

All her life, Hester had been bombarded with stories about England, yet she realised that the reality might prove very different. According to Trevor Elliott – and obviously to Mr Hetherington-Smith also – Liverpool was the hub of the universe, the most beautiful city in England and a centre of culture and trade. One or two of the sailors, on the other hand, had talked quite differently about their home. They had said it was a port like any other, full of inhabitants who would cheat you out of your last penny, shops whose goods were exorbitantly priced and wonderful markets where you could buy a hot meal for sixpence or get your pocket picked for free. Hester imagined that the truth was somewhere between the two, but she did not intend to disillusion Lonnie; time – and experience – would do that.

'Right! Since you feel like blowing some cobwebs away, you'd better pass me my coat and we'll go up together,' Hester said gaily. 'Twice round the deck is a mile and the last one back to the cabin is a sissy!'

The voyage through the Bay of Biscay was not too pleasant. A good many of the passengers on board suddenly disappeared from the dining saloon and the deck. They shut themselves in their cabins and kept the stewards busy, Hester told Lonnie when the child enquired as to the whereabouts of some of their new acquaintances.

'I wonder why we don't feel sick?' Lonnie said idly on the following day, as the *Pride of India* continued to butt her way through the stormy seas. 'After all, we've neither of us ever been on a ship before, have we, Miss Elliott?'

'No, but I've travelled all over India with my father,' Hester said. 'Once or twice I've been aboard river boats for several days . . . and don't you think that riding for a longish distance in a palanquin is rather like being at sea? I know you must have done that . . . and then there are elephants. They sway . . . I've known several people who were elephant sick.'

Lonnie giggled. 'I think I just have a very strong stomach,' she confided. 'I don't eat as much as some people, but what I do eat stays where it's put. How near to Liverpool would you say we were now, Miss Elliott? Are you getting excited? I am, I can't help it. My daddy talked such a lot about Liverpool and told me so many times all the things he had done there when he was a boy that I know I'll be happy there.' She turned to gaze solemnly at Hester. 'Only Daddy said you'd stay with me whilst I and Aunt Emmeline needed you, but once I was settled in you might leave me and get a different sort of job somewhere else, or even go to relatives of your own. I don't mind you leaving me, of course . . . after having to leave my dear *ayah* and my daddy, I suppose I'm used to leaving people . . . but I hope you won't go *too* soon.'

Hester, who had no relatives at all in England, or none that she knew of, and realised that she was ill-equipped to get any sort of job just yet, murmured that she would stay with Lonnie as long as Miss Hetherington-Smith wanted her and then changed the subject. 'Don't forget, your father will be visiting England to see how you are getting on in a year or two,' she reminded her charge. 'By then you'll probably have forgotten all about me.'

'Yes, that's true,' Lonnie said, blissfully indifferent to any feelings she might hurt, Hester thought ruefully. Not that her feelings were hurt. She had already realised that young Lonnie was so self-centred that it was almost impossible to like her, though she quite often felt sorry for the child. Still, you never knew. When they got ashore and moved into their new home things might be different.

The weather continued stormy as the ship entered

the Irish Sea and many of the other passengers stayed in their cabins. Then one morning Hester and Lonnie awoke to blue skies and pale sunshine, and when they went out on deck they realised they must be approaching the end of their journey. The ship was entering the mouth of a great river which must, Hester knew, be the Mersey, and she and her charge stayed where they were, leaning on the rail and ignoring their stomachs' insistent clamour that they had had no breakfast. Fascinated, they saw the distant blue of great hills, the golden strip of sand along the coastline. And then, as the ship continued on her way, the banks of the river grew closer and closer and the city itself appeared. It was a big, imposing city, Hester saw, with great white buildings and warehouses, shipyards and other signs of industry crowding close.

'Miss Elliott, are they the Liver Birds?' Lonnie said presently, as they steamed along. 'One of the deckhands told me that if a virgin passes by, those birds flap their wings . . . do you think it's true? And what's a virgin, anyway?'

Hester turned away to hide the smile twitching her lips. 'It's just one of those silly sayings that sailors know,' she said, keeping her voice level with difficulty. 'I should forget all about it if I were you. Oh, look, there's a train – it's actually above the ground! Oh, that must be the overhead railway . . . my father talked about it sometimes. He used to travel by it when he lived here. He told me to buy myself a ticket when I came Home. He said you got a wonderful view of the docks from up there.'

'I see it,' Lonnie said, and Hester, glancing at her companion's small, sallow face, saw it flushed with excitement. For once Lonnie was not simply thinking of herself, she thought, surprised. 'Oh, Miss Elliott, I really *am* excited now! Can you see all the people waiting for us to dock? I wonder which one is my aunt? She must be very nice, because she's Daddy's sister, and my daddy is the nicest man I know. Let's go to our cabin and start getting ready to go ashore!'

Chapter One

May 1934

Ben Bailey came along Heyworth Street heading straight for the pet shop. He was earlier than he had been on previous occasions, anxiety getting him out of bed well before his usual time on a Saturday, because he now had a vested interest in the contents of Mr Madison's pet shop. In fact, the kittens in the window were his, or practically his at any rate.

Reaching the shop, Ben pressed his nose against the glass and peered inside. It was so early that the shop was still closed and the kittens, in their nest of wood shavings, were asleep, curled into a ball in one corner of their cage. Anxiously, Ben counted them; one, two, three, four . . . his heart gave a little bound. Had Mr Madison already sold one of them? But then someone inside the shop pushed open an inner door and all in a moment the kittens were awake, rolling over to reveal a fifth kitten, a little gingery one, which had been hidden by the recumbent bodies of his brothers and sisters.

Ben heaved a sigh. He didn't know whether it was relief because all the kittens were still in the window, or disappointment because none of them had yet been sold. He wanted them to be sold, of course he did. It was the only way, he had assured himself, of seeing that they got good homes. Folk, particularly kids, would take on a kitten which had been given to them free and then cheerfully neglect it, believing that cats hunted for their own food and needed no help from their human owners. If you paid money for a kitten, however, you valued it more, perhaps even returning to the pet shop on a regular basis to buy the cat's meat which Mr Madison kept in the room behind the shop.

On the other side of the glass, the black kitten with a white tip to its tail detached itself from its fellows and stared up at Ben out of milky-blue eyes. Its small mouth opened in a soundless miaow, and Ben's heart melted. I'm the nearest thing to a mother they've ever knowed, he told himself, so it's natural they should miss me. Why, if it hadn't been for me, they'd have been dead weeks ago, poor little blighters. I wish I could have kept 'em, but as Mam said, there ain't enough food for all of us, let alone a brood of kittens. Still an' all, Mr Madison seemed to think he could sell 'em, so at least they'll get good homes.

Ben had found the kittens in a tumbledown warehouse some five weeks earlier. He had heard their hungry, agitated wailing as soon as he had climbed into the building and at first he had not realised they were motherless, but as soon as he touched one and felt its frantic mouth attaching itself to the tip of his little finger, he had realised that the kittens were starving.

For several days he had begged, borrowed or stolen milk for them, feeding them by dipping a piece of rag in the liquid and letting the kittens suck, one by one. Within a week, the little things were making progress, sucking at the bread which he dipped in the milk and growing round-bellied and bright-eyed. Ben had adored them, and named each one. Tip was obvious, Ginger more so and then there was Spot, who was white with black splodges, and Blot who was white with a black blotch on his nose. That left only the tiniest kitten, so Ben had christened him Joseph, since his coat was most definitely of many colours.

It would have been nice to have kept even one of the kittens, but Mrs Bailey had been firm. 'You've brung in two mangy old toms and that horrible black dog what must have been a hundred when you found it and died after six months,' she had pointed out. 'I know that cats fend for themselves pretty much, but a kitten's different. It'll want milk, just for starters. No, Ben, they can't come here.'

So Ben had begun to check on the pet shops in the area and had finally decided that Mr Madison's was the best one. On the previous day he had plucked up his courage and had tackled Mr Madison. At first there had been some confusion due to Ben's approach, which had been to go into the shop and ask Mr Madison if he sold kittens. Mr Madison was a heavily built man with thinning, gingery hair, pale-blue protuberant eyes and a dangling, wispy moustache. He wore a stained brown overall and large rubber boots but Ben noticed, with approval, that the little shop was beautifully clean and all the animals and birds looked well housed and fed. This was clearly the sort of place he was searching for. However, Mr Madison, joyfully seizing the wrong end of the stick, had assumed Ben to be wishful of owning a kitten and had immediately promised to get some in so that Ben could choose which one he wanted. When Ben had managed to explain that he was a purveyor of kittens rather than a customer, Mr Madison had turned quite nasty and had tried to order Ben out of the shop. But Ben had been too anxious for his kittens to take such an attitude lying down and had returned an hour later with the five kittens in his mother's canvas shopping bag, tipping them on to the counter when the shop was empty and drawing Mr Madison's attention to his protégés' shining fur, bright eyes and round little stomachs.

'They certainly look healthy enough,' Mr Madison had said grudgingly, having examined each kitten closely. 'Well, all right, lad, I'll take 'em on. They don't look as if they'll croak on me, at any rate.' He had leaned confidentially across the counter, lowering his voice. 'You'd be amazed the state some of the stock arrives in: dirty, neglected, underfed, yet folks still expect me to buy 'em and sell 'em on and who's the one to get cursed and complained at when the bleedin' little critter snuffs it? Why, me, of course! They wants their money back, sometimes they even want the price of the food they say they've give it. Not that they gets anything, 'cos that ain't how it works, but it makes for unpleasantness, like.' He eyed the kittens keenly then turned back to Ben. 'How much?'

Dizzily, Ben realised that the man actually meant to pay him for the kittens. Since he had not dreamed of such a thing – had rather feared Mr Madison might charge *him* for their keep – he had no idea what to reply, and merely shrugged helplessly.

'Thruppence a piece, then,' Mr Madison said briskly. He lowered his head then peered up at Ben, grinning like a shark. 'Now you'll still be at school, young feller-me-lad, so you'll be a bit of a mathematician, like. What's thruppence five times over, eh?'

'It's one and thruppence,' Ben had said at once. His mother often got him to do her messages and already, at the tender age of ten, Ben knew how to make sixpence do the work of a shilling. 'Thanks ever so much, Mr Madison. Mind if I pops in now and then to see how the kittens are doing?'

Mr Madison had confirmed that this would be all right but Ben had realised he must make such visits infrequently; he did not wish to wear out his welcome. So now he had no intention of entering the shop but had merely stopped by to see that the kittens were still thriving. Indeed, as he watched, a hand with a tin bowl in it appeared as if from nowhere, unfastened the top of the kittens' cage with a practised flick of the fingers and then descended. The tin bowl was placed in a cleared space, right against the glass, and Ben saw with approval that it contained a generous amount of bread and milk. The kittens must have smelt the milk, for they all dived across their cage and were soon enjoying an excellent breakfast, the larger of the kittens, Tip and Spot, actually standing in the bowl whilst gobbling as fast as they could. 'You greedy little tykes . . .' Ben was beginning, when a sharp elbow was driven into his ribs and a small, clear voice said imperiously: 'Go away, you common little slum child! I want to see the kittens have their breakfast, so you can just clear out and keep your filthy paws away from my nice clean coat.'

Ben was so astonished that he actually sidled away before realising that he had been mortally insulted, and by a girl, too! Hastily, he moved back to his previous position, saying gruffly: 'Just who do you think you are, Lady Muck? I've gorras much right as you to stand by the window – more, 'cos they're my kittens, so why don't you just shove off?'

'I shall do no such thing!' the girl declared. Ben saw that she was very small and very thin, with pale, unhealthy-looking skin and lank light-brown hair tied back from her face so tightly that her eyebrows slanted upwards at the ends. She had long, dark-brown eyes, thickly fringed with black lashes, a small dab of a nose and a sulky mouth. She was wearing a very smart red coat – a winter coat in May, Ben thought incredulously – woollen gloves and lace-up boots. Her expression, moreover, was so superior and scornful that she looked as though she thought Ben a worm beneath her feet.

'Well *I* ain't shiftin',' Ben said positively. His mam had always told him that women were the weaker sex and that he should treat them with a special care, but the girls he knew had never insulted him, though from time to time clacks had been exchanged when tempers grew frayed. So now Ben stood his ground and pressed his nose to the window once more, trying to ignore the stiff little figure beside him.

But the girl was clearly not used to such treatment and turned to a young woman standing nearby and watching them, Ben thought, with some amusement. 'Miss Elliott!' the girl said haughtily. 'Tell this . . . this untouchable to move away from the window! I wish to watch the kittens . . . and he smells horrible.'

'Why, you rude little bitch,' Ben said, his face growing hot with outrage. 'If anyone smells, it's you! Why, I were down bathing in the Scaldy no more 'un three weeks ago and me mam makes us all wash reg'lar.'

The girl laughed scornfully but Ben noted that her colour, too, had risen. '*Now* you'll be in trouble,' she said gloatingly. 'Miss Elliott! Come at once when I call!'

The tall young woman came towards them. She was dressed in a winter coat made of navy-blue wool with a matching felt hat. It looked a bit like a uniform and must, Ben thought, be far too hot in this mild May sunshine. The young woman looked down at her charge and Ben thought her lips twitched, but could not be certain. 'Yes, Miss Leonora?' she said. Her voice was low and pleasant and Ben thought he could detect a trace of a Welsh accent. 'What's up now?'

'This – this guttersnipe called me a *very* rude name,' the small girl, who appeared to be called Leonora, said impressively. 'Make him go away at once, Miss Elliott, or it'll be the worse for you.'

The young woman had large dark eyes and pale skin, whilst her hair, peeping out from beneath her navy-blue felt hat, was dark and shiny as a blackbird's wing. Ben saw now that something was definitely amusing her, though she surely could not find the small girl's rudeness funny? However, she said in a perfectly serious voice: 'Calling names is rude, Miss Leonora Victoria Hetherington-Smith, and a girl with as many names as you should know it, though I'm pretty sure you were the first to start calling names – you usually are. Anyway, why can't you *both* watch the kittens? Surely the window's big enough!'

'But he's an *untouchable,*' Leonora almost wailed, the colour in her cheeks darkening from rose to red. Ben thought she looked a good deal healthier when she was angry, but did not intend to tell her so. 'Oh, how I wish you'd stayed in India, Miss Elliott! If only my dear *ayah* were here instead, how much happier I should be! Why, you aren't even a proper governess. You're just the daughter of a common clerk, when all's said and done, and I won't share the window with a guttersnipe whatever *you* may say, I won't, I won't!'

Ben, looking from face to face, saw that though Miss Elliott was smiling, she was also angry. He thought she looked quite dangerous and waited hopefully for her to give Miss Leonora a clack across the ear, but though the young woman folded her lips tightly for a moment it seemed that her sense of humour was stronger than her outrage, for she shook her head gently and took hold of her charge by one skinny shoulder, turning her back towards the window. 'Watch the kittens and mind your manners,' she advised softly. 'And don't you ever let me hear you call my father a common clerk again. He was a civil servant, an important man with many responsibilities, and a better man never breathed. What is more, you know very well he was your own father's dearest friend. After my mother died, my father brought me up with almost no help and saw to it that I had a decent education and learned some manners, which is more than *you* ever did, miss. Now save your breath to cool your porridge and don't you threaten me again either, because it won't wash. I'm being employed to keep an eye on you but I don't believe your aunt would much care if I beat you black and blue so long as you didn't interfere with her life. Understand?'

Ben had expected the girl to be abashed by Miss Elliott's words but Leonora merely turned and gave her a glare, then swung round to face the window once more, pressing her nose against the pane. Ben, glancing sideways at her, thought that he had never seen a colder, harder expression on anyone's face and was accordingly astonished, a few moments later, when he shot another look at her to see two large tears making their way down her thin cheeks.

Ben had honestly thought her the most detestable person he had ever encountered, but at the sight of her tears he began to feel a tiny bit sorry for her. He thought she was probably a kid of only six or seven. He moved nearer, saying in an undertone:

'You don't smell, or only of something sweet at any rate. But there's no cause to go calling names, like the young lady said. Us can both see the kittens, can't us? And they *were* mine, honest to God they were, until I put them in the pet shop so's they could find good homes. I'll tell you their names if you like.' Then he added, with more than a touch of curiosity, 'What's an untouchable when it's at home, anyroad? I've been called a lot of names in me time, but never that one.'

Leonora pretended to cup her hands round her eyes so that she could see more clearly into the window, but Ben knew she was really wiping away those two tell-tale tears, then she turned to him. 'An untouchable is someone very low caste, someone who does the dirty jobs around the city which no one else would do,' she said in a subdued voice. 'I – I suppose it was rude to call you that, but how was I to know?' She sighed deeply. 'This country is very different from India. Oh, I wish I were back there with my own dear *ayah* to take care of me and my own beautiful house and garden to play in, and the river, and the willow trees . . .' Her voice faded into silence.

India! Ben had never known anyone who came from further away than Birkenhead, but he was pretty sure that India was a long way off. There was a globe in his classroom at school and their teacher, Mr Mallory, was fond of pointing out all the pink countries on it. 'Pink is the colour of the British Empire,' he had told them. And then he would name the various countries including, Ben was now sure, India. Yes, that was it! India was where the tea came from, and tigers, elephants, ivory, rice, sugar . . . Impulsively, Ben turned to his companion. 'India's a hot country, ain't it?' he enquired. 'But I thought Indians were brown, and wore turban things on their heads and long white robes. You dress quite ordinary, for a girl, and you're awful pale.'

With flashing eyes, the small girl drew herself up and turned away from the window with a flounce. 'I am *not* a native, you horrible boy,' she hissed. 'My father happens to be one of the most important businessmen in Delhi and he is one of the richest men in the city as well, *and* the most powerful. Why, he's a merchant prince!'

'Oh aye, and I s'pose you're a merchant princess,' Ben sneered, all his dislike of the girl coming to the fore once more. 'How were I to know . . .' But before he could say anything further, the girl had abandoned the window and set off along the pavement. 'Oh, bleedin' hell, trust a woman to scream at you and then fly off before you can explain.'

Miss Elliott, however, lingered, even though her charge was scurrying away as fast as her legs could carry her. 'Miss Leonora's been spoiled rotten,' she explained to Ben, giving him a friendly smile. 'She was born and raised in India with servants to do everything for her; they even laced her shoes and buttoned her coat. What is more, the only other children she met were like herself, over-indulged by everyone. She never got to know ordinary children like you, so I was downright pleased when I saw the pair of you chatting.' She heaved a deep sigh. 'But I might have guessed the little madam would start throwing her weight about the moment she got a chance; that's Lonnie all over. Won't I just give her a piece of my mind when I get her to myself. The trouble is, she's lonely, even though she doesn't know it. That aunt of hers has got a big house and loads of money but she doesn't want the bother, do you see? She's furbished up the old nursery at the top of the house and expects the child to spend her life in it, apart from the odd walk of a morning or afternoon. I told her Leonora'd have to go to school once she was settled in so that she could meet other children, but she's done nothing about it yet.' The young woman smiled ruefully down at Ben. 'I don't know why I'm telling you all this; I suppose it's because I'm as lonely as Lonnie is. By the way, what's your name, young man?'

'I'm Ben Bailey. You come from India, too, don't you? I'm sorry I fell out wi' that girl, but it fair made my blood boil, the things she said.' He glanced up the road and saw, with some satisfaction, that Leonora was retracing her steps, head down, feet dragging. 'Better say nowt else,' he said hastily, in a lowered voice. 'She's coming back.'

'Yes, she would come back. She'd never find her way home. We haven't been in England long enough for her to get used to your ways. Although she's eight years old, I doubt she could understand the road signs, let alone follow the route we took to get here.' Miss Elliott raised her voice as the girl approached. 'Well, Lonnie? Have you come back to say you're sorry to this young man? He was going to tell you the names of the kittens – aren't you interested?'

'Wait on a mo',' Ben said in an undertone. 'You said her name was Leonora Victoria something or other, but you just called her Lonnie. Why's that?'

'Shorter,' the other girl said briefly. 'Besides, her *ayah* could never get her tongue round Leonora, so she's been called Lonnie ever since she was knee high to a grasshopper.' Ben was not at all sure that he would ever like someone as stuck up and strange as Leonora, but already he realised that he liked Miss Elliott. She had talked to him as though he were grown up and she smiled a lot, not just with her mouth, but with those big dark eyes as well. So he turned back to the window and began to recite the names of the kittens and was presently struck by a wonderful idea. 'Why don't you ask Miss Elliott if she'll buy you one of the kittens?' he asked urgently, keeping his voice low. 'You'd like a little cat of your own, wouldn't you? You could have Tip, he's the biggest and strongest. Go on, ask Miss Elliott if she'll buy a kitten for you.'

He expected Lonnie to greet this suggestion with enthusiasm but instead she took a step away from the window, her expression a mixture of fear and of longing. 'Oh, but suppose it scratches me and gives me rabies or blood poisoning or something horrid?' she asked plaintively. 'Suppose it bites me? Miss Elliott's father was bitten by a snake and he died.'

'Why, ye-es, but that's India,' Ben pointed out. 'We don't have things like that in England, you know, and anyway, cats don't scratch or bite unless you tease 'em. My mam always says if you treat folk nice, they'll be nice back and I reckon it's the same wi' animals. If you're kind to the kitten and get its meals reg'lar, it'll be kind to you, see?'

'Oh, but suppose I tease it by mistake?' Lonnie said. 'I've never had a kitten, you know. I wanted a monkey ever so badly, or even a parrot, but my *ayah* screamed and had palpitations every time I suggested it, so I never got a pet of my own, though of course I had my own pony and a mongoose called Freddie, but he ran away when I was six and Father never replaced him.'

Ben stared. A pony of her own; she certainly was

a lucky kid. He began to say as much, then remembered that the child had been talking of her past. It was no comfort now that she had once owned a pony and a – a goose or whatever it was she had said. Lonnie turned her gaze back to the kittens in the window, then pointed a trembling finger. 'They've got teeth like little white needles and they *do* scratch . . . look at that one!'

Ben looked. Tip had finished cleaning the milk off his paws and was, rather unfortunately, sharpening his claws on a block of wood placed in one corner of the cage for that purpose. 'That's wood, stupid,' Ben said crossly. 'That's why it's in the cage, so's the kittens can sharpen their claws. They don't do it on *people*. Why don't we jest go into the shop and take a closer look at 'em?'

He half expected Lonnie to object but he had reckoned without Miss Elliott, who had evidently been listening to their conversation. She came briskly up beside them and took Lonnie's hand, saying bracingly: '*What* a good idea, Lonnie! A kitten will be company for you when I'm busy elsewhere and you'll soon grow fond of it, you know. As for monkeys, I've heard many a servant say that their bite is poisonous, though I don't believe it myself. Which of the kittens did you like best?'

Ben, leading the way into the shop, wondered if Lonnie might rebel, but though the small girl scowled frightfully and folded her lips into a long, tight line she said nothing, and when Mr Madison lifted the kittens' cage from the window and placed it upon the floor of the shop so that they might see the occupants more clearly she dropped to her knees and put a finger tentatively through the bars of the cage, gently caressing the tiniest kitten before looking up at the older woman and saying, rather breathlessly: 'I like this one best, Miss Elliott. I don't believe it would bite anyone – or scratch, either. Can I have this one?'

Mr Madison gave Ben an approving look; clearly, he thought the boy had been touting for business and appreciated his salesmanship. What was more, Joseph, being the smallest, was the one least likely to survive in the shop, for he would never get as much to eat as his larger, bolder brothers and sisters. Mr Madison extracted the kitten from the cage and put him straight into Lonnie's arms. 'You've chosen well, miss,' he said, beaming down upon his customer. 'This here's as pretty a kitten as I've seen in a long day, tortoiseshell being my favourite colour an' all. What'll you call her?'

'Oh! But this – this boy said its name was Joseph,' Lonnie informed him, clutching the kitten gently against the front of her red cloth coat. 'Can you change a kitten's name, then?'

Miss Elliott chuckled. 'Joseph's a boy's name,' she said. 'You could call her Josie, I suppose, but wouldn't you like to choose a name yourself?'

'Well, I'll call her Kitty,' Lonnie said immediately. 'There's a song . . . *Oh, I like little kitty, her coat is so warm, And if I don't hurt her, she'll do me no harm, So I'll not pull her tail, nor drive her away, But Kitty and I very gently will play.*'

'Well done, missie,' Mr Madison said unctuously, rubbing his hands together and cocking one gingery eyebrow at Ben. 'Now there's a few other things you'll be wanting, since, I'll be bound, little Kitty here will get nothing but the best from such a smart young lady. You'll be wanting a nice little bed for her to sleep on, a fluffy ball for her to play with, and later on you'll be needing a little collar wi' a bell on it, so's you know where she is.'

Leonora was nodding eagerly at every suggestion, but Miss Elliott was a trifle more practical. 'How do you know it's a female?' she enquired, digging in her pocket for her purse. 'I'm not sure we want a male, because they spray, I believe, and smell awfully.'

'All tortoiseshells is she's,' Mr Madison said sweepingly. 'Same as all gingers is fellers, or almost all, anyroad. Now you'll want a sizeable basket for her, 'cos she's a healthy little thing and will go off a pace once she don't have to fight the others for her share o' the grub. We do a nice line in woven reed, or wicker's a bit more substantial . . .'

'How much is the kitten?' Miss Elliott interrupted. 'We won't bother with a basket since a nice cardboard box with a piece of blanket in it will suit her for a while yet. But we'll have a fluffy ball, and when she's bigger we'll get a collar with a bell. Not that she'll be outdoors much, since the nursery's at the top of the house.'

Mr Madison looked uneasily at Ben, his eyebrows zipping up and down like a couple of caterpillars who have noticed a blackbird fixing them with its beady eye. Ben realised that Mr Madison would have been more comfortable if his young friend never discovered what he charged for the kittens. He was safe enough, however. All Ben wanted for his foundlings was good homes; if Mr Madison liked to price the kittens according to the customer, that was fine by Ben. Mr Madison turned his head away from Ben and dropped his voice. 'Three shillin' and that includes the fluffy ball,' he muttered. 'Does that suit, madam?'

From the willingness with which Miss Elliott dug

into her purse and produced a shiny florin and two sixpences, Ben surmised that Miss Elliott did not find the sum alarming. He had no idea what currency was used in India, but he did know something about the price of kittens and thought that a shilling apiece was what most shop owners asked.

Mr Madison beamed at the coins nestling in his palm and turned round to the shelf behind him, taking a large brown paper bag and a small grey object from it. 'D'you want to pop the kitten into this 'ere bag?' he enquired jovially. 'You don't want to lose her in the street. She ain't used to traffic, nor sudden noises – she's a country cat, she is.'

Ben gasped at this palpable lie and wondered whether Leonora would say something sharp, since he had told her the kittens were his, but Leonora said nothing, merely popping the kitten into the stout brown paper carrier and looking curiously at the little grey object Mr Madison was holding out. 'What *is* that?' she asked suspiciously. 'Oh, it's a horrid little dead mouse – take it away!'

Mr Madison chuckled comfortably. 'It ain't dead, nor it weren't ever alive,' he said. 'It's what they call a catnip mouse, missie. It's just a bit o' woollen cloth stuffed with catnip and your little kitten will have a grand time a-chasin' of it when you're safe home. Good day to you both and thank you for your custom. When the kitten's old enough, you'll be needin' fish ends, cat's meat and such, so I hope you'll be poppin' in again.'

The two females left the shop and Ben would have followed them, but Mr Madison stopped him. 'You're norra bad lad,' the older man said appreciatively. 'Fancy a Sat'day job and mebbe a bit o' work after school, like? Only I could do wi' a lad to clean out cages, food and water bowls and so on. I can't pay much but mebbe you'd be glad to earn the odd sixpence?'

'Oh, Mr Madison!' Ben said rapturously. Every kid he knew was eager to earn the odd penny for this was the Depression and money was hard to come by, even if you were a fully grown man. What was more, he had always loved animals and would enjoy nothing better than helping to keep them clean, fed and watered. 'It'd be grand to work here. Can I start on Monday? I can be in by half-past four, if I comes straight from school.'

Mr Madison laughed. 'That'll do nicely,' he said. 'But right now, just you go with them young ladies and make sure they get that kitten home safe.' He winked at his young companion. 'More money than sense, wouldn't you say? Though she parted with her dibs uncommon easy, an' who am I to complain when a customer pays up wi'out a murmur? Pretty gal an' all. Now off wi' you, young man . . . what's your name, by the way?'

'I'm Ben Bailey.'

'How d'you do, Ben?' Mr Madison said, bravely holding out a large, clean hand. They shook. 'Now off with you, because if your little friend loses that kitten there'll be hell to pay. I were listenin' when you was a-chatting together – I reckon she's a real handful, the young 'un, so I'd be happier if you kept watch till they's safe home.'

Hester Elliott ushered her charge into the big, imposing house in Shaw Street with an inward sigh of relief. She was beginning to wonder whether she would ever grow accustomed to being a governess. The trouble was, she mused, that she had led a highly unconventional life for as long as she could remember, which made it even more difficult to try to get Lonnie to behave conventionally.

Remembering her early years now, Hester thought that no childhood could have been happier or more strange. After her mother's tragic death, she and Trevor Elliott had grown closer than ever. As a district officer, Mr Elliott had had to travel over a very wide area, and because he trusted no one to look after his daughter save himself, Hester had gone with him.

For Hester, those had been halcyon days. She had had her own small tent, pitched beside that of her father, and during the day the young son of one of his employees had been responsible for her welfare. She had been ten at the time of her mother's death, and Sanjay only twelve, but he had spent his whole life in the jungles and forests of India and knew as much as any grown man of the perils and pleasures of such a life. Hester soon had implicit faith in his ability to take care of her. If he ran along a fallen tree, his bare, brown feet gripping the creeper-clad trunk, she would follow him, confident that it was safe to do so, but when he guided her round a thicket, telling her that some animal lurked within, she was careful to mimic his every move and to wait, still as a statue, until he gave the command to move on.

It was always hot in the jungle and most Europeans suffered from various forms of prickly heat, sores and sweat rashes, but Hester, wearing as little as possible, and following Sanjay into the coolest and shadiest spots when the sun was at its height, suffered scarcely at all.

This wonderful, free life had continued until she was fourteen, when Sanjay took up an official post as a sort of forest ranger and was no longer available to be her playmate and guardian. By this time, Hester's father had decided that her education had been ignored for long enough and had sent her to a first-rate boarding school in Paris, where the Sisters of Mercy had made her very happy during her time with them. It seemed that Hester had inherited her father's quick brain for she speedily caught up with and then overtook her contemporaries. When she was sixteen, she returned to her father's side once more, helping him with his work and typing out reports with two fingers on the battered old Remington machine he had always used. She had thought that this life would continue until her father's retirement, but once more tragedy struck. They had been camping in a tiny village and Hester had taken herself off, with a bearer to carry for her, to a bazaar in the nearby town. Upon her return, she found the camp in turmoil; it appeared that her father had been sitting beneath a large tree, dealing with a queue of natives, when a snake had dropped from the branches, close by the bare feet of a small child who had been playing in the dust. Trevor Elliott had snatched the child out of harm's way in one swift pounce but had not been quick enough to evade the cobra's strike. Someone had killed the snake, a king cobra at least six feet long, and though they had hurried the sahib to the nearest hospital, they had been too late. By the time Hester had arrived there, Trevor Elliott was already dead.

So when Mr Hetherington-Smith had first suggested that Hester should take on responsibility for his motherless child, she had almost fainted with relief. Her father had died only a matter of weeks before and she had been living with the family of his friend and colleague, Alfred Browning. Mary

Browning was the mother of five children, ranging in age from ten years to six months, and though she was perfectly pleasant to the young woman who had been foisted upon her, it was clear that she had no idea what she was to do with the uninvited guest. Members of the Civil Service in India had all the servants they needed, so there was little that Hester could do to help her hostess. Mr Hetherington-Smith's offer of work had, Hester felt, come in the nick of time and she accepted it gratefully.

What was more, it reminded her of the advice her mother had given her so many years ago. Kia had urged her daughter, almost with her last breath, to go back to England when she was grown up, if the chance ever arose. 'You should marry one of your own kind. I know you are fond of Sanjay – he is an admirable person, your father values him highly – but believe me, my darling, such a marriage as that would not do. You would be no more acceptable to Sanjay's people than he would be to yours. And great unhappiness would undoubtedly result. So please, little Hester, go Home when you are a young woman. Don't try to stay in India for your father's sake.'

'But why not, Mummy?' Hester had exclaimed plaintively. 'After all, you and Daddy met in India. You've never been Home yourself; you've told me so many times. Why must I be different?'

Kia's great dark eyes, burning with fever, had closed for a moment and then snapped open, as though she had suddenly been given some extra strength. 'Your father is a man in a thousand,' she had whispered. 'I was a very lucky woman, but such a love match is rare. Go to England, little sweetheart, where you will meet a great many young men. One of them will be the person with whom you choose to spend the rest of your life.'

Her voice had faded away and Hester's *ayah* had hustled her from the room, saying that the memsahib needed rest. Very soon afterwards, Trevor Elliott had come to Hester in her bare little bedroom in the bungalow in the hills and had told her, with tears running down his face, that her mother was dead.

Now, ushering her charge across the wide, tiled hall, Hester reflected that things could have been a lot worse. She might not be an ideal governess but she would do her best to see that Lonnie was decently educated and turned into a little English lady instead of the spoilt, over-indulged child she had known in India.

Life on board the ship returning to England had been a revelation, and not a pleasant one. By the time they reached Liverpool, Hester had been eager to hand over the responsibility for Lonnie to her aunt, although she expected to be retained as a governess until Lonnie started school, as surely she would. When Miss Hetherington-Smith made it clear that Hester's job as companion and governess to the child would continue indefinitely, she had been at first dumbfounded and then, as she realised how precarious her position was, almost relieved. She decided she would stay in Shaw Street until she had managed to obtain a decent position somewhere else, yet she knew in her heart that her task would not be easy. Lonnie was a little horror, although Hester had sense enough to realise that this was scarcely the child's fault. Lonnie had been whisked away from all she held dear, dumped on an aunt who did not want her in a cold, northern city where even the language was strange to her. It would have been a miracle had Lonnie taken to her new life, but at least, while Hester remained with her, the two of them could discuss the strangenesses around them and reminisce about the life – and country – that they had left.

For Hester herself was fighting a loneliness greater than any she had ever felt before. She knew nobody apart from the inhabitants of the Shaw Street house, and though the servants were friendly enough they kept her at a distance. Miss Hutchinson, Miss Hetherinton-Smith's paid companion, who might have befriended Hester, was far too afraid of her employer to risk her annoyance should she disapprove of such a friendship. So though Hester was secure enough, she longed for an ally in whom she could confide, and thought wistfully of her old life in India.

It did not help either Hester or Lonnie that Miss Emmeline Hetherington-Smith neither liked nor understood children. On the day they had arrived, she had made it clear to Hester that she was only accepting Lonnie into her household because the big house in Shaw Street was not hers at all, but her brother's. He liked to keep a home in Liverpool, the city from which his family had originated, and was quite happy for his spinster sister to live in the house whilst he himself paid all expenses. It seemed that he even made Miss Hetherington-Smith a generous quarterly allowance, so that the elderly woman felt she could not refuse a home to her niece. Accordingly, she had refurbished the nursery quarters at the top of the house which she, her sister Beatrice and the young Leonard Hetherington-Smith had occupied, and had installed Lonnie and Hester up there. The fact that she expected them to remain there, like prisoners, was due, Hester supposed, to a total lack of imagination, for no child wants to spend its entire existence shut away from the rest of the house and missing out on the rich street life it can observe from the nursery windows.

Hester had felt it her duty to point this out to Miss Hetherington-Smith and had accordingly received grudging permission to take the child out once or twice a day, so that she might visit the parks, the shops and other places of interest. 'She really should go to school,' Hester had added, emboldened by the fact that Miss Hetherington-Smith had reluctantly agreed to such outings, but the older woman had fixed her with a beady eye and reminded her that: 'You are employed as a governess, Miss Elliott, so a school is an unnecessary expense. The child never went to school in India, so why should she do so here?'

Hester had tried to explain the importance of Lonnie's meeting children of her own age, but Miss Hetherington-Smith brushed this aside as irrelevant. 'She will meet children in the park and very likely in the shops as well,' she had said. 'Please don't suggest school again, Miss Elliott, or you may well find yourself joining the vast numbers of unemployed who haunt the Liverpool streets.'

Hester had folded her lips tightly against a sharp retort, but very soon after this she had begun to examine the advertisements in the office bureaux and employment agencies, and had realised that Miss Hetherington-Smith was right. Work was hard to come by and poorly paid and for the time being at least she had best hold her peace.

So Hester and Lonnie began to fall into a routine. During daylight hours, they spent as little time as possible in the nursery quarters at the top of the house, although Hester made sure that Lonnie did her lessons regularly. They went for sedate walks in the park or strolled up and down the nearby streets, examining the wares in the shops with lively interest. Sometimes they hopped aboard a tram and visited the more sophisticated shops in the city centre and two or three times they had gone down to the Pier Head and walked along the waterfront, though the cold sea wind caused Lonnie to lament her lost India more fervently than ever.

If they met Miss Hetherington-Smith when they returned to the house, she always managed to look both astonished and outraged. Clearly, she felt that children – and their governesses – should be neither seen nor heard and did not allow for the fact that her niece could hardly be expected to enter the house by the back door or to reach the nursery via the servants' stairs.

Right now, however, the two of them were stealing quietly across the hall towards the stairs when the drawing room door opened and Miss Hutchinson came into the hall. Hester privately considered her a poor fish, almost unable to think for herself and very plainly in considerable awe of her employer. She was a tall, thin woman in her fifties, with light-brown hair braided into two earphones on either side of her narrow head, vague pale-blue eyes and an ingratiating manner. She saw Hester and Lonnie and put a conspiratorial finger to her lips. 'Hush,' she breathed. 'Miss Emmeline is interviewing the cook – we had a shockingly poor dinner last night – so I came out of the room because arguments bring on my palpitations and make me feel quite faint.'

As though her remark had triggered a response from

inside the room she had just left, Miss Hetherington-Smith's voice rose sharply. Miss Hutchinson clapped a hand over her mouth and shot towards the back regions of the house, murmuring between her fingers that she must speak to Mimms, the gardener, since dear Miss Hetherington-Smith wanted fresh roses in the drawing room.

Hester watched her out of sight, thinking what a shame it was that Miss Hutchinson had so little courage. When she and Lonnie had first come to Shaw Street and she had found Miss Hetherington-Smith so set against her charge, she had tried to persuade Miss Hutchinson to intercede on the child's behalf.

'A little girl needs companionship, and I need advice. I've tried to persuade Miss Hetherington-Smith to let the child have dancing lessons, riding or some other similar pursuit. But it seems she expects me to arrange everything, forgetting I'm in a strange city – a strange land, come to that.'

She had managed to catch Miss Hutchinson on her way to bed and the older woman had flattened herself against her bedroom door, looking absolutely terrified, as though Hester had suggested that she jump into a pit of poisonous snakes, Hester thought crossly.

'Oh, Miss Elliott, don't even suggest it,' the older woman had gasped, her pale face going even paler. 'Miss Hetherington-Smith would be so very angry and I can't bear dissension of any sort; it brings on my palpitations and the doctor says I must keep calm. Besides,' she had added, 'I know absolutely nothing about children or their requirements, so I can be of no use to you.'

At the time Hester had felt despair and anger mingling over the older woman's unhelpfulness, but as the days passed she realised that Miss Hutchinson's position was a difficult one and ceased to expect any support at all from that particular source. Now she watched Miss Hutchinson disappear through the green baize door which led to the servants' quarters and was about to continue crossing the hall when Lonnie tugged at her hand, pulling her to a halt, and jerked her head at the drawing room door, which had swung open a short way.

'I think I have shown a good deal of patience, Jackson, considering that most of the food which has appeared on our table has been all but inedible,' Miss Hetherington-Smith was saying in her harsh, commanding voice. 'We have had mutton so under-cooked that I was surprised it did not baa when I stuck my carving knife into it and lamb chops over-cooked until the meat shrivels on the bone, puddings which have to be dug out of their dish by main force, vegetables either boiled to a mush or served half raw, and lumpy gravy! Ever since you joined my staff, Jackson, my companion and I have suffered the cruellest pangs of indigestion. As for the food bills . . . well, they beggar description! What happened to the sirloin steaks, the leg of lamb and the joint of ham for which I paid the butcher such an exorbitant sum last week? Since they did not appear on our table, I assume that the staff must have eaten them in the servants' hall; unless, of course, they went up to the nursery, which I very much doubt.'

Mumble, mumble, mumble, went Mrs Jackson's voice. Hester could not hear what the woman was saying, but in any case her protest was soon cut off by Miss Hetherington-Smith.

'So you will kindly pack your bags, Jackson, and leave at once. I dare say you won't be surprised to learn that I do not intend to give you a reference.' Miss Hetherington-Smith's voice took on a note of deep sarcasm. 'Not that the absence of a recommendation will bother *you,* since I have no doubt that you personally wrote the excellent references which enabled you to get your position here.'

For the first time, Mrs Jackson's voice rose from a mutter to a squawk. 'I never. Oh, miss, I've been ill, norrable to do me wairk like what I normally would! Oh, miss, gimme another chance and I'll show you wharr I can do. Honest to God, miss . . .'

'No, Jackson.' Miss Hetherington-Smith's voice was now full of sweet reason. 'You have had four whole weeks in which to show me your skills, and according to your fellow servants all you've shown is a remarkable ability to pass work on to others' – here Miss Hetherington-Smith's voice dropped and Hester had to strain to hear the next words – 'and a great liking for the contents of the bottles which my dear father always kept in his cellars and are now only brought out when we have male company.'

There was another squawk from the cook but even to Hester's ears this protest lacked conviction. She could hear Mrs Jackson protesting that her mistress's words were a terrible libel on one who had never touched a drop and signed the pledge at the age of ten, but at this point the sound of footsteps came from the direction of the servants' quarters and Hester shooed her charge towards the stairs, saying nothing till they reached the security of the nursery. Then Hester blew out her cheeks and flopped into a chair, smiling at Leonora as she did so. 'Phew! I suppose you heard as much as I did, Lonnie, and I hope you realise that we were eavesdropping and of course eavesdropping is wrong. The truth is, I was so stunned to hear Miss Hetherington-Smith almost shouting that – that I forgot my duty was to ignore it and come straight up here. So we must forget we listened. Is that clear?'

'I don't see why it matters,' Lonnie observed. She knelt down on the rug before the nursery fire and took the kitten out of the paper bag. Settling herself comfortably on a cushion with the small animal on her lap, she glanced up at the older girl. 'I've never met the cook but I've eaten her awful food – or tried to, that is – and I can tell you, Miss Elliott, that if she had served food like that to my father in India, he would have ordered her to be torn to pieces by tigers.'

Despite herself, Hester laughed. Not knowing anything about English domestic habits, Hester had assumed that the cold tapioca puddings which had to be carved rather than spooned from their dish, the stews which lurked, almost meatless, below a thick icing of fat, and the inedible boiled potatoes, raw in the middle and falling to pieces on the outside, were considered unsuitable for the ladies of the house but good enough for children and governesses. Hester had taken to buying biscuits and milk and a bag of apples or oranges every time she ventured out, and she and Leonora existed mainly on such fare.

'Don't forget I've lived in India even longer than yourself, young lady,' she said. 'However, I agree that your father would not have tolerated such dreadful food for a week, let alone a month. If Miss Hetherington-Smith engages another cook, at least we may expect nicer meals in future.'

'I like the milk and biscuits,' Lonnie observed. Abruptly, she scrambled to her feet, putting the kitten carefully down upon the nearest chair. 'Should

I run down to the kitchen at once, Elliott, before the cook leaves, and ask her for some bread and milk for Kitty?'

'If you call me Elliott I shall confiscate the kitten and you will find yourself eating bread and water for a week,' Hester said, only half jokingly. 'You really must begin to treat adults with a little more respect.'

'But you're only a servant . . .' Lonnie began, then stopped short. 'I'm sorry,' she said humbly. 'My *ayah* was a servant but you're English, and I suppose that makes a difference, doesn't it?'

Hester sighed. Not for the first time, she felt considerable annoyance over the way Mr Hetherington-Smith had reared his daughter, though it was no different, she knew, from the way most English children were treated on the sub-continent. He had allowed her to consider the servants as inferior beings; in fact it seemed he had encouraged the little girl to believe herself superior to just about everyone. I am going to have to start from scratch, Hester told herself, picking up the kitten and holding it under her chin so that she could feel its purr vibrating through her throat. It really isn't the child's fault that she's so detestable; it's her upbringing. Aloud, she said: 'Lonnie, you have a great deal to learn and you may start by remembering that you are a small girl and therefore less important than anyone older than yourself. Can you understand that?'

'No, not really,' Lonnie said thoughtfully. 'But you haven't answered my question. What *am* I to call you?'

'I think it might be easiest if you used my Christian name, which is Hester,' Hester said. 'Since I call you Lonnie and not Miss Leonora, it seems fair enough that you should drop the "Miss" as well. But don't go calling other adults by their first names or they will think you very pert and disagreeable. And now that we're on the subject, it is not "done" in England to call people by their surnames only; my father used to say all names had a handle and the handle is Mr, Mrs, or Miss.'

'But Aunt Emmeline called the cook Jackson,' Lonnie objected. 'And you called the gardener Mimms yesterday morning, when you were asking him to cut some flowers for the nursery.'

'There's another saying which you would do well to remember: *don't do as I do, do as I tell you,*' Hester said, with all the patience she could muster. 'There are lots of sayings which you would do well to learn and abide by. I shall have to write them out for you so that you can learn them by heart.'

Lonnie was halfway to the door, but she paused and looked back. 'What sort of sayings?' she asked suspiciously. 'Perhaps I already know them – my *ayah* was very fond of sayings.'

'Oh, things like: *little pitchers have long ears; out of sight, out of mind; do as you would be done by; children should be seen and not heard,*' Hester said glibly, reeling off the well remembered phrases. 'Now you go off and fetch some milk and I'll go down to the garden and get Mimms to make up an earth box for Kitty here.'

The two of them left the room and began to descend the stairs. 'Can I carry the kitten?' Lonnie said hopefully, but Hester shook her head.

'Better not take her into the kitchens until you've found out how they feel about cats,' she advised. 'If Kitty were to puddle on the kitchen floor, it might set the servants against her and we wouldn't like that, would we?'

'What about Mimms? I dare say he may not like cats scratching up his garden,' Lonnie remarked, with quite astonishing shrewdness, considering that she had never owned a cat. 'And what's an earth box, anyway?'

'When kittens are very small and live at the top of the house, they can't get into the garden to – to attend to their business,' Hester said guardedly. 'Kittens are clean little creatures, however, and if we provide a box full of earth the kitten will use it as its WC. Of course, you will have to empty and refill it every day, but you won't mind that, will you?'

Lonnie, who had been trotting happily down the stairs by Hester's side, stopped short, eyes and mouth rounding in dismay. 'You want *me* to empty kitten poo?' she enquired incredulously. 'But Ell . . . I mean Hester . . . only an untouchable would do such a thing!'

'If you want a pet, then you must keep it clean,' Hester said firmly. 'Besides, who else could do it? There are no untouchables in England, Lonnie.'

'Mimms could; or – or the girl with the ginger hair and a tooth missing. Or you could,' Lonnie said promptly. 'I don't see why I should. I'm not even a bit like a servant!'

Hester bit her lip; the child was impossible! But if she did not deal promptly with Lonnie's queries, the girl would never learn. 'Don't argue all the time, Lonnie! Remember, *children should be seen and not heard*. There is no question of anyone else feeding, grooming or clearing up after Kitty. If you mean to keep her, then you must do all those things yourself. But it isn't too late; I'm sure the man in the pet shop will take her back if you've changed your mind.'

'Oh, I haven't, I haven't!' Lonnie squeaked, clearly

horrified at the mere suggestion. 'I'll clean the earth tray, honestly I will, Hester. But no one else may play with Kitty either, because if I have to do the dirty things, then I may have the fun as well, mayn't I?'

They had reached the hall by this time and Hester agreed that if her charge looked after the kitten, then she might be the only one to play with it as well. After that, she made her way into the garden to beg a seed box filled with earth for Lonnie's new possession while the younger girl trotted kitchenwards.

Ben followed the two girls and their kitten and was much impressed, when they reached Shaw Street, by the size and splendour of the house into which they disappeared. Joseph, he reflected, had certainly gone up in the world. The house was brick-built, slate-roofed and huge. The windows were tall and narrow, giving the house, Ben thought, rather a mean look, but the front door, large and imposing with a big brass knocker in its centre, an even bigger brass letter box and a huge bell-pull hanging beside it, looked so opulent that it offset the narrow windows.

'I wonder what it looks like round the back?' Ben muttered to himself. Ever curious, he walked down Everton Brow and turned left into Haig Street, realising that the house had a huge garden, bounded by a twelve-foot wall. When he stood on the opposite pavement and looked up at the house, he realised that the attic rooms would have a wonderful view and quite envied whoever lived up there; they would be able to see the docks and the River Mersey right across to Birkenhead, he thought enviously, and wondered if it was where the girl – Lonnie – slept. He also wondered what sort of a garden they possessed and whether it was any good for games. Although there was a small wooden door in the wall leading on to Haig Street, it was firmly bolted and in excellent condition; he tried peeping around the edges but it fitted snugly and he could see nothing. Tilting his head back, he looked up at the great, sooty brick wall, but it was far too high to even think of scaling it, which meant he would not be able to get so much as a glimpse of what lay beyond. He knew that there were trees since he could see branches swaying in the breeze above the wall, but other than that the garden was a closed book.

Since he was on Haig Street, he decided it might be worth while to take a look at the other properties; maybe they would not all be so well protected. Accordingly, he strolled along the pavement, peering curiously at the backs of the great houses as he passed them, and very soon found premises into which he could peer with ease. There was a board attached to the gate in the wall here, which read *Catholic Women's League Residential Club*. It appeared that the Catholic Women were not as fussy about the upkeep of their property as other residents, for the little door fitted very badly and in fact was hanging by one hinge. By standing on tiptoe, Ben was able to see into the garden. It was a pleasant sight on this sunny May morning. There was a terrace close to the house upon which a number of wrought-iron tables and chairs had been set out. Below the terrace was a wide lawn upon which Ben could see some small metal arches, and closer to Ben was a tarmacked area marked with white lines, with a net suspended about six feet from the ground, bisecting it. Not tennis, Ben mused, nor yet any of the other games he had seen being played in the city parks. He decided he would come back one evening to satisfy his curiosity, then moved on a bit further until he came to a somewhat run down property whose door actually stood open. Above the door the legend *Father Branningan's Orphan Asylum* made Ben start forward eagerly. Several members of the Branny attended his school; he might actually see someone he knew in the garden.

This, however, did not prove to be the case. There were half a dozen boys hunting a ball about on the rough ground within the walls, but though Ben took a good look at them they were mostly older than he and he knew none of them.

Retracing his steps, Ben decided that Miss Elliott and miserable little Lonnie were fortunate in their neighbours. The houses directly adjacent to their own were respectable and well kept and when Lonnie was a bit older she could, if she wished, go further along the road and get to know the Father Branny boys. Ben knew from his own experience that they were a friendly lot and guessed they would welcome a neighbour popping in for the odd game of football or cricket.

Walking past the house into which his kitten had disappeared, Ben glanced up at the attic windows and was gratified to see a small face pressed wistfully against the glass. So he had been right! The miserable little girl and her companion must occupy the attic rooms, for even at this distance he recognised Lonnie's limp hair and pallored, unhealthy-looking complexion. What was more, the child in the window was holding up something small and furry, clearly letting the kitten see what a grand home it now possessed. Much heartened by this, Ben waved and shouted and after a moment Lonnie waved back, though no one could have called it an enthusiastic greeting and indeed, immediately afterwards, she disappeared from behind the glass and did not re-appear again, though Ben waited for several moments more before turning his steps homeward.

Chapter Two

The first person Ben saw when he turned into the jigger at the back of Elmore Street was his sister Phyllis. She was crouching in the middle of the alley with a number of small objects spread out in front of her on a wooden orange box. Ben saw two pieces of broken china, some very weary-looking cabbage leaves, an apple core and several curled-up crusts of dried bread. On the other side of the orange box Phyllis's friend Annie stood, head on one side, contemplating the display of goods on the make-believe counter, for Ben knew at once that the little girls were playing 'shop'.

'I've very sorry, Mrs Jones, but me prices aren't to be argued over,' Phyllis was saying stoutly. 'Them cabbages is fresh as can be; look, they've still got the dew on them petals. So I'm afraid it's pay up or clear out, Mrs Jones.'

'But I've gorra make blind scouse for me whole fambly and I've got fourteen kids as well as me and me old man,' Annie said plaintively. 'I think your cabbages is too dear. I'll have a pound of carrots instead.'

'Well, Mrs Jones, you're missin' a real bargain,' Phyllis warned her friend. She dug out a greasy brown paper bag from somewhere about her person – Ben suspected her knicker leg – and grudgingly put a couple of crusts inside it, then screwed the bag closed and held it out towards her friend. 'That'll be sixpence please, Mrs Jones.'

'Sixpence! For two mouldy old carrots?' Annie squeaked. 'That's scandalous, Mrs Bailey. In future, I'll do me messages up on the Scottie, where a bargain's a bargain.'

'No you won't, 'cos your mammy won't let you go up the Scottie by yourself,' Phyllis said triumphantly. 'If you shops local, you pays local prices, I've heard me mammy say so many a time. Anyway, you can be shopkeeper now and I'll be the customer – and don't you try to cheat me or you ain't the only one that'll be shoppin' elsewhere.'

'No, I'm sick of this game,' Annie said discontentedly, throwing the paper bag down on to the counter. 'You're a cheat, Phyllis Bailey! When you're the shopkeeper, nothin' I want is ever under sixpence, but when you're the customer you nag and nag till I drops me price, so you always gets the best of it. I ain't playin' with you no more.'

Phyllis was nearly five and Annie a year older, but Ben knew that his sister usually got her own way and was not surprised to hear Phyllis say, as he walked past her: 'Here's me big brother Ben. If you won't buy from me, I'll tell him to give you a clack round the ear and that'll learn you.'

Ben turned and grinned down at his small, grimy sister. She had buttercup yellow curls, big blue eyes and a rosy, dimpled face, but today you would scarcely have known it, so covered in grime was she. He guessed that her previous game had been mud pies, or digging up drains, or something equally filthy and said, chidingly, 'If I give anybody a clack, it'll be you, you mucky little tyke. Just you get into the yard and have a swill under the tap before our mam sets eyes on you, and play nicely with Annie here or she'll leave you to your own devices and you wouldn't like that, would you?'

Phyllis, who was a sociable child and hated her own company, pulled a face at him, extending her tongue so far that Ben goggled at the length of it. 'Take care the wind doesn't change,' he said warningly. 'Come on, Philly, and I'll give you a hand to get the muck off you before Mam calls us for our dinners.' Phyllis hauled her tongue in board and followed her brother through the door in the wall into their own tiny yard, calling back over her shoulder to Annie, as though they had never disagreed, that she would see her in the afternoon.

Ben led his small sister across to the tap and filled the cracked china bowl which stood beneath it. Despite Phyllis's objections, he washed her hands and face, then rinsed her hair and rubbed it dry on the towel which hung from a nail on the nearby wall. Needless to say, the operation was accompanied by wails and grumbles from Phyllis, but Ben reminded her that their mother would have employed soap and a scrub brush on someone so filthy, and presently brother and sister, both considerably cleaner and wetter, crossed the tiny, cobbled yard and entered the kitchen. Though it was May and a sunny day, the fire blazed up cheerfully, for it was the only means of cooking that Mrs Bailey had. Right now she was dishing up from a blackened pot into six enamel dishes whilst Ben's older brothers, Dick and Ted, seated themselves at the wooden table, looking expectantly towards the food. Dick was twenty-three and a handsome young man. He had toffee-brown hair with a suspicion of a curl, golden-brown eyes and a long humorous mouth. He was a marine joiner at Cammell Laird's, making beautiful furniture and fittings for the ships which the yard built; the only member of the family bringing in good, regular money and though he had had several girlfriends, he had formed no permanent relationship. Ben thought this a rattling good thing, since his mother had once confided, as they searched for bargains in Paddy's market, that she did not know what the family would do without Dick's wages.

'I know he wouldn't lerrus go short if he could possibly help it,' she had told Ben. 'But when a young fellow weds, he needs every penny he earns for a home of his own and the upkeep of his family. Of course I know he'll marry some day,' she added hastily, 'and I hope he finds a real good girl to wed, honest to God I do. But until it happens, I'm that grateful for our Dick's help. And then Teddy's not doing badly. I know an apprentice doesn't get paid much, but he's well thought of is our Teddy. By the time Dick finds himself a wife, I dare say Teddy will be earning a real wage.'

'When our Millie was first married, she used to give me pocket money,' Ben said wistfully. 'But that were before the twins were born. I guess things get harder when you have kids, eh, Mam?'

His mother had agreed, with a sigh, that once you had children things did indeed become more difficult, but then a friend had hailed her and the conversation had moved on to other things. It had made Ben aware, however, of how dependent his parents were on their children's earnings, and from that time on he had been anxious to help in any way he could.

Now, Mrs Bailey looked up and smiled as her two youngest children came across the room towards her. She was a tiny, skinny woman with frizzy light-brown hair rapidly turning grey, rather protruding teeth and short-sighted eyes which gazed at the world through cracked and constantly mended spectacles. She was, as usual, clad in cast-off clothing far too big for her, for she had an elder sister who had married a plumber and was therefore in comfortable circumstances and able to pass on to her younger and less fortunate sister a good many of her outworn garments.

Ben admired his mother for she was a hard worker, having to bring up her family with very little assistance from her husband. Bob Bailey was suffering from lung disease and spent most of the day lying on a makeshift couch in the front room, trying to stuff and address envelopes or do accounts for small local businesses. Despite the money which the older boys brought in, Ben knew that his mother took on any job which would add to the family's income, cleaning offices and shops, taking in washing and earning whatever she could. Ben knew she was putting money away each week against the time when his father's illness grew worse and the doctor's bills became more frequent.

Phyllis, of course, was too young to help much anyway, and Ben did the best he could by doing the messages for his mother, fetching coal and water into the house, preparing vegetables and performing similar household tasks. He also delivered his father's work when it was completed, but so far he had not managed to obtain a paying job of his own. Now, with the comfortable assurance that he would soon be able to contribute something to the household expenses, thanks to Mr Madison, he took his place at the table and awaited the opportunity to reveal his wonderful news.

When they were all settled with steaming plates

before them – it was blind scouse, Ben noted without surprise – Mrs Bailey asked Ben how the kittens were doing. 'I were that sorry I couldn't offer 'em a home,' she said remorsefully, digging a spoon into her stew, 'but you know how it is, our Ben, it's a struggle for your dad and meself to make ends meet wi'out addin' another half dozen mouths to feed.'

'They's doin' fine,' Ben said, through a mouthful of scouse. 'The man in the pet shop took 'em – well, I telled you that last night – and he's already sold the littl'un. In fact, you could say *I* sold the kitten, 'cos there were this girl, lookin' in the window . . .'

Ben told the whole story, right from the beginning, though he omitted the offer of a job, saving that for a triumphant surprise later. The family listened with deep interest, even Phyllis refraining from interrupting, until his tale was told and then his father, from his place by the fire, remarked: 'India, d'you say, our Ben? I've always had a hankering to visit that country. And you say *both* them girls had lived in India all their lives? Well, blow me down. They'll have seen tigers, elephants, snake charmers – all sorts of wonders.' He sighed deeply. 'I wish they was living near enough to come a-visiting for I'd dearly love to chat with them, hear their adventures. Did they tell you anything, our Ben?'

'Norra lot,' Ben said regretfully. 'But I knows where they live and I'm going to keep my eye on that kitten, same as I will with the others when they're sold, so I'll mebbe get friendly with 'em. If I do, I'll try and bring one or other round some time, so you can have a yarn.'

'I doubt they'd come round here . . .' Mr Bailey was beginning doubtfully, when his wife cut in.

'Posh folks don't mix wi' the likes of us,' she said

briskly. 'But kids is kids. If that little gal doesn't have pals, then she'll be grateful for a decent lad to take her around, like.' She turned in her chair to smile fondly at her husband. 'So I wouldn't be at all surprised if young missy whatsername was to turn up here, bright as a button, to fetch our Ben one fine day.'

'She don't know where I live,' Ben pointed out. He felt the conversation was getting out of hand. After all, Miss Elliott and young Lonnie were simply the buyers of one of his kittens. Mr Madison, on the other hand, was his future employer, and as such would be of considerable interest to the entire Bailey family. It just showed, Ben thought triumphantly, that the kittens had been a blessing. Their acquisition had led to his first job, and that had to be good.

'Indians wear turbans and keep daggers in their belts,' Dick said dreamily. He shovelled a potato into his mouth and spoke thickly through it. 'Does that girl wear a turban, our Ben? I should think a kitten would be a pretty tame pet after tigers and monkeys and that.'

Ben decided it was time to announce his own important news. 'Hold on,' he said, with as much authority as he could muster, 'I haven't telled you all of it yet. Because Mr Madison saw that I'd helped to sell the kitten, he's offered me a job. I'm to go in each day after school – probably more during the holidays – and clean cages, feed the animals, and deliver ones what have been sold.' He beamed proudly around the table. 'What about that, eh? *And* he paid me one and threepence for the kittens, so here's me first wage, Mam.'

Ben fished in his pocket and drew out the money, tossing it lightly on to the table in front of his mother's plate and scarcely regretting at all the lost sweets, fruit and cinema shows which it had represented.

'Well I'm blessed,' Mrs Bailey said. 'Aren't I a lucky woman, to have all three of me sons earnin' a bit of money!' She swept the coins into the palm of her hand, then extracted sixpence and handed it back to Ben. 'Now you know me, young Ben; d'you think I'd take *all* of your wages, eh? You earned this money fair an' square, lookin' after them kittens as well as their own mother, so you'll take a share in the profits. Right?'

'Thanks, Mam,' Ben said gratefully, pocketing the sixpence. 'Still an' all, it's nice to know there'll be more where this came from. I were lucky to take Mr Madison's fancy but the kittens were such good 'uns that I guess he realised I like looking after animals.' He looked around the table. Phyllis was shovelling food into her mouth and seemed unaffected by his wonderful news, but Dick was smiling encouragingly at him and Ted leaned across the table and clapped him on the shoulder.

'Well done, young 'un,' Ted said bracingly. 'Next time you chop kindling for our mam, you might do some extra bundles and sell 'em door to door along Landseer Road. I heard some feller on the wireless saying he'd started out selling kindling and doin' messages for neighbours and ended up a millionaire with a huge house in Crosby and a dozen servants at his beck and call. Mind, I doubt he were as young as ten when he started, so you've an even better chance of making a heap of money one of these days.'

Everyone laughed but the laughter was affectionate, admiring, and Ben glowed with pride in his achievement. He might never become a millionaire but if he could keep his job and help his mam, then that would satisfy him.

Lonnie crossed the nursery, pulling off her outer garments as she did so and dropping them on the floor. She should have known from past experience that Hester would not countenance such behaviour, but at long last the weather had turned really summery and even Lonnie had found the heat in the streets oppressive. She had been clad in her coat, hat, gloves and boots, despite Hester's advising her to choose something lighter, and her pride had not allowed her to admit her winter clothing was a mistake, but as soon as she reached the nursery she had begun casting off the hot and heavy garments.

'Leonora Victoria Hetherington-Smith, what *do* you think you're doing?' Hester said reprovingly, entering the room hot on her charge's heels. 'Pick that clothing up at once and put it away tidily. Where's Kitty?'

'Why can't you pick it up?' Lonnie said aggressively. She was hot and cross and in no mood to be trifled with. 'As for Kitty, she's probably on my bed . . . but I'd better just check.' She went to pass Hester but was grabbed and turned to face her clothing. Hester said nothing, but gave her a little shake and pointed. Lonnie sighed. 'You asked where Kitty was so I was going to find out for sure,' she said plaintively. 'Whilst I do that, you might as well pick up my coat and things.'

This time the shake was harder and accompanied by a push in the back. Lonnie compressed her lips. Six weeks ago she would have pouted, run out of the room or demanded that a maid be sent up to do the task but time was already changing her attitude.

Despite her forays into the outside world, she had made no friends amongst the children who played in the parks. Some of them had made overtures but always seemed to draw back, and though Lonnie told herself it did not matter she was often lonely, so was careful not to antagonize Hester too much. Hester had made it clear, however, that if she herself were to remain at the house in Shaw Street, Lonnie must begin to do more. Looking back now, as she bent to pick up the clothing, Lonnie remembered how she had fought against doing such menial tasks at first. The first time she had had to empty Kitty's litter tray, for instance, she had stalked indignantly down the stairs and out into the garden, the reeking seed box and its nauseous contents held out in front of her whilst she muttered imprecations against Hester and every other member of the household. She had meant to tip the seed box out on to the lawn, hoping that one of the maids would step straight into the mess and carry it back into the kitchen to disgust the other servants. Mimms, who had been weeding a nearby flowerbed, had scotched this nasty intention by calling her over and telling her that there was a compost heap at the end of the garden, behind the shed.

'And don't think I couldn't tell from the way you was behavin' what you intended to do with that stuff,' he said severely. 'If you want to keep that kitten, you'll dispose of its messes where I say, for I won't have my flowerbeds or my lawn mucked up by cat dirt.'

Lonnie had looked at his rosy, countryman's face and stern eyes and had said pertly: 'How dare you speak to me like that! You are only a servant and an outdoor one at that. In future, I shall empty the litter tray as soon as I am outside the house. And don't you dare threaten my cat, you wicked old man.'

What had happened next had shocked Lonnie to the core of her being, for Mimms had made as if to turn away, knocking the litter tray as he did so. The contents had cascaded down Lonnie's front, staining her pink gingham dress, her white stockings and her brown leather sandals. Naturally, she had begun to shout, to accuse Mimms of deliberately attacking her, but the old man had just laughed.

'I reckon you got what was comin' to you,' he said. 'It were an accident, but unless you want a few more similar accidents, young woman, you'll not speak to me like that again. Why, I'm fifty years older than you – didn't no one ever tell you to show respect for your elders? D'you want everyone to think you're a nasty, spiteful kid? Most of the servants think it already, an' I don't blame 'em. I disagreed, I thought you were just spoilt, but now I'm not so sure. Mebbe they'm right and you're as black as you're painted. What d'you say to that, eh?'

Lonnie had looked down at her ruined dress and then up into the old man's face. Thoughts raced through her head. People, it seemed to her, did not like Leonora Victoria Hetherington-Smith very much, but this old man had not yet made up his mind. If she apologised . . . but why should she? He was only a servant after all.

She opened her mouth to tell him what she thought of him and with some astonishment heard her own voice saying penitently, 'I'm very sorry, Mr Mimms. Miss Elliott is always telling me that things are different here, but sometimes I forget. I'll take the box to the compost heap in future, truly I will.'

Mr Mimms's face softened and he held out the

spade he was carrying. 'Scrape the stuff up wi' this and purrit back in the seed box,' he said gruffly, 'then we'll say no more. Tell you what, Miss Lonnie, one of these days mebbe I'll give you a little garden plot of your own, then you'll appreciate me compost heap. You ain't such a bad little thing after all.'

This somewhat tepid phrase had thrilled Lonnie out of all proportion to the words used and she began to seek Mimms out when she visited the garden, even offering help should he need it.

Now, going into her bedroom and checking that Kitty was still queening it in the middle of her bed, Lonnie remembered that she did have a friend, for only the previous week Mimms had done as he had half promised and had given her a small piece of garden for her very own. She was eager to begin work in it as soon as she and Hester had had their tea.

Returning to the nursery – only now it was called the schoolroom – Lonnie assured Hester that the kitten was fine. 'We'll have tea early tonight, so I can start work on my piece of garden,' she said.

Hester heaved a sigh. 'May we have tea early tonight, please, Hester?' she said reprovingly. 'Does nothing ever stay in that butterfly brain of yours, Lonnie? You simply must learn to ask; little girls do not issue commands as though they were colonels in the army!'

'They do in India . . .' Lonnie was beginning, then saw the look on her companion's face and hastily changed it to: 'Please may we have tea early today, Hester?'

Hester, laughing, said she would do her best. After Mrs Jackson had left, it had been agreed between Miss Hetherington-Smith and Hester that nursery tea should be prepared and served by Hester herself. The new cook, Mrs Ainsworth, had set up quite a little kitchen in one of the spare attic rooms, even getting a small icebox so that milk would keep in all but the hottest weather. Each morning now, one of the maids toiled up the stairs with a fresh loaf from the local baker, a jug of milk, a large pat of butter and anything else which Hester thought suitable for their tea. Today it was to be cold ham and salad, accompanied by a plateful of bread and butter, followed by a square of seed cake. This last was regarded with abhorrence by Lonnie but Hester cheated by spreading jam over each slice and making a custard with the remains of the milk which she allowed Lonnie to pour over her portion.

Whilst they ate this repast, Kitty, who was now quite a well grown little cat, tucked into a bowl of bread and milk.

'Finished!' Lonnie said as soon as she had scraped the last trace of custard from her dish. 'That was really nice, Hester. I think I like nursery tea best of all our meals. I wonder if I might take Kitty into the garden with me? After all, she's getting to be quite big now and I'm sure she won't try to escape. Mr Mimms says it's agin nature for a cat to be always indoors and he says even if she does get out of the garden, she'll come back home of her own accord, 'cos cats knows their own place once they's fully growed.'

'Lonnie! If I've told you once, I've told you a hundred times not to imitate people's accents . . .'

'Yes, but it's what Mr Mimms *said*,' Lonnie pointed out. 'It is hard to know what's right and what's wrong, when you're in a new country and people talk differently. Can I take Kitty out with me, Hester?

I wonder if the other kittens get to go into gardens? They were all sold weeks ago! I bet that boy was pleased.'

'Yes, you may take her with you if you promise me not to go chasing after her if she gets out of the garden,' Hester said, after a moment's thought. 'You are still not used to the traffic on the streets, and dreadful though it would be to lose Kitty it would be even worse if I were to lose you! So remember, no straying outside the garden.'

'Kitty can't possibly escape unless someone leaves the street door open,' Lonnie pointed out, picking her pet up and giving her an exuberant hug. 'She's far too little to climb that huge wall and anyway she'll have heaps of exploring to do in the garden. She won't be interested in the outside world for a while yet. Call me when you want me to come in, because Aunt Emmeline still hasn't written to my father to ask if I may have a watch.'

'I'll come down when I've cleared up the tea things and see how you and Kitty are getting on,' Hester promised. 'Does Kitty's dirt tray need changing? If so, you might as well kill two birds with one stone and take it down with you when you go.'

'Oh – oh, pooh! I'll be carrying Kitty though, so couldn't you . . . ?' Lonnie was beginning, when she belatedly remembered that she was supposed to do everything for Kitty, and to do it willingly. Heaving a sigh, she went over and picked up the seed box, then headed for the door.

Hester went ahead of her to open the door, then took the seed box from her. 'Just this once, I'll bring it downstairs for you because you were a good girl and remembered the rules,' she said approvingly. 'You are beginning to learn some nice English manners, Lonnie, so I'm happy to help you out on occasion.'

'Thank you,' Lonnie said humbly, and together the two descended the stairs and presently emerged into the garden. How odd it was, Lonnie thought, as she set the kitten on the ground, took the box from Hester and watched her governess disappear into the house once more, that the sun which had seemed so oppressive in the streets should seem merely warming in the garden. But then she remembered that it was later in the day and that a pleasant breeze was stirring the branches of the tall trees.

'Well, missie? Have you come to do a bit of digging in your little plot? I said I'd find you a small spade and I've done just that – tek a hold on it and let's see whether it's right for you.' Mr Mimms stood before her, a miniature spade in one hand and a miniature fork in the other. Lonnie beamed at him, delighted that he had remembered how futile her efforts had been when wielding his enormous garden tools.

'Where did you get them?' she asked delightedly. 'Oh, thank you, Mr Mimms, how very kind you are! I'll try them at once but I'm sure they're both exactly right.'

The old man walked down the garden beside Lonnie, telling her that the tools had once belonged to his small son. 'All I had to do was clean 'em up a bit,' he assured her. 'My Ron were happy for you to have 'em since he's no young 'uns of his own.' They had reached the end of the garden and Lonnie seized the fork and began to dig, exclaiming with pleasure at how the brightly shining metal tines penetrated the hard-packed earth, for her little garden was close up against the wall and the soil had not been worked for many years.

'Don't try to do too much at once; pace yourself,' Mr Mimms advised, watching with approval as Lonnie began to turn the soil, breaking up the pieces with repeated blows of the fork. 'When you've dug the whole patch, I'll barrow over some compost, 'cos you have to feed soil if you want your plants to thrive, same as you do that plaguey kitten.'

Kitty, who had been cautiously investigating the newly turned earth, sprang back as a worm came wriggling to the surface. Lonnie laughed breathlessly. 'Right, Mr Mimms,' she said, wiping drops of perspiration from her hot face. 'Oh, Kitty, get out from under my fork or I'll spear you by mistake and that would be terrible. Go and play on the lawn or under the trees, where it's cool. I'm far too busy to amuse you now.'

Mr Mimms pulled a large gunmetal watch from his waistcoat pocket and examined it, then put it back. 'Time I were off,' he said gruffly. 'Sure you'll be all right, Miss Lonnie? Only Mrs Mimms gets that aerated if I'm late for me tea, life ain't worth livin'.'

'I'll be fine, Mr Mimms,' Lonnie assured him. She was very warm and her arms and legs were already beginning to tell her that this unusual work was not entirely to their taste, but she continued doggedly digging. In her imagination, her garden was already a mass of wonderful things. She would grow flowers, fruit, vegetables – oh, all sorts. But first, she knew, she must conquer the soil, enrich it with compost as Mr Mimms had advised, and find some means of earning a few pennies so that she might buy seeds. 'Thanks ever so much for my garden, Mr Mimms, and for my gardening tools. I'll take great care of them, the way you showed me last week, and put them ever so carefully into your shed and remember to lock it afterwards.'

'An' give Mrs Ainsworth the key, 'cos I don't want to find me shed burgled when I comes in tomorrer,' Mr Mimms said. He wheeled his rusty old bicycle towards the door in the high wall. 'Catch a hold of that cat, Miss Lonnie, or it'll be out through the gate and off down the road before you can say knife. Cats is that contrary, I've never known one what didn't want to be on the other side of any door it set eyes on.'

'Curiosity killed the cat,' Lonnie murmured, clasping Kitty to her chest and watching Mr Mimms as he wheeled his bicycle through the doorway into Haig Street. Kitty stared at the closed door, her golden eyes round with inquisitiveness, and Lonnie dropped a kiss between the little cat's pricked ears before returning her to the ground once more. 'Now we've got the garden all to ourselves,' she told her. 'I wish I could spare the time to play with you, Kitty, but I've got far too much work to do.' She took up her fork once more. 'I should like to get the digging finished before Hester calls us.'

The kitten miaowed and wound round her ankles, and then the little cat's attention was distracted by a passing butterfly. She leapt in pursuit, standing on her hind legs and batting fruitlessly at the air beneath the lovely insect. Lonnie watched her for a moment, then went back to her digging and had actually turned over a good half of her plot before she stopped for a rest and, looking round, realised with dismay that the kitten seemed to have disappeared. All thoughts of her garden forgotten, Lonnie cast down her fork and was about to begin searching Mr Mimms's vegetable plot and herbaceous borders when a loud miaow caused her to look up. Precariously balanced on an upper branch of the tall lime tree sat Kitty, eyes wide with fright, tiny white claws clutching desperately as the bough upon which she perched dipped and swayed in the breeze.

'Oh, Kitty, how ever did you get up there?' Lonnie cried, horrified at her pet's daring. 'Come down at once, and come down carefully!'

For a moment it seemed as though Kitty were going to obey her, but then the wind caused the bough to sway again and the kitten either lost her hold or decided to try for a safer perch, for one moment she was peering at Lonnie through the tossing leaves and the next she was sprawled on top of the brick wall.

'Oh, Kitty, hang on! I'll . . . I'll fetch a ladder from Mr Mimms's tool shed and rescue you,' Lonnie gabbled, even more afraid for her pet, for the wall seemed to have no sheltering spot into which the kitten might scramble and the wind caused the branches to sway and even brush against the bricks every now and then. 'Stay there! Don't move!'

Lonnie dashed towards the shed but before she so much as unlocked the door she glanced back towards the top of the wall upon which the kitten had been crouching. It was empty.

Without a second thought, Lonnie ran towards the green door in the wall, opened it and shot through. She dreaded seeing Kitty flattened on the pavement, but instead her pet was dancing jauntily along the road in the direction of Everton Brow. Lonnie shouted and felt a moment's relief when the little cat turned her head, but since Kitty then set off again at twice the pace, such relief was short-lived. Haig Street was a quiet road with very little traffic, but Everton Brow, stretching as it did between Shaw Street and Cazneau Street, was a different matter altogether. Traffic roared along it and the pavements were crowded with folk doing their messages before the shops closed.

By dint of running as hard as she could, Lonnie was only a few yards behind Kitty when she reached Salisbury Street. She was greatly relieved when the kitten did not attempt the crossing, but turned into Salisbury Street and ran along the left-hand pavement, occasionally glancing back as though keen to encourage her little mistress to continue the chase. The cat kept ahead of her with ease, for Lonnie was not used to running and was soon nursing a stitch in her side. She was gaining on the kitten, however, and beginning to feel confident that the chase was nearly over when a large, fat woman clad all in black, who was sailing down the pavement towards her, bent and picked Kitty up. Lonnie, thanking her stars, hurried up to the woman and began to explain that the kitten was hers, but the woman did not seem to understand. She shook her head, then addressed Lonnie in an accent so broad that the child had to strain every nerve to understand.

'Whazzup, chuck?' the woman wheezed. 'This 'ere's me own lickle cat what I lorst no more than a week ago. Whazzat you're sayin'? Is it like a cat you know, queen? But there's no doubt in me mind that this is lickle Tibby, what's been lorst and probably a-frettin' for kind Auntie Clara to find him . . . and now I have.' She beamed, toothlessly, upon Lonnie but her little grey eyes were calculating. 'Now orf wi' you, little missie! Tibby and me's goin' home so's he can have a nice saucer of conny-onny to fatten him up a bit.'

Lonnie began to protest, but the fat woman took no notice. She turned on her heel and presently dived across the road, but Lonnie, who was no fool, saw that the woman lingered as she crossed, as though to make certain that Lonnie was still following her. Perhaps this was some sort of game, Lonnie thought hopefully, as she stuck as close to the woman – presumably Auntie Clara – as she could get. She hoped that when they reached the further pavement, Auntie Clara would give her wheezy laugh and return the kitten to its rightful owner, explaining that it had all been a joke.

Nothing of the sort happened, however. The fat woman continued along the pavement, not hurrying, and glancing constantly at her pursuer, then turned down a narrow, blackened alleyway between the houses. Looking up at the street sign, Lonnie saw that they were now in Vine Terrace and thought what a shame it was that such a pretty name should belong to so ugly a street. Ahead of her, Auntie Clara had stopped walking and given a bellow, whereupon a dozen or so children, all ragged and filthy, clustered about her. Auntie Clara held up the kitten and addressed them. 'Hey, kids, look wharr I've got. If it ain't my own little Tibby wharr I lost last week, come back to his old mam. You remember my Tibby, don'cher, kids? 'Cos this lickle girl seems to think it's her kitten, but we knows better, doesn't we?'

Lonnie glanced hopefully at the children, then reflected bitterly that she should have guessed. These were kids to whom lying, cheating and probably stealing kittens came as naturally as breathing; she would get no help from them. Wondering what on earth to do next, she looked up into Auntie Clara's greedy face and saw, with distate, that the woman's skin was as grimed as that of the children surrounding her and that the thin strands of grey hair which fell from her headscarf looked as though they had seldom, if ever, been washed.

Lonnie was still wondering what on earth to do next when Auntie Clara spoke again. 'But it seems as though you've took a rare likin' to me lickle cat, young lady,' she said, leering down at Lonnie. 'I'm as fond of it as though it were me own child, but I won't deny I've hard work enough to feed meself and me brats, so I dare say it'd be better off wi' you. What say you give me half a crown? Then I'll hand it to you and no more said. Wharrabout it, eh?'

'But I haven't got half a crown,' Lonnie said helplessly. 'My aunt doesn't give me pocket money. I don't even have an *anna*.' She looked desperately around her. 'If you will come home with me, though, I'm sure my aunt would pay for the kitten.'

The fat woman laughed scornfully. 'Come home wi' you? An' have you tellin' everyone as how I'd stole your kitten and tried to sell it back to you?' She turned to the children, still hovering restlessly. 'That's likely, ain't it? I'm not such a fool as to put me head straight into the trap so's you can set the scuffers on me.' Her bright, mean little eyes swept over Lonnie from top to toe. 'That's a decent lickle dress you've gorron, an' them socks an' sandals is worth a penny or two down at uncle's. Hand 'em over and we'll say no more . . . I might even give you the kitten, just to show willin'.'

Lonnie stared at the old woman with disbelief. Surely she could not seriously expect Lonnie to take off her clothes and run home through the streets in her white pleated knickers, liberty bodice and vest? She was beginning to say she would do no such thing when the fat woman held up the kitten and began to squeeze. The kitten gasped and struggled and Lonnie saw its mouth open to miaow a protest and realised, with horror, that it could not do so. 'Stop it!' she shouted. 'You're hurting Kitty and she's never done anything to hurt you! I promise I'll give you money if only you'll let Kitty alone!'

'Tek your dress off and them nice sandals,' the woman said remorselessly. She squeezed the kitten again and Lonnie saw Kitty's eyes begin to bulge. The small mouth gaped and abruptly Lonnie lost her temper. Screaming abuse in Hindustani, she elbowed the children aside and went for her tormentor's face with her nails, stamping briskly on the woman's feet in their cracked old boots and kicking at her dirty white legs. The woman staggered back, loosing her hold on the kitten for a moment. Lonnie snatched the trembling bundle of fur, punched the fat woman as hard as she could in her enormous, drooping chest, and made off up the terrace as fast as she could run, all thoughts of her recent stitch forgotten. As she turned into Salisbury Street she glanced behind her, confident that the fat woman could not possibly chase after her, and saw, with real dismay, that the filthy, ragged children were pursuing. As she tore up the road towards Everton Brow, she heard shouts of 'Thief! Stop thief! She's stole our mam's cat! Stop her, someone!'

Lonnie continued to run and was passing Shaw Terrace when she realised that all sounds of pursuit had ceased and, glancing over her shoulder, saw that the children had abandoned her. Much relieved, she slowed to a walk and was comforting the kitten with promises of warm milk and many cuddles as she drew level with Elizabeth Terrace. Suddenly, with a triumphant whoop, the ragged children were before her. They must have cut round the back and lain in wait to trap her – hands outstretched to grab, mouths jeering defiance.

Desperately, Lonnie turned on her heel and fled the way she had come, with the pack in close pursuit. Doubling back and forth among the narrow streets and crowded tenements she was very soon lost, but when she emerged once more on to a main road she realised that the pursuit, at least, was at an end. Amongst so many people she would be safe, for though the children from Vine Terrace had been willing enough to bully her on their own ground she guessed they would not do so when surrounded by people who would probably condemn their behaviour – might even call the police.

It was a great comfort to be able to slow to a walk, and for the first time since her encounter with the fat woman Lonnie began to wonder what would happen to her when she arrived home. She had directly disobeyed Hester and it must be long past her bedtime, for the sun was very low in the sky and there were far fewer children about in the streets than there had been earlier. Glancing up at a street sign, she realised she was on Netherfield Road and felt tears come to her eyes. The road was a busy one with trams and a good many other vehicles roaring along it, but since she had no money she could not board a tram and in any case had no idea in which direction she should be heading.

For a moment she stood on the pavement's edge, glancing up and down and hoping to be able to orient herself, then turned to a passer-by. She was a tall and angular woman, with white hair pulled back into a bun on the nape of her neck, and a beaky nose.

Despite the warmth of the evening, she was clad in stout walking shoes and a swirling black cloak. She smiled very kindly upon Lonnie but admitted that she was a stranger in these parts and had never even heard of Shaw Street. It had taken Lonnie quite a lot of courage to ask directions and having made such a poor choice she hesitated to enquire again. In fact she was still hesitating when a voice spoke in her ear. 'What the devil are you doing out at this time o' night, and on your own, little Miss hyphenated whatsyername? Cor, an' you've got my kitten. Netherfield Road ain't no place for a kitten – trams don't stop for no man, they'd flatten a kitten soon as look at it!'

Lonnie turned and stared at the boy and had great difficulty in refraining from bursting into tears of relief. It was Ben, the boy from the pet shop! He might not like her – well, he did not like her – but at least he was a familiar face and she remembered that he had once owned the kittens and been kind to them. Convulsively, she grabbed at his arm with her free hand. 'Oh, oh, Ben, you don't know how glad I am to see you! I'm lost . . . this fat old woman tried to steal Kitty . . . some wicked children chased me, and I'll be in dreadful trouble when I do find Shaw Street again! Please, *please* can you take me home?'

She expected Ben to comply at once but instead he continued to stare severely down at her. 'Have you *seen* yourself?' he said incredulously. He took her arm and guided her to the nearest shop window, pointing at her reflection in the glass. 'Your dress is filthy, there's blood running down your knee and your elbow is scraped. Your hair's come loose and if them socks were white once, they ain't now. What's more, them shoes is caked with mud, if not worse, and how did you come by that bruise on your forehead?'

Lonnie, regarding her dishevelled reflection with fascination, remembered that she had fallen in her efforts to escape from the gang and was only glad that she had managed, on each occasion, not to fall on the kitten. 'I *told* you some kids chased me,' she said reproachfully. 'I fell once, rounding a corner too fast. The second time I tripped on an uneven paving stone and went down with a real bang. But Kitty's all right, although that wicked woman tried to squeeze her to death.' She heaved a deep sigh and held the kitten under her chin, feeling the small body vibrate with purrs. 'I don't care what they do to me, but suppose they send Kitty away? Because I *am* in a state, anyone can see that.'

'Tell you what,' Ben said, after a pause for thought, 'why don't you come back to Elmore Street where I live and let me mam tidy you up a bit? I dare say your folk won't be near so mad with you if you're clean and tidy and just say you got lost. After all, anyone can get lost. It's only when you get filthy as well that mams and dads holler at you.'

'Is it far to Elmore Street?' Lonnie said, rather timidly. 'And what o'clock is it, Ben? Hester was going to come down for me when it was time for my supper. Will your mam mind? Oh, if only Hester doesn't tell my aunt, it might be all right. My aunt doesn't like children, or cats – in fact, she doesn't like anyone very much,' she added truthfully.

'Mam won't mind at all. She's used to us kids comin' in pretty dirty, so one more won't make a deal of difference, and it won't be much past seven o'clock. You don't go to bed that early, do you?'

'No, but Hester could have come down at any

time, I suppose,' Lonnie said. Nevertheless, she fell into step beside him. 'But I'll come back with you if you're sure your mother won't mind.'

'I said she wouldn't mind and she won't,' Ben said. 'Shall I carry the kitten? It'd give you a bit of a rest, like.'

The two set off together and presently Lonnie found herself telling Ben the whole story, starting from her digging in the garden to the moment when she had burst on to Netherfield Road and lost her pursuers. Ben, holding the kitten gently, was deeply interested and whistled with either amazement or admiration – Lonnie could not tell which – upon hearing of Lonnie's attack on the fat woman. 'Serves her right for trying to strangle me kitten,' he said approvingly, when Lonnie described the kicks, scratches and punches she had administered to her foe. They stood on the edge of the pavement, waiting for an opportunity to cross, and Ben said instructively: 'This 'ere's Everton Road, queen, and Elmore Street is right there.' He pointed. 'We live at Number 27 but we won't go to the front door, 'cos no one ever uses that. We'll go down the jigger an' round the back and I'll fetch a bucket of water for me mam and you can wash as soon as we get inside. While you do that, I'll find Kitty a bite to eat and then our mam will tidy you up like what I said she would.'

Ben's mam was every bit as good as he had prophesied. The two children entered the kitchen to find Mrs Bailey ironing away at an enormous pile of white linen sheets. Ben explained briefly who his friend was and why she was there and Mrs Bailey immediately abandoned her iron and came across the kitchen to give Lonnie a quick hug before carrying her off upstairs. 'It'll be best if you strip down in my bedroom and have a good wash where there ain't no likelihood of someone bursting in on you,' she explained. 'And while I clean you up I'll send young Ben round to Shaw Street to explain where you are and what's happened.' She shook her head, helping Lonnie out of the pink gingham dress and tutting over the state of it. 'Good Lor', this *is* dirty. I'd best take it downstairs and give it a good brush while you wash. There's a bit of soap by the basin and plenty of cold water – will that do you?'

Lonnie agreed that it would do very well. Fortunately, for she had never washed herself in India, Hester had insisted that she learn how to clean herself up properly, so once Mrs Bailey had left her Lonnie struggled out of her underwear and lathered every inch of herself with the tiny piece of soap. The soap was red and smelt so strongly of disinfectant that it made Lonnie's eyes water, but it did its work well. Then she rinsed herself off in cold water, shuddering a little, for the warmth of the day was over and a cool breeze blew through the open window.

As she dried herself on the piece of rough towelling beside the china basin, she had leisure to look round the room. She had scarcely noticed the kitchen as she was hustled through it and up the stairs, but now she examined her hostess's bedroom closely. The room was very clean, the walls whitewashed, the worn linoleum on the floor speckless. There was a very old brass bedstead in the middle of the room, with one thin blanket folded over the faded counterpane, and when she investigated a curtain hanging beside the bed she found that it concealed a rail upon which several clean but well-worn garments hung. Apart from the washstand, there was nothing else in the room, though there was a broken piece of mirror propped up behind the enamel water jug and one ornament in front of it – a chipped shepherdess, with a headless lamb pressed against her skirts.

Lonnie had just finished drying and dressing herself in her underwear, and was draping the towel across the washstand and wondering how she could go downstairs without her dress, when she heard someone ascending the creaking wooden stairs. She opened the door cautiously and peered around it and Mrs Bailey beamed at her. 'I come up to tell you to fetch me tartan shawl from behind the curtain, and wrap it round yourself so's you can be decent,' she said, a trifle breathlessly. 'I didn't wash your dress but I've give it a good brush and sponged the worst marks off it. Your socks I had to wash and our Dick – that's Ben's big brother – is working on your sandals right now. He'll get 'em as clean as they was when you set out this morning, so in half an hour or so you'll be able to go home lookin' respectable, at least.' Mrs Bailey stared critically at what she could see of her uninvited guest. 'When you come down, we'll clean up your knee and your elbow. I don't have stickin' plaster, but there's plenty of clean rags what'll do duty as bandages, an' I always say carbolic soap is as good as doctor's salve any day.'

She began to descend the stairs again and Lonnie went back into the bedroom and found the tartan shawl which she wrapped round herself, sari fashion, before returning to the kitchen as Mrs Bailey had bade her. When she entered the room, Mrs Bailey was ironing once more – this time the pink gingham dress – and explained that she was drying off the sponged patches, since this would be quicker than putting the dress on the line. The socks, however, had been thoroughly washed and pegged out and would not, she suspected, be dry for several hours yet.

'It doesn't matter,' Lonnie said gaily. Suddenly she realised that she felt comfortable and at home in this small and shabby house, far more comfortable than she did in Shaw Street. She supposed, vaguely, that this was because Mrs Bailey was a real mother and not just an aunt or a governess. How lovely, she mused, it would be to live here, with Mrs Bailey to fuss over her and Ben, if he could only bring himself to like her, to go about with. She glanced contentedly around the kitchen. Kitty sat before the fire, gazing at the flames, none the worse for her adventure. Like the bedroom upstairs, there was nothing here that was not immediately useful. The enclosed fire had a mantel above it, but there were no ornaments upon it, only a series of tins which had once contained tea, biscuits or cake. Someone had stuck slips of paper on each, bearing the legends tea, sugar, money for messages, bread and dried beans. The kitchen floor was quarry-tiled but a couple of rag rugs, clearly home-made, added a touch of colour, and the big, scrubbed wooden table, upon which Mrs Bailey was ironing at present, seemed very much the focus of the room.

Lonnie was about to ask Mrs Bailey where everyone was when the door which led to the rest of the house opened and a man, so skeletally thin and white that Lonnie felt he was almost transparent, came into the room, accompanied by a small, fair-haired girl. The man held a pile of brown envelopes in one arm, and put them down on the end of the table, away from Mrs Bailey's work, saying in a thin, reedy voice: 'That's today's batch finished! I'll get Ben to pop these down to Bilverstone's first thing tomorrow.' He paused, then gave Lonnie a particularly sweet smile. 'I see we have a visitor. Would you be the young lady from India?'

Lonnie admitted that she had indeed come from India and Mr Bailey was beginning to ask her what she thought of England when the small girl sidled across the room and stood next to Lonnie, looking up into her face with great curiosity. 'Who's you? I'm Phyllis Bailey and on my next birthday I'll be five,' she announced proudly.

'I'm Leonora Hetherington-Smith and on *my* next birthday I'll be nine,' Lonnie responded bravely. 'I bought one of your brother Ben's kittens, which is how we became acquainted. See her, sitting on the rug in front of your mother's nice fire?'

Phyllis gave a crow of delight and cast herself down on the hearth. Her interest in Lonnie had paled into insignificance beside her interest in the cat and since Kitty seemed much inclined to play with the bit of string which Phyllis was dangling before her it seemed they would both be happy.

At this point, the back door opened and a young man came in. Since he carried her sandals, clean and polished, in one hand, Lonnie guessed that this must be Dick. 'I've done 'em, our Mam; they're good as new now,' the young man said briskly. He looked across at Lonnie, then smiled. 'You'll be the young lady from India. I've never seen a shawl worn like that before, but it looks grand, so it does. Want to pop your sandals on now? I expect Mam explained that your socks won't be ready for a while, but no doubt our Ben will deliver 'em tomorrer, before he starts work at the pet shop.'

He put the shoes down on the kitchen floor as

he spoke and Lonnie was struggling into them and trying to thank him at the same time when Mrs Bailey came across to her, sat her down on one of the wooden kitchen chairs, and began vigorously brushing her long, limp hair. 'D'you plait it or just tie it back?' she asked as she brushed. 'My word, there's leaves in your hair, miss! Whatever have you been a-doing?'

'I've got a little piece of garden,' Lonnie said eagerly. 'Mr Mimms gave it to me for my very own. I was digging there when the kitten escaped so I was already a bit dirty. Later, a fat woman who said her name was Auntie Clara tried to steal Kitty and after that some wicked children chased me and I fell. But I'm all right now,' she finished, smiling at Mrs Bailey.

'All right you may be, but you've had a nasty old time of it,' Mrs Bailey said. She began to pour water from a blackened tin kettle into the teapot standing ready. 'I know most rich folk use fresh milk, but all we've got is conny-onny – condensed – so that'll have to do you in your tea.' She stirred the teapot briskly, then poured the tea into five chipped enamel mugs. 'Get that down you, miss, and you'll feel much more the thing.'

Having handed everyone a cup of the strong, sweet tea, Mrs Bailey fetched a loaf from a cupboard, cut several thick slices, spread them thinly with margarine and a scraping of jam, and passed them round. She did not attempt to provide a plate, so Lonnie watched Dick fold his bread over and copied him, then began to eat. It was surprisingly good; the jam was sweet yet tangy and the bread home-baked and very much nicer than the shop bought loaves which Mrs Ainsworth provided in

Shaw Street. Lonnie, who had never before given much thought to where her food came from, said rather shyly: 'This is very nice jam, Mrs Bailey. What sort is it? I've never tasted jam like this before.'

Mrs Bailey smiled, but it was Dick who answered. 'It's our mam's home-made damson,' he explained. 'Us lads pick the damsons, come the back end, because the trees grow wild in the woods and the fruit's there for anyone to gather, same as blackberries, sloes, rose-hips and the like. Mam makes us a picnic and we tek off to the woods wi' canvas bags to hold the fruit and make a day of it. It's grand in the woods in the autumn and we'll be off again in a couple o' months. Why don't you come with us, miss? I dare say you'd enjoy it, though we can't promise you lions or tigers or monkeys, lerralone snakes! In England, you'll be lucky if you see a hedgehog or a fieldmouse.'

'I *should* like it, I'm sure I should,' Lonnie said, standing down her mug of tea. 'And we didn't see lions and tigers every day, you know! In fact, I never did see a lion. I've seen tigers, though. My father went on a tiger shoot once. The tiger had been killing children when they went to the river to fetch water, so the sahibs got up a party and I went too, though I wasn't allowed to see the man-eater until he was dead.'

There was a respectful silence, broken by Dick's whistling beneath his breath. 'A man-eating tiger!' he said reverently. 'What wouldn't I give to go to India! I don't suppose I'll ever get the chance, though. What about monkeys, miss? I've heard tell monkeys is everywhere, even in the big cities. I see them in the zoo, but that isn't the same, somehow.'

'There are loads of monkeys all over Delhi,' Lonnie

admitted. 'When my *ayah* took me to the gardens at Connaught Place, we would see monkeys swinging from the peepul trees. If we took a picnic, they would come really close, hoping to snatch some food. I thought they were charming, but my *ayah* – that's my nurse – didn't like monkeys, she said their bite was poisonous. My daddy said that wasn't true; he said she was a superstitious old woman, but of course it is dangerous to be bitten by any animal, or it is in India at any rate.'

Dick whistled again. 'You make monkeys sound as common as sparrers,' he said rather wistfully. 'Did you have a garden? Were there any monkeys there?'

'Yes, there were monkeys in our garden and I thought they were really sweet because they have such pretty, sad little faces, but the servants hated them. They said if you left the door or the window open the monkeys would come in to thieve, and they were right, because once I went into the kitchen and there were four monkeys emptying a flour barrel.' She chuckled reminiscently. 'You should have seen them! They looked like four little white clowns and the mess in the kitchen was unbelievable. They're very destructive, so all the women hate them. They'll steal washing off the line or a cake off the kitchen table, and if they get frightened they'll rip curtains or mosquito netting in their hurry to escape.'

Everyone laughed and Phyllis, abandoning the kitten, begged for more stories of monkeys.

'Well, when you go into the jungle,' Lonnie said, 'you have to be careful, because the jungle is where the big monkeys live – gibbons and baboons – and they can be as strong as a man and cause a lot of damage. But the little ones would make lovely pets, I'm sure, if only I'd been allowed to have one.'

'I've seen monkeys dancing to a barrel-organ in the city centre; folk throw pennies and the monkey gathers them up, quick as a wink, and gives them to the organ grinder,' Dick offered. 'But I feel bad when I see their sad little faces. They're always cold, huddled in little red coats and hating what they have to do. I'd let 'em go back to India, if I had my way.'

'Pity Ted isn't here, because he's mortal fond of animals, same as our Ben is,' Mr Bailey remarked. 'Tell us about live tigers, little miss, ones that ain't man-eaters I mean. How can you see a tiger without riskin' it fancying you for its dinner, eh?'

In fact, Lonnie could not really remember having seen live tigers, though she knew she had done so when her mother was alive. The two of them had accompanied Mr Hetherington-Smith when he and a party of friends went into the jungle and her mother had described how she and her little daughter had taken their seats in a *howdah*, perched on the swaying back of a great elephant. She had told Lonnie how the huge beast had made its silent way along the narrow jungle paths and how they had seen tigers, antelopes and that most feared of Indian game, wild boar, from the safety of their high perch.

She had actually taken a deep breath to describe the tigers she could no longer remember when the back door opened and two people entered the room. One was Ben, grinning broadly and looking a little self-conscious, and the other was Hester.

Hester had not missed Lonnie until almost seven o'clock, when she had gone into the garden to see how the child was getting on with her digging. She usually gave Lonnie a supper of milk and biscuits at about eight o'clock, an hour before she went to bed, but this simple meal needed no preparation and could be served in a moment. So she went about her work calmly, with no need to hurry. She washed up their tea things and dried them on one of the tea-towels the cook had provided, then stacked the china and cutlery in the cupboard in the kitchen, as she now thought of the spare attic room. Then she went to the window, which had a bird's eye view of the garden, or a good deal of it, and of the city of Liverpool, spread out like a particularly fine drawing, and of the docks, the Mersey, the sea . . . and even of the town of New Brighton, on the opposite bank.

She had hoped to see Lonnie, but here she was disappointed, for the overhanging trees hid the child's small garden plot completely from her view. However, she left the window, threw a light cardigan over the shoulders of her cream cotton blouse, and descended the stairs. She did not much fancy helping Lonnie with her digging, but she intended to praise the child for her endeavours, for she knew, probably better than anyone else in the house, how hard it must be for Lonnie to come to terms with doing things for herself. Even in the short time she had worked for Mr Hetherington-Smith in Delhi, she had realised that she had been very lucky. Her own parents, though they had had a great many servants when they were in the city, or in their bungalow in the hills, had made sure that their little girl knew how to wash and dress herself, how to cope with ordinary life. When she and her father set off on a tour, what was more, she had had to be self-reliant.

She had done some rudimentary camp cooking, had helped her father's servant to carry clothing down to the nearest stream for laundering, and had waded into the water, thigh deep, to rinse shirts and shorts in the faster current in mid-stream.

Gardening, however, was a closed book to her, but one she was pleased to see young Lonnie eager to tackle. So she set off down the stairs and across the hall full of good intentions. No matter what sort of mess Lonnie was making of her plot she, Hester, would praise her for her efforts.

On her way out, she met Miss Hutchinson coming in. They exchanged a few words and then Miss Hutchinson had to hurry away, since she was dining, as usual, with her employer at seven o'clock and dreaded keeping that difficult lady waiting. 'Where are you off to, Miss Elliott?' she said archly, as they parted. 'Not meeting a young gentleman friend, I trust? Miss Hetherington-Smith would not approve of that, I can assure you!'

'No, I'm not meeting anyone. I'm going to bring Lonnie in, if she's had enough digging for one day,' Hester said, trying to hide the annoyance she felt. As if she could possibly have met a 'young gentleman friend' whilst under the Hetherington-Smith roof! Why, she was always with the child; when she had once suggested that one of the maids might keep an eye on Lonnie whilst she went to a concert at the Philharmonic Hall, she had been sharply taken to task.

'Mr Hetherington-Smith assured me that you would be in charge at all times,' Miss Hetherington-Smith had said smoothly. Hester believed the older woman was lying, had never had any such assurance from her brother, but she realised that this was not the moment to say so. 'In time, Miss Elliott, I may make arrangements so that you can have a few hours off, but not whilst Leonora is so dependent upon you. Now please don't mention the matter again. As for sparing a maid to do your job, certainly not!'

'Digging?' Miss Hutchinson said now, raising sparse eyebrows. They were as grey as her skin and almost invisible, Hester saw. 'Why on earth should the child be digging?' She giggled. 'Not trying to escape by tunnelling her way out of the garden, surely?'

Hester sighed; it would have been nice to tell Miss Hutchinson that sarcasm was said to be the lowest form of wit, but she refrained. She guessed that because of her position in the household and the treatment meted out to her by her employer, Miss Hutchinson was simply having a go at the one person in the house who could not revenge herself upon her. 'No, Miss Hutchinson, she's been given a piece of garden of her own to cultivate,' she said patiently. 'It was very kind of Mr Mimms and means a good deal to the child. She's not very comfortably situated, so far from home and with only myself for company, for I dare say we both know that her aunt has no time for children, and no interest in her niece.'

Miss Hutchinson sniffed, but looked a little conscious. Possibly she was comparing her own lot with that of Lonnie, and realising that they were both to be pitied in their different ways. 'It's nice for the child to have an interest,' she admitted over her shoulder as she went into the house. 'Not that I saw her when I was selecting a few blooms for the drawing room . . . but I expect Mimms has given her somewhere out of the way, in case she grows tired of her new pastime. Good evening to you, Miss Elliott.'

'Good evening,' Hester said levelly, and continued into the garden.

The first thing she noticed, once she had crossed the lawn and wended her way between the rows of vegetables in the kitchen garden, was the open back door in the wall.

Chapter Three

For a moment Hester thought that Mimms had just gone out and was about to close the door behind him, but then she looked towards the plot that Lonnie had been given, saw the cast down fork, the general air of abandonment, and cold fear clutched at her heart. She did not yet love Lonnie the way she ought but she was growing fonder of the child with every day that passed, and was horrified at what might befall one small girl, alone in the city of Liverpool . . . and there was the kitten! Oh, mercy, Hester thought, breaking into a run, what on earth could have happened?

She reached the open doorway and went into the street beyond, looking swiftly up and down, for who knew when Lonnie had left? It might have been minutes or hours ago! The street was a quiet one, with the houses and shops opposite all tiny, close-crammed dwellings whose inhabitants, Hester thought, were probably indoors at this hour, for no children played on the narrow pavement or invaded the road with their tops and skipping ropes. Truth to tell, she had never before used this doorway, never set foot in Haig Street, and it was a surprise to her, and not a pleasant one, that such poor dwellings should crowd so close to fashionable Shaw Street. But it had been just the same in Delhi, she remembered, beginning to hurry along the pavement towards Everton Brow. The rich rubbed shoulders with the very poor and seemed, most of the time, not to notice them. Her father had often remarked upon the indifference of the rich to the beggars, many of them horribly mutilated, who sat patiently outside the doors of those so much more fortunate than themselves. He had told the young Hester that he had often seen athletic young Englishmen trip over an armless beggar's drawn-up feet, only to curse the man and pass on without parting with so much as an *anna*.

'It's not wickedness so much as a total lack of imagination, a feeling that because a man's skin is a different colour from your own he is not a man at all, not capable of suffering, as one is oneself, but more like an animal,' he had told her. 'Don't ever get like that, little Hester. Feel for others, as I do, as all right-thinking men and women do.'

Having searched Haig Street both to right and left, Hester returned to the garden, gnawing her lip with indecision. Should she admit defeat and return to the house and tell her employer that she had lost her charge, and persuade Miss Hetherington-Smith to get the police to search for Lonnie? Or should she go further afield, knock at the doors of the houses which had a view of the roadway, and ask for help herself? She supposed it was her duty to tell Miss Hetherington-Smith, but the thought of those cold, indifferent eyes suddenly blazing into icy wrath – and, it must be admitted, the thought of her own plight should her employer decide to dismiss her without a character and without notice – determined her to search alone for a while, at any rate. What was more, it was now seven o'clock or past, which meant that the two ladies would be in the dining room, eating the excellent dinner which Cook had sent up, and in no mood to be interrupted with something as trivial as news of a lost child.

Accordingly, Hester went to the dwelling directly opposite the back of the Hetherington-Smith house, and was lucky. The woman who came to the front door was harassed and clearly in the middle of a meal, for she was still chewing and held a small baby in her arms whilst two more children clung to her skirt, but she was both knowledgeable and helpful. 'A little gal in a pink gingham dress? Oh, aye, I see'd her when I called me kids in for their grub,' she said, wiping the baby's nose on a piece of rag and then using the same piece of rag to do similar duty by the children at her knee. 'She come out, looked up the road, then chased off after summat . . . I think it were a kitten, one o' them ones wi' a patchwork sort o' coat, if you understand me.'

'Yes, you mean tortoiseshell . . . lots of different colours,' Hester said eagerly, recognising the description of Kitty without difficulty. 'Which way did the little girl go, ma'am? She's a stranger in the city; she's lived in India all her life, and may easily get lost.'

'Oh, she ran off down the Brow,' the woman said at once. 'She runs funny, don't she? She sort o' turns her toes in and her knees out, like.'

Despite her worry, Hester had hard work not to giggle. Lonnie hardly ever ran but when she did it had occurred to Hester before that she ran like a rickshaw boy, though no doubt unconsciously. The rickshaw boys, Hester remembered, were the only people who ran much in the streets of Delhi.

Once Hester had made up her mind to search for Lonnie herself, things became easier, for she did not hesitate to ask everyone in the street whether they had seen a child in a pink gingham dress, either chasing after or holding a tortoiseshell kitten. And on the corner of Salisbury Street, a fat man in a faded brown overall, with a pipe gripped between his teeth, leaned in the doorway of his small shop, benevolently eyeing the passers-by. When Hester posed her question, he nodded vigorously. 'Aye, I see'd her twice,' he said, beaming at Hester. 'The first time she were a-chasin' a kitten – that was when she dashed down Salisbury Street like a scalded cat – and the second time she were comin' back again an' bein' chased herself by a crowd of them horrible dirty little Vine Terrace brats. They was hollerin', "Stop, thief!" But o' course no one took a blind bit o' notice because them Vine Terrace kids is all thieves and robbers to a man.' He chuckled richly at his own joke. 'Or woman,' he finished.

'I don't suppose you happened to notice where she went after that,' Hester asked hopefully. 'Did she turn towards the docks or up in the direction of Shaw Street? Only she's a stranger in the city and not yet nine years old.'

'She didn't do neither, queen. She lit off across the Brow as though all the devils in hell were on her heels. Which in a way they was, 'cos them kids from Vine Terrace, especially the Lambert kids, are as near devils from hell as you'll get on this earth,' he added, rather grimly.

Hester felt the blood drain from her cheeks. Horrid visions of poor little Lonnie lying beaten to a pulp in some lonely alley filled her mind. If the child was hurt, it would be all her fault for letting Lonnie out of her sight. Miss Hetherington-Smith had made it clear, God knew, that she held Hester totally responsible for anything Lonnie might do. 'What had she done to offend the Vine Terrace kids?' she asked, her voice quivering with suppressed emotion. 'Why should they chase her? She doesn't know anyone around here . . . unless she was rude to them, of course.'

'Kids is like animals in some ways,' the shopkeeper said shrewdly. 'They don't like anyone who is different to what they are. Your little lass were wearin' shoes and socks as I recall; them Vine Terrace kids are allus barefoot. But I dare say your gal will be all right, 'cos they wouldn't folly her outside their own territory, if you understand me. And she went down Watmough Street, which is well off their stamping ground. So don't be afeared you'll come across a corpuss, 'cos they ain't that desperate villains, though I won't let 'em into me shop without I've got my till locked up safe.'

'Thanks ever so much,' Hester said gratefully, turning to leave him. She glanced back. 'Can you tell me what time all this happened? Am I very far behind her?'

Here the shopkeeper was unable to help her much, saying vaguely that it were probably forty or fifty minutes ago, or maybe a little more. 'I comes out to smoke me pipe an' keeps poppin' back into the shop whenever a customer appears, see,' he explained. 'Time don't mean much when you're doin' the same thing for five or six hours together, but I'd say it were early evenin' when the little gal passed me first.'

'Thanks again,' Hester said. She crossed Everton Brow, turning left along the pavement, and then dived into Watmough Street. Very soon she was as lost as ever the child could have been and when she emerged on to a busy main road, with trams roaring along, was tempted to give up and go home. She had traced Lonnie this far, but what chance had she of finding the child with the pavements so crowded and the streets so busy?

However, there was a woman selling flowers on the opposite pavement and it seemed worth at least asking her if she had seen Lonnie, so Hester crossed the road and approached her. As soon as she mentioned a little girl with a kitten, the flower seller nodded her head. 'Oh aye, only the feller were holding the kitten,' she said, in a thick country accent. 'I noticed the pink dress pertickler, 'cos pink's me favourite colour. They crossed the road together and cut through the Place to Everton Terrace, I reckon.'

Hester, with her heart in her mouth, was beginning to ask the flower seller what sort of a man Lonnie's companion had been when the woman gave a crow of triumph. 'There's the feller, only he's by hisself now,' she exclaimed. 'Well, ain't that the strangest thing? See him? Dodging in front o' that tram?'

Hester followed the direction of the woman's pointing finger and her heart gave a great leap of relief. It was Ben Bailey, frowning with concentration as he crossed the road and clearly intent upon some errand which was taking all his attention. When Hester shouted to him, he looked blankly across at her for a moment, then a wide grin bisected his face and he came towards her, speaking as he advanced.

'Fancy seein' you, Miss Elliott! I were on my way to Shaw Street to tell you that Lonnie is safe. She's wi' me mam and dad; Mam's cleaned her up a bit, 'cos she got in quite a state, one way and another. Will you come back to our place now and see for yourself she's all right? She didn't mean to worry you, only the kitten escaped and of course she ran after it . . .'

On the way back to Elmore Street Ben tried to make the governess see that Lonnie had meant no harm when she had lit out after the kitten. Indeed, Hester was so relieved to hear that Lonnie was safe that she would have forgiven her most things, and when Ben threw open the back door of Number 27 and ushered her inside she was actually smiling, thinking that Lonnie had had a horrid time and would doubtless think very carefully before leaving the safety of the Shaw Street garden a second time.

Ben waited until she and Lonnie had exchanged an embarrassed hug before briskly beginning introductions all round. 'This here's me mam, that's me dad, this 'un's me little sister Phyllis, and the tall feller is me elder brother, Dick. Ted's stayin' over wi' me Aunt Jemimah an' that cat sitting on the hearthrug is Kitty, what I believe you've met before.' He chuckled. 'Oh, an' this here's Miss Elliott, what takes care of Lonnie,' he added belatedly.

Hester murmured greetings and heartfelt thanks but was unable to stop her eyes returning to the tall, dark-haired figure of Dick Bailey. She thought he had quite the kindest – and handsomest – face she had seen since reaching Liverpool and presently, when she was seated at the table with a hot cup of tea so that she might recover from her anxiety before taking Lonnie home, she realised that Dick was looking at her with equal interest.

'Ben tells us that you and young Lonnie here lived in India until recently,' Dick said, his dark eyes fixed on her face. 'I've always wanted to travel but never had the opportunity. Our dad's the same; I gets him old copies of the *National Geographic* magazine whenever I can, but pictures ain't the same as visiting somewhere yourself. Me and Dad would dearly like to hear you talk of India sometime.'

Hester, agreeing that she would come round and chat to them one evening, was aware of a distinct feeling of disappointment. So it was not *she* who interested him, but her experiences in the great land of India. She reminded herself that since he was Ben's brother, he was unlikely to be the sort of man she ought to be searching for if she had marriage in mind. She doubted if Dick's education rivalled her own and her mother had always impressed upon her the advantage of marrying into a similar background. And anyway, wasn't she leaping ahead rather? He was a nice young man with a sympathetic air but that did not mean her thoughts should automatically fly to marriage. The truth was, she had met so few young men since coming to England that anyone she did meet was immediately assessed, as she would once have assessed the young subalterns, district officers and civil servants who had comprised her father's circle in Delhi. Not that she had had marriage in mind then, any more than she had now. Now, as then, she was simply trying to place herself in the context of new surroundings.

'Another cup o' tea, Miss Elliott? And how about a slice of me fruit loaf? I expect you've been rare worried over young Lonnie here, so mebbe you've not noticed it's nigh on eight o'clock. Lonnie telled us you normally have supper around now.'

Jerked back to the present, Hester looked about the room, noticing for the first time its stark simplicity and air of poverty. The fruit loaf was on the table and contained, Hester saw, very little fruit. Thanking Mrs Bailey for her kind offer, she accepted a second mug of tea but refused the fruit loaf, though despite her trying to catch Lonnie's eye that young lady was devouring a large slice as though she had not eaten for a month.

When Hester had finished the tea, she stood up, announcing that it was really time they returned to

Shaw Street. Ben offered at once to accompany them, but Dick was already at the door, holding it open. 'I'll walk the young ladies home, then go on to see Mr Nicholls,' he said gruffly. 'You help our mam to clear away the tea things, Ben, and tidy the kitchen while she puts Phyllis to bed.'

Hester fully expected Ben to object, to say that it was his place to return them to their home, since it was he who had brought them to Elmore Street, but he did no such thing. 'Sure I'll do that, Dick,' he said equably. 'I'll see you another day, Lonnie. And I'm real sorry if we worried you, Miss Elliott, by bringing her here instead of taking her home, only she were in such a state, her aunt would have turned her out if she had set eyes on her.'

'You did the right thing,' Hester assured him, and watched whilst Lonnie swooped on the kitten, still playing on the hearthrug with Phyllis, and tucked her under her arm, assuring Phyllis, who was inclined to be tearful at the loss of her new friend, that she would bring Kitty back as soon as might be, indeed she would, and then Phyllis could play with her again. 'And thank you very much, Ben, both for rescuing Lonnie and for coming to find me,' Hester said. She turned to Mrs Bailey. 'You've been so good to us both,' she said warmly. 'I can never thank you enough . . . and the rest of your family, too. I hope we'll see you all again.'

'You'll be truly welcome, Miss Elliott,' Mrs Bailey said, beaming. 'Why, Mr Bailey was only saying t'other day that nowt would please him more than to hear you talk about your life in India, so when you've a bit o' time to spare . . .' She accompanied the small group into the back yard, adding in a lowered tone as soon as they had left the kitchen: 'As I'm sure you could see, miss, me husband ain't in the best of health. He don't gerrout much no more, and though I does me best, he gets mortal tired of addressin' envelopes, shut up in the house. It 'ud be doing us all a good turn if you and the young 'un came round now and then. He's a good man, he don't deserve wharr's happened to him . . .'

Her voice died away and Hester hastily assured her that they would most definitely come back again. 'Though how we shall find you I'm not quite sure,' she admitted, as Dick held the back gate open for her. 'We know the way to the park and the nearest tram stop, and of course we often walk up Heyworth Street to look at the shops, but other than that . . .'

'I reckon Ben will be happy enough to bring you round,' Dick interrupted before his mother could reply. 'Or I could do so, weekends. Anyroad, from what young Ben said, you come the back way this time. I'll tek you home by the main roads, then you won't have no difficulty. Just remember that Elmore Street is off Heyworth Street and you're home and dry.'

'Of course it is,' Hester said, remembering. 'The fact is I got myself in a rare state, trying to follow Lonnie's path through all those little side streets. I'm sure you're right and I'll find my way back easily, when I'm calmer.' She turned to Mrs Bailey, smiling and holding out her hand. 'Goodbye, Mrs Bailey, and thanks again.'

Mrs Bailey shook the proffered hand rather hesitantly, then she bent down and gave Lonnie a hug. 'Don't forget, you'll always be welcome at Number 27,' she said. 'You and your kitten, of course. I'll see there's always a saucer o' summat nice a-waitin' for Kitty, and a nice cup o' tea for yourself.'

Once they were in the street again Lonnie stayed close to Hester, but chattered away to the kitten as though she did not much want to hear what her governess probably meant to say to her. She must have guessed, Hester supposed, that some explanation of her behaviour was due, as well as a promise that such a thing would not occur again. But very soon Hester was talking animatedly to Dick, telling him a little of her life in India. Compared to Lonnie, she was widely travelled, having accompanied her father around the enormous area over which he reigned as district officer. Their family dwelling had been in Delhi, however, and she thought of that city as her home. Describing the beauty and barbaric splendour of its many mosques, bazaars and palaces, she was forced to admit that it was a good deal more impressive than Liverpool. 'But the climate is horrendous and the terrain flat as a pancake,' she told him. 'Rich people and most of the women and children go to the hills when the heat is at its worst, and stay there until the monsoons are over, but I stayed with my father all through the year. I can't imagine ever grumbling about the temperature here in England!'

Dick, laughing, assured her that she would soon feel differently when the snows and winds of winter took over. 'You'll think back to India then and wish you'd never crossed the sea and settled in a land where half the year is freezing,' he teased her. 'Tell me more about the bazaars, they sound fascinating.'

Hester obliged, but she asked questions too. 'What does a carpenter *do* aboard a ship?' she enquired as they walked. 'I know that Cammell Laird make ships – everyone knows that – but what do you actually do? I thought they were made of steel, not wood, these days!'

Dick gave her his slow, attractive smile. 'That's a tall order,' he said. 'At the moment, we're working on a five thousand ton cargo ship. She's called *Clementine* and there's no end of work for a good carpenter, only they call us joiners. Have you ever been aboard a ship when she's being fitted out?'

Hester shook her head. 'No. In fact I've only been aboard a sea-going ship once in my whole life and that was when Lonnie and I came back to England from India. I was really amazed at how elegant the ship was, though,' she added. 'We had a beautiful cabin, Lonnie and I, with lovely wardrobes for our clothes, ever such comfortable beds, a dressing-table, chairs . . . and all beautifully polished.'

'Oh aye. You were on a passenger liner, and from the sound of it you came first class,' Dick observed. 'Most of the first class furniture is made by Waring and Gillow. Us ship's joiners get to make the actual fittings such as companionways – that's stairs to you, Miss Hester – and the contents of the crew's quarters, dining rooms, saloons and so on.' He smiled his slow smile once more. 'At the moment, I'm working on a beautiful sideboard made of walnut. I love the feel of good wood, always have, which is why I signed on as a joiner's apprentice as soon as I left school. Most of the workforce live in Birkenhead and when I marry and move away from home, I reckon I'll cross the water. It's nice over there. Have you ever taken the ferry across the Mersey, Miss Hester? If not, perhaps you might like to do so some day. When our dad were fit, Mam used to pack us a carry-out and the whole family would go off to New Brighton for a day at the seaside. I doubt he's well enough to do that now, but the rest of us could go, make a day of it. So if I arrange it, would you and young Lonnie like to come along?'

'I suppose I ought to ask Miss Hetherington-Smith's permission before I take Lonnie anywhere,' Hester said doubtfully. 'However, since her aunt seems totally uninterested in what we do and probably wouldn't even miss us, if you tell me the day you've chosen, then I'm sure we'll be happy to come along. We'll contribute to the picnic, of course,' she concluded.

She half expected Dick to demur but he nodded, seeming to take her offer for granted, and she realised once again that the Baileys would have a struggle to feed themselves, let alone two virtual strangers, and Dick would not willingly add to his mother's burden.

As they neared Shaw Street, Dick began to question her about India once more and Hester, answering him as best she could, was astonished by the breadth of knowledge his questions revealed. She thought it would be tactless to remark on it but Lonnie, hopping along between them as she dodged the cracks in the paving stones, had no such inhibitions. 'Have you ever been to India, Dick?' Lonnie enquired. 'Because you know an awful lot about it – more than I do, and I've lived there all my life, until now.'

Dick reached out a large, capable hand and rumpled Lonnie's hair. 'No, the furthest I've been in one direction is Southport, and New Brighton in the other,' he observed ruefully. 'But I'm a great reader, queen. I'm a member of the library and go to the Central on William Brown Street. I've been working me way through the International Library since I were ten and for some reason I've always been interested in India.' He whistled softly. 'It's a grand country, full of fascinating people and animals. You don't know how I envy you your years there.'

'I loved it too,' Lonnie admitted. 'But I hated the heat. It was lovely in the hills – we went there from April to October when my mother was alive, but after she died I had to return to Delhi when my daddy did, in July. That's when the monsoon starts and the city is hot and wet and full of fevers. I think everyone hates the heat and the monsoon, even the Indians, don't you, Hester?'

Hester, agreeing, thought fleetingly of the child she had first met more than three months before. A sickly, pallid little girl with dark circles under her eyes, always dressed up in stiffly starched white dresses with half a dozen petticoats beneath them, long white stockings and dark leather strap shoes, and a head-hugging bonnet of white straw, decorated with ribbons. It had been the standard dress for English children when they were in the city, changing only to jodhpurs and hacking jackets when they rode out on their ponies and God knew the second costume was as hot as the first. Her own mother – and her father, for that matter – had dressed their little girl sensibly, in loose silky-white dresses and open sandals. That was city wear, of course. When she was taken to the jungle, she wore loose baggy trousers and shirts and went barefoot whenever it was safe to do so.

She was beginning to tell Dick something of this when they turned into Haig Street and walked along the pavement until they reached the green wooden door. Here Dick stopped and went to open the door for her, then turned to her, looking puzzled. 'Do you have a key?' he asked.

Hester shook her head. 'One of the servants must have locked it after I went. I think I left it open when I chased out after Lonnie. I've no recollection of shutting it, anyway.' She turned away from the door and headed for Everton Brow once more. 'I don't have a key to the front door either but I can ring and Fletcher will come and let us in.'

When they reached Everton Brow, Dick stopped her with a hand on her arm. 'I won't come any further, because I don't want to make trouble for you,' he said quietly. 'In my experience, there's always someone looking out of the window and taking note of what's going on outside. I don't know Miss Hetherington-Smith but I'd lay a bet she wouldn't approve of the likes of me being with her niece.'

Hester stared up at him, her eyes rounding with astonishment, then she laughed. 'You certainly *don't* know Miss Hetherington-Smith,' she told him, her eyes sparkling. 'She wouldn't care if Lonnie and I stayed out all day and all night too, so long as we didn't make a nuisance of ourselves. As for who our friends are, she should be grateful that we've met a nice family like yours – except that we see her so rarely, we never have a chance to tell her anything. Honestly, Dick, you can come right up to the house with us, no problem.'

This Dick resolutely refused to do, however. He shook hands with Hester, told Lonnie that he was sure he would see her again quite soon, touched his cap to both of them, and set off the way he had come. Hester and Lonnie approached the front door and Hester rang the bell, belatedly realising that since Dick had dived down Everton Brow he must have come out of his way to bring them home. She was reflecting on how nice he was, and how kind, when the door opened. Expecting to see Fletcher's thin, cadaverous countenance, she was surprised and even a little shocked to find Miss Hetherington-Smith herself glaring at her in the doorway. Hester opened her mouth to apologise for disturbing her employer, but she had no chance to say more than a few words. Miss Hetherington-Smith cut across her, mouth grim, thin brows drawn into a deep frown.

'Come into the drawing room, Miss Elliott. I have a great deal to say to you, none of which I wish to be overheard by the servants.'

'Wouldn't it do later, Miss Hetherington-Smith?' Hester said, rather desperately. Suddenly, she felt both young and inexperienced and wished fervently that she really was twenty-four, as Miss Hetherington-Smith had been informed, and not merely eighteen. The loneliness and the sense of overwhelming responsibility which had left her while she was in Elmore Street came flooding back. 'It's way past Lonnie's bedtime and she's had a rather frightening and tiring day.'

'That is beside the point, Miss Elliott,' Miss Hetherington-Smith said icily. 'I know very little of children, but I imagine *Miss Leonora* is perfectly capable of remaining awake for another thirty minutes or so while we . . . discuss . . . your behaviour.'

Hester, with Lonnie leaning wearily against her, followed Miss Hetherington-Smith into the drawing room. She reflected that her initial determination to base her behaviour upon that of Lonnie's governess in Delhi, Eleanor Andrews, was going to be tested to the full, from the sound of it. The trouble was, she had only known Miss Andrews for the few weeks she had lived in Mr Hetherington-Smith's imposing mansion and had never seen that lady in any situation of which she was not mistress. However, she braced her shoulders and faced Miss Hetherington-Smith across the hearth, hoping that she looked pleasant and in control, though she suspected it was likelier that she looked both exhausted and frightened, for Miss Hetherington-Smith was clearly in a blazing temper.

'Miss Elliott, I have it on good authority that you and your charge abandoned this house without telling anyone that you intended to remain away from it for many hours,' her employer began. 'It so happened that one of the maids went upstairs at half-past eight to bring down your supper dishes and any remaining milk. She was much disturbed to realise that, despite the lateness of the hour, your supper had not been touched, so went into the schoolroom to ask the reason for this.'

Interfering, nosy little beast, Hester thought wrathfully, continuing to eye her employer steadily, hoping she gave no hint of her inner turmoil. She knew instinctively that it would never do to let Miss Hetherington-Smith realise how inexperienced and unsure she really was. 'I'm sorry if the maid was worried,' she said politely. 'I did not realise I was supposed to apprise the servants of my movements, though I would have been hard put to it to do so, since I had no idea we would be away from the house for so long.'

'I think, Miss Elliott, that you had better explain your absence from the moment you abandoned the schoolroom until you rang at the front door just now,' Miss Hetherington-Smith said. It was clear that she was still very angry and Hester had no doubt that the older woman was looking forward to handing out a blistering set-down, if not worse. Nevertheless, remembering Miss Andrews, she calmly drew up a chair and sat down on it, pulling Lonnie on to her knee as she did so.

'Since this may take some time and Lonnie is extremely tired, I think we had both better sit down,' she said, guiltily aware that her tone of sweet reasonableness was probably enough to infuriate a saint, but quite unable to stop herself imitating Miss Andrews, once she had begun. 'As I'm sure you know, Mimms has given Miss Leonora a plot of garden for her own . . .'

Hester told the bare bones of the story as well as she could, emphasising the fact that Lonnie had not meant to disobey, had merely tried to rescue her pet and had been attacked by a group of rough, unpleasant children who had tried to take the kitten from her and had chased her, so that she had fallen twice, hurting herself quite badly on both occasions, but still managing to escape her pursuers.

Miss Hetherington-Smith sniffed disdainfully and, for the first time, took a good long look at her niece. 'I can see that that part of your story, at least, is the truth,' she said grudgingly, 'since Miss Leonora looks like a guttersnipe and not like the young lady she is supposed to be. Go on with your tale, Miss Elliott.'

Hester continued with her story, mentioning in passing that the child had been rescued by a young boy who had taken her to his mother and had then returned to fetch Hester.

As she spoke, she watched Miss Hetherington-Smith for some sign of softening but saw none, and when she finished her narrative she suspected that the older woman was disappointed that she could find so little fault. But it was soon apparent that she underestimated her employer's abilities in that line.

'This young boy,' Miss Hetherington-Smith said. 'I take it you met him in the park? Where do these people live? Are they respectable?'

Lonnie's hand had been lying against Hester's knee; now she felt the small fingers give her a warning pinch and answered glibly: 'Very respectable I should imagine. The boy has a delightful little sister and they often visit the park. Their home is not far from here though I'm afraid I didn't notice the address.'

'Well, it seems that though you are clearly at fault, Miss Leonora had no right to behave as she did. In fact, had it not been for the kitten . . . yes, I see my way clear now. The kitten must go. I cannot have my whole household disrupted by a pet which is out of control, and clearly one cannot teach a kitten to behave in a responsible manner.'

Hester began to protest but Lonnie, Kitty still tightly clasped in her arms, bounced to her feet. 'How dare you try to take my cat away, you wicked old woman,' she shrieked at her aunt. 'If I tell my daddy that you have done so, he will come over to England and chop off your head, or – or send you away from this house, which is his, and let you live in a miserable slum somewhere.'

Miss Hetherington-Smith actually blinked and a tide of red mottled her neck and her thin cheeks. She glared furiously at Lonnie, then directed the glare upon Hester. 'If this is the way you teach your charge to behave, then it is you who needs disciplining,' she said harshly. 'I really feel that my niece would do better if I took your advice, Miss Elliott, and sent her away to a boarding school, where she might be properly disciplined. Why, when I was a girl, if I had spoken to anyone like that, I would have been locked in my room for a week and fed on bread and water. In fact, I've a good mind to keep Miss Leonora on bread and water until I receive a proper apology.'

'You may shut me in the nursery for a month if it gives you satisfaction,' Lonnie said angrily, 'but don't you dare try to take my kitten away from me.' She turned imploring eyes upon Hester. 'You won't let her take Kitty, will you, Hester?'

'And you should not call your governess by her Christian name,' Miss Hetherington-Smith said, almost triumphantly. 'She is Miss Elliott to me, and should be the same to you. Really, I don't know what has been happening in my own house. The idea!' She turned to Hester. 'Have you taught the child no respect? I can see, if it is left to you, she will become a disgrace to our family name.'

Hester heaved a sigh and stood up, setting Lonnie down on the floor beside her. 'I'm very sorry you find me so unsatisfactory, Miss Hetherington-Smith,' she said pleasantly. 'Lonnie – I mean Miss Leonora – please apologise to your aunt for your rudeness. I am sure Miss Hetherington-Smith did not mean to threaten Kitty and understands how much your pet means to you. Why, your letters to your father are always full of Kitty's antics and I'm sure he'd be greatly distressed if you wrote and said that your aunt had sent your pet away.' She smiled sweetly at the old woman. 'Isn't that so, Miss Hetherington-Smith?'

'On this one occasion, I am prepared to overlook what has happened,' Miss Hetherington-Smith said, after a long pause, during which she glared balefully at both Lonnie and Hester. 'But in future, Miss Elliott, I shall want a detailed account each morning of how you mean to spend the day.'

'Very well, Miss Hetherington-Smith,' Hester said

dutifully, and turned away to hide a smile. Would Miss Hetherington-Smith expect a written report, including such things as visits to the WC and the time spent in the bath on a Friday night?

Once they had regained the schoolroom and Lonnie had settled Kitty in her basket, the two girls stared at one another. 'I know it's wrong to lie, Hester,' Lonnie said, after a moment, 'and anyway, you didn't, not exactly, because the Baileys *are* respectable. But wasn't Aunt Emmeline horrid? If I hadn't thought to threaten her with my daddy, I do believe she really would have turned Kitty out. She is horrible, isn't she?'

'She's old-fashioned and narrow-minded and doesn't understand children in the least,' Hester said guardedly. She was uncomfortably aware that Lonnie, when in a rage, was quite capable of repeating some casual remark of her own in order to score over her aunt. 'But remember, dear, she isn't actually going to do anything, not this time at any rate, so in future we must both be very careful not to behave in a way which could annoy her.'

'Huh! If that means I mustn't go round to the Baileys' again, then I'm going to annoy her the very next chance I get,' Lonnie said roundly. 'I won't let her choose my friends, I won't, I won't!'

Hester agreed, but pointed out that if they were careful, they might continue to lead their own lives without too much interference. 'I don't approve of blackmail,' she said, trying to sound a good deal more disapproving than she felt, 'but there's no doubt your aunt is in some awe of your father and does not wish to offend him. It is a card we cannot afford to play too often, but it has certainly come in useful today.'

'I don't quite know what you mean when you

talk about playing cards, but I know very well that Aunt Emmeline is living in my father's house, and should remember it when she tries to boss me about,' Lonnie said grandly. But though Hester was amused by this remark, she kept her face straight and merely recommended Lonnie to come to her room and have a good wash before tumbling into bed.

'For your aunt was quite right when she said you looked a real little guttersnipe,' she told her charge. 'And I can see you're absolutely exhausted. As for calling me Miss Elliott, perhaps you'd best do so in your aunt's hearing, but when we're up here or outside the house, I think we'll stick to "Hester", don't you?'

'Yes please, Hester,' Lonnie mumbled, speaking round a huge yawn. 'And you'll call me Lonnie, won't you? Daddy only called me "Leonora" when he was cross.'

'I'll do that,' Hester agreed, ushering her charge into her small, whitewashed bedroom and beginning to pour cold water from the jug into the basin. 'And now let's get to bed, young lady, before we fall asleep on the linoleum!'

Emmeline Hetherington-Smith watched her niece and the governess depart and then sat down heavily in a velvet-upholstered armchair drawn up by the empty fireplace. She was trying to tell herself that she had won the encounter, that she had put the hateful Miss Elliott in her place and frightened her niece with the threat of taking the kitten from her. But even as she sat down in the chair, she could feel the heat of fury and frustration rising to her cheeks. How dare that impudent chit of a governess speak to her the way she had! And as for Leonora, nasty, spoilt little thing, she had been worse. If only, oh, if only her brother, Leonard, had not been such a fond father, had not laid the law down regarding her employment of Miss Elliott! The truth was she was financially dependent upon her brother for almost everything. True, her father had provided for her generously in his will, but that had been fifteen years ago and what had seemed a large sum then seemed so no longer.

Leonard had advised her to invest the money in one of his thriving companies but she had ignored him; he was a dozen years her junior and her choleric temper – and her pride – would not allow her to accept advice from someone she regarded as a mere stripling. So the money had remained where her father had placed it and of course there had been calls upon it when she needed extras, such as a holiday on the Continent, a trip to Scotland for the shooting or a visit to London when her wardrobe needed replenishing. The result was that her inheritance had shrunk frighteningly, leaving her unable to imagine existing without Leonard's help.

Sitting in the empty drawing room, Miss Hetherington-Smith wished, not for the first time, that she had taken her brother's advice and invested her money. After all, it need not necessarily have been in one of Leonard's companies, he had always made that clear. He had advised buying shares in the India Rubber Company, or even in a local firm such as Lewis's or Blackler's and, though she had not taken this advice, she had been unable to resist following these companies' fortunes in the financial press. She had very soon realised that, had she done as Leonard suggested, she would by now be a rich woman, but there was no point in repining. Before she could reinvest her money the Depression was upon them, and though Leonard still believed she should capitalise upon her shrunken income, her cautious nature would not allow her to do so. To lose her little bit of money, her 'independence', would have killed her, she believed, so when Leonard had suggested that she should take care of the child, adding that he would provide and pay for a governess, continue to pay all household expenses and triple her own allowance, she had been quite unable to resist.

Now, with the flush of anger still heating her thin cheeks, she wondered whether she would have accepted the challenge had she known what a pert, disagreeable child Leonora was and how arrogant and self-possessed the governess. Of the two, she really thought she disliked Miss Elliott the more. A child could be punished, humiliated, reduced to tears and repentance, but a grown woman of twenty-four, experienced in the ways of the world, would have her own ways of combating aggression, no matter how such aggression was disguised.

Miss Hetherington-Smith began to dream of the revenge which she longed to wreak upon the heads of her two uninvited guests. If she played her cards right she could get her own back on both of them. She could criticise the governess for a thousand faults, real and imaginary, say she was bringing the child up to be rude and selfish . . . and this would mean Leonora could indeed be shut in her room and fed on bread and water for her sins.

For quite half an hour, Miss Hetherington-Smith sat in the velvet armchair, indulging herself by planning a campaign which would end in her victory over Miss Elliott and her charge. In fact it was only the opening of the drawing room door and the timid voice of Miss

Hutchinson, asking her whether she would like a hot drink before bedtime, which brought her abruptly back to the present. Sighing, she stood up slowly, hearing her knees creak a protest, for she had sat in the same position for far too long. 'Yes, Miss Hutchinson, tell Maud to bring hot milk and a plate of digestive biscuits to the small parlour,' she said grandly. 'I have a problem I should like to discuss with you.'

Alone in her neat first floor bedroom that night, getting ready for bed, Miss Hutchinson considered the problem which her employer had laid out before her. At the time, she had tried to sound sympathetic, admitting that the situation was a difficult one, but in her heart she had been dismayed. She had known, of course, that her employer was a spiteful woman, full of self-importance, who needed careful handling. Her own approach from the start had been to agree with everything Miss Hetherington-Smith said, to try to placate her when she was in a bad mood and to soothe ruffled feelings in the servants' quarters. When she had first been told of the impending arrival of her employer's niece and her governess, she had been truly dismayed. She had worked very hard to win a place in Miss Hetherington-Smith's confidence, had believed herself to be a valued employee and companion, and immediately feared that she would be pushed into the background, possibly even dismissed, when the newcomers arrived. So it had been with real pleasure that she had seen how the child's mere presence irritated Miss Hetherington-Smith. Her employer had banished both intruders to the attics and had made it plain that she expected the governess both to take care of her pupil and to keep her out of the way of the adult members of the household.

Miss Hutchinson had expected Miss Elliott to dine with them, perhaps even to share their luncheon, but this had not proved to be the case. Miss Hetherington-Smith had informed her companion that though she meant to do her duty by her niece she had no intention of changing her way of life by one iota, and this had satisfied Miss Hutchinson very well. A niece and a governess who seldom saw the mistress of the house were unlikely to worm their way into that lady's cold heart.

However, after her discussion with her employer that evening, Miss Hutchinson had speedily realised that her employer actually hated both Leonora and Miss Elliott and intended to do her very best – or worst – to see that they were unhappy in her house. Indeed, she had made no secret of the fact that if it were possible she would turn them both out, and this had sent a spear of terror through her companion's quivering heart. Although Miss Hetherington-Smith probably did not realise it, Miss Hutchinson was well aware that it was her employer's brother who paid all expenses and consequently called the tune. She was deathly afraid that Miss Hetherington-Smith's vicious temper would get the better of her, and if her brother withdrew his support – as he surely would – then it was not the governess or the child who would find themselves on the street, but Miss Hetherington-Smith and her companion.

Miss Hutchinson knew all too well what such an event would mean to her. She was far too old to get another job, and anyway she had lived in a gentleman's house for twenty years and doubted if she could survive alone so much as a twelvemonth, knowing nothing of marketing, managing, rent and the like.

Having washed, brushed out her thin hair and plaited it, and slid her voluminous nightdress over her head, Miss Hutchinson turned off the gas and climbed into bed. Settling down, she reminded herself that she rather liked Miss Elliott, had liked her ever since she had realised she had no cause to be jealous of the younger woman. Would it not be politic, therefore, to confide in Miss Elliott regarding the danger in which she and the child stood? If she could put the governess on her guard, perhaps she would begin to be more conciliatory towards their mutual employer and then life could go on as before.

Snuggling down beneath the sheet and deciding that she would do her best to calm these very troubled waters, another dreadful scenario presented itself to Miss Hutchinson. Suppose Miss Hetherington-Smith found a good excuse to dismiss Hester Elliott? Surely the obvious thing to do then would be to command Miss Hutchinson to deal with Miss Leonora? Just the thought of having to climb all those stairs up to the schoolroom set Miss Hutchinson's joints aching, whilst the idea of having to deal with a lively eight-year-old almost made Miss Hutchinson swoon with horror. So great was her dismay that she sat bolt upright in bed, staring out into the darkness as though Leonora was the devil himself. Then, with a sigh, she lay down again. It must not happen, she vowed; it could not be allowed to happen. The very next morning, she must seize the opportunity of speaking to Miss Elliott alone. Between them, surely they could hatch a plan?

Satisfied that there was a way to avoid the fate

she feared, Miss Hutchinson turned over, heaved the blankets up to her ears and was soon asleep.

After the excitement of Kitty's escape, life returned to normal. Hester and Lonnie did lessons for a couple of hours, either in the morning or in the afternoon, and when the weather grew hot and sunny the pair carried their books and a picnic lunch out to Prince's Park, where they sat on the grass in the shade of the big trees and struggled with sums, writing and reading.

Hester noticed increasingly how Lonnie was changing in the more temperate climate. Her hair, which had been lank and lifeless in India, grew shiny and healthy-looking and roses bloomed in cheeks that had once been pale and sallow. The child began to fill out, too, and Hester thought it would not be long before she would have to appeal to Miss Hetherington-Smith for new clothing for her charge.

Although she knew that it was Mr Hetherington-Smith who paid for such things, she had begun to realise that his sister had come insensibly to think of the money as her own and accordingly grudged every penny which was spent on the child or her governess. Hester suspected that the staff had grown used to their mistress's penny pinching and largely ignored it when it was a matter of running up bills for food for the household, but she did not have sufficient confidence to do the same and she and Lonnie continued to wear unsuitable clothing, even in the heat of summer.

Lonnie grew rebellious as the heat increased, however, and told Hester bluntly that her gingham dresses hurt across the chest and shoulders and her woollen dresses were far too hot.

'Since it's Daddy who pays for my clothes, why can't we ask Aunt Emmeline to give us money for bigger ones?' she enquired plaintively. 'And why does that Hutch keep hanging round us? She starts to speak and then breaks off in the middle of the sentence and rushes away with some silly excuse. If you don't want to ask Aunt Emmeline, Hester, why don't we get Hutch to ask for us?'

Hester heaved a sigh. It was another hot and sunny day and they were sitting in Prince's Park in the shade of a mighty oak, doing their lessons. 'I don't think you ought to call Miss Hutchinson Hutch,' she said reprovingly. 'Oh, I know your Aunt Emmeline does so when she's in a good mood, but that's different. As I keep on telling you, Lonnie, there is one set of rules for grown-ups and another for children and children must be respectful towards their elders.'

'All right, then, why don't we get Miss Hutchinson to ask Aunt Emmeline if I can have some bigger dresses?' Lonnie said. She was lying on her tummy, picking daisies for a daisy chain whilst learning her French verbs. 'In India, I made daisy chains with marigolds and sometimes my *ayah* put frangipani blossoms in my hair.' She sighed reminiscently. 'They smelt so sweet. Does frangipani grow in England, Hester?'

'I don't think so,' Hester said absently. 'As for asking Miss Hutchinson to put in a word for us, it would never work. Miss H is far too nervous; she'd be afraid of offending Aunt Emmeline. But it's funny you should have noticed how Hutch hovers round us whenever your aunt's out of the way, because . . .'

She was interrupted by a shriek of delight from Lonnie. '*You* said it! You called her Hutch and though I know you are a grown-up I don't believe Miss

Hutchinson or Aunt Emmeline would like it one bit if they heard you. I'll tell you what, Hester, let's call her Hutch when there's just the two of us – she reminds me of a rabbit because of the way she keeps chewing invisible lettuce and twitching her nose – and go back to Miss Hutchinson when anyone else is around.'

Hester thought this was rather dangerous and said so but Lonnie assured her that she would be most careful. 'After all, Hutch is a sort of pet name and since I really don't like Miss Hutchinson one bit I'm not likely to call her by it, am I? I forget whether you told me why she keeps starting to talk to you and then stopping short and going all red. Do you *know* why, Hester?'

'No I don't, but I mean to find out,' Hester told her. 'Have you learned those wretched verbs yet? You ought to be really good at French because you've been speaking Hindi and English ever since you were tiny. Most children who find they can speak two different languages pick up a third, and sometimes a fourth, without too much trouble.'

'I have learned the verbs and I do like French, but speaking it is very much easier than writing it down,' Lonnie observed. She rolled over and sat up, then closed her book. 'Do you want to test me, Hester?'

Hester had already realised that Lonnie was both bright and quick to learn and was not surprised to find her charge word perfect in the three verbs she had been learning. As soon as Lonnie had recited the last one, she told the child to pack up her books, saying that they would go across to the lake and eat their sandwiches by the water.

'Can we take a boat on the lake?' Lonnie asked

eagerly. 'It's such a hot day and it's always cooler on the water.'

Hester agreed that it would have been pleasant but reminded Lonnie that they had not brought any money with them. 'My salary is supposed to be paid monthly but your aunt frequently forgets to pay me at all,' she said ruefully. 'What is more, I don't believe the money she does give me is quite what your father intended. Before she pays me, she deducts a sum for my keep and for the clothing which was provided when we first came to England, so I don't have very much left over. However, the next time I'm paid we will hire a boat on the lake . . . and have ice creams as well, and that's a promise.'

Hester had not previously mentioned her salary to anyone; for all she knew, it might be common practice for governesses to pay for their own keep, but she was beginning to find it increasingly hard to manage on the tiny amount of irregularly paid money which Miss Hetherington-Smith saw fit to hand over. Tram fares, soap, tooth powder, stockings and such things as the odd packet of biscuits, or a few sweets, were all little extras which Hester had expected to be able to buy with her salary, but this was not always the case.

Lonnie, getting to her feet and hefting the bag of books on one shoulder, looked astonished. 'She makes you pay for your own food?' she said incredulously. 'I'm sure that's not right, Hester. I bet rabbit-Hutch doesn't pay for her own food! Why, did Daddy make you pay for your food when you were living with us in India?'

Hester, still smiling over the term 'rabbit-Hutch', admitted that Lonnie's father had most certainly done no such thing. 'He was exceedingly generous, considering that I did very little teaching in those early days,' she said. 'If he knew how your aunt was treating me, I think he would be most perturbed.'

'Write to him,' Lonnie ordered at once. 'Do it as soon as we get home, Hester, then I can put your letter in with mine and save you a stamp. What a good thing I've always given my letters to Fletcher to post – at least I don't have to pay for stamps.' A thought occurred to her. 'Do you pay for stamps, Hester?'

'I don't write letters,' Hester admitted. 'Now that my parents are dead, there is no one for me to write to, but I will take your advice and put a sheet or two in with your next letter to your father. He will know exactly how he intended his money to be spent.'

Two days after their conversation in the park, they met Miss Hutchinson on Heyworth Street as they were returning from a window shopping expedition. Window shopping was, at the moment, the only form of shopping they could afford, since despite Hester's timidly mentioning to Miss Hetherington-Smith that her salary was some weeks overdue, it had not yet put in an appearance.

Miss Hutchinson had clearly been shopping since she carried a string bag bulging with small purchases. Hester saw notepaper and envelopes, a bottle of royal-blue ink and a paper bag which she guessed would be full of extra strong mints, for which Miss Hutchinson had a passion. There were other things in the string bag, but they were all wrapped and, in any case, Hester was less interested in Miss Hutchinson's shopping than she was in the reason for that lady to waylay her and then to say almost nothing. Accordingly, she stopped, smiled at Miss Hutchinson, and put a detaining hand on the older woman's stick-like arm. 'Miss Hutchinson, I wonder if I might have a word?' she said, and saw Miss Hutchinson's eyes swivel doubtfully to her young charge. 'Lon . . . I mean Miss Leonora, why don't you run along to Madison's and see what new pets he has in his window? I'll catch you up in a moment.'

As soon as the child had gone, Hester smiled beguilingly into Miss Hutchinson's frightened eyes. 'I realise you've been trying to speak to me for the past couple of days but didn't want to do so in front of Miss Leonora,' she said gently. 'However, she will be happily occupied by the pet shop for some time, so I assure you you can now speak freely.'

Miss Hutchinson began to blink rapidly and to make the small mumbling movements with her lips that Lonnie had rudely referred to as chewing lettuce. Her eyes darted uneasily from side to side, and for a moment Hester feared that she would deny any desire to talk to anyone, but then Miss Hutchinson took a deep breath and began to speak. 'Oh, my dear Miss Elliott, I've been at my wits' end to know what to do for the best, but finally decided that you should be warned in what peril you stand. Miss Hetherington-Smith is a very fine lady but she cannot bear to be crossed, and after her interview with yourself and Miss Leonora she was – she was deeply upset. She called me into the small parlour and – and it was clear she was very angry indeed, and – and . . .'

'And looking for some means to punish us both?' Hester said, still gently, though within herself she could feel her own temper rising. 'Is that what you're trying to say, Miss Hutchinson?'

'Yes. The fact is, Miss Elliott, she is searching for an

excuse to dismiss you. She feels she has been slighted, by both you and the child, and would do almost anything to see both of you settled elsewhere.'

'Well, she could dismiss me, of course,' Hester said at once, 'but she can scarcely dismiss her niece!'

'No-o, but she could send her away to a boarding school which would agree to keep her during the school holidays. There are such establishments, I know, because when I was very much younger I taught in such a school. A great many of our pupils had parents living and working in India and sometimes their children were very unhappy, though I'm sure the staff did their best to be agreeable,' she added, rather self-consciously.

'But surely her father would never agree to such a thing?' Hester said. She had guessed that Miss Hetherington-Smith would have liked to dismiss her, but had never considered that she might plan to send Lonnie away. 'I'm sure Mr Hetherington-Smith would be very angry indeed if his sister tried to do any such thing.'

'Oh, I agree,' Miss Hutchinson said fervently. 'But if his sister made it appear that you were a bad influence – he's so very far away, you know – he might be forced to accept the situation.'

'I . . . see,' Hester said slowly. She regarded Miss Hutchinson closely. 'It's very good of you to warn me, especially since you've never shown any particular interest in either myself or Miss Leonora. To be blunt, I thought you disliked us nearly as much as Miss Hetherington-Smith does. So why say anything?'

Miss Hutchinson's cheeks began to mottle red and her eyes darted about more furiously than ever, but when she spoke her voice was steady, though low. 'I – I was jealous, I'm afraid. Miss Hetherington-Smith is not an easy lady and has frequently told me that many other women could do my job a good deal better than I can. I was afraid she might dismiss me when you and the child arrived and you must see how – how vulnerable I am. I could not get another post, and though I have been saving up for many years I have not managed to amass a decent sum. In short, I am as dependent upon Miss Hetherington-Smith's goodwill as on the money she pays me.'

'I do understand, and I'm very grateful,' Hester said. 'Indeed, if Miss Hetherington-Smith charges you three-quarters of your salary for your keep, as she does me, you must be in a desperate situation indeed.'

'Three-quarters of your . . .' Miss Hutchinson gasped. 'Why, Miss Elliott, you should not be paying *anything* for your keep. Only – only please don't tell Miss Hetherington-Smith that I said any such thing or I know she'll dismiss me out of hand.'

'I won't say a word,' Hester assured her. 'I wonder, Miss Hutchinson, that it did not occur to you that, with my dismissal, you yourself might be expected to take charge of the child.'

Miss Hutchinson heaved a huge sigh and dabbed at her mouth with a tiny lace-edged handkerchief. 'It did,' she said baldly. 'Yes, such a thought did occur to me and quite frankly, Miss Elliott, it terrified me. I am far too old for such a charge and though I've seen very little of Miss Leonora I know a spoiled and wilful child when I see one. She would run rings round me and have the house in an uproar and, of course, I should be blamed. And there are the two flights of stairs up to the schoolroom – I have rheumatism in my knees and ankles – oh, Miss Elliott, just ascending and descending those stairs would kill me, I know it would!'

'Then I shall do my very best not to be dismissed,' Hester said, smiling. 'It's been good of you to talk so freely, Miss Hutchinson, when I know how dangerous you must have felt it to be. I shall certainly heed your advice, though now that I see Miss Hetherington-Smith each morning to tell her of our plans for that day, I always do my best to be polite. Perhaps, however, I could be a little . . . humbler . . . if you think that would be more acceptable than mere politeness. And I hope you know me well enough by now to be sure I shan't breathe a word of this to anyone. If I tackle Miss Hetherington-Smith about my salary, I shall tell her that I met another governess in the park and she told me that neither she nor any of her friends contributed towards their keep. But I'm hoping it will not be necessary, since, after all, it is Mr Hetherington-Smith who pays me. His sister only passes the money on – or doesn't, as the case may be. Shall we join Miss Leonora now, or are you in a hurry to get back to the house?'

'I think I had best be getting back,' Miss Hutchinson said regretfully and Hester realised that once she had begun to talk, the older woman had positively enjoyed sharing her worries. 'I feel very much better for having told you what has been happening, Miss Elliott, and I trust we may have other, though happier, conversations in the future. Ah, here comes Miss Leonora. She must have grown tired of waiting for you. And now I'd best be off or Miss Hetherington-Smith might begin to ask awkward questions.'

'Oh, Hester, isn't it a perfectly lovely day? Daddy always used to say that spring in England was the most beautiful season, but then he'd sort of look at me out of the corner of his eye and say, "Except for autumn!" and he and Mummy – and me – would laugh like anything, because Mummy used to say Daddy liked to have his cake and eat it, even when he was talking about the seasons. Well, I know we didn't really see the spring, because we were too late, but autumn . . . !' Lonnie took a deep breath and gazed expressively around her. They were crossing St John's Gardens, bound for the fashionable shops on Church Street and Bold Street, but had paused to better appreciate the brilliant foliage of the autumn-tinted trees and the blue arc of the sky overhead. Lonnie thought suddenly that this was as lovely as anything India had offered. Lovelier in a way since it was gentler, more peaceful. She realised with an inward start that she was beginning to like England for itself, though she still remembered India and her life there with wistful pleasure. 'Oh, autumn is just *lovely*, don't you think?'

'Yes, it's even better than I had imagined. The colours are indescribable, which is probably why your father prefers it to spring,' Hester began, only to be interrupted.

'I don't think he really preferred it to spring, I think it was a sort of joke between him and Mummy,' Lonnie explained. 'It's a bit like me when I'm talking about India. Looking back, the bungalow in the hills seemed the most beautiful place on earth, except for the garden of our Delhi house, but sometimes I think you don't really remember things exactly as they are, you remember the good bits and sort of cut the bad out of your memory. What do you think, Hester?'

'I think we ought to get a move on, since we've got a full day's shopping ahead of us,' Hester said, setting off at a smart pace and emerging into William Brown Street. 'I know you want to visit the library, but perhaps we should leave that for later? After all, it isn't every day that your father sends us a money order for winter clothes, is it?'

'No, but I'm awfully glad he's done so,' Lonnie said pensively. 'He must have understood what was going on from your letter, though I was afraid he wouldn't. You didn't really grumble about Aunt's meanness and you didn't say how hard it was to get your salary paid, yet Daddy has come up trumps. But fancy sending the money order to you, Hester! Whatever did you say to my aunt? She can't have been pleased, she's so fond of telling us that she can't afford this, that or the other. I suppose you felt you had to admit you'd had the money?'

'Goodness, yes, though I didn't tell her what a large amount your father had sent! And she wasn't too bad at all, in fact. I told her that your father was going to write to her but apparently she had already received the letter. She knew all about the money order, you see . . . so what a good job I had decided to tell her about it! If I had not . . . well, we won't even think about that!'

'So what did she say?' Lonnie persisted. She could not imagine Aunt Emmeline being pleased to find that her niece's governess had been sent money to buy clothing and secretly hoped that her aunt had been both furious and humiliated, but it seemed that it was not so.

'Say? Well, nothing very much except that Mr Hetherington-Smith had been more than generous and she hoped I would make sure that the clothing we purchased would last for at least three years. And . . . well, I shouldn't really tell you this, Lonnie, and you must be sure to forget I've done so, but when she waved your father's letter at me I'm pretty sure there was a money order in it. So you see, she's had a present of some money for clothes as well as us.'

There was a short pause whilst Lonnie considered this, then she gave a crow of amusement. 'He's bribed her!' she exclaimed joyfully. 'That means he understands what sort of a woman she is . . . oh, I am glad you told me, Hester! In my heart I've always felt a little worried and anxious in case she wrote lies about us to Daddy and he believed her. But he won't, will he? Because he knows how she is.'

'I think you're right, but remember, forget I ever said anything like that,' Hester said. 'And now for a real shopping spree – did I tell you that Mr Hetherington-Smith said we were to buy such things as a sled and ice-skates for when the weather gets really cold?'

'Yes, you did, though since neither you nor I have ever seen frost, let alone snow, I don't suppose we'll be able to use such things . . . unless we get Ben Bailey to show us how,' Lonnie remarked, skipping along beside her governess and eyeing the passing shops with more than her usual interest. 'I really hated him when we first came to England, but I don't now. I can't say I like him very much, but he isn't as bad as I first thought. Mr and Mrs Bailey and Dick are really nice, though. Easily the nicest people we know.'

'That's because we've seen more of them, I expect,' Hester said. 'Ben works whenever he can . . . he really is a help to his parents, you know, Lonnie. You should like him because of that.'

'But you can't like people just because they're good or noble or stuff like that,' Lonnie pointed out. She felt that this was a fact too often ignored by grown-ups, even such nice ones as Hester, of whom she was by now truly fond. 'There's something inside you and something inside them and if the two clash, well, they clash. It's a bit like me and old rabbit-Hutch. You keep telling me she's all right really, she means well, she warned you to be a bit smarmier with Aunt Emmeline, but unfortunately every time I see her chumbling away and blinking and twitching her nose I just think *that person isn't to be trusted,* and that's that!'

'You sound like a little old woman,' Hester said, laughing, as they crossed the road and headed for the nearest shops. 'I do hope you're wrong, though. Hutch – I mean Miss Hutchinson – really does mean well, or so I believe.'

Lonnie, who still distrusted her aunt's companion, was beginning to disagree when her governess paused outside a large plate glass window. 'Here's Lewis's. It's an excellent place to start for there is a great deal of choice in such a big department store.' Hester said. 'Shall we take a look inside?'

Lonnie agreed eagerly and the two of them entered the store's imposing portals and made their way to the children's clothing department. The shopping expedition, to which they had been looking forward ever since Mr Hetherington-Smith's letter and money order had arrived, was about to begin.

By lunchtime the two girls had so many bandboxes, packets and parcels that they were quite unable to carry them and had to leave them in the charge of the store whilst they made their way up to the beautiful restaurant on the top floor. 'We'll have a really good luncheon,' Hester said, and Lonnie saw that her governess's eyes were sparkling with excitement and pleasure, for Lonnie had not been the only one buying new clothes. Hester had bought two skirts, one navy pleated to be worn with a white blouse and navy jacket and the other pale green with a diamond pattern around the hem and a matching cardigan. She told Lonnie that she had sufficient underwear and stockings to last her for some time, but admitted that she could do with more warm clothing for the winter days to come.

After they had had luncheon, they returned to the fray and Lonnie was soon provided with warm woollen dresses, cosy cardigans, woollen stockings and an overcoat so ample that the shop lady had told them it would do Lonnie for at least three winters. Then boredom crept in. Clothes were all very well but choosing them, Lonnie realised, was not the fun she had imagined it would be. The shop assistants did not seem to like it when she wanted to take the first garment they produced and kept bringing out alternatives, saying she must have a good choice. However, as soon as Hester pronounced herself satisfied with their purchases from the children's department, they moved on to hats and gloves, and once Lonnie had seen her governess absorbed she made her way unobtrusively to a wide window seat, settled herself on the cushions with her nose pressed against the glass, and, with her eyes fixed on the panorama of Liverpool rooftops, proceeded to let her imagination wander.

Naturally enough, with her father's generosity so much on her mind, Lonnie's thoughts flew back to her former life. When her mother had first died, she had been unable to think of her without becoming overcome by the sadness of her loss, but that had been almost two years ago. Now, she could remember her mother and the happy times they had had together with a sort of nostalgic pleasure. Her father, too, was a favourite subject to dwell upon, as was her *ayah* and Diga, her *syce*. Diga had been fourteen years old when he had first begun to take the missie-sahib out on Domino, her favourite pony. Together they had roamed the streets and parks of the city, although never going more than a short distance from home. Diga had been friendly but firm and had never allowed her the freedom for which she had longed. 'It is dangerous for a missie-sahib to venture too far from home,' he had told her instructively. 'I know you long to visit the old city because that's where the best bazaars are to be found. But such places are dangerous and the gardens surrounding Connaught Place are very beautiful and spacious. Far more suitable for pony riding than the narrow streets of the old city, which is full of bad people who might try to do you harm. That is why your father employs me to keep you safe, and I cannot keep you safe if we go into the dangerous places.'

Lonnie had thought that this was just an excuse to deny her the bazaars, the little narrow streets thronged with Indians, the riverside walks and the places where snake charmers, tight-rope walkers and other such entertainers exhibited their mysteries. These things had been glimpsed in passing when she was riding in one of her father's motor cars, but even her indulgent parent refused to linger in such places. Now, Lonnie thought sadly that when people talked of the mysteries of the East, they might have been referring to the very delights which her father had denied her. She and Hester sometimes talked of India and she had speedily realised that her governess's experiences had been very different from her own. Hester knew the real India, the India which Lonnie dreamed about, and when she could be persuaded to talk freely of it she held Lonnie as spellbound as she held the Baileys, though Lonnie always tried to hide the fact and pretend that she, too, knew all about the great jungles and the creatures that inhabited them.

For after their first visit to the Baileys' household, she and Hester had revisited Elmore Street several times, usually going in the afternoon and returning in time for nursery supper. On the last occasion Hester had bought a cake at Fuller's, a walnut cake, covered thickly with white frosting, and Lonnie had been astonished at the almost reverent pleasure with which Mrs Bailey had greeted it when Hester had handed it over. The older woman had offered to cut it there and then and when Hester had refused a piece, saying it was more suitable for teatime, Mrs Bailey had admitted that an object so magnificent would thrill the whole family and had put it away in a sort of wire cage beneath the kitchen window so that the others might see it, untouched and splendid, before they began to eat it that evening. Hester and Lonnie had lingered, sharing the Baileys' supper and enjoying a slice of the beautiful cake.

As generally happened, Bob Bailey began to talk about the India he only knew through books, and this was a sign to Hester to tell the family something of her own recollections of that country. This time, she talked about the great city of Delhi; the Yamuna river which bisected it and the various bazaars which she remembered so well. She told them of the spice market in Khari Baoli street, with its huge sacks of herbs and spices being trundled along on narrow barrows, pushed by tiny dark and sweating labourers. As she spoke, her mind reconstructed the scene so well that she felt she could smell the spices and see the colourful stalls piled with lentils, rice, nuts and tea.

'But rice and lentils aren't spices,' Mrs Bailey said, leaning forward. 'Do they sell all sorts?'

Hester laughed. 'Yes, though everything there is edible,' she said. 'Now if you wanted household items, you would go to the Sadar bazaar. Believe it or not, they even sell saucepans, teacups and crockery by weight. It always used to make me laugh to see someone point out a big pan and ask the price, and the Delhi-wallah or stallholder put it on his scale.'

'Tell about the trees and the flowers,' Mrs Bailey said eagerly. 'Do you know, when you told us about the spice market, I could smell spices, I swear I could! But we love to hear about the trees and flowers, and birds and beasts, don't we, Bob?'

'Well, Delhi's pretty flat, but the North and South Ridges have a number of native trees on them: babul, arjuna, tamarind, peepul and neem trees. Shade is a valuable commodity in a country as hot as India, and the trees seem to attract what breeze there is, so the Ridge is a pleasant place to visit,' Hester said. 'A great many of the gardens are planted with flowering trees, too. The coral tree has brilliant scarlet flowers; the jacaranda is covered with wonderful blossom of the most brilliant blue in the spring and the amalta has bright yellow blooms. They make the gardens delightful and the houses and walls are often almost hidden by pink and purple bougainvillaea. The scent may not be as strong as the spices in Khari Baoli, but it is even sweeter.'

'Wharrabout the animals and the birds?' Ben asked eagerly. 'When I have a pet shop of me own, I'm going to send away for all sorts of exotic birds. Pet shops aren't much good for lions and tigers and that, but birds are a different story. Go on, Miss Elliott, tell us about the animals.'

'Well, jackals and nilgae antelope still live on the South Ridge; I know that because I've seen them myself,' Hester told him. 'And in the tombs of Hamayan and the Lodi gardens there are quantities of wonderful birds. Parakeets – you've seen parakeets in pet shops over here, Ben – sunbirds, bulbuls and bee-eaters are very nearly as common as sparrows are in England.'

'Bee-eaters? And bulbuls? What do they look like?' Ben asked excitedly. 'Bulbuls don't even sound like birds; nor do bee-eaters really.'

'It's difficult to describe them, apart from telling you that bee-eaters are just about every colour under the sun. But next time I come round, I'll bring a book,' Hester said, laughing. 'I can see I shall have to educate myself on the flora and fauna of India; nothing less will satisfy you!'

Soon after that, Mrs Bailey had reminded them about their proposed trip across the water and Hester had fallen in gladly with the suggestion. The talk at the table had then revolved around New Brighton, a place which the girls had never visited, and so it was rather later than usual when Dick offered to walk them home. They usually left Elmore Street in time to reach Shaw Street whilst Miss Hetherington-Smith and Miss Hutchinson were enjoying their dinner and could be relied upon not to come snooping through the hall as the girls climbed the stairs to their own domain. As they hurried up Everton Brow, with Dick's hand beneath her elbow, Hester had had the uneasy feeling that someone was watching her from the tall side window of Number 127 and hoped that it might be Fletcher, or one of the maids. This hope was dashed, however, when she and Lonnie were tiptoeing across the hall towards the stair, as Miss Hutchinson had met them, a finger to her lips. 'A word, Miss Elliott,' she had hissed, and she and Hester had disappeared into the servants' quarters, Hester first telling Lonnie to make her way up to the schoolroom. Hester had joined her there no more than ten minutes later, looking grave. 'Miss Hutchinson has just told me that your aunt saw Dick Bailey accompanying us along Everton Brow just now,' she had told Lonnie. 'Miss Hutchinson said they finished dinner early tonight because Mr and Mrs Mullins from next door are coming in for a game of bridge. She said Miss Hetherington-Smith was setting out the card tables in the small drawing room when she saw us coming up the hill. She was very angry and seemed to believe that it was some sort of clandestine meeting. Miss Hutchinson advised us most earnestly not to go to visit the Baileys for a few days, so I think we shall have to cancel the trip to New Brighton. She thinks your aunt would consider them unsuitable friends for you, and might make this an excuse for dismissing me.'

Lonnie was disappointed, for she had been looking forward to the treat, but quite saw that it would not do to antagonise her aunt further. 'But we can't just not visit them,' Lonnie had said, much aggrieved, 'it would hurt their feelings and be awfully rude. Even *I* know that and you're always telling me I've got no manners!'

Hester had laughed but agreed that it would certainly be most dreadfully rude to stop seeing them, particularly since the planned trip to New Brighton had been regarded by the whole family as a high treat. 'We'll have to go round and explain that for the time being we shall be unable to visit Elmore Street or go to New Brighton,' she had said. 'I'll go by myself one evening, when you are in bed and asleep, only you must promise me, Lonnie, not to get out of bed or do anything which might call attention to my absence. If I go in the evening, Dick should be there and I'm pretty sure he'll understand. If you remember, he was worried that someone might see us together when he brought us home that first time, so he'll realise that it isn't our fault and won't think we're being – being snobbish or horrid.'

Lonnie had been sorry not to be included in the expedition to Elmore Street but had understood the gravity of the situation. When Hester returned she was sad, Lonnie could tell by the droop of her mouth, but she assured her charge that the Baileys had understood and sympathised. 'Ben says if we go and look in Mr Madison's window, he'll nip out and stand beside us as though he were just a customer and we can let him know how things stand,' she had said. 'They were all so nice about it, Lonnie, which made me feel even worse. Dick said there's a way round everything and he's sure we'll all meet up again when he's thought of a plan.' She had smiled down into Lonnie's eager eyes. 'He's quite right, we'll think of something. So cheer up! This is just a temporary set-back, not the end of a friendship.'

But that had been in August; now it was October and though they had chatted to Ben from time to time, Hester had been far too nervous to risk visiting in Elmore Street. Once, when they had been heading towards Heyworth Street, Lonnie had noticed the gardener's boy dodging along the pavement behind them, as if on their trail. When he had seen her eyes upon him, he had dived into a shop doorway and Lonnie had wondered if she had just imagined that he had been following them. When they reached home, however, Hester had asked Lonnie if she had seen young Greg lurking behind a pillar-box whilst they pretended to examine the pets in Mr Madison's window, and Lonnie had known that her original suspicion was correct: the gardener's boy had indeed been spying on them.

After that, it became a sort of game to spot young Greg, or Fletcher, or Edie the kitchen maid – and also to pretend ignorance of their presence. 'It's Miss Hetherington-Smith who puts them up to it,' Hester said grimly. 'Honestly, Lonnie, I'm doing my very best to please her, to be the sort of governess she wants for you, but it doesn't seem to work. She must really hate me!'

'I shouldn't let it worry you; she can't hate you as much as she hates me,' Lonnie had said. 'Every time she looks at me, I see it in her eyes – I can read her like a book! She thinks about how nice and quiet the house was before we came and how she had all Daddy's lovely money to herself. She never had to send the maids up to the attics with hot water, or the milk and bread and other tea things, and when she walked into the garden she was always the only one there. She could cut roses or pick some tomatoes from the greenhouse, or just stroll around sniffing the flowers. But now Kitty and I are often out there and Mr Mimms chats to me and tells my aunt what a good little gardener I am becoming, so she can't forget about me no matter how hard she tries.'

Now, sitting on Lewis's window seat, Lonnie regarded a line of seagulls perched on the ridge of a roof just below her and thought, crossly, that she had considered herself hard done by in India because she was not allowed more freedom. Yet when her father had told her that he was sending her to England, one of the things he had promised her had been a less restricted life. 'Children in England go to school, visit their friends and play games in the park without needing adult supervision,' he had assured her. 'Provided you are sensible, you will be able to please yourself much more than you can here.' He had lifted her on to his knee and given her a hug, then rumpled her hair. 'Dear little Lonnie, I shall miss you most dreadfully, but it is for your own good, I promise you. You are beginning to look peaky and sallow and you are far too thin. You are a little English girl and you need the English climate, no matter what you may think. But as soon as you're old enough I shall want you with me once more, so be sensible and make the most of your time in England. I shall write to you every week and shall expect you to reply as regularly, sweetheart.'

If I wrote to Daddy and told him that Aunt Emmeline sets spies on us and won't let us visit our friends, I wonder whether he would tell her off and insist that we were left alone, Lonnie thought, still eyeing the large herring gulls only ten feet away from her. But she knew that she should not worry her father over something which he could not do anything about. She was in her aunt's charge and at her mercy and could not expect her father, thousands of miles away, to intervene.

Sighing, she turned away from the window for a moment to see how Hester was getting on. Her governess was nodding, ferreting in her purse, whilst the shop assistant wrapped something up in blue tissue paper. I mustn't expect Daddy to do anything about his sister, Lonnie decided. It wouldn't be fair, but oh, I do wonder what he's doing now!

Leonard Hetherington-Smith was about to leave his office. He had run his business for so long now that he was able to leave it for quite lengthy periods, confident that his well-trained staff would be able to manage in his absence, and today he intended to put that confidence to the test.

After Lonnie and her governess had left he had gone up to the hills, feeling that he needed the coolness and quiet of his large and airy bungalow whilst he grew accustomed to being without his adored little daughter. At first, the bungalow had seemed *too* quiet, too peaceful. There had been no point in uprooting his entire household as he had done in the old days, when his wife and child had been with him, so he had only taken a couple of servants to augment the staff who spent the whole year in the hills. Naturally, however, the neighbouring properties had been full of Europeans who had fled from the heat of the plains, and as soon as it became common knowledge that Leonard was in residence invitations began to pour in. Parties, balls and masquerades were offered for his enjoyment, as well as picnics and expeditions of pleasure into the surrounding countryside. Leonard soon found himself at least occupied, and within a week of beginning to socialise once more he had met Rosalind Bright.

Rosalind had come out from England, a member of what the Anglo-Indian aristocracy rather unkindly called 'the fishing fleet': young ladies of impeccable lineage and considerable charm and good looks, usually from military families. Most had been sent by parents who had once served in India and were keen to see their daughters suitably married to bright young men who would, in the years to come, both make names for themselves and earn a good deal of money.

Leonard had met Rosalind at a dance. The hosts' bungalow being too small for such an event, it was held in the grounds, where coloured lights were strung from the branches of the trees and soft-footed servants padded amongst the small tables, offering the guests champagne, wine and exotic food.

Leonard had noticed Rosalind at once, partly because of her extraordinarily white skin and light, ash-blonde hair, and partly because of her gaiety. She was wearing smoke-grey chiffon which swirled as she moved and when Leonard asked her to dance, thinking to find a frail, ethereal spirit, he was both astonished and pleased to realise that, in fact, she was very down to earth. She joked and laughed with him, linked her arm in his to take a closer look at the fairy lights clustered in the trees, and agreed to meet him the following day for a ride in the pine woods, despite the fact that he was more than twenty years older than she.

A great many people in New Delhi considered Leonard to be immensely wealthy but he had never thought of himself as a 'catch', possibly because he and his wife had been married young. Even now, when he proposed marriage to Rosalind – which he did on their fifth meeting – and she accepted, it never occurred to him that it might be his money which had attracted her. After all, he lived in no particular style and spent no more lavishly than any other European in a country where the cost of living was low. If people sniggered behind their hands at this meeting of May and September, Leonard merely considered that they were jealous. There were not many men of his age who could both captivate and capture someone as beautiful and as charming as Rosalind Bright.

At first he had simply fallen for her face and delightful personality, but he soon realised that she was very intelligent and quite capable of keeping her end up in the older and more sophisticated circles in which he moved. Before leaving her in the hills to return to his various business interests in the city, he had taken her for a day's outing to Simla. They rode up the Western Mall in a rickshaw, for the way was steep, and did not get down until they reached Scandal Point. From there they dived into a narrow alley fringed with elaborately decorated houses. The alley was roughly cobbled and Rosalind was wondering aloud why her companion chose to scramble up such terrain when Leonard led her into a tiny shop, so crammed with gold and jewels that they dazzled the eye. There, he had bought her a diamond ring of such breathtaking beauty that even the merchant from whom they had bought it saw it go with regret, saying it was the finest gem he had ever owned. Rosalind had been enchanted with it, saying that she particularly liked it because it was not huge or ostentatious but simply the most beautiful jewel she had ever seen. Certainly, she had never expected to own such a one, and as they made their way back to the hill station she looked at her companion speculatively, her large grey eyes wide with curiosity. 'Darling Len, can you really afford a stone like this?' she asked in her usual straightforward manner. 'I'm afraid I never thought of the cost when the old man produced tray after tray of stones, but if it's going to embarrass . . .'

Touched both by the naiveté of her question and

the simple kindliness of it, he had laughed out loud and given her an exuberant hug. 'Ros, light of my life, I could afford to buy every gem in the shop if I really wanted to,' he assured her. 'I have a great many business interests all over India. I have homes in three major cities and the hill bungalow which you've already seen, besides a house in Liverpool and property in central London. Your ring is well within my means.'

Rosalind had laughed and returned his hug and then, standing on tiptoe, she had kissed his cheek. 'Well, at least you know I'm not marrying you for your money,' she remarked. 'To tell you the truth, Len, I'd marry you if you were just a box-wallah, peddling pins and hair ribbons and cheap jewellery to half the housewives in Delhi.'

Leonard heard the sincerity behind the words and felt his heart swell with pride. His first wife, Deirdre, had been his second cousin, so he had known her all his life. Her family had lived on the Wirral and there had been coming and going between the Radnors and the Hetherington-Smiths for as long as he could remember. He had always thought of Deirdre as a sweet and simple country girl and after two years in India, struggling with the business and being cheated over household expenses by his staff, he had decided his best course would be to marry.

He had returned to England, proposed to his little country cousin and gone back to Delhi with his blushing bride. He had never regretted his marriage and had taken it for granted that, as the stronger personality of the two, he would always have to look after Deirdre, but she had done her best to keep up with him and had proved popular with his friends and acquaintances.

Lonnie had been born long after the couple had given up all hope of ever having a child and Deirdre had been besotted by her daughter, wanting to protect her from every wind which blew and anxious over the many health risks with which India abounded. Other children played in their gardens, taking the risk of snake bite, scorpion sting or the snapping of a stray dog, should it gain access, but Lonnie was five before her mother allowed her to play out of doors and even then she was always accompanied by her *ayah* and seldom allowed to invite other children on to their property.

When Deirdre had died, Leonard's grief had been deep and totally honest. He had loved her and would miss her gentle loving ways for the rest of his life, he had thought, but now, when he was with Rosalind, he found to his shame that it was hard to bring Derdre's small oval face and shining, toffee-brown hair to mind. What was more, he knew that Deirdre had never been his intellectual equal, whereas there were times when he ruefully suspected that despite the age difference Rosalind was at least as clever as he, if not more so.

So now Leonard made his way to the railway station where he would catch a train up into the hills, where Rosalind waited. They intended to get married as soon as they returned to the plains and to have a honeymoon aboard one of the many cruise ships which took on passengers in Amritsar, for though Leonard longed to introduce his beautiful young wife to his dearest Lonnie he had no desire to visit England in winter, when he could scarcely expect Liverpool, the city of his birth, to look its best.

As soon as he and Rosalind had tied the knot

he meant to write a long, chatty letter to his sister informing her of his new status and another to Lonnie, assuring her that her new stepmother was the most wonderful person in the world. Rosalind loved children and was good with them; Leonard had seen many evidences of this since his fiancée was staying with the Cuthbertsons who had half a dozen children with ages ranging from four months to eight years.

As he boarded the train, taking his place in the first-class sleeper and pouring himself a generous *chota-peg* from the decanter of whisky on the little sideboard, he reflected that the letter to Lonnie must be tactful in the extreme. He would have liked to tell her that Rosalind's presence would mean she might return to India once more, to live with him and his new wife, but he knew this was impossible. The educational and social advantages of living in England could not be lightly dismissed, and then there was the continuing health hazard which India's extreme heat and the prevalence of diseases such as cholera represented to growing children.

Having thought about his responsibilities, Leonard leaned back in his comfortable seat, just as the train began to move forward. Through the window, he could see the crowded platform with its little knots of people cooking meals, sleeping or indulging in fierce arguments gradually being left behind. The journey would take almost four days and this period was always one to which he looked forward because he could relax completely and enjoy the varied scenery through which the train passed whilst allowing his thoughts free reign. It was an opportunity to draft out the letters which he meant to send when the time was right, so he fished in his attaché case and brought out his writing pad, his fountain pen and a sheet of pink blotting paper. He pulled out the flap of the small writing desk and laid the things out on it. Then he pulled his chair closer and picked up his pen. Presently, with his eyes gazing straight ahead, he began to think of Rosalind.

Chapter Four

'There's a letter for me from Daddy!' Lonnie came dancing up the stairs and into the schoolroom where her breakfast porridge was awaiting her attention. 'Oh, Hester, I do love Daddy's letters. They are always exciting and quite often he tells me about my friends, if you can call them friends, that is. Last time he wrote, he told me how naughty Arnold Cuthbertson had been.' She giggled, sliding into her seat and picking up her porridge spoon. 'Doesn't the cold make one hungry, Hester? I took Kitty down to play in the snow but she didn't like it one bit. She picked up her paws one at a time and shook them, then she sneezed and went hoppity hop back into the house.' She took a large spoonful of porridge and crammed it into her mouth, then began to wrench at the envelope. 'Daddy said that Arnie Cuthbertson put a big dead bull-frog in a guest's bed and nearly made her faint. She's got ever such a funny name – the guest I mean – she's called Miss Bright. Daddy says she's ever so nice and was a real sport about the bull-frog, but Mr Cuthbertson didn't think it was funny and wouldn't let Arnie ride his pony or go on a picnic for a whole week.'

'That sounds fair,' Hester said. She did not mind bull-frogs in their natural element but would not have cared to discover one in her bed, particularly if the discovery was made by a naked toe. 'Just you put that envelope down, miss, and eat your porridge.

We don't have many rules up here but one of them is *hot food should be eaten hot and letters can always wait*, and you don't want to get porridge all over Daddy's letter, do you?'

Lonnie laughed but began to ply her porridge spoon energetically and presently was scraping the dish clean. 'That was lovely; you *do* make nice porridge, Hester, much nicer than Cook's,' she said, pushing back her empty plate. 'May I open the letter now?'

'Wouldn't you like a piece of toast?' Hester said. 'I can make you some in the twinkling of an eye.'

Lonnie, however, shook her head. 'No thanks, I'm full to the brim with porridge,' she said, reaching eagerly for the envelope. 'I wonder where Daddy is now? He went back to the hills, you know, but I don't suppose he stayed there very long. I expect by now . . .' She had ripped open the envelope and immediately began to read the flimsy pages, her lips moving silently as she perused every word. Hester got up and began to clear the table, carrying the dishes through into the small kitchenette. She had got into the habit of always washing their crockery and cutlery and both cooking and clearing away their meals, since this saved the servants a job and would, she hoped, endear her to Miss Hetherington-Smith, who was constantly grumbling that Hester and the child made a great deal of work for the maids. Hester had acquired a second gas ring, upon which she boiled a large pan of water for washing up, and close to the basin which she used for this purpose stood three enamel buckets holding cold water. Hester put the sticky porridge dishes, spoons, knives and side plates into the bowl and splashed boiling water on to them, then added a judicious amount of cold. She set to work with her little mop and had very soon finished the task, leaving the dishes to dry in the rack which Cook had provided. She was about to return to the schoolroom and suggest that they start lessons at once in order to go out into the snow as soon as they had finished, when the door shot open and Lonnie appeared. Her face was bright red and her dark eyes were flashing dangerously. 'You'll never guess what my daddy's been and gone and done,' she said in a high, furious voice. 'He's been and gone and married that Bright woman! Oh, Hester, I can't *believe* my daddy would do such a thing! If he was lonely, why didn't he have me taken back to India again? Or he could have married *you* – you're ever so pretty and we know each other so well that it wouldn't have made much difference. Why, you could still have stayed with me over here because lots of mummies do that. They visit India every other year for three or four months and the daddies come back to England for their long leaves whenever they can.' As Hester turned away from the washstand, Lonnie hurled herself across the room and into her governess's arms, still too furious for tears, though Hester thought they were not far off. 'Oh, Hester, what shall I do? I hate Miss Bright, hate her, hate her! How *dare* she marry my daddy the moment my back's turned! Daddy says she will be my stepmother and I must love her and be good to her, but I won't, I won't!'

'Darling Lonnie, I don't suppose you'll see much of her for the next few years,' Hester said gently. 'Remember how lonely your daddy must have been with you far away and your mother gone.'

'Mummy's only been dead two and a bit years,' Lonnie said resentfully. 'People don't marry again so quickly as a rule. Anyway, Daddy *isn't* lonely, he's got heaps and heaps of friends, and if he *was* lonely, why couldn't he have kept my dear *ayah*? She would have looked after him as well as any wife could.'

Over the top of the child's head, Hester allowed herself a small grin. She knew very little about marriage herself, but guessed that no *ayah*, no matter how good, could perform all the duties of a wife. However, it would not do to say so to the child. 'Your father is an Englishman, dearest, and needs an English woman as his partner,' she explained gently.

Lonnie gave a derisive sniff. 'Why?' she said baldly. 'My father speaks perfectly good Hindi and my *ayah* spoke quite good English. Oh, Hester, I *don't* understand.'

Hester took a deep breath and her mind searched feverishly through various similes, at last coming up with one she hoped Lonnie would understand. 'Kitty is a cat, right? She's a very young cat at the moment but one day she will look round her for a mate, a he-cat. She will want to be with him and perhaps they will have baby kittens of their own later on. Do you understand that, Lonnie?'

Hester had sat herself down in the upright kitchen chair, with Lonnie sucking her thumb, a thing she rarely did in the daylight hours, leaning against her knee. The child did not speak, but after a moment nodded her head.

'Well, if you had a little dog, do you suppose that the little dog and Kitty would become excellent friends? If they wanted to do so, could they live happily together and have kittens or puppies?'

Lonnie looked up, then gave a watery giggle. 'That's

silly,' she mumbled around her thumb. 'But . . . but I know what you are trying to say. My *ayah* was a dear but she was nothing like my mother. Yes, I suppose Daddy does need someone of his own kind, though I wish it could have been me, or you. Then things needn't have changed. And he says in his letter that he's taking Rosalind – that's her name, Rosalind – on a world cruise. He'll be gone six months – six whole months, Hester – so I shan't even be able to write to him, though he says he'll send me cards and presents from every port.' She sniffed dolefully. 'So things will change even more, don't you think?'

'Dear Lonnie, things *won't* change,' Hester insisted. 'You must not imagine that your daddy will love you less because he also loves Miss Bright. There are two quite different kinds of love, you know, so you needn't worry that you will be displaced in your father's affections. You are his dear little girl and nobody can take that away from you. As for the cruise, six months will soon pass and you'll have your daddy's letters and presents every week or so. You can write to him regularly, you know, as you have always done, then when he gets home he'll have all the fun of reading what you've been doing while he was away.'

'When he comes home he *says* he'll bring that woman to England for a nice long stay,' Lonnie admitted grudgingly. 'He *says* she wants to meet me – and you and Aunt Emmeline of course – but I dare say that's just one of the promises grown-ups make and never mean to keep.'

Hester laughed. 'You mustn't be so determined to believe the worst of people,' she said, giving Lonnie's thin shoulders a little squeeze. 'Now put your letter somewhere safe and we'll forget lessons for this morning and go out and play in the snow.'

Lonnie removed her thumb from her mouth and rubbed her face with her sleeve, then smiled up at Hester. 'I can't put the letter away; I threw it in the fire,' she said briskly. 'I was very cross and upset and I wanted to punish Daddy for being so – so secretive. If he had come back to England and got married here, I might have been a bridesmaid. I've always wanted to be a bridesmaid but now I don't suppose I'll ever get the chance,' she finished dolefully.

Hester leaned down and gave Lonnie's tear-wet cheek a quick kiss. She had never been particularly demonstrative but had realised for some time that Lonnie missed the cuddles and caresses which had been a part of her life, both with her parents and with her *ayah*. Hester had felt awkward at first, for her own father had not been a demonstrative man, but now Lonnie took it for granted that she could sit on her governess's knee when she was unhappy and would always be kissed good night and good morning. 'You shall be bridesmaid if I ever get married,' Hester promised recklessly. 'Now I think you ought to wash your face before you're seen in public, or everyone will guess you've been upset. I'll pour you some warm water so you can make a proper job of it.'

Later that day, Miss Emmeline sat at the window with her brother's letter spread out on the large desk in front of her, watching the snow whirl past. She was thinking hard. Her first reaction to his news had been one of incredulity and rage. She had never liked her sister-in-law – had never really known her in fact – but ever since Deirdre died she had begun to consider herself the natural heiress to the enormous fortune which her brother had built up. Without actively wishing him harm, she had begun to take it for granted that he was unlikely to outlive her, despite her being a dozen years the elder, for everyone knew that men aged much quicker than women and that those in tropical climes frequently fell prey to misadventures and diseases unknown in England.

She had accepted, of course, that Leonard would leave most of his money to Lonnie but guessed that, as the child's guardian, she would hold any such monies in trust until the child either married or was considered old enough to manage her own affairs. Yet now, out of the blue, came the news that Leonard was married, and to a young and lovely woman who would undoubtedly outlive both Leonard and Emmeline herself.

Emmeline picked up the letter and read it through again. In the back of her fertile mind was a thought which would not quite come to the surface. Something in the letter could be turned to her advantage, only she could not quite see . . . if she read the letter again, slowly . . . if she consulted Hutchinson . . . except she did not wish to let her companion see how baffled and frustrated she felt. She simply must work out the puzzle for herself. She would get no rest until she had done so.

She had read the first three paragraphs when it suddenly occurred to her just how she could use the information her brother had given her. He and his new wife were embarking on a world cruise for six months. For six whole, glorious months they would be incommunicado, unable to receive letters or information from anyone, including the wretched child who had turned the Hetherington-Smith household upside down and whose smug, self-satisfied governess had dared to defy the mistress of the house and make her feel small and petty. She had never let Miss Elliott know it but she had received an extremely unpleasant letter from her brother, regarding the payment of Miss Elliott's salary. He had been very angry and had not scrupled to tell his elder sister that she had no right to charge a dependent employee for her keep. He had added that unless she wanted him to pay Miss Elliott direct she had better mend her ways at once, assure the governess that a mistake had been made, reimburse her for the money already withheld, and never attempt to do such a thing again.

At the time, Miss Emmeline had been in danger of having an apoplexy from sheer rage and frustration. She had only been able to bring herself to comply with her brother's wishes by dwelling on the revenge she would wreak upon Miss Elliott when the opportunity presented itself. She had planned to dismiss the governess without a character as soon as she possibly could, playing with the lovely notion of accusing the younger woman of theft, immoral behaviour or contaminating the mind of a child. She knew, of course, that unless such an accusation could be substantiated her brother would be very angry with her, might even stop her allowance or cease to pay the household expenses. But since she knew in her heart that such dreams were unlikely ever to come to fruition, she scarcely considered her brother's reaction.

But now it seemed that fate had delivered Miss Elliott into her hands. She could make use of the girl in any way she wished and Leonard would not find out what was happening for six whole months. She had long thought that the job of Lonnie's governess was not a particularly exacting one. A couple of hours of lessons each morning and perhaps a walk around a museum in the afternoon were tasks, she felt, that could be undertaken by almost anyone. As her brother paid the governess's wages, however, there was no point in dismissing Miss Elliott since she herself would have to employ someone in her place. But in the meantime, she would see that the young woman was kept fully occupied. Already, Miss Elliott was responsible for nursery tea and for clearing away and washing up the tea things. In future, she could undertake other, similar tasks. If Miss Elliott – I shall call her Hester in future, Miss Emmeline told herself – could keep her own room tidy, then she could do the same for the whole of the second floor. She could easily fit such tasks as dusting, polishing and cleaning windows into her duties without disturbing the child's lessons. Warming to her theme, Miss Emmeline realised that with her governess busy the child might become a nuisance, for everyone knew that Satan could always find work for idle hands to do. Therefore, while Miss Elliott – Hester – busied herself with cleaning the rooms on the second floor, the child might as well either assist the governess or come down into the kitchen and make herself useful there.

Yes, there were many things which an intelligent young girl could do. In fact, Miss Emmeline thought, the work which she would set the child could be regarded as a much needed lesson in housekeeping. Frequently, Miss Emmeline had to send one of the maids to the grocer's, greengrocer's or fishmonger's for some item the household needed. If her order was a large one, the shop delivered, so there was no reason why Lonnie should not be sent on errands such as this. The wretched governess was always pointing out that children needed fresh air; well, she would get plenty of fresh air on her way to and from the shops and if Hester thought the distance too long for short legs, then a child's tram fare was only half that of an adult. Miss Emmeline began to smile. At present the household employed three maids. With Hester doing a good deal of the housework and the child helping with such tasks as the preparation of vegetables, the washing up after dinner and the running of messages, it might be possible to dispense with the services of one, or even two, of the other maids.

Outside, the snow still fell and as she stared, unseeingly, at the whirling flakes, Miss Emmeline's attention was caught by two figures emerging from the front door. Both were well muffled up in caps, scarves, coats and boots, the taller one carrying what looked like a parcel, whilst the shorter was rolling a snowball along the pavement, now and then stopping to turn it so that it retained a rounded, rather than a wheel-like, shape. Gadding about without a thought for who will have to clear up the mud and snow they will bring in again, Miss Emmeline thought viciously. She glanced automatically at her watch as the dusk deepened to make sure that the governess and her charge had not broken their curfew. It was still only half-past three, however, so she turned from the cold scene outside with a little shiver. The sight of the snow made the small study in which Miss Emmeline sat seem even warmer by contrast, though the fire in the grate needed making up. She smiled and stood up and tugged at the bell pull; it crossed her mind how pleasant it would be to tug at the bell pull, as she had just done, and to have Hester – the once proud and beautiful Miss Elliott – come creeping in with her hair in a tangle and her cap on crooked, to answer the summons. How enjoyable it would be to order Hester to fetch up a new scuttleful of coal; how delightful to see her returning with sweat running down her face. Even more delightful would be the sight of Hester, the once proud governess, heaving lumps of coal on to the fire and then pushing back her hair to leave coal streaks all over her brow.

Give me a month, just a month, and she'll be sorry she ever told lying tales of me to my brother, Miss Emmeline told herself grimly. At the end of two months, she'll be quite crushed and the child along with her. There will be no more snooty looks and impudent answers from either of them.

Presently, the maid, Mollie, entered the room, glanced at the fire and seized the empty scuttle without being asked. Miss Emmeline was quite surprised to see how neat and trim the girl looked, but then she had been a housemaid for months, she comforted herself. If Hester had answered the bell, how different things would be!

'Shan't be a tick, miss,' Mollie called cheerfully as she left the room. 'You should ha' rung earlier, the perishin' fire's near on out.'

'Mollie! I do have a name, you know; how many times do I have to tell you . . . ?'

'Sorry, Miss Smith,' Mollie said promptly, pausing in the doorway. 'I means to remember but you know me, I gorra rotten mem'ry.'

'For the hundredth time, Mollie, my name is Miss Hethering . . .'

But it was too late; Miss Hetherington-Smith was speaking to a closed door. Sighing, she turned back to her desk in the window embrasure. Mollie will be the first to go, she told herself. As things stood at present, she had little choice but to employ the girl, since despite the Depression live-in servants who were as poorly paid as Mollie were difficult to find. But if she could use Hester and Lonnie . . .

Miss Emmeline smiled at the whirling flakes and continued to plot.

Ben was selling firewood and feeling quite pleased with himself. It was early December and trade in the pet shop was thriving, for a good many indulgent parents bought pets for their children as Christmas presents and though trade always fell off lamentably after the holiday, such pets still had to be fed and Mr Madison made sure he kept plenty of fodder in for the lean months. The shop was well stocked with small animals and birds at present and they all had to be fed and watered and cleaned out daily, so Ben did not have very much time to himself, but he was keen to make some money so that he could buy presents for his family and had begun to haunt any shop whose goods were delivered in wooden boxes. Having acquired a good supply of such boxes, he had then used his parent's small wood axe to chop them into kindling which he tied into bundles with short lengths of twine and sold for a ha'penny each.

He could not sell his kindling whilst he was at work or at school but the shop did not open on a Sunday and he generally finished work by eight on a week-day, so despite the cold and snow he usually managed about an hour's selling each evening and spent most of Sunday renewing his supplies.

Ben looked into the large canvas bag slung around his shoulder and sighed. He had six more bundles to sell and though his feet were so cold he could no longer feel them, his hands ached with the chill and he knew that when he did get home and began to warm up, his extremities would be agony. However, he was halfway down Everton Road and the next few houses were large ones; if they were short of kindling – and you never knew your luck – they might easily buy at least two bundles, which would shorten his toil considerably.

Ben trudged up the next short pathway and rapped on the door. He was in luck today, having finished early at the pet shop, since trade had been slow because of the snow. He and Mr Madison had cleaned down and moved the animals back from the window by three in the afternoon; then the blinds had come rattling down – it helped to keep the interior of the shop warm, Ben knew – the tiny oil stove which was kept behind the counter during daylight hours was carried into the centre of the shop, and he and Mr Madison went about their own business. Ben had gone straight home, picked up his supplies of kindling and set out for a part of the city he had not yet covered. He had done pretty well, he considered now, waiting for someone to answer the front door. He had started out with twenty bundles of kindling and now had only six left, which meant – he struggled with mental multiplication for a moment – that he was the richer by sevenpence to add to his hoard.

'Yes? What d'you want?' A small, pert-faced girl in a long draggly apron, a cap perched on her greasy hair, looked at him enquiringly. 'If you're sellin' something . . .'

'It's kindling, only a ha'penny a bundle,' Ben said

quickly, diving into the canvas bag and producing one. 'They're ever so cheap, miss, only a ha'penny.'

'We don't want none,' the girl said quickly. She tried to swing the heavy door shut but Ben pretended to drop the kindling, which was not hard because of his numb fingers, and shot out a boot, successfully preventing the door from closing.

'You could ask in the kitchen,' he said persuasively as he straightened up. 'A ha'penny ain't much and it's good kindling. I chopped it meself out of orange boxes and it's dry as dry, so when you put a match to it it'll go up like a rocket.'

The girl gave him a long, calculating look, then turned away, not attempting to shut the door again. 'I'll nip an' ask Mr Sedgewick, though since I'm the one that has to light the fires I'd be pleased enough to use dry kindling; the stuff what comes in from the woodshed is always damp,' she remarked over her shoulder. 'But people in big houses always seems careful wi' their splosh,' she added, in a lowered tone. 'It ain't as if they'd even notice partin' wi' a copper or two either. So I'll have a go for you.'

Ben, who had not thought her a particularly pleasant girl, was delighted when she came back with tuppence, informing him grandly that Mr Sedgewick himself had parted with the money and she would take four bundles, if he pleased. 'Thanks ever so much, miss,' Ben said earnestly, grinning from ear to ear. 'I were that cold I were on the point of giving up and now I've only got two more bundles to sell, then I can go home. Thanks again!'

The girl grinned at him, an elfin grin which lit up her small, narrow face, and made her look almost pretty. 'That's all right, chuck,' she said, preparing to close the door behind him. 'Good luck wi' your last two bundles!'

Ben glanced up at the next house and was about to ascend the steps when someone caught hold of his arm. He looked down and saw a small girl, warmly dressed in a navy-blue serge coat with a fur collar and a scarlet, fur-fringed hat. It was Lonnie. She had a long scarlet and white scarf wrapped around her neck and the woolly glove on his sleeve was scarlet too. She was beaming up at him, her face rosy with the cold and her eyes bright, clearly delighted to see him again. Standing nearby, also smiling broadly, was the governess.

'Ben!' Lonnie squeaked. 'Oh, how maddening that I didn't realise it was you earlier! It would have been much more fun to get your attention by throwing a snowball at you, but I threw the last one at the gas lamp on the corner. It seems ages since we saw you! How are Mr and Mrs Bailey? Oh, I do miss them, but I expect they told you how horrid Aunt Emmeline had been and how we dare not go round to Elmore Street just yet.'

'Yes, Dick did tell us your aunt didn't approve of us,' Ben said grudgingly, after a moment. 'But he telled us you were goin' to call round at the shop when I were there working, and you never did. I've allus looked out for you, too,' he ended virtuously.

The governess stepped forward, smiling. 'We have been to the pet shop at least half a dozen times since then, but the trouble is, with the shorter afternoons, we don't have much spare time which coincides with yours,' she said apologetically. 'Miss Hetherington-Smith now insists that we return to the house before dusk begins to fall. Nursery tea has to be served at four o'clock and we aren't allowed to leave the house after teatime, and on Sundays it's even worse. We attend morning service at St Augustine's church, then we have our midday meal with Miss Hetherington-Smith and her companion, and during the afternoon Lonnie has to read to her and tell her what stage her studies have reached. After that, we go to evening service, which gives us very little time to ourselves.'

'It isn't as though she listens to what I've been doing, either,' Lonnie put in resentfully. 'She usually falls asleep, doesn't she, Hester? And quite often she snores so loud, I can't hear myself speak. Once, I laughed, and she woke up and told Hester I was a rude, impertinent brat, and needed a good whipping.'

Ben looked at the small girl doubtfully. Was she simply making excuses for not visiting the shop? Probably. 'But it's past four now. If you aren't allowed out after four . . .'

'We aren't,' Lonnie said, giggling. 'But Aunt Emmeline wanted some letters taking to the post. My father wrote a week ago to say he had married again and I suppose she wanted to congratulate him – at any rate, one of the letters was addressed to Delhi. She wanted some knitting wool as well, from Wendy's on Heyworth Street. She didn't tell us to get it, mind, she told old rabbit-Hutch, but *she's* got a shocking cold in the head, so when Hester offered to go in her place, she jumped at it.'

Ben raised his eyebrows. Old rabbit-Hutch? Had the snow turned the girl's brain? He glanced interrogatively across at Hester, who was smiling and nodding. 'Poor Ben, he must think we've run mad,' she said cheerfully. 'The fact is, Lonnie's aunt has a companion by the name of Miss Hutchinson, but I'm afraid we've taken to calling her Hutch, because it's shorter. I rather like her, but Lonnie does not and since she thinks Hutch looks like a rabbit . . .'

'I get it,' Ben said quickly. 'But if you've been snowballing lampposts, young Lonnie, you must have been out for longer than an hour! What'll happen when you get home again, eh?'

'Nothing much,' Lonnie said cheerfully. 'We've got awfully cunning, haven't we, Hester? You see, my aunt's a creature of habit, who does everything by the clock. At six, she goes to her room to change for dinner and whilst she's there she usually sends for a glass of madeira. We reckon she'll be safely tucked away in her room between six and six thirty, so if we *do* manage to escape, we always return to the house around that time. We go in the back gate because Mr Mimms had a key cut for us and though the servants must know we're breaking the rules they never tell on us. They don't like my aunt any more than I do,' she ended triumphantly.

Ben nodded. Dick had said gloomily, after Hester's last visit, that he doubted whether they would ever see the two young ladies again but he had told Ben to keep his eyes peeled for a sight of them. 'They'll be round to Mr Madison's so any gossip that's going, any change in their circumstances, they'll tell you,' he informed his young brother. 'And you can pass it on to the rest of us, our Ben. That way, we won't lose touch entirely and things is bound to get better as young Lonnie gets older.'

Ben hoped that this would be so, but when he talked to Ted, his brother was a trifle doubtful. 'They live in a posh house, in a smart part of the city. They may ha' been glad to visit us when they were strangers and didn't know many other people,' he had said. 'But that'll all change when the gal goes to school or that aunt of hers begins to introduce her to her own friends and relatives. Still an' all, they's only a couple of gals.'

A touch on his arm brought Ben's attention back to the present. 'Ben? You do believe me, don't you?' Lonnie asked anxiously. 'It's been horrid, not being able to come and go as we like. We didn't mention it, but Aunt Emmeline actually set the servants to spy on us, only we knew we were being followed, so we were very careful.'

'*Spying* on you?' Ben said incredulously. 'I thought you said the servants didn't like your aunt. If that's so, why would they spy for her?'

Lonnie heaved an exaggerated sigh. 'Don't you know *anything*?' she said, her incredulity rivalling Ben's own. 'Servants have to do as they are told, whether they like it or not. But since they've never been told to tell Aunt Emmeline if we come in late, they can choose, see? And though they did follow us at first, that's not to say they would have told Aunt Emmeline if we *had* been up to something. Mollie and Maud wouldn't, anyway. They're ever so nice, aren't they, Hester? They know we do our best not to make a mess in the schoolroom or our little kitchen or our bedrooms, to save them work, so they do little extras for us, like nicking a few of Aunt Emmeline's biscuits, or fetching up the remains of a trifle the grown-ups had for dinner, so we can have a taste too.'

'Oh,' Ben said, taken aback. He reflected that this Lonnie was a very different child from the one who had been so rude to him outside the pet shop that first time. What was more, he could not help noticing how different she looked. She had grown taller and sturdier; her coat fitted her neatly instead of being far too loose and her cheeks were pink and her face more rounded. Despite himself, Ben grinned at her. 'Tell you what, young Lonnie, the city suits you,' he said. 'You look much better than when you first come from India.' He glanced around him, but this was a quiet residential district and he could see no clock. 'If you've gorra minute to spare, I'll show you a sport what's much more fun than snowballing lampposts. Any idea o' the time?'

Lonnie shook her head but Hester shot back the cuff of her thick wool coat and consulted a small gunmetal wrist watch. 'It's five o'clock,' she said. 'We've just been to pick up some shoes which Sarah Jones has soled and heeled for me – she's made a grand job of them, thank goodness, which means I shan't need new ones for a while yet – and the only other visit we have to make is to the confectioner's on Rupert Lane. D'you know Ada Staig's shop? We've tried most of the confectioners near home but Lonnie positively adores Mrs Staig's iced buns and of course she sells the most delicious home-made toffee, so I dare say we'll be buying a couple of ounces of that as well.'

Ben swallowed and tried not to look wistful. He did indeed know the shop, which was famous for its delicious produce, but was rarely a customer there. However, the fact that they were going to walk down Rupert Lane fitted in very well with his bright idea. 'Yes, I know Staig's all right,' he said. He rummaged in his canvas bag and drew out a smallish object which he waved at Hester and Lonnie. 'But do *you* know what this is?'

Both girls stared. 'It looks like the lid of a round biscuit tin,' Lonnie said at last. 'So what? Did Mrs

Staig make the biscuits that were in it? Is that why you're carrying it around?'

'Nah, you woolly-head,' Ben said scornfully. 'It's me sledge. When I've sold all me bundles of kindling, I were going to make for Everton Brow and have a bit o' fun. How about you coming along as well?'

Lonnie looked at the biscuit tin lid. 'But how could we all get on it?' she said doubtfully. 'I've got a sledge – a real one – at home, only Aunt Emmeline doesn't approve of playing games in the street. Hester did say she'd take me out into the country at the weekend, if the snow lasted . . .'

'We don't all gerron it at once, we goes one at a time,' Ben said patiently. 'It's gerrin' dark now, so there won't be much traffic about, particularly on Everton Brow 'cos it's steep and too slippy for either horses or motors. Well? Are you going to come wi' me to have a go, or ain't you?'

They were talking as they made their way along Rupert Lane and presently they stopped outside the brightly lit window of Mrs Staig's confectionery shop. The two children gazed pensively through the glass, whilst Hester checked the money in her purse, then turned to Lonnie. 'I'll buy a bag of those delicious iced buns and a piece of slab cake for nursery tea,' she announced. 'You've got tuppence left of your pocket money, haven't you, Lonnie? So what's it to be? Toffee, mint balls or midget gems?' Hester turned to Ben. 'How about you, young Ben? Do you like midget gems? I'm sure Lonnie will share whatever she gets.'

Ben grinned up at her, suddenly acknowledging the warmth and friendliness he could read in her face. Abruptly, he dismissed all his doubts over the truthfulness of their story. Why should they lie, after all? If they had simply not wanted to know him or his family, they would scarcely accompany him along the crowded pavements, or offer him a share in the nice things they meant to buy. 'If you'd like to take me last two bundles of kindling – they cost a ha'penny each – then I could buy me own sweets,' he said grandly. 'That way, Lonnie and me could have a bit o' choice, like. Now how about it, eh? Are you going to have a go on me tiddy little sledge?'

'I will, I will,' Lonnie squeaked, obviously over-joyed at the prospect ahead of them, but Hester shook her head, though she was still smiling.

'I'm afraid my b t m is too big for even the largest biscuit tin lid, but I'll come and cheer you on with pleasure,' she said. 'And yes, dear, I'd be happy to buy your two bundles of kindling because the maids are always complaining that when it's snowing or raining, and they have to run from the woodshed to the house, the kindling and the logs get wet.'

'Well this ain't wet, nor it won't get wet,' Ben said cheerfully. He had wrapped the kindling in old newspaper but did not hand it over to Hester at once, though he accepted the penny gratefully. 'I'll keep it in me canvas bag until we reach your back gate and then it can go in wi' the shoes and the buns and that,' he said cheerfully. 'Now what'll I blow me penny on?'

They went into the shop and after considerable thought, Lonnie bought an ounce of midget gems, 'because they last longer', and an ounce of acid drops. Ben decided on a whole penn'orth of toffee and both children emerged from the shop with one cheek satisfactorily bulging. After that, they made their way to Everton Brow and by the light of the street lamps Ben climbed aboard his biscuit tin lid and shot off down the pavement, using his heels both to steer with and to break when it was necessary. When he came panting up again, all aglow with the delight of the ride, he found Lonnie eager for her turn, though he noticed that Hester was looking distinctly troubled. 'I wonder if Lonnie might try to have a turn in Haig Street, rather than Everton Brow?' she said, rather timidly. 'It's pretty dangerous, you know, Ben, even for someone as experienced as yourself. My blood turned to water when you had to steer round that big fat woman with all the shopping bags.'

'I see what you mean,' Ben said, having thought the matter over. 'But Haig Street's got no sort of slope to it. She'd just sit on the tin lid and look silly. Tell you what, though, if I go down behind her – on me bum like – I could brake for her with me boots and make sure she doesn't tip over sideways or career into Cazneau.'

Hester agreed to this, though still a trifle doubtfully, Ben realised, but Lonnie had no such qualms and squeezed on to the biscuit tin, clutching Ben's knees, and presently the two of them shot off, ending up in a snowdrift at the corner of Soho Street. Lonnie was laughing helplessly when Ben dragged her out of the drift, and told her that she wasn't bad at sledging, for all she was just a girl. Lonnie, clearly delighted with this temperate phrase, demanded another turn, then another. But Hester, who had kept an eye on her wristwatch, called a halt to their fun and told Ben, regretfully, that they would have to go home now or risk being in real trouble.

'I don't want to go,' Lonnie wailed, clutching at her

governess's sleeve. 'It isn't half-past six yet, surely. Oh, it can't be!'

'No, but it's ten past and your coat, boots and stockings are all wringing wet,' Hester told her. 'Come to think of it, Ben, you must be even wetter because you didn't have the benefit of sitting on the tin lid.'

Ben glanced indifferently down at himself. 'Me kecks is ruined, I wouldn't wonder,' he said. 'Never mind, Mam always makes me wear old rags when it's snowy 'cos she knows I'd likely ruin decent things. These 'uns are more patch than trouser, if you know what I mean, but me mam's a rare one with her needle. She'll patch 'em again, never fret, once they's been hung on the clothes horse to dry.'

'I hope you're right,' Hester said, rather doubtfully, then held out a brown paper bag. 'Give these to Mrs Bailey, Ben, and tell her I'm sorry if I've led you into mischief. And now you'd best give me the kindling and we'll be off.'

'What's this 'ere?' Ben said, peering suspiciously into the bag. 'Hey, you can't give me your tea, Hester! Them buns was for your tea, I heered you say so.'

'Yes, but I bought eight buns altogether, six for you and two for us. After all, you've given Lonnie the most fun she's had since we came to England – wouldn't you agree, Lonnie?'

Lonnie nodded vigorously and beamed at Ben. If she regretted the loss of the buns, she clearly did not intend to say so. 'Go on, Ben, take 'em,' she urged. 'Oh, and we never asked why you were around so early, because you're usually in the shop until six o'clock, or even eight. Did Mr Madison close sooner than usual because of the snow?'

'That's right. Well, to be honest it were more

because there weren't no trade to speak of,' Ben admitted, continuing to walk along beside them. 'Norra soul came in after we'd ate our sandwiches, and it were mortal cold in that shop, even for us, behind the counter. The animals in the window – we've got four lovely spotted puppies, have you seen 'em? – fair freeze, Mr M thinks. So when we close we empty the window and stand the paraffin burner in the middle of the shop. Then we put the cages all round it, like Injuns surrounding a covered waggon in a cowboy fillum, then o' course we heads for home ourselves, so we're all better off.'

'That's nice,' Lonnie said. 'Ben . . . you *do* believe us, don't you? About being followed, I mean? Only we don't tell lies, do we, Hester? Well, only to our enemies, and people who want to do us harm, like Aunt Emmeline,' she added darkly.

Ben grinned at her. They had reached the green door in the tall wall now and Hester was fumbling in her bag for her key. Ben was extremely eager to see into the garden which he had so often imagined, and stood close, the kindling in its newspaper wrapping already in his hands. 'Oh aye, I guess you were tellin' the truth,' he assured his young companion. 'I try not to tell lies meself, but sometimes you have to say something which ain't quite right. Our mam calls it tellin' white lies, like saying to your pal that his new suit's real sharp, when you think it's too short in the sleeve and too wide in the body . . . that sort o' thing.'

Hester unlocked the door and held it open so that Lonnie could slip through, then held out her hands for the kindling. 'Thank you very much, Ben. It was kind of you to carry the wood for me, and kind to give Lonnie such a treat, too. I don't know how long the snow will last, but if it is still thick at the weekend, perhaps you'd like to come into the country with us? We'll either take the ferry across to Woodside, or a bus along the coast to Crosby or Formby, somewhere like that. How are you fixed on a Saturday?'

'I'm working,' Ben admitted gloomily. 'Dawn to dusk on a Sat'day, just about. Now if it were a Sunday . . .'

But Hester and Lonnie assured him, in a sad chorus, that Sundays were impossible for them. 'Never mind, we'll manage that outing some time,' Hester said. She hesitated. 'Umm . . . I suppose the men at Cammell Laird's work on a Saturday?'

Ben, admitting that some weeks they only worked up to lunch-time, noticed that Hester's cheeks turned very pink and idly wondered why, but before he could say anything Lonnie squeaked: 'The back door's opening. Come on, Hester! Let's hope it's just one of the maids, or Fletcher!'

Ben took a quick and comprehensive glance around the winter garden with its neat rows of cabbage and sprout plants. Beyond the kitchen garden, he could see a long, green lawn, deep flower beds and a terrace surrounded by a stone balustrade. To the right of the terrace was a range of brick-built, slate-roofed buildings which he imagined were storage sheds. Then he moved quickly out of the way as Lonnie flew towards the house, her small feet pattering on the cleared pathway. Hester began to close the green painted door. Seconds later he heard the governess's key snick in the lock and her more measured tread growing fainter. He wished quite desperately that he could know who had come to the back door and whether his friends would be caught by Miss

Emmeline, but it was impossible. To try to discover just what was happening in that tall, imposing house could only mean real trouble for the two girls. He was beginning to walk back along Haig Street when he suddenly remembered the glimpse he had got back in the summer of a pale little face at the attic window. Hastily he crossed the road and stood beneath one of the few gas lamps which adorned it, gazing earnestly up at the house. At first he could see nothing, then a light bloomed and to his joy a small black figure appeared in the window and waved, making some sort of gesture before, reluctantly it seemed, drawing dark curtains across the lighted panes.

It's all right, Ben told himself, making his way slowly along Everton Brow once more. They got in safely, without being questioned by that old brute of an aunt. I'm almost sure Lonnie give me the thumbs-up before she pulled the curtain. And with that cheery thought – and nine lovely brown pennies in his canvas bag, as well as his sweets and the iced buns – Ben set off for Elmore Street, already enjoying the sensation he would cause when he told the family how he had spent the afternoon.

'That's the last piece of holly, thank goodness,' Hester said, balancing it along the top of the big gilt mirror which decorated the right-hand wall, and rubbing her fingers thoughtfully, for the holly was prickly. She and Lonnie had been told to put up the Christmas decorations and had thought it would be good fun, but in fact it had turned out to be very hard work. Mimms had provided the holly, ivy and mistletoe, and Fletcher had brought the other decorations down from the narrow attic room where they spent most of the year, but even so, putting up such a quantity of stuff had not been easy. Mimms had erected the large Christmas tree and had left them to decorate it with the Hetherington-Smiths' Victorian beads, baubles and delicate glass novelties, and Lonnie had acknowledged that it had been fun, but when they saw the vast quantity of greenery which must, Aunt Emmeline said, decorate all picture rails, door frames and banisters, their hearts had failed them.

'Why does she *do* it? It isn't as if she's got lots of children or young relatives who will come to the house over the holiday,' Lonnie had wailed. 'I believe she's done it to make sure we work like galley-slaves and have a miserable Christmas, that's what I think!'

At the time Hester had scoffed, said it was nice of Miss Hetherington-Smith to decorate the place, but a word with Mollie had revealed that though Miss Hetherington-Smith had always put up the Christmas tree and decorated the main drawing room, that had been the extent of her Christmas preparations. 'She allus goes to one of the neighbours on Christmas morning and they have drinks an' that,' Mollie had said vaguely. 'Then several of 'em comes back here for tea an' a slice o' her plum cake. But as for all them twinkly fings, an' the green stuff everywhere . . . well, I dare say that is to make Miss Lonnie feel more at home, like.'

But Hester was learning that Miss Hetherington-Smith did nothing without a reason, and so far as she could see the reason was often to 'put someone in their place', as their employer herself would have said.

Miss Hetherington-Smith had begun the procedure

within a couple of days of her brother's going off on his cruise. Hester had gone down to her in her study, as she did each morning, to report on what she and Lonnie meant to do that day, and was told to sit down because there was 'quite a lot to discuss, this morning'.

The discussion, it seemed, was to be somewhat one-sided, however. 'The maids in this household are fully occupied, and since the arrival of yourself and the child have been hard put to it to get their work done,' she had said frostily, eyeing Hester over the top of her little round spectacles. 'In future, you will keep the attic rooms which you use clean. I have instructed the maids that they are no longer to go up to that floor.'

'I do most of it already . . .' Hester was beginning, but got no further. 'In future, you will do it all,' Miss Hetherington-Smith said. 'You may go.'

Hester, used to the older woman's abrupt, not to say rude, way of talking, had not replied but had quietly left the room. However, in the days that followed she found that though she went to the study each morning to report on the day's doings, she was there mainly, now, in order to be given a list of the jobs which Miss Hetherington-Smith had decided she must do. Wash all the picture rails and skirting boards in all the attic rooms with warm, soapy water. Scrub the linoleum in the schoolroom one day and in their two bedrooms the next. On a cold December day she was ordered to get all the curtains down, wash them, and hang them in the garden to dry. When she had pointed out that the curtain material was heavy and unlikely to dry on such a cold day Miss Hetherington-Smith had said, grudgingly, that if she was right, if the weather remained cold and windless, then she might use the drying rack in the kitchen.

'You will then have to iron the curtains,' her employer added, a good deal of malice in her chilly tones. 'I believe you purchased one of those new-fangled electric irons when I told you the kitchen staff could no longer launder for you and your charge. No doubt it will also iron curtains?'

'Certainly it will,' Hester had said drily. There had been a good deal of envy and some mutterings from the maids over her purchase of the iron; they were expected to wash, starch and then iron all Miss Hetherington-Smith's clothing and the household linen the old-fashioned way. As soon as she realised how much easier the electric iron made her tasks, Hester suggested that the maids might borrow it for their own work and the offer was eagerly accepted. Sometimes, Mollie carried the iron reverently down to the kitchen, but at other times she came up to the schoolroom and she and Hester chatted as she worked, smoothing the big white damask tablecloths and the old-fashioned leg o' mutton blouses which Miss Hetherington-Smith favoured.

Needless to say, however, Hester said nothing of this to her employer, but merely left the room without another word. To mention that she lent the iron to the staff would have been asking for trouble, she knew. Fletcher had told her that when Mr Hetherington-Smith had made a hasty visit to Britain on business some five years earlier, he had been shocked by the inconvenience of the old house.

'This will never do, my dear,' he had said to his sister. 'I will have the house wired for electricity and the gas-lighting done away with, and I'll have running water piped to the bathrooms and to the servants' quarters in the basement. You'll find the house runs a great deal more smoothly, I assure you.'

Unfortunately, it had not occurred to him that the attics would ever be occupied, so though she and Lonnie had the advantage of electric light they had to cart their water up from the floor below . . . though at Hester's insistence they took baths twice weekly in the guest bathroom on the lower floor. When Hester and Lonnie had first arrived in Shaw Street, Miss Hetherington-Smith had told her that she and her charge might use the guest bathroom and since she had never rescinded the offer they continued to take their baths there, though Hester always cleaned every inch of the place as soon as they had finished with it in order to pre-empt any grumbles from her employer.

But now Hester stood back and regarded the hallway with considerable satisfaction. Whatever Miss Hetherington-Smith's reason for insisting that they decorate the whole ground floor of the house, it certainly looked a good deal more festive than it usually did. The Christmas tree looked particularly beautiful, for Miss Hutchinson had provided them with a number of tiny candles, and when these were lit every flame would be reflected a dozen times in the delicate glass baubles, making the tree seem alive and alight. Hester knew just how wonderful it would look because the previous evening, after Lonnie had gone to bed, she and Miss Hutchinson had lit the candles and Hester had seen the older woman's eyes fill with tears at the beauty of it.

'I don't know what's got into her,' Miss Hutchinson had whispered. 'I suppose it's because the child is living here now, but oh, I'm glad! I've never seen anything so beautiful!'

'Hester, do you think we might go out and do some last minute shopping?' Lonnie said, bringing Hester abruptly back to the present. 'After all, we've spent a whole day – and most of yesterday – putting up the decorations, so surely we might have a little time to ourselves now?'

'Yes, I think we might,' Hester said. 'Now that your aunt gives us so many tasks to perform, she is less interested in how we spend our spare time.' She laughed, then clapped a hand to her mouth and headed for the stairs, with Lonnie close on her heels. 'Come to think of it, we don't *have* much spare time any more, do we? So I see no reason why we shouldn't put on our warmest coats, boots and scarves, and go shopping. Thank heaven the snow's all gone, so we aren't likely to get soaked – and you haven't bought your present for Aunt Emmeline yet!'

The schoolroom felt pleasantly warm after the icy hall and stairwell, though Hester noticed that the fire needed making up. The servants were very good and often sneaked a scuttleful of coal or a bag of logs up to the second floor, but Miss Hetherington-Smith had insisted that Hester should perform this task, so the maids could only bring fuel up when their employer was engaged elsewhere. Since the scuttle and log box were both full, Hester guessed that Mollie had been up whilst Miss Hetherington-Smith was paying afternoon calls. Quickly, she put a couple of lumps of coal on to the small fire, then closed down the damper and covered the grate with coal dust so that it would not burn up whilst they were out. Then she and Lonnie got into their outdoor things and clattered down the stairs, not troubling to go quietly.

'When the cat's away the mice will play,' Lonnie said cheerfully, as they let themselves out of the front door. 'As for giving that horrible old woman a present, how about a feather duster? Then *she* could clean the beastly picture rails and the chandelier in the hall instead of making poor Mollie risk her life on a rickety stepladder.'

Although it was still only mid-afternoon, the cold took Hester's breath away as they stepped on to the pavement and began to walk to the nearest tram stop. 'I don't think a feather duster would be tactful,' she said. 'Though it's very tempting, I admit. How about one of those boxes of embroidered handkerchiefs? I dare say she would prefer gloves, but they are much more expensive.' She giggled. 'If either of us were any good at embroidery, we could buy plain lawn handkerchiefs and embroider her initials on each one. Oh, dear. I don't suppose she will buy us anything we want because she doesn't understand us at all, does she?'

Lonnie was beginning to reply when a tram came roaring down the street and drew to a halt beside them. The two girls hopped on board and presently hopped off again outside a large store. 'Here we go!' Lonnie said gleefully as they pushed their way into the huge emporium. 'I do wonder what Daddy has sent us, Hester. Mollie told me that several lovely big parcels had arrived for us with Daddy's writing on the labels.'

'I'm sure whatever he gives you will be delightful,' Hester said. 'Shall we go to hats and gloves first? I think they sell hankies as well.'

It was Christmas Eve and Dick was finishing work in the captain's cabin of the *Fearless*, a destroyer being built for the Royal Navy. The sideboard was of walnut, which Dick always enjoyed using, and now he ran his hand appreciatively over the softly gleaming surface. He had made this particular piece from scratch, starting with the bare wood, and now that he looked at his creation he felt justly proud of it.

'Well, old Dick? If you've finished a-gloatin' over that there bit of furniture, then how about comin' up on deck for a quick sup of cold tea and a mouthful of hot bacon sandwich? Sammy Wills is doin' the necessary for everyone – a sort of Christmas treat – so you'll not want to miss out.'

Dick turned round and grinned at the speaker. Joey Frost was a small, cheery little man, almost as broad as he was long. He had small, bright blue eyes and a rosy face and though his hair was grey it was no indication of his age, for he had once told Dick that both he and his father had been grey as badgers before their twentieth birthday. He had been a joiner foreman at the shipyard ever since Dick had come to Laird's as an apprentice, and since they both lived in the same area of Liverpool and caught the same tram and ferry to work they had speedily become good friends, despite the fact that Joey was ten years Dick's senior.

Joey would have been the first to admit that, though he was capable enough, Dick was his master as regards fine furniture, for the younger man enjoyed the fiddling, precise work needed for such articles. Joey, on the other hand, could knock up a companionway or a large article of galley furniture in half the time that it took Dick to lovingly carve the decoration of leaves and fruit which embellished each drawer of the captain's sideboard. Both men admired the other's abilities, and because Joey was a well-liked and trusted foreman he was able to make sure that Dick was responsible for the finer furniture whilst he and others like him undertook the more straightforward joinery so necessary on any class of ship.

'Yes, I reckon it's finished,' Dick said now, in reply to Joey's question. 'And I could do wi' a bite to eat and something to wet my whistle.'

Joey produced his pocket watch and held up the face so that Dick could see it. 'It's high time we wasn't here,' he said breezily. 'Norreven the boss would expect us to work over on Christmas Eve.' He sighed gustily. 'Tomorrow's the great day; me kids look forward to it all year, I reckon, and they wakes long before it's light and start badgering me to tell 'em if Santy Claus has come and if it's time to have their stockings.'

'I shall have a real lie in,' Dick said, as the two men gained the deck. 'I've gorra little sister – and a younger brother as well – but they both know breakfast comes first and stockings next. It'll be a good Christmas for us this year, now that Ted's been took on as apprentice plumber at Laird's and young Ben is part-time at Madison's – you know, the pet shop on Heyworth Street.'

'Aye, it won't be so bad for us Frosts,' Joey remarked, seizing a large tin mug full of tea and a hot bacon sandwich from the skinny lad who was handing them out. 'Ta, Freddie.' He turned back to Dick, who had also been provided with tea and a bacon wad. 'Doin' anything special on Boxing Day? Wharrabout that young woman you met up with a few months back? The one who come from India, I mean.'

'Hester Elliott,' Dick said wistfully. Whenever he spoke her name, a picture of her appeared in his mind. The smooth oval face, the long-lashed dark eyes, the dimple in her cheek when she smiled. At first, he had thought about Hester constantly but he had not seen her now for weeks and he supposed, ruefully, that he was unlikely to do so over the holiday. He said as much to Joey, admitting for the first time that the girl was really a young lady, a governess in a large household, and unlikely to cross his path again.

'You never know,' Joey said. 'You're a grand lad, Dick, a feller any gal would be proud to walk out with. Governesses is only human, after all.'

'It's a bit more complicated than that,' Dick said, rather guardedly. He glanced around at the men crowding the deck, then took Joey's arm and propelled him to the stern rail, where the two men stood looking over the side at the choppy grey waters of the Mersey. 'She's all alone in the world, d'you see? So far as I can make out she's got no relatives living and the old woman she works for has made it plain she thinks us Baileys is low. She doesn't want her niece – or her governess for that matter – associating with the likes of us. I had hoped we might manage to see her again, but no luck so far and it's been months since we last met.'

Joey looked at him thoughtfully. 'I've knowed you for eight years and in all that time you've never been really interested in a gal,' he remarked. 'Oh, I know you've took girls dancing and to the cinema, or for picnics on trips up the river, but you was never really interested, if you know what I mean. So why this gal, eh?'

Dick whistled tunelessly between his teeth for a moment, still gazing down at the water, then he lifted his eyes to Joey's face. 'I don't know, and that's

God's truth,' he said simply. 'Hester isn't just pretty, though, she's really beautiful. And it isn't just her looks, neither. There's a deal of sweetness in her. My mam says she's got a generous spirit . . . well, she's ever so good and patient with that young Lonnie Hetherington-Smith and she's not an easy child, nor a nice one, truth to tell. Yet I reckon that after living with Hester for a few more months Lonnie'll lose a whole lot of her superior ways and probably end up a decent little girl like our Phyllis.'

'Tell you what,' Joey said presently, having thought the matter over, 'the old lady don't know me from Adam, do she – any more than the servants do? What say I go there, pretend I'm a small shopkeeper – I always fancy I look like a shopkeeper – and say the young lady left a glove or some such thing in me shop afore Christmas. I could go Boxing Day. Then I could have a private word, like, wi' your Miss Hester Elliott, arrange a meeting betwixt the pair of you, and you could take it from there.'

Dick would have been the first to say that he was not a quick thinker, that he needed time before taking the lightest decision. He was cautious, considering all aspects of every question before giving his own reply. Accordingly, he regarded Joey's generous offer from every angle, though he found himself replying before he had anywhere near thought it through. 'Would you, Joey?' he said in a low voice. 'It were what I hoped young Ben would do when he telled me he'd met up wi' the pair of 'em. The trouble is, there's things you can tell a young lad who ain't yet eleven and there's things you can't. A couple o' times I began to suggest that he might arrange a meeting with Hester and Lonnie if they came into the shop when he were working there. But somehow

I couldn't bring meself to say it.' He looked earnestly down at Joey's rubicund face. 'I'm not saying as Ben would have laughed at me – he ain't that sort of feller – but I felt it gave away me feelings for Hester when I wasn't even sure meself how I felt. And then, there's Hester herself. She can't possibly know how I feel, far less feel the same. She's very young and she's still a stranger in this country . . . mebbe I'm being unfair to her. Mebbe it wouldn't be right to even try to gerrin touch.'

Joey looked at him, his small eyes widening. He tipped his bowler to the back of his head and whistled soundlessly. 'Well, I never did know such a feller!' he gasped. 'In the space of half a minute you've talked yourself right round from one point of view to another. Tell me straight, young Dick, do you want me to go to this here gal's house or don't you? This is last chance time, 'cos I ain't going to offer again.'

Dick saw that there was amusement in his friend's twinkling blue eyes, but that there was understanding, too. He took a deep breath, intending to prevaricate, to say that he would let Joey know later in the day, and heard his voice saying quickly: 'Yes, yes please, Joey. I'd be right grateful if you'd arrange a meeting for Hester and me. Tell her I'll be outside . . . let me see . . . St Augustine's church at two o'clock on Boxing Day. If she can't make it then, tell her any time, any day, when I'm not working.'

'That'll be grand,' Joey said approvingly, beaming at his friend. 'You leave it to me, our Dick. If she can't manage two o'clock on Boxing Day – come to think of it, hadn't you better make it three, in case they have a late dinner and she's held up – then I'll arrange for some other time, 'cos I know when we're not working – none better!'

'Thanks, Joey, you're a real pal,' Dick said gratefully. 'Just thinking about seeing Hester again has made me Christmas, honest to God it has. So what time will you go round there, Boxing Day? If you go early enough, we can meet for a pint at the Vaults and you can tell me what happened.'

The Crescent Vaults was a favourite pub with most of the men who lived in the warren of tiny streets off Everton Brow. Dick knew Joey regarded it as his local and was to be found there a couple of nights a week, nursing a pint of Guinness, his favourite bevvy. He was not surprised, therefore, when Joey fell in with this suggestion at once. 'I'll go round to the girl's place at eleven,' he said. 'No, better make it half-past ten in case they's going out. That'll mean I'll be in the Vaults by eleven o'clock. Does that suit you?'

'I'll be there from half ten onwards,' Dick said fervently.

Christmas Day dawned bright but extremely cold. Hester and Lonnie were grateful for the bright fire burning in the school grate, for Mollie, as a Christmas treat she had said, had come sneaking up the attic stairs whilst the house was dark and still, and had lit their fire for them.

'It don't do the old lady no harm if I lights your fire in my own time,' she had told Hester on a previous occasion when she had done the same thing. 'If you asks me, Miss Hester, Miss Lonnie's father would be mad as anything if he knew the way that old woman treats the pair of you. Still an' all, me, Maud, Edith and old Fletcher does our best to make you a bit more comfortable. Why, even old Hutch snitched a few chocolate biscuits out of Miss Hetherington-Smith's supply and smuggled 'em up to Miss Lonnie. She daren't do much, poor old dear, but she does what she can.'

Lonnie, fully dressed and with her hair braided into a long plait, was hopping up and down with excitement and eyeing the parcels piled on the schoolroom table. 'May we open just one or two, Hester?' she pleaded. 'I know my aunt said they were to be carried downstairs and put under the tree until after Christmas luncheon, but surely we might undo one of Daddy's presents. Or two?'

Hester, however, did not think this wise. She had noticed Miss Hetherington-Smith making a note of parcels received – and sent – and knew it would not be sensible to antagonise the older woman. 'I don't think we'd better open your father's presents,' she said. 'But you may open my present if you wish.'

Lonnie gave a squeak of delight and hurled herself at the pile of packages. She ripped off the brown wrapping paper to reveal a white angora wool hat and matching mittens and of course immediately put them on and stared with admiration at her reflection in the small looking glass. 'Thank you ever so much, Hester,' she said earnestly. 'Do you remember seeing that little girl in Bold Street . . . ?'

'Yes, of course I do,' Hester said, smiling. 'Why did you think I bought them, you little goose? I wished I could ask the little girl's mother where she had got them but I didn't want you to guess what I was buying so I simply had to search the shops until I found the right things. They do look well on you. And now I think we ought to go down for breakfast, since your aunt has insisted that we join them for all meals today.'

'Well, it isn't because she loves us,' Lonnie mumbled, as they set off down the first flight of stairs. 'It's because everyone will be at eleven o'clock service and after that we've been invited round to the Russells' for pre-luncheon drinks. I expect they'll have champagne and whisky and things and you and I will get lemonade,' she added gloomily. 'Oh well, at least there's roast turkey with all the trimmings and delicious plum pudding, as well as nuts and fruit and mince pies to look forward to.'

'And after luncheon, there's the present opening,' Hester reminded her. 'And Mollie says that Christmas breakfast is pretty good as well. There's bacon and egg, and mushrooms, and those specially fine sausages which Eli Alper makes . . .'

'Ooh, lovely,' Lonnie said rapturously. 'Do you know, Hester, I was never really hungry in India. I don't know whether it was the heat, but I used to push my food round and round my plate and long for the end of the meal to come. I never wondered what was for dinner or asked for a second helping, but now I really enjoy my food and look forward to meal times.'

'It's the cold, I think,' Hester said. 'When it's cold you are much more active because you're trying to keep warm, and when you're active it gives you an appetite. I'm the same; yet despite eating much more than usual, I don't think I've put on any weight, which means I'm using up the food in energy.'

'Yes, I know what you mean. Scrubbing floors, dusting picture rails and brushing carpets does use up a lot . . .' Lonnie was beginning, when the drawing room door opened to reveal Miss Hetherington-Smith and Miss Hutchinson, both smiling benignly.

'Good morning, Leonora, good morning, Miss Elliott,' Emmeline greeted them. 'I expect you're eager for your breakfast. And then you must wrap up warmly, because though I'm sure the dear vicar does his best, the church is bound to be chilly on such a frosty day.'

She led the small procession into the breakfast parlour where they took their places round the table in the window embrasure whilst Mollie and Maud brought the tureens over from the sideboard. 'Isn't it nice to see the sun shining?' Miss Hutchinson said presently, when they were all served. 'I'm sure this is going to be a wonderful Christmas for all of us!'

Chapter Five

Christmas Day had been as enjoyable as Miss Hutchinson had predicted, Hester thought as she tidied round the schoolroom and served the porridge she had made earlier, in two round, blue porringers. Mr Hetherington-Smith's gifts had been delightful and generous. Hester had received a length of rose-coloured silk, so beautiful that she was sure she would never dare cut into it to make the dress for which it was intended. Lonnie had received dress lengths in kingfisher blue silk and warm scarlet wool as well as a game called Monopoly which had greatly intrigued her and made her long, she told Hester, for a quiet afternoon so that the two of them might learn its intricacies.

There had been other gifts, of course. Boxes of chocolates, gaily coloured hair ribbons, soaps and talcum powder and, from Miss Hetherington-Smith, a leather-bound bible and matching prayer book. Lonnie, Hester knew, had been hard pressed not to giggle when she had unwrapped her aunt's gift, but Hester thought she had behaved impeccably. Lonnie had admired the rather prosaic black and white illustrations in the bible and had said it would be nice to have her own prayer book so that she might learn by heart all her favourite passages. Miss Hutchinson had shot her a suspicious glance – her own gift to Lonnie had been a copy of *The Wind in the Willows* by Kenneth Grahame, beautifully illustrated by Ernest Shepard –

but Miss Hetherington-Smith merely seemed gratified by Lonnie's words and thanked the child, with apparent sincerity, for the beautifully embroidered handkerchiefs.

Later in the afternoon, the guests had arrived for tea and to Lonnie's joy the party had included two children of about her own age, a boy and a girl, called Peter and Eunice. They were staying in Shaw Street with relatives and immediately tea was over – it was various exciting sandwiches, little cakes and biscuits and of course a towering, white-frosted Christmas cake – Lonnie carried them off to the schoolroom, begging Hester to accompany them so that they might meet Kitty and have four people to play Monopoly.

Kitty, stuffed with Christmas treats, for Hester had smuggled up a supply of the roast bird, was much admired, and, fortunately perhaps, Peter and Eunice knew the game of Monopoly well. They seemed to enjoy instructing Hester and Lonnie and by the time their mother decided to take them home they were all on excellent terms. Lonnie extended an invitation to her new friends to come to the park with herself and her governess next day. 'It'll be much more fun with the three of us – and Hester – to play Hide and Seek and Catch and so on,' she exclaimed. 'And then there are the swings and boats on the lake . . . If only it might snow again. Then we could make a slide!'

Unfortunately, Mrs Hopwood had already made arrangements to spend Boxing Day visiting her sister in Southport. They would set out early in their motor and probably not return until after dinner, she told Lonnie apologetically, but there was no reason to cancel the trip to the park since Peter and Eunice would be quite free to accompany her on the following day, the twenty-seventh.

Lonnie, with a number of other games beside Monopoly to play, not to mention a brand new skipping rope and a pair of roller skates, had been happy enough to accept the change in her plans gracefully and had gone to sleep that night clutching the roller skates to her bosom, as though they had been soft as swansdown. Hester, afraid she might roll on them and do herself an injury, had gently removed them before seeking her own bed, replacing them with the angora hat and mittens. She had put the roller skates down on the bedside table and by morning Lonnie seemed to have forgotten her unusual sleeping companions. She jumped out of bed full of plans for their day and then took so long to get dressed that when Hester called through to tell her breakfast was ready, she entered the schoolroom in her underwear, with her dressing gown slung hastily around her shoulders. 'I'll dress in a minute, honestly I will, Hester,' she promised. 'But I do hate cold porridge and I don't want to waste your lovely food. Besides, there are only the two of us and you don't mind if I eat my breakfast in my dressing gown, do you?'

'No, I don't mind. And there are sausages afterwards,' Hester told the child. 'You can thank Mrs Ainsworth for that. She smuggled a parcel of sausages to Mollie, who brought them up last night, after you'd gone to sleep. Cook said we might as well have 'em as they'd go to waste otherwise. She's nice, Mrs Ainsworth. She told me the other day that though Miss Hetherington-Smith is a difficult woman to work for, at least she insists that only the best ingredients are bought and never grumbles over household expenses provided she can see what she's paying for.'

'My father pays,' Lonnie said virtuously, tucking into her porridge. 'If Aunt Emmeline had to pay out of her own purse it would be a different story. That I *do* know.'

'True,' Hester acknowledged. 'If you've finished I'll just nip through and fetch the dish of sausages.'

Although Miss Hetherington-Smith always made sure that there was plenty of good food available, she did not consider that a cooked breakfast was necessary for children or their governesses, so the sausages were a real treat and both Lonnie and Hester tucked in with a will. What was more, Kitty was given a piece, finely chopped, and Lonnie got a good deal of satisfaction from watching her pet, paws tucked in and tail curled round, enjoying the treat. After the sausage the cat had a saucer of milk, then Lonnie got out the ball of wool with a string attached that had been Miss Hutchinson's present for the kitten. The two of them began an energetic game and Hester, with a sigh, reminded her charge that if they were to get some fresh air before luncheon she ought to think about getting dressed. Lonnie, tearing round the room just ahead of Kitty, replied indistinctly that she would get dressed presently, so Hester went into the attic kitchen and took the kettle off the gas ring, poured hot water into the basin, and began to wash up. Since she had no wish to get anyone into trouble she disposed of every sign of the sausages, then washed and dried all their breakfast things, including the frying pan. She was stacking everything tidily away in the old and battered cupboards which Fletcher and young Alf, the boot-boy, had rather reluctantly carried up the attic stairs, when Mollie's familiar bouncy step sounded on the flight. Hester went to the door and smiled an enquiry and Mollie, out of breath, stopped a dozen steps short of the landing.

'Oh, miss, there's a feller at the door for you,' she said breathlessly. 'I said as he could give the glove to me – though I didn't think it looked like one o' yourn, miss, nor Miss Lonnie's either – but he said as how he'd not give it up to anyone but the young leddy as left it on his counter. So could you come?'

'Glove? But I've not lost a glove, or I don't think I have, at any rate,' Hester said, puzzled. 'I suppose Lonnie could have done so, though. Was it a woolly glove, Mollie?'

'Yes . . . no . . . oh, I'm not sure, miss,' Mollie said distractedly. She glanced nervously down the stairs behind her and Hester remembered that the staff had been told that they must no longer go up to the attics. 'Shall I tell him to go away, then?'

'No, no, I'll come, of course. Tell him I'll not be a moment,' Hester said at once. It had suddenly occurred to her that it might be Ben – or even Dick – at the front door. Mollie, glad to have delivered her message without seeing Miss Hetherington-Smith, ran down the stairs and headed for the next flight, but paused a moment as Hester said in a conspiratorial whisper: 'This man . . . is he young, Moll? Just a boy, I mean? Or . . . is he older?'

'He's ever so old, miss,' Mollie hissed back. 'He's little and fat and . . . oh, mercy, there's the breakfast room bell. I'd best hurry.'

Well, it's neither Ben nor Dick, Hester told herself. She had meant to go back to the schoolroom and tell Lonnie of the visitor, but decided against it. The child and the kitten would be happy enough for a good while yet, and she herself would not be two minutes at the door. What was more, she could fetch up an armful of logs whilst she was about it, which would save another trip downstairs to the woodshed later in the day.

Descending the last flight of stairs, a sharp wind reminded her that whilst the front door remained open it was cooling down the entire house, which would presently bring Miss Hetherington-Smith from the breakfast parlour to demand who was thoughtless enough to have left the door ajar. Not wanting trouble on a holiday, Hester almost ran down the hallway, went out into the chilly morning and pulled the door half closed behind her. This way she was less likely to be accused of freezing the entire household, though she, of course, would be an icicle if she stayed on the step for more than a moment or two.

The small, round man standing outside, hat in hand, grinned at her and replaced the bowler on his head, covering a thick mop of grey hair. 'Morning, miss,' he said. 'I noticed you come into me shop afore Christmas, along o' a little gal, and when you left I found this glove . . .' he flourished a very plain, black woollen glove '. . . a-lyin' on the floor. We was mortal busy but I ran to the door to see if I could call you back, only you an' the little gal had gawn. So I come along here this mornin' . . .'

'How did you know I lived here?' Hester said. She could not remember the small man and thought him more memorable than otherwise. Was this some trick to take a look at the house of a well-to-do family? If so he had been foiled, since Mollie had clearly not thought to invite him to step inside to wait and she herself meant to do no such thing. 'Surely my name and address are not inside the glove?'

She spoke sarcastically and was rather surprised when the small man beamed at her. 'No, Miss Elliott, nothin' o' that sort,' he said in a lowered tone. 'To tell the truth, a friend axed me to call, and this were the best excuse I could find. A friend by the name o' Dick Bailey.'

'Dick!' Hester said, and at the small man's alarmed expression clapped a hand over her mouth. 'Dick Bailey did you say?' she added in a much quieter tone. 'Oh, Dick is very much our friend, but things have been so difficult . . . I was terrified that he might come to the house to wish us the compliments of the season . . . not that there would have been anything wrong in his so doing but my employer has some very odd ideas and we – Lonnie and me, that is – get so little time to ourselves . . . but what is the message? And who are you, if you don't mind my asking?'

'I'm Joey Frost, miss,' the little man said hoarsely. 'I'm foreman joiner at Laird's and Dick's one of me best mates as well as the best wood carver we've got.'

Hester's hands flew to her throat. 'Is – is anything wrong?' she quavered. 'I know Mr Bailey is a sick man . . . or has Dick been injured in some way?'

'No, no, nothing of that sort,' Mr Frost said reassuringly. 'Dick wanted to come to the house himself, but we thought it would be safer if I come instead, using the glove as an excuse to get to see you. Dick's rare keen for a meetin' and suggested three o'clock today, outside St Augustine's church, if that would suit? I'll be seein' him in about half an hour so I can tell him what we've arranged then.'

Hester smiled down at the small man. 'It's very good of you, Mr Frost, to do so much for Dick, and you may tell him I shall certainly be outside the church at three o'clock this afternoon,' she said, keeping her voice low. 'I shall have to bring Lonnie of course, but I dare say Dick will understand.' She was about to bid Mr Frost goodbye, when it occurred to her that she was not her own mistress. Miss Hetherington-Smith might easily tell her, when she went to the study to outline her plans for the day, that she wanted some tasks doing or messages run that afternoon. Unless she could think of a cast-iron excuse for leaving the house at around three o'clock, she might either be very late or have to miss the appointment altogether.

She said as much to Mr Frost, then took the glove in her hand and examined it closely, just in case her employer was already seated in the study, watching her from between the dark velvet curtains.

Mr Frost, however, seemed equal to the challenge. 'Tell her ladyship there's to be a children's carol service in the Liverpool High School, further down Shaw Street, this afternoon,' he said. 'Say Lonnie's very keen to go and you reckon it'll be a grand afternoon, wi' lemonade and mince pies throwed in for the kids and a nice cup o' tea for grown-ups. It's true, too,' he added virtuously. 'There'll be a mort o' kids there so even if she were walkin' past at comin' out time, likely she'd not see her niece amongst all the others. Come to that,' he added, struck by a sudden idea, 'why don't you leave young Lonnie there whiles you and Dick have your chat? I'll lay she'd have a grand time.'

'Mr Frost, you're a genius!' Hester said admiringly. 'I'll ask Miss Hetherington-Smith if she would like to come with us, because if there's one thing she hates, it's kids. Besides, she and Miss Hutchinson were talking the other day and I'm pretty sure she's ordered Allsop, the chauffeur, to bring the motor round at two, so that she may go and visit friends who live out at Great Sutton.'

It was Mr Frost's turn to look doubtful. 'But suppose she asks you to go along,' he said worriedly. 'What excuse could you give? Would a kiddies' carol service be a good enough reason for missing a trip in a motor car?'

Hester laughed. But she was beginning to shiver for she had not thought to drape a coat around herself before emerging from the front door. 'She never invites either of us to go out with her,' she explained. 'So we'll be quite safe on that score.' She held out her hand, and after a second's hesitation Mr Frost did the same and they shook. 'No, Mr Frost, I'm afraid you've had a journey for nothing,' Hester said, in her normal voice. 'The glove belongs to neither myself nor Miss Leonora. However, it was exceedingly good of you to come all this way and I hope you have better luck with your next customer, though if I were you I should simply pin it up in your window and wait for the owner to come past and recognise it. Good day to you!'

'Aye, I'll do that,' Mr Frost said, heartily, in his booming voice. 'Sorry to have troubled you, miss; may I wish you all the compliments of the season and a happy and prosperous New Year!'

Hester, still shivering, let herself back into the house, closed the front door and leaned on it for a moment, vigorously rubbing her upper arms with both hands. She was thrilled that Dick had made the first move and that they were actually going to meet again at last, but more than a little apprehensive over Mr Frost's visit. She realised that she had spent a good deal longer talking to him than she would have done had a missing glove been their only subject of conversation. She was still planning what she should say if questioned when the study door opened and Miss Hetherington-Smith's long pink nose and beady eyes – how like a mongoose she is, Hester thought irreverently – appeared in the doorway.

'Just what was all that about, Miss Elliott?' Miss Hetherington-Smith enquired frostily. 'You and that fat little man seemed to have a great deal to say to one another.' She sniffed disparagingly. 'A shopkeeper, I presume? I could smell trade even through the front window.'

What a disgusting old woman you are, Hester thought. A snob through and through and with no reason to think yourself better than anyone else since you live here by courtesy of your brother and are, in fact, his pensioner. Aloud, she said: 'Yes, he is a shopkeeper, Miss Hetherington-Smith, a most respectable and honest man. Miss Leonora and I were in his shop just before Christmas, purchasing wrapping paper and some tobacco to give to Mimms. Apparently, one of his customers dropped a glove on her way out of the shop and he has been visiting the homes of all those he knows to see whether the lost glove belongs to one of them.'

'And how did he come to know you, miss, since it can't be every day that you buy tobacco?' Miss Hetherington-Smith asked suspiciously. 'And you could not possibly have spent so long simply discussing a lost glove which did *not* belong to you.'

'One of next door's housemaids came into the shop just as we left and must have told him where we lived,' Hester said, with a glibness which astonished her. 'And whilst he was telling me about the glove, he happened to mention the children's carol service at the High School this afternoon. He has a niece who sings in the choir and wondered if Lonnie and I might like to go along. Apparently, they will sell some tickets on the door and he told me it's a very popular event. I asked him whether respectable people went and he assured me that it is well attended by folk from the big houses, since the tickets are not cheap.' She gazed innocently at her employer. 'I wondered if you might like to come along, Miss Hetherington-Smith? Children's voices are so sweet and I know you are fond of music.'

This explanation must have satisfied Miss Hetherington-Smith for she half turned away, saying as she did so: 'I'm visiting friends this afternoon, Miss Elliott. At what time does this carol service end?'

'I don't know, but I imagine about half-past four, maybe five o'clock,' Hester said. 'A longer service would be trying for the little ones. I'm sorry you can't come with us, but I'm sure Miss Leonora will enjoy it and probably meet several of her little friends from the park.'

Miss Hetherington-Smith did not deign to reply but re-entered the study, then suddenly appeared to think of something and turned back. 'Since you are out this afternoon, I take it that you will assist with the housework this morning,' she said over her shoulder. 'The dining room will need a good clean which will include brushing the carpet, dusting and polishing all the furniture and beating the Persian rugs. Kindly see to it.'

Hester opened her mouth to reply but was given no opportunity. The study door slammed almost in her face and, with a shrug, she turned towards the stairs. One of these days someone will teach you some manners, you nasty old crab, she said to herself. If Lonnie's father really does mean to visit England when his honeymoon is over, then Lonnie will make sure that he learns the truth about his sister.

But she could not think about revenge or Mr Hetherington-Smith's possible visit. Right now, her mind was too full of Dick and the meeting planned for later that day. With a light step, she ran up the two flights of stairs, eager to tell Lonnie what had transpired.

Dick had not realised that the streets would be so crowded on Boxing Day. He had known nothing of the carol service at the High School, which was only a stone's throw from St Augustine's, and when Joey had mentioned it had scarcely taken it in. Now, however, watching the animated crowd surging past, he could only hope that when Hester arrived the majority of the audience would have disappeared into the school.

He had had no doubt that he would recognise her, yet when a slender figure in a navy-blue coat, scarlet scarf and matching perky little hat stopped beside him he drew back, thinking she wished to go into the church, before he looked into that small, perfect face and knew her at once.

Abruptly, he was overcome by shyness. She was smiling up at him but when he did not speak her smile faltered and a tide of rosy pink invaded her cheeks. She made as if to turn away and Dick knew that if she did so their conversation would never take place. He grabbed for her sleeve, saying hoarsely as he did so: 'Miss Elliott! I'm that sorry I didn't know you straight away, but last time I see'd you it were summer and I hadn't thought . . . hadn't expected . . . you look ever so smart!'

To his great relief, Hester laughed and turned back towards him. 'Don't worry. I nearly walked straight past you, as well,' she said gaily. 'After all, we haven't met for some time and, as you say, when we did meet it was summer. Now where on earth has Lonnie got to?'

Even as she spoke, the small girl Dick remembered appeared at her side. The child was wearing a matching cherry-red coat and hat, both fur-trimmed, and the face that she turned to Dick, though still recognisably the Lonnie of last summer, was altogether rounder and rosier; healthier in fact, Dick told himself.

'Hello, Dick!' Lonnie said cheerfully. 'Have you brought Ben?' Her face fell when Dick admitted that he had not.

'I weren't sure if either of you would be able to get away,' he explained. 'Me pal Joey met me this morning and I've not been back home since.' He grinned down at the small girl, finding it easier to address her than to talk directly to beautiful, self-confident Hester. 'If I'd thought you'd enjoy a chat wi' Ben I might ha' brought him along, but you'd not always been too friendly, had you?'

Lonnie giggled. 'Oh, that was when I didn't know him very well,' she said frankly. 'I was still thinking like someone who has spent her whole life in India, but now I'm quite different. Did Ben tell you about the sledging?'

'Aye, on a biscuit tin lid,' Dick said, grinning. 'I wish I'd ha' been there!' He turned to Hester. 'Don't tell me you took part in their games,' he said, twinkling down at her. 'When I were a kid,

I were nearly killed shooting out on to Netherfield Road, squatting on a saucepan lid. I shot between a tram and a dray, the horse reared, the tram driver swore, a barrow boy wheeled his barrow straight off the edge of the pavement and tipped oranges all over the road . . . my, were I popular! Luckily for me, they were all so keen to have my hide that I managed to slip away whiles they were squabbling over who could get to me first.'

Hester and Lonnie laughed heartily with him and Dick realised that he had unwittingly broken the ice by recounting his hair-raising ride. He was seeing Miss Elliott once more not as his social superior but merely as a sweet and friendly girl whom he would like to know better. Confident now, he took her hand and tucked it into his elbow. 'I thought we'd go along to Shaw Street gardens and have a stroll around there to get our circulation going,' he said. 'How long can you be away from the house, Miss Elliott? I've all the time in the world, but I know it's not the same for you.'

'I think we're safe until about five, five thirty,' Hester said. 'I waylaid Allsop, the chauffeur, when he came down to the kitchen this morning and he said his orders were to pick madam up at two, take her to Great Sutton and call for her at half-past five since she and her companion would be having tea after the game of bridge was finished. It takes about half an hour, if not a bit more, to do the journey from Great Sutton so wouldn't you think, Dick, that we'd be all right if we got back to the house about six? And by the way, please call me Hester, because I intend to call you Dick. After all, I hope to be able to visit your parents again some day and there will be two Mr Baileys . . . three if you count Ted.'

'Four, if you count Ben,' Lonnie contributed, laughing up at them as they turned into the gardens. 'We're pretending to go to a carol service, Dick, but won't we get terribly cold, just strolling round the gardens? I know our coats and hats must look warm and cosy to you, but to Hester and me they feel pretty flimsy.'

Dick looked down at his thin jacket and flannel trousers. He would have scorned to wear gloves and had left his muffler at home, thinking it was not smart enough for such distinguished company. Even so, he did not think it particularly cold. However, he understood from Lonnie's remark that she and Hester were still what he would have called 'nesh' from having spent almost all their lives in India's sunny clime. 'Tell you what,' he said, struck by inspiration, 'we'll gerron a tram and go to the Pier Head. There's a canny-house not too far from there where I'll bet they'll still be serving, despite it being Boxing Day. What do you say?'

'Grand idea, but what's a canny-house?' Hester asked curiously. 'Is it – is it the sort of place I ought to take Lonnie, Dick? Only if it's by the Pier Head, it might be a – a disreputable sort of place.'

Dick laughed. 'A canny-house is a sort of working men's dining room. In fact, Miss Annie Conboy's place really is a dining room, but in times past it was just a canny-house and the fellers still tend to call it that,' he explained seriously. 'Miss Conboy is a very respectable woman. She's an excellent cook and would be most insulted if you suggested that her customers were disreputable. Most of them come off the ferries from Birkenhead and Woodside and are respectable working people, popping in for a hot meal or perhaps just a mug of tea and a bun, before returning to their lodgings in the city.'

'It sounds *lovely,*' Lonnie squeaked, before Hester could reply. 'If we have a nice meal there, then Hester won't have to bother with making our tea when we get back to Shaw Street. And that means no washing up either!'

'Aye, our Phyllis don't think much to washing up,' Dick agreed. He smiled to himself at a mental picture of Phyllis, standing four-square on the stout wooden box which brought the smaller children of the family up to sink level whilst she lashed around in the greasy water, grumbling all the time that none of her pals did washing up, so why should she? 'She's only just five, mind, so I guess she's got reason to have a bit of a moan now and then. It's good training for later, though, when you've a home of your own,' he added encouragingly.

By this time they had reached the tram stop and presently a green goddess, as the modern trams were nicknamed, drew up alongside. Dick saw the girls aboard, then sat down beside Hester with a sigh of relief, for although trams were notoriously draughty it was still a good deal warmer than out in the open street.

It was almost impossible to talk much, for trams are noisy vehicles and this one was no exception, but it did not take long to reach the Pier Head and the three of them disembarked. The wind was blowing straight off the Mersey and Dick turned his two companions towards St Nicholas Place. 'We'll walk up to the floating road and go across it on to the landing stage,' he said. 'That'll bring some colour to our cheeks. I'll show you where the Birkenhead ferry docks. I catch it every day along with a couple o' hundred others who work over the water,' he added.

As they reached the floating road and faced into

the wind, Lonnie actually staggered from the force of it and Dick put an arm round her. He could see that Hester, too, was having difficulty remaining upright, so it seemed only natural to put an arm round her as well. He half expected her to pull indignantly away but instead she clutched his jacket, laughing up at him and screaming into the wind: 'Gracious, this is a gale, isn't it? I truly believe the wind is strong enough to carry me over the rooftops if I spread the skirts of my coat and held them out like wings.'

Dick chuckled and tightened his hold. 'Well, I wouldn't like that to happen so I'll hang on even tighter,' he shouted. 'Are you all right, though? Would you rather walk inland?'

'No indeed,' Hester assured him, rather breathlessly. 'This is wonderful. It makes me feel so – so alive! And when we get to the canny-house, I'll have a *huge* appetite. I hope your pockets are deep, Dick!'

Dick assured her solemnly that he had been saving up for this moment for a month and, in fact, this was in a way true. He had dipped into his savings in order to make sure his family had a good Christmas, and the remainder of that money was in his pocket now. Joking with Hester about how much they could all eat, he reflected ruefully that neither girl had any conception of the hardship suffered daily by people such as the Baileys. And at present, we are luckier than most, he reminded himself. Dad's little pension doesn't go far but with me and Ted both earning at Laird's and young Ben contributing a share, at least we can be pretty sure of paying the rent and getting a square meal each day. But any extras – treats, clothing or doctor's bills – are a terrible worry.

But it did not do to dwell on such things, so he drew the two girls to the railings and pointed at the surging river and the ferry moored close to the landing stage. 'There you are, that's one of the ferries me and the fellers catch each workday morning,' he said. 'This place heaves wi' workers all pushing and jostling to get aboard the ferry so's they'll be in work on time. Me and my pal Joey – he's me foreman joiner – usually gets here ten minutes at least before the ferry sails, so as to be sure of a place. It's worse coming home, though, because when the hooter goes you all stream out at once, running downhill as fast as you can to get aboard.'

'Why is it worse, though?' Lonnie shrieked. 'Isn't it nicer to be going home than going to work? I'm sure I should like it better!'

Dick laughed, smiling down at her. 'Now just you think it out for yourself, young Lonnie,' he said with mock severity. 'First thing in the morning, us fellers can choose what time we leave home and there's always some slug-a-beds who take a chance on catching a tram which will get them to the ferry by the skin of their teeth. Then something goes wrong and they miss the tram or a bootlace breaks or they have to go back for their carry-out. That means folk arrive at the ferry in the mornings a few at a time, see?'

Lonnie frowned over this for a few seconds, then her brow cleared. 'Yes, I *do* see!' she shouted. 'When the hooter goes, *everyone* is free at the same moment. That means whoever runs fastest gets to the ferry first; am I right?'

'That's right, queen,' Dick said. 'You're not as green as you're cabbage-looking!'

Lonnie gurgled with amusement and Hester laughed outright. 'That's an expression we never heard in India,' she said, just as Dick swung them back on to the floating road once more. With the wind behind them, it was no longer necessary for Dick to keep his arm around either girl, but no one seemed too anxious to change position and the three of them marched happily back across the bridge. When they turned right into the Goree Piazza they were partially sheltered from the wind by the large buildings on their right and only then did Dick, rather regretfully, release his hold. But since Lonnie immediately grabbed his hand and Hester walked very close to him, Dick still felt warm and comfortable and proud of the company he was keeping.

'What is this place?' Lonnie said, looking curiously round the piazza. Dick shot a glance at Hester. Would she rather the child did not know some of the more disreputable history of the city in which she now lived? But Hester was looking at him with equal interest, so Dick decided he might as well enlighten them – if he did not, someone else would.

'In times past, Liverpool was the centre of the slave trade,' he told them. 'The slaves were sold on the Goree Piazza here.'

'I say! *Real* slaves? Black Africans with gold bangles round their ankles and spears and such?' Lonnie asked. 'Poor things! They must have felt worse than we did when we first came from India. They would be used to warm sunshine as we were, and they would hate this cold wind. Who bought the slaves, Dick? What did they want them for? Were there little boy and girl slaves as well as the grown-ups?'

Dick blinked at this volley of questions. In truth, he knew very little about the slave trade, save that it had been a blot on the history of the city in which he had been born and bred. He took a deep breath but was saved from having to reply by Hester, who cut in at once.

'Lonnie, Lonnie, Lonnie! Dick is not your schoolteacher, nor your governess, and doesn't want to be bothered. If you want to know all about the slave trade, I will take you along to the reference library and you can look up slavery there. Or we might try the museum, which would be more entertaining, I dare say.'

Lonnie groaned at the suggestion, but at this point they turned into Crooked Lane and when Dick began to talk of the various delicacies available at the dining rooms she forgot about slavery and began to speak of the nice things she intended to eat.

Presently, the three of them were seated at a quiet corner table with a generous meal spread out before them. Dick had ordered what the proprietress called a 'ham tea' which meant a plateful of thickly sliced ham, four pickled onions and a pile of bread and butter. To follow this there were sultana scones, gingerbread and a seed cake as well as mugs of tea for Dick and Hester and milk for Lonnie.

Despite the fact that, on the previous day, she and Hester had enjoyed a delicious Christmas dinner and a very large Christmas tea, as well as a supper of various cold meats and left-over cake and biscuits, Lonnie's eyes glistened as she munched the ham and contemplated the cakes to come. 'My aunt believes that too much meat heats a child's blood, whatever that may mean,' she informed Dick. 'As for sugary cakes and puddings, she says if I eat them, all my teeth will fall out.' She snorted disdainfully. 'As if they would! Why, when we lived in India, my *ayah* was always giving me sweetmeats from the bazaar and though, of course, my baby teeth *did* fall out, that was nothing to do with what I ate. It happens to every child, doesn't it, Hester?'

'Yes it does,' Hester agreed. 'But sweet things really are not good for one's teeth. Or one's complexion for that matter,' she added thoughtfully, 'since they are said to give you spots.'

'Then Aunt Emmeline should be covered in spots as well as having no teeth,' Lonnie said, triumphantly. 'D'you know, Hester, that she doesn't have any? Mollie told me that when she takes my aunt's tea to her in the morning, she sees Aunt Emmeline's teeth grinning at her from a glass on the bedside table. She says it fair gives her the willies and she doesn't like it much when my aunt tries to talk to her without putting the teeth in first. Did you know that, Hester?'

Dick looked across at Hester; she was smiling, her eyes alight with amusement, and Dick thought she had never looked lovelier. The wind had whipped colour into her normally pale cheeks and the food and warmth, after the chill outside, had given an added brightness to her eyes and reddened her softly curving lips. 'Well, Hester?' he said, teasingly. 'Were you fooled by Miss Hetherington-Smith's china choppers? Or did you think they were rooted in gum, like what ours are?'

'Rooted in gum? That makes it sound as though you and I glue our teeth in with gum each morning,' Hester said, twinkling up at him. 'As for Miss Hetherington-Smith's false teeth, I really don't think they're a very suitable subject of conversation whilst we're trying to eat our tea. Let's change the subject, shall we?'

But Dick, having watched the dimple come and go in her cheek, wanted to see her laugh again. 'I understand you invited Miss H to accompany you this afternoon,' he said gravely. 'Of course it wasn't an invitation to tea, but if it had been she could have had the best of both worlds. She could have gone off in the motor to Great Sutton and sent her teeth along to have tea with us. We could have put them on a little side plate with some ham and a pickled onion or two, and watched them chomp it all up.'

Lonnie gave such a shriek at this idea that Hester had to reprove her, though she was laughing so much herself that it was difficult to do so. Even Dick found himself laughing, and when he tried to calm down by taking a big swallow of tea he choked on it and had to turn away from the table and use one of his Christmas handkerchiefs to mop his streaming eyes.

The whole afternoon continued in this pleasant vein and Dick was delighted with the success of his outing.

'I haven't laughed so much before in my whole life,' Lonnie said as they left the dining rooms and turned back towards the Pier Head where they would catch a tram heading for home. 'At first I was sorry you hadn't brought Ben, but he might have eaten my share of tea as well as his and I *did* enjoy all that lovely ham with no one to scold me for being greedy or make excuses to stop me eating cake. Oh, Dick, it's been easily my best thing since we've come to Liverpool.'

'What about the sledging, you ungrateful young thing?' Dick asked, but he was secretly extremely flattered by her words. He had never been inside a house belonging to the rich, but imagined that it must be a sort of fairyland. Especially the nursery floor where there would be games in plenty and toys and treats for half a dozen children, so to have his little outing favourably compared with such things must be praise indeed.

'Ye-es, the sledging *was* wonderful,' Lonnie agreed. 'I'm not sure whether it comes absolutely level with this afternoon, but I think it falls a little behind because there was no ham.'

Dick laughed outright at this self-confessed greed and assured Lonnie he would tell Ben that next time they went sledging he must bring along at least an old ham bone so that he and Lonnie could suck at opposite ends of it when their sledging was done. This sent Lonnie off into more shouts of laughter but before she could answer him a Number 13 drew up alongside them and they all piled on board. The lower deck of the vehicle was already almost full so they climbed the spiral stair to the upper deck and took their places right at the front. 'I dearly love a tram ride,' Lonnie sighed. She had not taken a seat but was standing in front of Dick and Hester with her nose pressed to the glass. 'Everything looks so much more exciting from up here! We're in Dale Street now . . . I can see the brewery where Maud's brother Cecil works.' She turned briefly to her two companions. 'I knew it was Dale Street because I saw the sign at the corner . . . whoops, here we go across a huge street . . . there's the library and the Walker Art Gallery . . . could we really go there one day, Hester? Oh, I wish I could have a tram ride like this every day! Aren't the streets empty, though? Usually the pavements and the roadways are crowded but today there's hardly anyone around.'

Lonnie continued to chatter, more to herself than anyone else, and presently Dick suggested to Hester that they should make some arrangement to meet again. 'For I can't expect my foreman to act as messenger every day of the week,' he said. 'Even Miss Hetherington-Smith might get a bit suspicious like if tradesmen kept a-calling with one glove of a pair! Now what day is best for you and Lonnie?' He lowered his voice. 'Mebbe I'm being a bit forward, but speaking for meself I've had a grand time, and young Lonnie's certainly enjoyed it. Only – only you may feel different, o' course.'

'I'd like to meet again very much,' Hester said, rather shyly. 'It *is* difficult because you work quite long hours, don't you, and Sundays are impossible for us. Miss Hetherington-Smith makes sure we have very little spare time but we do get out occasionally. Didn't Ben say you sometimes have a half day on a Saturday, for instance?'

'Yes, though not very often,' Dick said briefly. His mind was racing. There must be a way of meeting, if only he could think of it! The trouble was, darkness fell early at this time of year and Hester had already explained that she and the child had a curfew and were, in any case, never allowed out after dark. But there were exceptions to every rule, he reminded himself, and he did not think that even so dictatorial an employer as Miss Hetherington-Smith could prevent Hester from attending a night-school class, a concert of classical music or a church function. Of course she would have to get someone to keep an eye on Lonnie, but in a household which included, from what Hester had told him, at least three maids, this should not be an insuperable objection.

He said as much to Hester, who brightened. 'It's true that Mollie, Maud and Edith are all well disposed towards us,' she admitted. 'I see no reason why Miss Hetherington-Smith should object if I make such an arrangement with one of the maids. After all, they have regular time off and Miss Hetherington-Smith never tries to stop them from going about their own business at such times. What do you suggest we do then, Dick?'

'How about the flicks?' Dick said, greatly daring. It was almost obligatory to hold a girl's hand if you took her to the cinema; a good-night kiss was also taken for granted by most young women, though seldom on a first date. He looked sideways at Hester's delicate, rose-petal cheek and swallowed hard. Oh, oh, oh! If only she would agree to a cinema trip, how happy he would be! 'How about going to see Johnny Weissmuller in *Tarzan The Ape Man*? It's on at the Evvie Palace on Heyworth Street, which isn't too far from Shaw Street,' he suggested and found his heart was in his mouth in case she should guess his amorous intentions and say no. 'Some of the fellers from Laird's have seen it and thought it were grand!'

'A trip to the pictures,' Hester said, her voice almost awed. She knew the Everton Electric Palace quite well, though she had never been inside it. 'I haven't been to the cinema for years . . . in fact, I've only ever been twice. Oh, Dick, that would be really lovely, but I shall have to tell Lonnie's aunt I'm doing something more worthy, otherwise I shall never get permission to have an evening off. I wonder what it could be?'

'Tell her you're going with a girlfriend to a concert of classical music at the Philharmonic,' Dick suggested. He was amazed at the speed with which his mind had worked, especially when he considered that he knew nothing of classical music and had never visited the Philharmonic Hall on Hope Street. 'Do you think that would serve?'

'It's worth a try, anyway,' Hester said, her eyes still alight. 'It isn't that I long for pleasures, or riotous living, or anything of that nature, it's just that I'm living a sort of unnatural life, if you understand me. The maids are nice girls, kind and often amusing, but their idea of a good book is *Peg's Paper*, or the *Red Letter*. It wouldn't occur to them to go to a library, as you do, Dick. And come to think of it,' she added in an aggrieved tone, 'I'm not even a member of the free library because Miss Hetherington-Smith keeps forgetting to sign the form saying I'm a resident on Shaw Street.'

'Hang on tight, we're coming up to Shaw Street now,' Lonnie squeaked as the tram lurched around the left-hand bend. 'Will we get off at our house, Hester, or shall we go on a bit? Dick won't get off for ages yet, will you, Dick?'

'I'll get off at Abram Street and cut through,' Dick said. 'Better that way, don't you think? Now let's decide what day we'll meet, and where.'

Hester nipped his arm and nodded warningly towards Lonnie but the child had turned back to her perusal of the outside scene and was ignoring them once more. 'Should we say next Thursday?' she suggested timidly. 'I can walk down to the tram stop on Shaw Street at, say, seven o'clock, and you can be there waiting. That is, if I can get permission to go out, of course.'

'Yes, that sounds fine,' Dick said. 'If you can't make it, would you be able to nip into Madison's and leave a message with Ben? He's there most days in the school holidays.'

This was agreed, and far too soon for Dick the tram began to slow down as it approached the stop while below the conductor bellowed: 'Everton Brow!' at the top of his not inconsiderable voice.

'Oh, oh, we're almost there. I'll go first so's you'll have something soft to fall on if you trip on the stairs,'

Lonnie said cheerfully. 'Goodbye, Dick – and thank you again. I wish it were Boxing Day a hundred times a year!'

Dick stood up and took Hester's hands in his and even as she began to thank him for the treat, he interrupted her. 'It's me who has to thank you for your company,' he said softly. 'It's been a real pleasure, honest it has. I dunno how I'll wait till Thursday but I guess I won't think of much else till then.' And before he allowed himself to wonder whether he dared or dared not, he had bent and kissed her cheek.

Hester walked home on air. She liked Dick better than any other young man she had yet met and the thought that he obviously liked her too was heady stuff for a girl who was not yet nineteen to take on board. What was more, she thought that Dick would not try to hurry her or persuade her to do anything she disliked or felt was wrong. He had talked a little about his work at Cammell Laird's and she had got the impression of a sober and industrious young man, liked by his workmates and respected by other craftsmen – in other words, she told herself, the sort of person her father would have thought a – a suitable friend for his daughter.

The thought made her blush. How embarrassing it was, but how true, that a woman's mind went from meeting a man to marriage in one leap. How equally true, she suspected, that a man's mind made no such leap – or, if it leapt at all, leapt in a far less moral direction.

But that was just what Dick's mind had not done, she was sure. He liked her, wanted to get to know her better, but had no intention of trying to persuade her into a deeper, more serious relationship before she was ready for it.

And then there was his sense of humour. Hurrying towards home, with Lonnie's small hand firmly clasped in her own, she thought of his smiling, teasing face, the way his eyes lit up, the strength of his jaw, the cleft chin, and the long laughter line which sprang up by his mouth whenever something really tickled him. Thinking of it, she gave a small gurgle of amusement and immediately Lonnie said, as though Hester been voicing her thoughts aloud: 'He really is nice, isn't he, Hester? Dick, I mean. I thought he was awfully good-looking the first time we saw him, but now I just like him best of everyone I know, except for my daddy, of course. Oh, and you, dear Hester!'

'Yes, he is nice. But we mustn't talk about him any more, because we're getting far too close to the house, and you know we agreed that your aunt would not be at all pleased if she discovered that we were meeting a young man,' Hester reminded her charge. 'I wonder, are all elderly English ladies like your aunt? Do you suppose none of them approve of a member of their household seeing someone of the opposite sex?'

Lonnie chuckled. 'If that was true no one would work for my aunt for very long,' she pointed out. 'Mollie has a young man – he's the butcher's assistant from Davies's shop, on Hibbert Street – and Maud has a young man as well, though hers lives in Formby, so she doesn't see him all that often. No, I think it's probably that they don't much like their nannies or their governesses having gentlemen friends.'

'I don't see why that should be,' Hester said, genuinely puzzled. 'What's the difference between one employee and another?'

'Oh, a nanny or a governess might corrupt the mind of a child in her charge,' Lonnie said, giggling. 'I heard one of the nannies in the park saying that, only she was joking, I think. So are we going to meet Dick again? Next time he might bring Ben, then we could . . .'

But they had reached the house and Hester gave Lonnie's fingers a warning squeeze before saying loudly: 'Ring the bell, my dear. Wasn't the carol service lovely? But the hall was rather chilly so I shan't be sorry to get back to our nice warm schoolroom.'

The door opened and Fletcher, tall, stooped, grey-haired and kindly, stood smiling down at them. 'Did you have a good time, young ladies?' he asked in his slow, creaking voice. 'I've heard the Boxing Day carol service is always very well attended and generally greatly enjoyed.'

'Oh, thank you, Fletcher!' Hester said, smiling up at him. 'Yes, the carol service was very enjoyable but the hall was rather chilly, so we shall hurry upstairs and get the fire lit, then we can make ourselves a snack and a nice hot cup of tea.'

Fletcher ushered the two girls inside and then said in a lowered voice: 'Miss Hetherington-Smith and Miss Hutchinson have only just got back themselves, miss. They're in the drawing room and have ordered sherry before dinner, because Miss Hetherington-Smith was complaining that it was far from warm in the motor, despite the fur rugs. But, miss, as it's Boxing Day, was you not to dine downstairs? Only there's a boiled fowl in white sauce, far too much for the two ladies, and you don't want to go spoiling your appetites with nursery tea if you're to dine on boiled fowl later.'

Hester paused at the foot of the stairs. 'Nothing was

said about dining downstairs, Fletcher,' she assured him. 'I expect that the remains of the fowl will be eaten cold tomorrow night. But it was kind of you to think of it. Has all gone well in our absence? Mollie took Kitty down to the kitchen, so perhaps we should go straight down there and collect the cat.'

'Yes, that might be a good idea, miss,' Fletcher said, looking rather relieved. 'Mollie's a good girl but when she gets to playing with the kitten, and Mrs Ainsworth with a dinner to cook . . . well,' he chuckled. 'You might say the fur flies, miss.'

Lonnie giggled. 'I want to fetch Kitty up to the nursery anyway,' she observed. 'I've not seen her for ages – it seems like ages, anyway.'

'I'm sure it does, Miss Leonora,' Fletcher agreed. 'And did you enjoy the carol service? I'm told it is usually first-class.'

Lonnie began to speak, then remembered and nodded enthusiastically. 'It was one of the nicest things I've ever been to,' she said, casting a glance so full of mischief at Hester that the governess had hard work not to smile herself. 'Come on, Hester. I'd better take Kitty into the garden for a few minutes, in case . . . you know.'

The two of them hurried down the stairs and into the large basement kitchen to rescue Kitty, who had been penned in with a couple of old fireguards whilst Mrs Ainsworth made chicken liver pâté for a savoury course. Kitty, it seemed, was far too fond of chicken liver to remain meekly on the floor whilst Mrs Ainsworth chopped and mashed, and had persistently leapt on to the kitchen table, causing much hilarity from everyone but the beleaguered cook.

'She's kept us all amused, miss, but I don't deny that the kitchen's no place for her when it comes to cookin' a meal,' Mrs Ainsworth commented as Lonnie swooped on her pet with loving cries. 'I've put up a plate of scraps, though, so you can take them up wi' you when you go back to the nursery.'

'It ain't the nursery no more, Mrs A,' Mollie said with a giggle. 'It's the schoolroom, ain't it, Miss Lo . . . Leonora, I mean.'

Lonnie, carrying her pet out through the back door, agreed that this was so and Hester left her to deal with the kitten whilst she herself took the proffered plate of scraps and began to climb the three flights of stairs which would lead, at last, to the nursery – or schoolroom, she reminded herself drily as she climbed.

In her old domain once more, she decided that as they had eaten so recently she would just prepare a snack for Lonnie and herself. She put the plate of scraps down on the floor for Kitty when she returned, made up the fire, which she had banked up with ash before leaving earlier in the day, and began to cut bread and butter it. There was strawberry jam, a whole jar, and half a jar of apricot, and there was a sizeable piece of Christmas cake which Mrs Ainsworth had sent up the previous day. She checked in the small cupboard where the milk was kept and saw that there was still plenty, both for their tea now and for a hot drink later. Satisfied on that score, she soon had the food prepared and when Lonnie and the kitten returned they sat down to a simple meal.

'Have a wash and then go straight to bed, Lonnie,' Hester said as soon as the bread and butter and the cake were no more than a memory. 'When I think of the tea you ate at that dining room it's a wonder to me that you could manage another morsel. However, the cold makes one hungrier than usual, I suppose.'

'You ate all your ham tea when we were with Dick, and now you've had three pieces of bread and butter and apricot preserve as well as quite a large slice of cake,' Lonnie said cheerfully, slipping off her chair. 'Actually I'm very tired; I don't mind going to bed early at all.'

As soon as Lonnie was safely tucked up in bed, teeth cleaned, hands and face washed and hair plaited into a long braid, Hester got out the ironing board, set it up before the fire and began on the pile of clothing in the wicker linen basket by her side. She selected a pillowcase with a lace trimming and began to smooth it flat, thinking back with real pleasure over the day that had passed. From the moment that Mr Frost had appeared on their doorstep, the day had begun to glow in Hester's mind, and she knew that it had been the happiest day she had enjoyed in England so far. Dick, she decided, was a very special person. He seemed the sort of young man who was at ease in any company. Mr Frost seemed a pretty rough diamond but he must be truly fond of Dick to have come seeking her out in her employer's house. Lonnie thought Dick the nicest of all the Baileys, though she had taken to the whole family, even accepting that Ben was not as black as she had previously painted him.

More important even than the day that had passed, though, were the days ahead. Hester was looking forward eagerly to her next meeting with Dick and even as she thought of it she realised that it was not simply the prospect of a visit to the cinema which was making her heart dance, it was the fact that, for the first time since arriving in England, she had something to look forward to. With Dick a part of her life, if only as a friend, she would be eager for each new day. It was not that she was unhappy with

Lonnie and her work, it was simply that she had no life of her own. When she took Lonnie to the park or the shops she met other young women but since they were mostly nannies or nursemaids they had held back from her, content with the company of their peers, assuming that she, as a governess, would consider them inferior companions. This was not so, but Hester had never bothered to break down the barrier of reserve the other girls had erected, partly because Miss Hetherington-Smith saw to it that she was too busy for social intercourse.

Now, however, things would be different. Hester did not intend to ask Miss Hetherington-Smith for time off at first She meant to arrange for Molly to come up to the schoolroom next Thursday with a pile of ironing which she could do whilst keeping a weather eye on young Lonnie. If she and Dick enjoyed their outing – and she had little doubt that they would do so – then she thought that she might suggest another evening entertainment or two before taking the plunge of telling her employer that she meant to take Miss Leonora out somewhere on a Sunday afternoon. Thinking it over, as she worked her way through the sheets and pillowcases, she decided that Miss Hetherington-Smith would probably quite enjoy a respite from her niece's company on a Sunday afternoon, for though Leonora was always careful not to try her aunt's patience too far, she found it amusing to skate around the thin ice of her aunt's displeasure, pretending to mis-hear questions, answering in an ambiguous manner, and generally behaving in such a way that Hester herself – and probably Lonnie's aunt – were secretly relieved when such sessions were over.

And when I've got her used to the idea that Lonnie

and I need a little time to ourselves on a Sunday, then I shall explain that I have discovered everyone else of my acquaintance has at least a half day and a couple of evenings off each week, Hester planned busily, skilfully edging the iron around the buttons of Lonnie's frilly white blouse. I shall tell her I now have friends in my profession – she smiled at the choice of word – and need to see them socially sometimes in order to keep up with current trends. Hester laid the little blouse over the back of a chair and picked up the next garment. Suddenly she was full of optimism. Surely Miss Hetherington-Smith would realise that everyone, from the highest to the lowest, should have a little time to themselves? It was not as if whichever maid who sat upstairs in the nursery would be idling their time away for, as Miss Hetherington-Smith had pointed out, silver cutlery could be cleaned, brass ornaments polished and table linen patched and mended while one was sitting by the fire in the evening. It was true that Hester herself performed a good number of these tasks but she knew that neither Mollie, Maud or Edith would object to doing them in her place while seated cosily by the schoolroom fire with the kettle hopping on the hob and a tin of fancy biscuits to hand. For her part, Hester was happy to spend some of her salary on tea and biscuits for the other maids if it meant that she might have a couple of evenings off each week.

The pile of ironed linen had grown considerably and Hester's shoulders were beginning to ache, reminding her that the day had been a long one and it was high time she took herself off to her own bed. She ironed the last garment, a petticoat of her own, unplugged the iron and stood it on the side of the fender to cool, and went through to check on Lonnie.

The child was fast asleep with her thumb in her mouth and her old rag doll, Jenny, clasped in her arm. Kitty, as usual, had abandoned her basket as soon as Hester had left the room and was curled up against the curve of Lonnie's tummy. Hester leaned over the bed, careful not to disturb the kitten, and gently removed Lonnie's thumb, scarlet from sucking. It remained on the pillow for perhaps ten seconds before Lonnie popped it back into her mouth once more and Hester, smiling and shaking her head, went off to her own room. She was well aware that if Miss Hetherington-Smith knew her niece sucked her thumb there would be trouble, but since her employer had never yet mounted the stairs to the nursery floor there seemed little fear of discovery. Children, Hester concluded as she undressed, sometimes needed the comfort of thumb-sucking whilst they accustomed themselves to a new situation. In time, her charge would stop sucking her thumb naturally. Hester stood in front of her small mirror and unpinned her hair from the bun which she wore during the day. She brushed the long rippling length of it, enjoying the feel as it swirled well below elbow length. Her father had never approved of short hair for women and Hester was glad that fashion seemed to be turning away from bobs and shingles to a softer, more feminine look. When the brush had performed the necessary one hundred strokes, she plaited her hair into its bedtime braid and climbed between the sheets. What a lovely day it had been, she mused. And there would be lovely days to come. Even if she and Dick were only to be friends, her life was bound to become more interesting as a result. But she acknowledged now that the little leap her heart gave whenever she thought of him augured well for their future relationship. She lay for a little while reliving her day once again until sleep overcame her.

'Hester, are we going to do lessons today? Only if I were in school it would be holidays, and holidays usually last until the fifth or sixth of January, which is ages away. I know Aunt Emmeline says that we don't do a proper school day, but if we did we wouldn't be able to help in the house so much, so I don't see . . .'

'Stop, stop!' Hester said, laughing. The two of them were eating their breakfast porridge whilst Kitty lapped at a saucer of milk and the cold grey light of a winter's day came in through the frosted window. 'Whatever made you think we were going to do school work today? As it happens you were wasting your breath since I had already decided we should visit the museum on William Brown Street this morning. It's a dreadfully cold day, far too cold for the park to be an enjoyable trip, but the museum will be warm and it will get us out of the house for the morning. I had thought of suggesting that we might pop into Madison's to see if Ben is free. He might like to come with us, because I know he has said before that he's mainly needed first thing in the morning and last thing in the afternoon. And after we've been round the museum I thought we might have a snack luncheon at Lyons on London Road. Would you like that? The food is very reasonable and delicious.'

'Oh, Hester, you do have the most scrumptious ideas!' Lonnie said, clasping her hands before her chest like a child in a storybook. 'I should think it would be a most tremendous treat for Ben, because his family are very poor, aren't they? I did think that Dick might have brought him along on Boxing Day, only then I remembered Mrs Bailey saying what a big help Dick's money was; she didn't know how she would go on without him. She said it was because Mr Bailey is so poorly that he can't work, and his bit of a pension gets eat up in doctor's bills, mostly.'

Hester, murmuring faint agreement, felt very ashamed of herself. It had simply never occurred to her that Dick, who was in a good job, might have to hand over most of his wages to his mother to keep the family going. Yet Lonnie, so much younger and less worldly than herself, had put two and two together and realised that Dick's money probably would not stretch to another ham tea. Hester felt deeply mortified that she had let Dick spend his money on her and Lonnie without so much as offering to pay a share. But I'll do so on Thursday, she told herself grimly. This is 1934 – very nearly 1935 – and I'm a working girl, not some spoiled little ninny dependent on her family for pin money. I'll explain to Dick that I want to pay my share since he has the whole family to support whereas my salary is for my use alone. I'm sure he won't mind; he's such a sensible, down to earth sort of person.

'And of course, I think the museum will be a great treat for me as well,' Lonnie said excitedly, spooning porridge at a great rate. 'The only thing is, I expect Ben's been to the museum lots of times. Wouldn't it be better if we arranged to meet him after the museum instead of before?'

'Why?' Hester asked baldly.

Lonnie wriggled uncomfortably. 'We-ll,' she said slowly, 'the fact is, Hester, he's such a knowall! I thought I might get one over on him so I'd know a bit more than he does, because he's always telling us where the best places are for shopping, how much the ferry costs, and things like that and why certain places have odd names. So I thought I'd find out all about the slaves and tell him, for a change.'

Hester shook her head reprovingly at her charge, though she could not help smiling at Lonnie's very obvious human failing, for everyone likes to be knowledgeable sometimes. 'We'll visit Madison's and ask Ben when he'll be free,' she decided. 'If he can't get away until later he can wait for us outside the museum, but if he's going to be free earlier then he shall come with us. You wouldn't want him hanging about in this cold weather whilst you and I were snug and warm inside the museum, would you?'

Lonnie was reluctantly admitting that this seemed fair when she suddenly jumped to her feet with an excited cry. 'It's snowing!' she shouted, darting over to the window. 'Oh, Hester, you don't know how I've longed for more snow. Now we can go sledging, on the beautiful little sled we bought with the money Daddy sent us! I do believe I'm the luckiest girl alive.'

Ben agreed with apparent eagerness to accompany Hester and Lonnie to the museum, though it speedily became apparent that he was not entirely at ease. He said nothing in front of Lonnie, but when the child had wandered ahead to take a look at one of the further exhibits, Hester asked Ben why he was so quiet. 'You've usually got plenty to say for yourself,' she said smiling down at him. 'But today you've scarcely said a word. You never even contradicted Lonnie when she read the showcards all wrong. Nothing bad happened at work, did it? I hope Mr Madison wasn't displeased when you decided to come with us.'

'No, it ain't nothing to do with Mr Madison,' Ben told her. 'The fact is, when I left home this morning, me mam were in a fair state. Me dad went to sit down by the fire to take his breakfast as he usually does and he suddenly started to cough. Mam gorrup to give him a clean handkerchief and when she took the used 'un off him it was soaked in blood. I were ever so frightened but me dad said it were just a nose bleed an' I weren't to gerrin a state. He said to go to work same as usual, only Mam tipped me the wink to fetch Dr Perkins on me way an' to get old nurse what lives round the corner. I s'pose it's all right,' he added doubtfully, ''cos it has happened before. They have him in hospital for a few days until the bleedin' stops and then they sends him home. Mam will go with him to wharrever hospital Doc Perkins suggests, so there's no point in me goin' back to Elmore Street before this evening. Mam said not to worry but you know how it is. I'm that fond of me dad . . .'

'Of course you are, and I'm not surprised you're worried. Is there anything I can do to help? Would you rather we all went to your house just to check that your father really is all right? Honestly, if we could help . . .'

But Ben insisted that this would never do. 'We'll finish goin' round the museum 'cos we're nearly through with it anyway,' he said. 'But I'll have to skip the meal,' he added regretfully,' and go straight home. You never know, if me dad is in hospital, Mam may have left a message with a neighbour tellin' me where she is an' so on. She might even have left Phyllis with Mrs Arbuckle down the road and if so I'll collect the kid an' take her home with me, 'cos Mrs Arbuckle's got eight of her own and our Phyllis don't like her overmuch.'

'Right. I'll tell Lonnie . . .' Hester was beginning, but Ben cut her short.

'No! Don't you go tellin' young Lonnie owt about me dad. Our mam never lerron to Phyllis that it might be hospital, 'cos kids worry, don't they? I'll say I forgot I'd some messages for me mam and make off before she can ask questions.'

'All right, Ben, but will you please let us know what's happening,' Hester said anxiously. 'I'll come into the shop early tomorrow, if I can get away, but if not, late in the afternoon. If you won't be there yourself, leave me a message. And remember, anything I can do to help . . .'

Ben agreed to this and presently, as they emerged from the museum, he clapped a hand across his mouth and said: 'Oh, wharra fool I am! Mam telled me to go straight home 'cos she had some messages for me. I'm awful sorry, miss, but I gorra go.'

Lonnie gave a moan of disappointment and began to remind Ben of the meal they were about to enjoy but the boy had already gone, slipping into the crowd and making off at a trot. Lonnie turned large despairing eyes on Hester. 'But he said he could come with us,' she wailed. 'Besides, he never goes home to have luncheon, you know he doesn't.'

'No. But when Ben left home this morning his father was not feeling too well. I don't imagine there's much to worry about but I could see Ben felt uneasy so I advised him to go home and promised that we would have a meal together some other day,' Hester said. She did not see why Lonnie should not know at least some of the truth. 'Now shall we have our own luncheon? Afterwards, we'll go back home and play one of your games by the fire.

Lonnie appeared to derive some comfort from this

suggestion and the two of them had cheese on toast and fizzy lemonade in Lyons. It had snowed on and off all morning as though it could not quite make up its mind what to do, but by the time their luncheon was finished large flakes were falling fast. This made the prospect of an afternoon playing games by the nursery fire quite attractive and the two girls turned up their coat collars, pulled their hats low over their brows and set off for the tram.

'We'll cut down Fraser Street on to Islington; we can pick up a tram there which will take us all the way to Shaw Street,' Hester said breathlessly. Hand in hand they hurried along the pavement and were lucky enough to arrive at the tram stop just as a green goddess was drawing to a halt. Unfortunately, a large number of people had decided to abandon shopping because of the snow and the tram was crowded. Hester and Lonnie managed to get aboard and were so speedily followed by others that when the conductor called their stop they got down with considerable relief and headed straight for home.

Usually they went in through the garden gate, but today Hester pulled her charge to the front door. They rang and Fletcher ushered them inside, tutting in a fatherly way over their soaked garments and advising them to take off their boots and leave them with him so that they might be dried and polished before they were next needed.

Hester and Lonnie hastily took off their boots and sped upstairs, their dripping coats over their arms. 'We'll hang them over the fireguard and they'll soon dry off,' Hester was saying as they entered the schoolroom. 'Hello, Kitty! Aren't you glad you're a nice little indoor cat today? I don't think you would much enjoy all that horrid snow!' As she spoke, she was making up the fire to a real royal blaze but since this merely resulted in the coats' giving off a good deal of steam, she told Lonnie to get out the Monopoly board while she herself took the coats down to the kitchen. 'For I don't see why we should have to breathe in steam and probably catch consumption,' she said frankly, 'when there is an enormous drying rack, probably empty on such a day, in the kitchen.'

'All right, Hester, but don't be long,' Lonnie said. She was setting out the Monopoly board and the pieces on the schoolroom table. 'Which will you be? The boot, the top hat, the car . . . ?'

'I'll be the car. It's faster than the boot or the top hat,' Hester said gaily, piling their coats, hats and scarves on her arm and heading for the door. 'Sort out the Chance and Community Chest cards and don't you dare look at them while I'm away.'

In the kitchen she was greeted warmly, though she thought she noticed a certain restraint. However, Mrs Ainsworth and Maud helped her to drape the wet garments across the rack whilst Edith hauled on the rope which carried it up to the high ceiling. 'Thanks ever so much,' Hester said, turning back towards the door. 'Anyone want a game of Monopoly? Lonnie's upstairs setting out the board this minute.'

Maud began to speak, but Mrs Ainsworth cut across her words. 'The ladies is in, miss,' she said heavily. She glanced around her as though expecting Miss Hetherington-Smith or Miss Hutchinson to appear through a trap door in the floor like the demon in the pantomime. 'There's always a heap o' work to do, especially since . . . but there, you go off and have your game. You'll come down later for cold meat and cakes for nursery tea?'

'Yes, I'll do that,' Hester assured the older woman. She was about to leave the kitchen when it occurred to her that she had not seen Mollie since the previous day. Probably it was the girl's day off. I really must tackle Miss H about Thursday evening, but perhaps I ought to have a word with Mollie first, she decided. 'Mrs Ainsworth, is Mollie out? Only I'd like a word with her if possible.'

Mrs Ainsworth looked uncomfortable. 'I reckon she's in her room,' she said heavily. 'Third one along after the butler's pantry. Only perhaps Maud might go along and fetch her out for you . . .'

'It's all right, I won't barge in, I'll knock on the door loudly and wait until she answers,' Hester said. 'I rather want to speak to Miss Hetherington-Smith about having an evening off occasionally, only I thought I'd have a word with Mollie first.'

Maud began to speak but Hester was already closing the door and hurrying along the passage in the direction of the maids' rooms. As she went, she could not help noticing how scratched and dirty was the linoleum and how scuffed the paintwork of the walls, but servants' quarters, she supposed, were seldom seen by their employers and therefore such niceties as redecoration were usually ignored.

The door to the butler's pantry stood open and so, when she reached it, did the third door along. Indeed, within six feet of it, she could hear what sounded remarkably like muffled sobbing which so disturbed her that she entered the room at once, saying as she did so: 'Mollie! You poor child! What on earth has happened?'

Mollie had been lying face down on the bed, her shoulders heaving with sobs, but at the sound of Hester's voice she sat up and scrubbed desperately at her reddened, tear-swollen eyes with a damp and well-used hanky. 'Oh, miss!' she said, her voice distorted with weeping. 'Did they tell you? I dunno what to do, it'll break me mam's heart, 'cos I'm the only earner apart from me dad and he's a farm labourer, as you know, and winter's hard on such as him. Me mam relies on the money I takes home just to feed the other kids . . . oh, miss, whatever will I do?'

Hester glanced around the mean and shabby room, the three narrow beds made up with thin blankets and the wash-stand with its burden of chipped china, then back at Mollie's face. She sat down on the bed and put an arm round the younger girl. 'No one has told me anything, Mollie dear,' she said gently. 'Tell me what's upset you so and I'll see if I can help.'

'No one can't do nothing,' Mollie said wildly. 'She's give me the sack, telled me she'd pay me for the rest of the week but I'm to go tonight. I axed wharr I done wrong and she said since you come, Miss Hester, she found she could do wi'out a housemaid. She said as you were beginning to be useful so she didn't need me no more. She said she pays you a good salary so it would help a great deal if she could save on my wages. She did say she'd give me a reference but Cook says her references ain't up to much, 'cos she won't admit she's got rid of someone for no real reason, see? Oh, miss, wharrever shall I do?'

'Well, stop crying, wash your face and go and see to Miss Lonnie. Tell her I'm afraid there'll be no game of Monopoly tonight and see her into bed. I'll be up as soon as I can, but if you wouldn't mind staying with her whilst I go and speak to Miss Hetherington-Smith,' Hester said. How dare the old woman try to turn Mollie on to the street just because she, Hester, was now doing a good deal of the housemaid's work! Well, she would soon put a stop to that! She would tell Miss Hetherington-Smith that she had been employed as governess and companion to Miss Leonora, that she had helped with the housework out of a desire to be useful, but she would do so no longer if it meant Mollie's losing her job. If she stuck to her guns Miss Hetherington-Smith would have no option but to keep Mollie on because the large, rambling old house needed all its staff to clean and maintain it.

Full of this resolve, and completely forgetting all about her desire to have some time off, Hester went straight to her employer's study. She knocked on the door and walked in without waiting for an invitation to do so. Miss Hetherington-Smith sat behind her old-fashioned desk, apparently doing household accounts for she had a pile of bills by her left hand and a large ledger open on the blotting pad before her. She looked up enquiringly as Hester entered, though her face darkened as soon as she saw who her visitor was. 'Yes, Miss Elliott?' she said. 'May I ask the reason for this rather hasty intrusion? A gentlewoman, Miss Elliott, waits to be invited to enter; you, I noticed . . .'

'I'm sorry if it's offended you, Miss Hetherington-Smith, but I'm in rather a hurry,' Hester said. Buoyed up by anger, she scarcely considered her words or what effect they might have. 'I've just come from Mollie. I went to have a word with her and found her very much distressed. She tells me you've given her notice.'

Miss Hetherington-Smith's thin grey eyebrows rose in simulated surprise. 'And what business is it of yours, Miss Elliott, if I choose to dispense with the services of every member of my staff?' she asked icily. 'As it happens, I no longer need the girl and have no intention of paying wages for someone to sit idle about my house. But I repeat, Miss Elliott, what business is it of yours?'

'It became my business the moment you decided to start giving me Mollie's work to do,' Hester said bluntly. 'I was happy to help, Miss Hetherington-Smith, but not to supplant a young girl whose wage, small though it is, is helping to feed a large family. I was employed to act as governess and companion . . .'

Miss Hetherington-Smith clearly guessed what Hester was about to say and cut her off before she was able to do so. 'I imagine you were about to say that you will no longer assist with household tasks,' she said, and there was a thin suspicion of triumph in her voice as she spoke. 'In that case, I shall of course have no option but to keep Mollie on, though I think it will be best, Miss Elliott, if you and I parted company. Since you are paid monthly and the month ends today, I will pay you what is owed and you may leave at once.'

Hester felt the blood rush to her face. She was furious with herself for not anticipating this. She began to say that it was Mr Hetherington-Smith who employed her and not his sister but her words were cut short immediately by her employer's harsh voice. 'You are quite wrong, Miss Elliott. Whilst my brother is out of touch, I run this house in the way I think fit and I decided some while ago that you were not a good influence, either on the staff or on my niece. To tell you the truth, your attempt to interfere with my running of the house by endeavouring to prevent me from dismissing my own staff is just the sort of behaviour I cannot tolerate. Get your things together at once; you will leave my employment forthwith.'

'I shall do no such thing,' Hester said bravely, but with a shrinking heart. 'If your brother knew . . .'

'But he does not,' Miss Hetherington-Smith pointed out. 'Besides, Miss Elliott, have I not made it perfectly clear that you may choose? Either Mollie or yourself leaves this house tonight; it's entirely up to you. But think how different are your circumstances! Mollie has a large family, you say, and very little money. She has no qualifications for any sort of work except that of a housemaid and there is a Depression in Liverpool as elsewhere. Furthermore, she is not yet sixteen, quite a child in fact, whereas you are twenty-four years old, well educated and intelligent. I will certainly provide a reference so you should have no difficulty in finding employment elsewhere. That will be all, Miss Elliott.'

Chapter Six

The hotel on St John's Lane, the Victoria, to which she had fled was quiet and respectable, but within a few hours of taking a room there Hester had realised that it was far too expensive for someone in her position. She was without a job or any immediate prospect of earning some money and she was so appalled by what had happened to her that for the moment at least all she wanted was a refuge; somewhere to lick her wounds and recover from the shock of being almost forcibly ejected from the house in Shaw Street.

During the interview with Miss Hetherington-Smith, her employer had suddenly stopped speaking in mid-sentence and swept out of the room, shutting the door behind her with a slam. She had returned moments later not attempting to apologise or explain her absence and had taken up her argument where she had left off as though there had been no interruption. It was only when there was a tap on the door and it opened to reveal Maud standing there, looking thoroughly scared, with a bulging suitcase in either hand, that Hester realised why Miss Hetherington-Smith had abandoned her for those few moments.

'I done what you said, madam,' Maud said timidly. 'I packed up all Miss Elliott's things – her clothing and that – though I couldn't get her coat nor her leather boots into either case so they're hung over the banister at the end of the stairs.' The girl turned to Hester, though shooting a scared glance towards her employer as she did so. 'Miss, what's happening? You ain't leaving us, are you?'

Before Hester had a chance to reply, Miss Hetherington-Smith began to hustle Maud out of the room. 'Miss Elliott has decided to seek a position as governess somewhere where she will not be required to help in the house. I'm sure it's very understandable that she should wish to do so since, of course, she is fully trained and very competent. However, I feel Miss Leonora will do very much better at a school for young ladies, where she can meet other children of her own age.' She shot a triumphant look at Hester. 'Indeed, Miss Elliott has told me many times that the child was leading an unnatural life and should be educated amongst her peers; is this not so, Miss Elliott?'

Hester gave her a look of withering scorn but said nothing in reply and Miss Hetherington-Smith turned to Maud. 'You may go.'

The maid, with another worried glance at Hester, scuttled along the corridor in the direction of the basement.

As soon as she had gone, Hester crossed the hall towards the stairs. Immediately, she felt her arm taken in a spiteful grip. 'You will not go upstairs; nothing of yours remains there and I won't have Miss Leonora frightened,' Miss Hetherington-Smith said firmly. 'If you persist, I shall call Fletcher to eject you, and that would not look well for either of us.'

'Kindly remove your hand this moment,' Hester said, feeling her cheeks flush with rage. 'I have no intention of going upstairs, but I do intend to put on my coat and boots before leaving this house.

And I should like my salary immediately, if you please.'

Miss Hetherington-Smith looked rather wildly around the hall and Hester said bitingly: 'Don't worry, I've no intention of stealing the silver while you go to your room to fetch the money that is owed me. But I tell you to your head that I don't intend to leave here with scarcely a penny piece to my name. If I am not paid properly I shall go straight to the nearest police station and lodge a complaint against you.'

'Hutch! Miss Hutchinson!' Miss Hetherington-Smith shouted. But her companion did not appear and bidding Hester to remain just where she was Miss Hetherington-Smith hurried into the study, opened a drawer in her desk and removed a small leather bag. She tipped the contents on to the pink blotting pad, counted out the required sum and, returning to Hester, pushed it into her hand. 'I shall give the staff instructions that you are not to be admitted if you come calling,' she said harshly. 'And don't think to complain to my brother, for by the time he returns to India my niece will have forgotten all about you.'

Hester had already donned her boots and, struggling into her coat, did not reply. She still felt dazed, as though this was not happening but was some weird sort of nightmare. All the fight seemed to have gone out of her and all she wanted now was to escape from the malevolence and spite emanated by Miss Hetherington-Smith. She was trembling from reaction but buttoned her coat, pulled her hat down as far as it would go and headed for the front door. When she opened it, a swirl of snow blew in and it was with some pleasure that she threw the door wide in order to pick up her cases. Head held high, she had marched into the road, turning right along Shaw Street and making for the tram stop. The snow whirled past her face, planting cold kisses on her skin, and she had no idea whither she was bound. She only knew she wanted to put as much distance as possible between herself and Miss Hetherington-Smith, and when a tram drew up alongside her she climbed aboard and let the conductor lodge her cases under the stairs. When he said: 'Lime Street Station, miss?' she made no demur but paid her fare and sank wearily on to the nearest slatted bench.

Arriving at Lime Street, she had gone up St John's Lane to the Victoria Hotel, simply because it seemed respectable, and had booked herself a room for one night. The sum required had been enough to frighten her, however, and the very next day she had moved to a much smaller and cheaper hotel on Lord Nelson Street.

Now, sitting in a chair by the window of her tiny room in the St Anthony Hotel and contemplating the snowy scene outside, Hester was wondering what she should do next. The truth was, she had no faith whatever in her ability to get work as a governess. She never doubted that any reference given by Miss Hetherington-Smith would be unlikely to help in her search for employment and though she knew that Lonnie's father would assist her in any way he could, it would be some time before he was in a position to do so.

But tomorrow I meet Dick, Hester told herself now, rubbing her hands together, for it was bitterly cold in the bedroom, though downstairs in the lounge there would be a good fire burning. I'm sure Dick will help in any way he can – why, he might even know of someone who's advertising for staff – because, for the time being at least, I'll do any job which will keep body and soul together until I can find something suitable.

Thinking of Dick cheered her considerably. At first she had felt friendless and alone, unable to return to the house in Shaw Street to explain to Lonnie why she had left so suddenly, but whenever she thought of Dick she remembered how resourceful he had been. He had sent a workmate to the door in order to get a message to her, so once she was more settled surely she could do the same. If Lonnie was really going to school then she, Hester, had only to find out at what hour she left the house each morning and she would be able to meet the child en route and discuss what had happened. It worried her most of all that Lonnie might feel herself deserted and might blame Hester for such desertion. She knew Miss Hetherington-Smith well enough by now to realise that the older woman would have no compunction in simply inventing a story which would put Hester in a bad light and herself in a good one, and though she had faith in Lonnie's good sense and knew the child loathed her aunt, she supposed that Lonnie would be bewildered and hurt by her absence, not realising what had actually taken place.

At this point, Hester got resolutely to her feet and began to don her outdoor clothing. It's no use sitting here feeling sorry for myself; I'll go out right now and search for an employment bureau and see what sort of jobs are on offer, she told herself. Wouldn't it be a grand thing if, by the time I meet Dick tomorrow, I've already got myself a job. Besides, I can't afford more than two more nights in this hotel so I've really got to search for somewhere cheaper and I can do that once

I've visited the employment bureau. Another thing I can do is get a tram to Heyworth Street and explain what's happened to me to young Ben. What's more, I can find out whether his father was really taken to hospital. I suppose I could go round to Elmore Street, her thoughts continued, but I really don't want to do that. They have troubles of their own and somehow I feel I must speak to Dick first. After all, the young woman he asked to go to the cinema with him was in a good job and earning a respectable salary. Who knows, when he discovers I'm almost penniless and have no job and no home of my own, he might not want to meet me after all! But Hester did not believe this for one moment and presently set out, well wrapped up, to tackle the employment bureaux in the surrounding area.

Dick and his mother sat by the hospital bed, Mrs Bailey holding her husband's frail hand. Dick thought he had never seen his father look paler and more bloodless, yet when the older man's eye rested on Dick he gave a broad and cheerful smile.

'Don't look so worried lad,' he said in a thin, reedy voice, 'they are going to make me better, same as they always do. Oh, I know it takes a bit longer each time, but there are some wonderful doctors in this here hospital and they say I'm a fighter and fighters usually do best. Now just you take good care of your mam and the little 'uns and I'll do me best to get well so's I can come home and moither the lot of you with me wild demands.'

Dick and Mrs Bailey smiled dutifully, but Dick could see how the long speech had worn his father out and presently he gave his mother a nod and told his father gently that they really ought to be going. 'We left Ted in charge of Ben and Phyllis,' he explained, 'and though Ted's a right sensible lad he's no sort of cook, so Mam and me thought we'd bring in fried fish and chips, 'cos we have to walk past the chippy on our way home.' He stood up, then bent over the bed and took his father's hand, gently squeezing the frail fingers. 'Is there anything we can bring in for you, anything you fancy?'

The white face on the pillow tried to smile and the pale lips parted but it seemed speech was too much of an effort, for Mr Bailey merely shook his head.

'Well, if there's nothing special you fancy, we'll mebbe bring you in a baked custard; I'll buy the eggs and milk and Mam'll do the work,' Dick said, with a gaiety he was far from feeling. 'I doubt I'll be in tomorrer, Dad, 'cos it's Ted's turn, but I'll see you the following day.'

Mrs Bailey bent and kissed her husband, then the two of them made their way out of the hospital. On the pavement once more, they headed for the tram stop and it was not until they were walking up Heyworth Street with newspaper packets of fish and chips that Dick said what was probably in both their minds. 'He's the best and bravest man I know, Mam, but I've never seen him as bad as this before. If only we could get him away to somewhere healthier . . . weren't that what the doctor were saying?'

'He said your dad might last a bit longer if he could get him into one of these here sannytoriums,' Mrs Bailey said worriedly. 'There's one in Blackpool and another miles and miles away in Wales. But I know your dad – he won't want them to take him where we can't visit. What worries me, Dick, is if we persuade him to go and he gets worse . . .' Mrs Bailey gulped and could not go on, her voice suspended by tears.

Dick reached out and gave her hand a comforting squeeze. 'I know what you mean, Mam,' he said gently. 'You can't bear the thought that our dad might die alone, surrounded by strangers. But – but shouldn't we take a chance, if there's any hope . . . ?'

Mrs Bailey stopped dead in the middle of the pavement and turned to face her son, her tear-wet eyes meeting his steadily. 'Dick, as you know, the doctor sent for me while you were talking to your dad,' she said resolutely. 'I didn't meant to tell you and you mustn't tell the young ones, but – but there ain't no hope, not really. My poor old boy can't live more than a few weeks. The doctor says his lungs are in rags. He doesn't know how he can keep so cheerful, feeling as he must. He suggested this here sannytorium because there'll be fresh air and scenery and that and because the food's better and likely the nursing is too. It ain't because a sannytorium would give our dad a better chance, because it wouldn't. Oh, Dick, I'm that sorry to put it on you, but I can't take a decision like that on me own. What the devil should we do, chuck?'

All the way home they discussed the problem and continued the discussion when the young ones had gone to bed, but in the event the decision was taken out of their hands. Next afternoon, Dick was called out of work by the manager and told he must make his way back to the hospital as his father was gravely ill and his mother needed him. When he arrived at the hospital, his father's bed was surrounded by screens and Dick's heart sank into his boots, but his mother, emerging presently, told him that the doctors thought their patient was holding his own.

'It were the suggestion of going away to that

sannytorium what brought on a bad attack,' she explained in a breathy whisper. 'He says he won't go nowhere, says he'd sooner die here than live in some godforsaken spot where he couldn't see his wife and his kids for mebbe weeks at a time. He wants all of us to swear we won't let them take him away, so as soon as they've revived him after this latest bout we're to make him any promise he wants. Understand?'

Dick, still shaking with an icy coldness, nodded dumbly, and never gave a thought to his plans for the evening which, in any event, had crumbled into dust.

Hester arrived early at the Everton Electric Palace, in no very bright spirits. Despite the best of intentions her efforts to find herself a job before meeting Dick had proved fruitless. As she had intended, she had visited the nearest employment bureaux but none of the staff she met had been able to help her. At Miss Strong's bureau, she had consulted the proprietress herself and Miss Strong had been blunt. 'You are far too young for a post as governess, Miss Elliott,' the severe-looking lady had told her. 'Besides, due to the Depression, most families are sending their children to school rather than paying out what they consider to be large sums for private and personal education.'

'Yes, I do understand that; it was the reason Miss Hetherington-Smith decided to end my employment with her,' Hester said, ruefully – and untruthfully. There was no point in telling anyone more than was necessary. 'But what about nannying, Miss Strong? I was advised to give my age as twenty-four when I first became a governess – I am not yet nineteen, as you know – but from my experience nannies are usually a good deal younger than governesses . . .'

'Not nannies, nursery maids,' Miss Strong interrupted. 'Of course some nannies are younger, but the majority of girls that you see in the park with their charges are actually nursery maids. It is not a well paid job and it often includes a good deal of housework and to be honest, Miss Elliott, most families would be embarrassed to offer such a post to someone of your obvious education and class. Have you ever considered office work?'

'No, because though I used to type my father's reports with two fingers I have no experience in the secretarial field,' Hester had said honestly. 'I have neat handwriting but I understand one has to be able to use a typewriter and to have some skill in book-keeping and I'm afraid I have neither.'

'Oh dear,' Miss Strong said mournfully. 'That does rather limit us, I'm afraid. What about shop work? It is not terribly well paid – in fact, it is quite poorly paid – and you would have to look for lodgings of some sort, but you have a good appearance and a pleasant, unaccented speaking voice. The big stores are always on the lookout for someone who has pretty manners and an engaging smile.' She rifled through the papers on her desk. 'Now let me see . . . yes, Lewis's want someone for their haberdashery counter. You would only be learning for the first three months or so, but I do think you might find promotion came quite quickly in such employment.'

Armed with Miss Strong's recommendation, Hester had gone straight round to Ranelagh Street. She had been directed by a shopwalker to the upper floor but to her intense disappointment she was not asked to attend for an interview. 'We're really looking for a girl of fourteen or fifteen to train up,' the woman behind the desk told her. Her eyes swept Hester from the tip of her head to the toes of her shoes. 'When a girl is your age, Miss Elliott, she is usually experienced in shop work. I take it you've not worked commercially before?'

Hester had been uncertain exactly what these words meant but explained she had been a governess to a small girl who was now to be sent to school. The woman behind the desk nodded her understanding. 'And of course you are too young for most governess posts, yet too old to enter a department store as a beginner,' she stated. 'I advise you to look in the smaller shops where your appearance and accent would be very much in your favour and perhaps less experience is needed. Good morning.'

Despite her disappointment over gaining employment, however, Hester looked around her at the hurrying crowd with lively interest. It was annoying that she still had no job but she realised that her faith in Dick's ability to help her was considerable. When he arrived, she was sure he would have a solution to her problem; he might even be able to point her towards some affordable lodgings. Huddling her coat round her, she wished it were not so cold and began to look forward to the moment when Dick would usher her into the warm picture house, so that her fingers and toes might thaw out as they watched the film.

Hester waited for two hours at the rendezvous, though she got steadily colder and colder and very rapidly became deeply depressed. Dick was so sturdily reliable that she had never dreamed he might not even appear. When she had at last given him up, she still could not believe that he had deliberately failed her. There must have been an emergency at work, or perhaps his father was, indeed, more ill than Ben had imagined. Walking miserably back to her hotel room, she determined to go to Madison's the next day to see if she could get news of Dick from his brother.

Next morning, she visited the shop to find it closed, with a notice in the window saying briefly that the premises would only be open on Wednesdays and Saturdays until the weather cleared. She did remember, vaguely, that Ben had said something about saving some of his earnings so that he still had money in January and February when Mr Madison would not need him for more than a couple of days a week, if that, but finding the place closed was still a nasty shock. Hester played with the idea of going round to Elmore Street, but once again her conscience prevented her from doing so. It would simply not be fair on the family to add to their burdens, and besides, the next day was Saturday and Madison's would be open then. In the meantime, she must cease to rely on Dick – or anyone else for that matter – and find cheaper lodgings on her own account. With this in mind, she set off towards the Pier Head, thinking that she might find affordable lodgings near the docks. She guessed that there would be disreputable places which she must avoid but the speed with which her money was disappearing alarmed her. She decided that she would not return to the hotel until she had found herself either a job or suitable lodgings, or ideally both, and somehow, having made the decision, she felt both more cheerful and more optimistic. Surely *someone* would be glad of the services of a young and healthy person like herself?

* * *

By lunch time, Hester's search had led her to the Scotland Road, an area which she had not previously visited, and for a while she forgot her own troubles as she examined the fascinating shops, stalls and barrows which thronged the wide pavements. She guessed that there would be flats above the shops but also guessed that these desirable premises would be owned by the shopkeepers below and unlikely, therefore, to be available for rent.

She had abandoned the Pier Head area hastily when she had been accosted by no fewer than three sailors, clearly looking for more than just a night's lodging. But here on the Scotland Road, surrounded by women with large shopping baskets doing their messages, she was spared such embarrassment, though she was aware that passers-by eyed her curiously. Looking at her reflection in the window pane, she began to realise that she was rather too well dressed for someone wanting work of almost any description and decided that she had best explain her position to the first would-be employer she encountered, rather than letting an interview take its normal course.

Having made this decision, she then chanced upon Paddy's market and, whilst examining the clothing on one of the stalls, had a piece of luck. The woman behind the counter, if you could call it that, saw her wistfully examining a respectable, though worn, grey skirt and jacket and was beginning to assure Hester that the material was of excellent quality and would last her for years when something seemed to occur to her. She was a tall, raw-boned Irish woman with sparse sandy hair and a merry, though almost toothless, grin, but her small eyes were shrewd and she suddenly stopped in mid-sentence and changed tack. 'It's a grand suit, alanna,' she said. 'And isn't that a grand coat you're wearin', sure enough? How's about if we did a kind o' swap, like? I'll give you the suit and two shillin' for that nice warm coat.'

Hester hesitated, but only for a moment. The coat was almost new and had cost a great deal more than two shillings but there was no doubt that she would feel far less out of place amongst these friendly but clearly working class people without it. She had seen a couple of notices in small dress shops saying that they wanted full-time or part-time staff, but had hesitated to enquire, feeling certain that her appearance would go against her. However, in the grey suit and without her smart felt hat, at least she would look as though she needed the job.

'Well? What d'you say, alanna? Is it a deal?'

Hester pretended to examine the material as though in doubt, then raised her eyes to the Irish woman's. 'Two shillings is too little,' she said briskly. 'But if you will give me five shillings . . .'

'Five shillin'! That's wharr I'd charge a customer for a coat like that, seein' as the folk round here aren't made o' money,' the woman observed. She sighed deeply. 'I'll give you three bob, and that's me final offer.'

'Four, and that's *my* final offer,' Hester said firmly. 'Why, you must know that this suit has been worn and worn, whereas my coat was only bought just before Christmas. So it's four bob or nothing. And what's more, I'll want to try this suit on before I agree to any bargain in case it's too small for me.'

'It'll fit you a treat, but if you're set on tryin' it out I'll hang me curting over the stall supports and make you a bit o' privacy,' the Irish woman said.

She had clearly accepted that she would have to pay four shillings for the coat. As she hung the curtain around one corner of the space behind the stall, she added curiously: 'What's a well-dressed gal like you doin' on the Scottie, anyhow? Fallen on hard times, have you?'

'You could say that; I lost my job,' Hester said briefly, struggling into the grey flannel suit. The skirt, which was pleated, fitted her as though it had been tailored to do so and the jacket, though a little short in the sleeve, looked both neat and respectable and was warmer than she had anticipated. 'I'm looking for some cheap lodgings as well as a new job; I don't suppose you know of any?'

As she spoke, Hester emerged from behind the curtain and the Irish woman gave a gap-toothed grin and held out two florins. 'It fits you a treat, just like I thought it would,' she said triumphantly. 'D'you mind sharin'?'

For a moment, Hester wondered what on earth she meant; was she suggesting that they should share the skirt and jacket? Then she realised that the older woman was referring to lodgings. 'I'd be happy to share if it meant that the rent would be cheaper,' she said honestly. 'Until I get work, I really have very little spare money.'

'There's a room-share in Stansfield Court off the Scottie,' the Irish woman said thoughtfully. 'It's cheap, that I *do* know since me niece, young Maggie O'Reilly, has lately taken a bed there. There's nowt provided, 'cept the bed and a blanket or two, but the gals manage all right and seem happy enough. Want to go round, see if they've a space?'

'Thank you ever so much,' Hester said fervently. 'I'll go round at once; who do I ask for?'

'Ask for Mr or Mrs Maskell, 'cos they's the owners, only they ain't always in at Number 10 – it's Number 10 where me niece lives – 'cos they owns Numbers 12 and 14 an' all, but no doubt you'll find 'em somewhere in the Court.'

'Thanks again. I don't suppose you know what your niece pays Mrs Maskell, do you?' Hester asked hopefully. 'Because until I get work, there's only your four bob between me and the workhouse!'

She had spoken half jokingly but the Irish woman took her up on it at once. 'If you're that hard up, why don't you sell some more of your clothes? There must be good stuff that you're prepared to part with. That skirt you were wearin' – the navy-blue – that's quality, that is.'

Hester laughed and patted the garment she held in one arm affectionately. 'I may well be reduced to selling my clothing unless I get work pretty soon,' she admitted. 'But I'm not thinking of doing so yet. How far away is Stansfield Court from here?'

An hour later, Hester was in possession of both a job and lodgings. She had run Mr Maskell to earth, finally, at Number 16. He was a small, pug-faced individual with red-rimmed, watery eyes and protruding teeth, half veiled by a straggly grey moustache. He also had a blunt, wide-nostrilled nose which jerked and quivered spasmodically as he spoke, reminding Hester of a white guinea-pig she had seen in the pet shop window.

He had been quite willing to show Hester the room and she had followed him obediently up three flights of dirty, narrow wooden stairs and on to an even narrower landing. 'Here we are, then!' he had said grandly, throwing open the nearest door. He looked into the room himself then peered rather anxiously at Hester. 'It ain't much,' he said, almost apologetically, 'but the gals manage well enough and it is cheap – you won't get no cheaper in the city centre, I can tell you. It's rare enough we have a vacancy but now and again someone gets a live-in job and leaves, which is why we've a bed goin' beggin', so to speak.'

Hester stepped into the room, bending her head as she did so, for it was an attic room with a low and sloping ceiling. The window was at knee level and there were four beds crammed in so tightly that she could not help wondering whether the occupants kicked each other every time they turned over. The beds were all on the right-hand side of the room, leaving a narrow corridor at their feet. Against the window was a wash-stand with the usual utensils upon it, and beside the wash-stand a tiny paraffin stove. Above each bed was a short wooden rail upon which were hung various garments. Hester made her way to the window and looked out. Rooftops met her gaze and, far below, the dirty paving stones of the court. It was not an inspiring view and she turned quickly back into the room to find that Mr Maskell had followed her and was standing so close that she knocked against him as she turned.

'Washin' facilities, and there's your cookin' stove,' Mr Maskell said grandly, indicating the paraffin stove and the wash-stand. 'Each gal has a box – sometimes more'n one – under her bed, for her personal things, like. The missus and meself don't interfere wi' our lodgers so long as there's no trouble, and the gals in this room is all good gals, which is more'n I can say for some of 'em,' he added darkly. 'So will you be takin' it, miss? It's half a crown, but seein' as you're norra local gal, we'll say two bob for starters, eh?'

Hester looked doubtfully around her. The floor was bare boards, the bedsteads iron, and the white-washed walls in sad need of re-painting, but it was clear that the girls kept the place as clean as they could, and anyway, it might only be for a few nights. At two bob, I can scarcely expect a palace, Hester told herself and took a deep, steadying breath. 'Yes, please, Mr Maskell, I'll be glad to take it,' she said formally. 'I'll bring my possessions around tomorrow morning, if that's all right with you.'

'That suits,' Mr Maskell said. His pink little piggy eyes surveyed her again from head to heel. 'The only thing is, miss, as I'll need a fortnight's rent in advance, 'cos you might take the room and light out, leavin' me to find a lodger all over again. Or you might find somewhere better . . . different, I mean, and not bother to come back at all.'

Hester began to lift the flap of her handbag to get at her purse, then hesitated. 'Certainly I'll pay you a fortnight in advance, Mr Maskell,' she said. 'But I shall need a receipt. Otherwise you might deny that I'd paid you anything, might you not?'

She half expected Mr Maskell to show indignation, if not fury, at her lack of trust but to her surprise he beamed at her, now looking like a happy guinea-pig, though she could not recall ever seeing a guinea-pig in Mr Madison's shop with a smile on its face. 'You're a sensible young woman, miss,' he said jovially. 'A real businesswoman, that's what you are! You come along o' me now and I'll write you out as nice a little receipt as you'll get anywhere.' He led the way down the stairs to an extremely untidy kitchen at the back of the house, sat down at a rickety deal table and wrote her out a receipt. 'What do they call you, miss?' he enquired. 'You'll need a name on the receipt and besides, though this is Liberty Hall, we like to know who our lodgers are!'

'My name is Hester Elliott,' Hester said. 'I wonder, Mr Maskell, if you know of anyone in this part of the city who needs a – a shop assistant or a clerical worker, or something of that nature? I've recently moved from Shaw Street and would like employment nearer at hand.'

'Well, I dunno,' Mr Maskell said doubtfully, handing her the written receipt and watching as she tucked it into her handbag. Hester felt sure that he had priced every garment she had on and was noting that the handbag was made of good, solid leather. 'What you wants to do, miss, is look for cards in shop winders. Round here, they don't go in much for them bureau places.'

'Thanks very much,' Hester said, rather gloomily, but she still left the Court with a spring in her step. At least she had a roof over her head now and one which she could afford. Even if she did not immediately find work, she would be able to feed herself for the next couple of weeks with the money she had saved from her salary.

Now, taking Mr Maskell's advice, she began to look into every shop window she passed, and presently she reached a large dress shop displaying cheap-looking gowns in its window, in one corner of which was a card offering full-time work to a suitable applicant. She went into the shop to enquire about the job and the woman behind the counter, dark-haired, dark-eyed and weasel-featured, gave her what amounted to an arithmetic examination before admitting, almost grudgingly, that she seemed suitable and might start work the following day, for what Hester considered the tiny wage of twelve shillings a week. 'But this ain't to say the job's permanent, 'cos you'll be on trial for the first three months, which means I takes money off you if you make mistakes or lose me customers,' the woman said quickly, when she saw how relieved Hester was to have been offered the position. 'I'm Miss Deakin and I'm the proprietor of this shop, so naturally I want things done right and won't tolerate laziness or anything which puts me customers out of temper, is that understood?'

Hester said that it was and although she thought the older woman was being not only mean but also unfair to dock her wages she agreed unhesitatingly to the conditions laid down. After all, she had left her name with Miss Strong's bureau and intended to try again for work in one of the big stores, if a position should crop up, but in the meantime at least she would be able to pay for her lodgings and feed herself on her meagre wage from the dress shop. And I don't intend to make any mistakes or lose any customers, she told herself as she stepped into the street once more. Now if only I can contact Dick and explain what has been happening to me, and if I can get in touch with Lonnie, I shall be on the right road.

The next morning, when she awoke, Hester immediately remembered that today her life would change once again. As she washed and dressed she thought that by now she should be well and truly accustomed to change, because ever since her father's death her life had consisted of nothing else. But now it was difficult to think about her life in India, save with a sort of reminiscent wistfulness, because her life in England had demanded so much more of her. She had never shirked independence, had expected it, but had not realised that she would be quite so totally flung on her own resources. Her father had talked vaguely of her getting a job of some sort but had clearly expected that it would be of short duration since, naturally, she would soon be married. But I believe he'd be proud of me if he could see me now, Hester thought, picking up her suitcases in either hand and heading for the stairs which led down into the foyer. She was wearing the thinner coat which she had brought with her from India and was glad of her thick woollen muffler and sturdy woollen gloves, for though it was no longer snowing there was a keen wind and the gutters were laden with slush, making walking an unpleasant business. She wondered whether she should hail a taxi cab, for it was some way to Scotland Road and she had to deliver her cases and then reach the dress shop by nine o'clock. Taxi cabs were bound to be expensive, however, so she had best catch a tram.

By the time she reached Stansfield Court, Hester's arms were aching and she viewed the prospect of climbing three flights of stairs with considerable dread. As she entered the front door, however, she had a piece of luck. A hefty young man was emerging from the kitchen, calling something over his shoulder as he did so, and as soon as he saw Hester and her two suitcases he came forward with a broad smile and one hand held out. He had short, bristly fair hair, twinkling blue eyes and a rather upturned nose and he reminded Hester of someone, though she could not say of whom. 'You'll be Miss Elliott, I've no doubt,' he said cheerily. 'Lemme take them cases off of you – you're in the attic room wi' Flossie, Rose and Trixie, ain't you?'

'Thank you very much; I don't know who the other

girls are, but I am in the attic,' Hester said gratefully. 'I've got myself a job in a dress shop on the Scotland Road and I have to be there by nine, so I'd be most grateful . . .'

She had been following him up the stairs but at her words he stopped short, put down the cases and turned towards her. 'Orf you goes, then. I'll shove these here cases under your bed where no one can't see 'em – not that anyone comes here with robbing in mind, 'cos they know we ain't none of us exactly rich!'

'Thank you,' Hester said again. 'It's awfully good of you, I really am grateful. The lady I'm working for wouldn't be best pleased if I were even a second late, let alone a few minutes. Do – do you lodge here as well, then? And please tell me your name.'

'I ain't a lodger exactly, or p'raps I am in a way,' the young man said cheerfully. 'I'm Roy Maskell; me mam's your landlady and we live at Number 16 but, o' course, I'm always in and out, so you'll be seein' a good bit o' me.'

'Well, thanks again, Mr Maskell,' Hester said over her shoulder, as she headed, once more, for the front door.

Lonnie awoke. Half forgetting her change of circumstance, she sat up on one elbow and looked wildly about her. A bare and unwelcoming room met her gaze. Beside her own small bed, there were five others, each one containing the curled up body of a girl of about her own age. Beneath her breath, Lonnie recited their names and descriptions: Amelia, with the curly red hair and freckles; Marion, with the long dark pig-tail which reached well below her waist; Barbara, who wore hideous little metal-framed spectacles and cried herself to sleep each night; Shirley, who was silent and sulky, a rebel against the nuns and their teachings; and Abigail, Lonnie's favourite, who took life as it came and seldom stopped smiling, no matter how the nuns scolded. These were her companions in misfortune and misfortune it most definitely was, though Lonnie was determined to escape just as soon as the opportunity arose.

However, it was freezing cold in the little room. Jack Frost had wielded his brush on the narrow windows so that it was impossible to see out and when Lonnie snuggled down the bed again and pulled the blanket up round her ears, she realised that her breath had condensed on the blanket and was now ice.

She had raged against her aunt's wickedness in dismissing Hester, despite the older woman's insistence that it had been Hester's wish to leave her employ. 'You are a wicked, evil, lying old harlot,' she had raged, fishing the word out from some dim recollection of a remark made by her father concerning the servants of the temple. 'You never liked Hester and you hate me and this way you think you can make both of us unhappy. But you're wrong, you horrid old tyrant. When my daddy hears what you've done, he'll turn *you* out on the street! I shall write to him this very day and tell him how wicked you are.'

She knew her aunt had been furious by the tightening of those thin lips and the slow rise of pink colour which had blotched her sagging old cheeks, but she had not realised the lengths to which the older woman would go. Lonnie had written the letter, sealed it in an envelope and had been crossing the hall on her way to post it when Miss Hetherington-Smith had pounced upon her. '*I'll* take that,' she had said, wrenching the envelope from Lonnie's grasp with such violence that it tore. 'Not that it matters what you say, since your father cannot receive any correspondence until he returns to India in three months' time. In the meantime, Leonora, you are going to go to school. You are a rude, ungrateful, ill-disciplined child and I won't have you turning my house upside down and behaving so badly that half my staff – including your governess – are threatening to leave my employ.'

Lonnie had been almost speechless at this twisting of the facts but even as she began to rant at her aunt once more, a terrible helplessness seized her. Children never win a battle against a grown-up. Her father, who would have been on her side, was out of reach and Hester had gone, she had no idea where. Stifling a sob, she had turned and rushed up the stairs, flinging her hat, coat and scarf down on the schoolroom floor.

She had spent the rest of the day fruitlessly plotting to contact her father and to find Hester but when she awoke the following morning, her aunt had come up to her bedroom and had told her that the arrangements had been made. A convent school on the outskirts of the city, a very respectable place indeed, whose pupils were mainly children of parents serving their country abroad, had agreed to Lonnie' starting there at the beginning of term. Uniform and a great many other things would be provided by the nuns, though Miss Hetherington-Smith told her niece repressively that, naturally, she would pay for all these things as well as for her niece's education.

'I shall have a little more money available, since

Miss Elliott is planning to return to India and naturally I don't intend to replace her with another governess,' she had said. 'No doubt, as soon as she is settled, she will write to you, giving you her new address so that you may keep in touch. At the moment she will be living temporarily in some hotel or other. You can scarcely write to her there.'

Now, trying to will herself into warmth once more, Lonnie thought desperately that she would have run away from the school had she had anywhere to run to. Shaw Street was clearly out, though she assumed she would be returning there for the Easter holiday. Her aunt had grudgingly promised her as much when Lonnie had threatened to make a terrible scene if they would not allow her to take Kitty to school with her. 'Mollie will look after your cat; Cook says the creature is already useful and keeps the basement clear of mice,' she had told her niece. 'You will be able to see for yourself, when you come home for Easter, that everything I do is for your own good. Now hurry up and get your coat and hat; Allsop is waiting in the Bentley.'

Remembering the cosy kitchen in Shaw Street made Lonnie's hands and feet feel colder than ever and she was just contemplating fetching her brown school jumper and pulling it on over her white cotton nightdress when a tremendous clangour broke out. Immediately, feet thumped to the ground and with many a groan and grumble her companions proceeded to get out of their beds. Lonnie followed suit – just in time. The tall, brown-painted door opened and a monitor's head appeared. 'Everyone out of bed? Well done,' the older girl said briskly. 'Get yourselves washed and dressed and be downstairs in twenty minutes.' She looked almost kindly at

Lonnie. 'You're new, so you'll be the last to get washed. Better pop back into bed until it's your turn, 'cos it's freezing sharp outside.'

The monitor withdrew and five of the girls immediately returned to their beds, grumbling as they did so that there should be some other washing arrangements than those provided by the nuns. 'Other schools have proper washrooms and hot water,' Shirley said. It was her turn to wash first which meant, on such a day, breaking the ice in the blue and white enamel jug and gingerly dipping her sponge into the ice-cold water. 'Oh, how I wish my mother knew what sort of place this was! She would never have made me come here!' She rubbed her hands and face briskly dry on a rough towel and padded back to her bed, saying as she did so: 'Next one!'

Already, after only five days, Lonnie knew the drill. She was third in line for washing and heard Abigail, who was second, shouting at Shirley for not emptying her slops. Shirley, muttering grudgingly, returned to the wash-stand and emptied the small amount of water she had used into the slop bucket. There were two buckets, one for washing water and the other for the contents of the girls' chamber pots, which lived beneath each bed. One was supposed to swill out the pot with one's washing water, but because it was so cold the girls tried hard not to use them but to go down to the cloakroom on the ground floor.

'Next!'

Lonnie jumped out of bed and hurried over to the wash-stand. 'I don't believe you washed at all, and I know you didn't clean your teeth,' she said accusingly as Abigail passed her. 'Oh, Abby, isn't this the most hateful place in the world? I've never been so cold before in my life, not even when Hester and I first arrived from India.'

'Oh, damn! I quite forgot my teeth; I'll do them when you do yours then I won't spit in your washing water before you've used it,' Abigail said. 'Oh, how we used to grumble about the heat on the plains when it was time to go to the hills . . . well, when I get back to India, I won't ever grumble again.'

Abigail, Shirley, Marion and Lonnie had all spent their formative years in India, though they had never met there, since they came from such disparate locations as Peshawar, Benares, New Delhi and Bombay.

'What's this place like in the summer? Are we allowed any more freedom when the weather's fine?' Lonnie asked, beginning to clean her teeth and motioning to her friend to do likewise. 'It won't be as cold as it is now, that's one comfort.' Lowering her voice, she added: 'Not that I mean to be here when summer comes – no, indeed! I'd like to run away except that I've nowhere to run to, but my father returns from his world cruise in April and he will certainly take me away from this horrid place.'

'Most of us say that, to start with,' Abigail remarked. 'The trouble is, Lonnie, if you've no relatives to take you in and your father and mother are not rich, then this school is just about all they can manage. I hate it here, of course I do, but I know it's all my parents can afford, and I know the younger children will have to come here as well one day, so I try to behave myself and do more or less as I'm told. Otherwise, when the little ones come, the nuns will be horrible to them because of me; do you understand?'

'Yes, in a way,' Lonnie said. 'But I'm an only child

and I intend to be really difficult and awkward, see if I'm not! And my father *is* rich. I'm sure he'd hire a house for me and servants and things and let me go to a day school, rather than stay on in this awful place. Next!'

Lonnie and Abigail returned to their beds and began hastily dressing, for the nuns bore down heavily upon lateness or disobedience. Each nun carried a short strap at her waist which she would ply vigorously upon any wrong-doer and though Lonnie intended to be as disruptive as possible, she had already discovered that strapping was exceedingly painful and best avoided.

Presently, descending the stairs with her dormitory companions, she saw Sister Martha standing in the hallway, gently swinging the strap and eyeing the girls' woollen-stockinged legs covetously. She was clearly longing to send her strap whistling across someone's calves but thus far had been denied the opportunity of so doing by the exemplary conduct of her pupils. Lonnie considered climbing aboard the banister and shooting downstairs at top speed, knocking the nun over like a nine-pin as she reached the hall. It would be enormous fun and would mark her out as a girl not to be trifled with, a girl determined to court not merely trouble, but also expulsion. However, there was the strap to be considered . . . Sighing, Lonnie decided to leave disruption until after breakfast, since her stomach was already growling with hunger and anyway she had an uncanny feeling that the nuns would not willingly expel any pupil. That she would be punished severely she had no doubt, but like the other girls she could not possibly be expelled because her relatives were far away. Already, in five short days, she had heard of the punishment cupboard, a dark and dreadful basement prison where the truly bad were locked in total, spidery darkness for as long as eight hours. Older girls swore that, in times past, disobedient and difficult pupils had been incarcerated for longer, not even being allowed out to seek their beds but forced to spend the night sitting miserably on the dank earth floor, praying for release.

Lonnie tripped off the stair and drew level with the nun. Sister Martha's expression was almost friendly and Lonnie realised why when the strap whistled threw the air and caught her across the calves. The nun gave her a brief, mad smile, saying as she did so: 'Good morning, Sister Martha! Where are your manners, Leonora?'

Lonnie gasped, for the cut had been a painful one, and opened her mouth to tell the nun what she thought of her, but to her own astonishment heard her voice, very small and prim, saying: 'Good morning, Sister Martha!'

As they entered the dining room and took their places at the long wooden tables, upon which bowls of porridge already steamed, a subdued chatter broke out. It was forbidden to talk on the stairs and corridors or in the classrooms – except when addressing or being addressed by a teacher, of course – but quiet conversation in the dining room was permitted. Wedged on a bench between Abigail and Shirley, Lonnie accepted a mug of weak tea from a dining room monitor and then turned to hiss in Abigail's ear that her leg was still smarting and that she hated Sister Martha.

'We all do,' Abigail said frankly. 'She's the worst of the lot, if you ask me, but you'll feel her strap over and over, Lonnie, if you don't fall in line. After all, it doesn't hurt you to say good morning, does it?'

'No – oh, no-o, but I forgot,' Lonnie explained. 'Why did she have to hit me, though? She knows I'm new.'

On her other side, Shirley gave a derisive snort. 'She was longing to hit someone, that's why,' she informed Lonnie. 'She always stands there, at the foot of the stairs, hoping to be able to punish someone for something. The best way to treat them is to obey all the rules on the surface whilst they're watching, and undermine them in any way you can whilst they're not.'

Lonnie thought this over. 'Yes, I know what you mean,' she conceded at last. 'I'll try to do as you say, Shirl, but they make me so angry! Oh, and isn't the food *dull*? Don't we ever have eggs and bacon for breakfast? Or something other than stew for lunch?'

'No, breakfast is always porridge, bread and margarine and weak tea,' Abigail admitted. 'But it isn't always stew for luncheon and sometimes we have quite nice high teas. If only they weren't so strict – and so fond of using the strap – I suppose life here would be bearable, but as it is, every girl in the school feels she's serving time, as though this were a gaol.'

'Which it is,' Shirley chimed in. 'Tell you what, girls, we'll form a secret escape committee and see if we can break out some time!' She turned to Lonnie. 'We go out into the great big world twice a week. They walk us around the streets in a crocodile as far as Prince's Park where we are allowed to play hop-scotch or other games which they consider ladylike. Apart from that we never leave the school and in my opinion it's not right. If only the parents knew . . .'

'Why don't you write and tell them?' Lonnie said bluntly, finishing her porridge and reaching for the bread and margarine. 'We're allowed to write letters on Sunday afternoons, Sister Bernardette told me so when I first arrived. She's my favourite, Sister Bernardette, she's really nice.'

'Oh, we can write letters all right,' Abigail said. 'But the nuns read them and if you say anything against the school, Mother Superior will send for you and tear your letter up. Then she will dictate another letter and that is the one your parents see.'

Lonnie ground her teeth. She said nothing more but concentrated on eating her breakfast, whilst inside her mind she was already plotting against the school and its regime.

A week after his father's admission to hospital, Dick came home to find his mother in a state of great perturbation. Her hair was on end, there was no meal on the table and various objects were strewn about the room.

'Mam! What on earth's happened?' Dick said, his heart sinking into his boots. When he had left the hospital the previous evening, his father had seemed better, actually sitting up in bed and talking almost brightly of how he would soon be home. Surely he had not had a relapse? Oh God, let me dad be all right, let Mam just be flapping about some small thing, Dick prayed.

Mrs Bailey must have guessed what he would think for she said quickly: 'It's all right, chuck, don't get to worriting, but the consultant had a word wi' me when I popped in this afternoon to take your dad a bottle of milk stout. Sister said to build his strength up in any way I could . . . but that's not the point. The consultant telled me that your da' needs fresh air and quiet, and you know, our Dick, Elmore Street ain't exactly a backwater. There's a deal o' traffic comes past our house now, going between Heyworth Street and Landseer Road . . . and then there's the tannery – when the wind's in the right direction, the fumes from that place are enough to turn you sick.'

'So what's the plan?' Dick asked bluntly. 'You know we promised our dad we wouldn't let them send him to the sanatorium, no matter what.'

'Ah, but that's the point,' his mother explained. 'The consultant talked a good deal o' sense to your da'. He says the air's cleaner over the water provided you steer clear o' the docks an' that. He says there's a sannytorium on the Wirral which we could reach each day, easy as easy, by bus or even on foot. It makes sense because you and Ted both work over there and rents ain't so high and believe it or not, our Dick, he's talked your dad round. So what do you say?'

'Oh, but wharrabout Ben's job and the work you do, Mam? Can we afford to manage wi'out what you and Ben bring in?'

Mrs Bailey crossed the kitchen, took Dick's hands in hers and gazed straight into his eyes. 'Could we manage wi'out your dad's pension . . . wi'out your dad?' she asked bluntly. 'Because according to the doctor, that's what we'll have to face within a few weeks if we don't up sticks. I talked to Ben when he came back from school earlier an' he's agreeable. There's a lot to be arranged – this house for instance – but I reckon if all goes well we can find ourselves a little place to rent across the water and be out of here in a week to ten days.'

Dick gaped at her. He knew his parents had lived in Elmore Street ever since their marriage, thirty years earlier, guessed what a wrench it would be for his mother to tear up her roots. But he had never doubted the depth of the love between his parents and knew that his mother would give everything she possessed to have his father fit once more.

'What about the house?' he asked. 'I'm sure the landlord could let it easily, 'cos you've always kept it nice, Mam, but . . .'

'We ain't lettin' it go to no one through the landlord, 'cos if we did that we might never gerrit back,' his mother explained. 'I'm goin' to sub-let it to Mrs Kinnerton's daughter Ethel.' She glanced round the kitchen furtively, as though she expected to find listeners everywhere, then lowered her voice. 'It – it may not be for all that long, son. The – the consultant says fresh air can't cure the damage done, it – it just means we'll have your dad for a bit longer, and that's good enough for me. What d'you say, Dick? The others are all with me, but you're the main wage earner, so it's up to you.'

'We'll go as soon as we've got somewhere suitable,' Dick said at once. 'I'll ask around at work, but there's usually places to rent on the outskirts of the city.' He had not yet removed his outer clothing but now he took off muffler, jacket and cap and hung them on the kitchen door before turning back to his mother. 'As soon as I've had me tea, Mam, I'll nip round to Shaw Street. I've been meaning to go ever since I let Miss Hester down because I were meant to meet her the day Dad were taken bad. I'm surprised she hasn't come calling, but I dare say she's been busy, same as I have. I'll let her know our new address when I know it meself, but in the meantime, wherever we're living, the pair of us can always meet up for a few hours of an evening.'

'I thought you didn't want to go round to the house in case you made trouble for the gal,' Mrs Bailey remarked, going to the pantry and fetching a loaf of bread and a large piece of cheese. She thumped them down on the table and returned to the pantry for a slab of margarine and a jar of pickled onions. 'There you go, la'. Sorry it ain't a proper cooked meal, but I want to get off to the hospital as soon as Ted comes in. Phyllis is in bed and Ben's round at the Madisons', explaining about the move, so you'll have to make do wi' bread and cheese tonight.'

'Bread and cheese is fine,' Dick said, taking a seat at the table. 'As for not wanting to visit the house, what choice have I got, Mam? But I won't ask for Hester straight out, I'll . . . no, I've a better idea. There's a devilish high wall at the foot of their garden, and I reckon I could gerrover it if I took a couple o' sturdy boxes to stand on. That way, I can speak to the servants wi'out the old gal hearin' what's up.'

Mrs Bailey came and sat down opposite her son. 'You go to the front door, like a Christian,' she said instantly. 'You've nowt to be ashamed of, young Dick, but if you goes sneakin' round the back everyone will think you're up to no good. Why, if a scuffer were to catch you . . .'

Dick, with a mouthful of bread and cheese and pickle, laughed and nearly choked himself. His mother rushed to give him a cup of tea and presently, mopping his streaming eyes, Dick told her that she was right. It was far more sensible to go to the front door and ask to see Hester. If she were not available, he would produce a letter from his pocket and give it to the butler or maid who answered the door, requesting that it be delivered as a matter of urgency.

His mother applauded his decision, but reminded him to come straight to the hospital when he had finished his business in Shaw Street. 'Your dad will want to hear from your own lips that you'll be just as happy in Birkenhead as in Liverpool,' she told him. 'The most important thing, the consultant said, is to keep your dad calm and happy. Ah, here comes Ted. I hear his step on the cobbles!'

Dick stood on the pavement in Shaw Street, staring up at the house where Hester and Lonnie lived. It was a large and imposing building and somehow unwelcoming, as though it divined that its mistress would turn him away from the door at once if she knew his errand. Dick looked up at the windows which must, he supposed, be bedrooms but could see no sign of life. He wondered if it were possible that Hester and the child were downstairs, for both the long windows facing the road were well lit, though the glow of the lights came only dimly through thick red curtains.

Heartened by the thought that, if they were downstairs, either Hester or Lonnie might come to the door to see who was calling, Dick stepped forward and reached for the bell. He pressed it firmly, then snatched his hand away as he heard its shrilling sounding horribly loud in the evening hush. In his pocket, the letter crackled when he moved and he found himself almost hoping that whoever answered the door would refuse him admittance but would accept the letter and promise to see it delivered. That way, he would not have to beard the dragon Hetherington-Smith in her den. Not that he expected to have to do so, but he had just seen the curtains to the right of the front door twitch, had even glimpsed a long, pale face peering out at him for a moment before the curtains were closed once more. If it had been Miss Hetherington-Smith he had seen, he supposed, dismally, that it was quite possible that she would demand to know his business. If he entered the house, she was within her rights to question him, for Hester and Lonnie were in her charge whilst they lived under her roof.

Dick did not have to wonder for long, however, for the door opened, revealing an elderly, white-haired man, his brows raised in question.

Dick cleared his throat. 'I wonder if Miss Elliott is available?' he said hesitantly. 'She has been very good to my mother, but since my father's illness we've not seen her. Usually they meet in – in the park, but of late . . .' Since the man made no move to ask him into the house, Dick began to fumble in his pocket for the letter. 'If – if she isn't available, my mother sent a letter . . . If you would be kind enough to see that she gets it . . .'

The elderly man cast a quick, furtive glance all around him, then stepped out of the house, pulling the big, heavy front door half closed behind him. 'Miss doesn't live here any more,' he said, in a low, breathy tone. 'She's been gone more than a week and no one hasn't said where, except Miss Hetherington-Smith, who says she's gone back to India. But if you ask me . . .'

The old man had been holding the door handle as he spoke and suddenly it was wrenched from his hand, almost tipping him over backwards. Dick saw a tall, thin woman, with a mean mouth, standing in the hallway. The butler straightened up and turned towards her, saying with what dignity he could muster: 'I'm very sorry, madam, but I didn't see fit to ask the young gentleman inside and if I'd stood in the hall with the door open, I'd have chilled the whole house in minutes. Were you wanting something, madam?'

'Yes, I want to know this young man's business,' Miss Hetherington-Smith said, in an aggressive, grating voice. 'If he's come sniffing around after that governess, the one who left us in the lurch by going off home back to India, then he can take himself off smartly. And what was that about a letter?' She held out an imperious hand, 'I'll take that, if you please.'

So domineering was her tone and so commanding her attitude that Dick was glad he had not succeeded in removing the envelope from his jacket pocket. Pulling himself together, for he had been considerably startled by the old woman's jack-in-the-box appearance, Dick looked her straight in the eye, then raised his brows. 'Of what use would it be to give you the letter if Miss Elliott is no longer living under your protection?' he asked slowly. 'And if, as you say, she has returned to India, she will no doubt get in touch with my mother as soon as she is able to do so. Is Miss Lonnie available? I should like to have a word with her.'

'If you mean Miss Leonora Hetherington-Smith, she is not here either,' the woman said. 'She has returned to India with her governess.' She raised thin, pencilled eyebrows. 'I am surprised that your mother did not know that, since she must have noticed their absence in the park. Surely these nannies and nursemaids chatter amongst themselves.'

'Then I'll say good evening to you,' Dick said, turning away from the doorstep. Miss Hetherington-Smith started to speak, her voice rising angrily, but then appeared to realise that he did not intend to bandy words with her and slammed the door in mid-sentence.

Dick walked slowly back along Shaw Street, his heart sore. Whatever had happened to send Hester flying back to India, he was sure it had something to do with the mean-spirited and despotic woman he had just left. Indeed, now that he began to think about it, he wondered if Miss Hetherington-Smith had been speaking the truth. To be sure, the butler had told him Hester no longer lived in Shaw Street, but thinking back carefully, he remembered the butler's very words: *She's been gone more than a week and no one hasn't said where, except Miss Hetherington-Smith, who says she's gone back to India. But if you ask me . . .*

Dick's steps slowed even more. To his way of thinking, the butler had no more belief in his mistress's words than did Dick. Certainly, Hester was no longer living in the house, but it seemed doubtful that she had gone back to India. Dick knew all too well what a complicated business it was to book a passage on one of the great liners leaving the port, particularly if you did not have much money, and though Hester had seemed comfortably off compared with the Baileys, he did not think she would have been able to raise such a large sum at short notice. He was just wondering if Hester had borrowed the money from Miss Hetherington-Smith when he heard the clack-clack of shoes on the pavement behind him and someone seized his arm. For a wild, joyous moment, he thought that it was Hester, then realised it was a little servant girl in a thin print dress with a plaid shawl wrapped around her shoulders. He stopped in his tracks and looked down at her enquiringly. 'Hello! Where have you sprung from?'

'Mr Fletcher – he's the butler at the Hetherington-Smith place – axed me to catch you up and explain a thing or two,' the girl said breathlessly. 'I'm Mollie Hardwick what works in the house.'

'I'm Dick Bailey. I don't suppose Miss Hester talked about me much, but I'm anxious about her. We'd arranged to meet again on the Thursday after New Year but that were the day my father were took bad in hospital and in all the fuss and fright I never got to the meeting place. So I'm desperate to gerrin touch with her and explain, like.'

'We guessed at something of that sort, 'cos Miss Hester seemed so happy all of a sudden. She were me pal – straight up, she was. Why, she stopped the old crow from giving me the sack, and then got sacked herself. I were that fond of Lonnie, too. Mr Fletcher says as how madam telled you that Lonnie had gone back to India wi' Miss Hester, but I knows it ain't true. I dunno about Miss Hester – she were sacked on New Year's Eve – but I do know that young Lonnie is still somewhere in Liverpool. You see, I'm friendly wi' Mr Allsop, the chauffeur, and he telled me Miss Lonnie had gone to some convent school or other, out Smithdown Road way.'

'Thank you, Mollie,' Dick said fervently. 'D'you think young Lonnie will know where Miss Hester has gone? Well, I'm sure she will, because those two girls were like sisters. Hester would tell Lonnie as soon as she had an address, though if she really has gone to India . . .'

'We talked it over in the kitchens and we don't see as how she could have gone to India,' Mollie interpolated. 'The old baggage paid her up to date, that's true, but she didn't give her a penny extra. A passage to India costs, and besides, you have to know sailing times and where to go to book your cabin and so on. No, she might go as soon as she's earned the money for her fare, but we don't reckon she's gone yet.'

'Has she got a job then?' Dick said eagerly. 'D'you know where she's working? I'm over at Cammell Laird's so I won't get much opportunity for scouring the city in search of her, but if I knew where she was working . . .'

'Madam telled her not to come near nor by the house or she'd set the scuffers on her, tell 'em she thieved money afore she left,' Mollie said sadly. 'That old baggage deserves to be thrown into a scorpion pit, as Miss Lonnie would say. Though I dare say,' she added reflectively, 'that Miss H's tongue's a good deal sharper than a scorpion's tail. She'd probably kill 'em all off before they could get so much as one sting into her skinny old body.'

Dick laughed ruefully. 'Look, Mollie, I'm going to give you a letter which I'd like you to deliver to Miss Hester if you ever come across her. The truth is, my whole family's moving away from the city over to Birkenhead. My dad's very ill and has to go into a sanatorium, so we're upping sticks and taking a place across the water, to be nearer him. That means that if Miss Hester tries to find us in Elmore Street, she'll not do so.'

'Tell you what, the old crow don't open my letters

– not yet she don't, at any rate. You knows my name and address, so when you're settled in Birkenhead, mebbe you could drop me a line, telling me your new address? I know the old crow telled Miss Hester she weren't ever to visit in Shaw Street but it's my belief she'll get in touch with us as soon as she can safely do so. We're her only link wi' Miss Lonnie, after all.'

'Yes, and I'll leave a forwarding address with the new tenants of our house in Elmore Street,' Dick said, much struck by the good sense of this idea. He seized Mollie's hand and wrung it, then patted her shoulder and turned her in the direction of Number 127 once more. 'Off with you, before you turn into an icicle,' he said cheerfully. 'Many thanks, Mollie Hardwick; you're a wonderful girl.'

Chapter Seven

It was Monday morning and Hester was hurrying along to the shop, for on a Monday Miss Deakin expected her junior assistant to arrive an hour early. The rest of the week, the two of them and an older girl, Betsy Fleming, worked from nine o'clock until six, except for Fridays and Saturdays, when they were liable to be on the go from the moment the shop opened until ten or eleven o'clock at night, when it closed, and this meant that cleaning down was usually left until after the weekend. The lighting in the shop was not good enough to reveal to tired eyes all the fingermarks on the polished wooden counter, or the scuff marks and boot dirt all over the polished wood-block floor.

So every Monday morning – and there had been three of them – Hester arrived whilst it was still dark, switched on the lights and began the lengthy task of cleaning down. Since this included both the inside and the outside of the large windows it took her until ten o'clock at least, and she worked alone since Miss Deakin did not deign to enter the premises until the church clock had chimed ten. On reflection, she decided she probably preferred it to the manageress's acerbic presence.

On this particular Monday, Hester was feeling rather down. On Saturday it had rained from dawn to dusk and few customers had entered the premises, so she had asked Miss Deakin, humbly, if she might go at eight, as she needed to contact a friend who worked on Heyworth Street. Miss Deakin had cut a shilling off her wages, but she had actually dismissed her at seven o'clock, saying crossly that she supposed she and Betsy could manage since there were so few people about.

Hester had gone first to Elmore Street and had been totally dismayed to find the little house occupied by strangers. A sulky, slatternly girl of fourteen or fifteen had answered the door, but when Hester had enquired for the Baileys had not been helpful. 'They've flitted,' she had said briefly. 'Gone over the water – I dunno where.' And with that she had closed the door – almost slammed it in fact – in Hester's face.

Hester had knocked again, to ask whether Mr Bailey was still in hospital or whether something bad had happened to the family, but despite both knocking and calling the door had not been opened again and presently Hester gave up and returned miserably to Heyworth Street, knowing that Mr Madison, like most shopkeepers, worked late on a Saturday night.

She had had a little more luck here since Mr Madison told her, regretfully, that his excellent young helper had moved across the water to Birkenhead. 'I dare say you knew that the lad's dad were took bad,' he informed her, whilst busily cleaning out cages and spreading fresh sawdust. 'It seems one of them there doctors up at the hospital said as how Mr Bailey would stand a better chance of regaining his health if he moved away from the city. Clean air and fresh country food would do him a power o' good, the doctor said. But the old feller wouldn't go 'cos he said he'd sooner die with his family around him than live miles away where he couldn't see them every day. So o' course the Baileys upped sticks and moved across the water and the old feller went into the sanatorium like what the doctor wanted.'

'You don't know which sanatorium?' Hester asked hopefully. 'I – I don't want to lose touch with Ben and the rest of his family; they've been good friends to me. The trouble is, I'm not living in Shaw Street any more. Lonnie's going to school, I believe, so she doesn't need a governess and that means that if the Baileys try to contact me there, they will be out of luck.'

Mr Madison looked up from his cage-cleaning and raised a gingery eyebrow. 'Ben said as how the old woman didn't have no time for her niece – or for you either, for that matter – so I suppose you didn't leave of your own accord, like?' he said shrewdly. 'And you'll be wanting to gerrin touch with the Bailey family 'cos you know they can't gerrin touch with you, now you've left Shaw Street, is that right?'

'That's it, Mr Madison,' Hester said gratefully. 'So if you see young Ben could you tell him I'm working on the Scotland Road, in a shop called Paris Modes, owned by a Miss Deakin. I'm there till six most evenings, but on Friday and Saturday we shut when the customers stop coming, which can be very late.'

Mr Madison had whistled under his breath. 'Some of these dress shop women treat their staff like slave labour,' he had observed. 'I'll bet she takes money off you at the slightest excuse. But never mind, gal, you're bound to get something better soon; you'd add class to any establishment, that's what I say.'

So now, Hester wielded her cloth, soaked in vinegar and water, on the inside of one of the large windows and told herself that she really must make time to call back at the employment bureau and see whether anything better had turned up. The trouble was, Miss Deakin worked her so hard and kept her so late that all she wanted to do when she did reach her shared room was to fall into bed and sleep till morning. In fact, when she was free, on her afternoon off, she usually went straight to Paddy's market to sell some item of clothing which she felt she could do without, in order to give her a little extra money for food.

The girls with whom she shared her room were, unfortunately, a constantly changing group since the moment one of them got a decent job she moved to more salubrious and spacious accommodation. The attic room at Number 10 Stansfield Court was the only room in any of the Maskell houses to contain four beds and was generally seen as a refuge for the desperate. As soon as a girl could afford better, she would take a room-share in one of the other houses and settle down there until she either married or could afford even better accommodation.

Hester, still stunned by her staggering change of circumstances, did not really attempt to become friendly with the girls in her room. For one thing they all seemed to know one another already, and when Hester arrived home she was far too tired after her long and exhausting day to go down to the shared kitchen, where she could have cooked herself a proper meal. Instead, she toasted bread and heated beans over the small paraffin stove in their room, ate without much enthusiasm, and then got straight into bed. When the other girls came up, chattering and laughing, she simply shrank further under the covers and longed for the lamp to be turned off so that she might sleep.

Another reason for a slight coolness between Hester and the other girls was an incident which had happened during the first week in her new abode. Beneath her bed were the suitcases which contained all her possessions. In one was the light and summery clothing she had brought with her from India, together with such items as soap, toothpaste, her face flannel and a large – and expensive – sponge. The second held her winter clothes, and it was these that Hester was gradually having to sell to the cheery Irish woman in Paddy's market. She told herself she might have managed had she been more domesticated; as it was, she usually treated herself to a proper cooked meal every other day, in one of the many dining rooms and cafés which abounded on the Scotland Road.

That first week it had not occurred to her to check the items in the suitcase, so when she decided she must sell her best navy-blue wool skirt and the matching bolero jacket with its shiny pearl buttons, she had been amazed and furious to find that the garments had disappeared. Urgent enquiries had brought bold stares and some unsympathetic sniggers from all the girls except Bridget O'Hara, who waited until the two of them were alone before saying, in her thick Irish brogue, that she knew which one of the girls had prigged the clothing.

'Without a doubt 'twas that Annabel, the girl wit' the spots and greasy hair, who left to take a live-in job in Southport,' she told Hester. 'The other girls all know it were her, so they do, but they don't want no trouble and they ain't above snitching odds and ends themselves, if they t'ink no one will notice. Don't your cases lock?'

'Yes, they do,' Hester had said grimly. 'It didn't occur to me to lock them, to tell you the truth, but in future I'll make sure they're locked all the time, even when I'm at home.'

Bridget nodded. She was a small, plump girl of sixteen with bristly black hair, round dark eyes and a fresh complexion which made Hester assume her to be a country girl, though it later transpired that Bridget was a product of the city of Dublin, over the water in Ireland. Though Hester did not know her very well she thought her the pleasantest of her room mates. Bridget worked as a cleaner in a gent's outfitters in the mornings and she also cleaned in a fruiterer's shop in the afternoons. Her combined wages probably came to no more than Hester's, yet she managed what money she had a good deal better than the older girl. When Hester remarked on it, Bridget said that she came from a poor family and had always had to scrape a living and to make every penny do the work of two. 'My mammy and daddy didn't want me to leave home and come over the water, but sure and Liverpool has plenty of jobs if you're prepared to work hard. In Dublin, though, there's ten girls queuing up for every post and the money's real poor,' she explained. 'You think the wage you get is pretty small, but I send three shillin' home to me mammy every week and still manage to survive, so I do. But you're used to something better, Hester, so you don't know the tricks of makin' money go round.'

'The trouble is, I don't have the time to shop carefully, and I was never taught to cook,' Hester said. 'At least you're able to take a good look at the shops in the interval between finishing at the outfitter's and starting at the fruiterer's. Miss

Deakin keeps me at it until pretty well all the shops are closed.'

'You should go to the markets,' Bridget told her. 'There's stalls along Great Homer Street what stay open even later than your shop. They're cheap enough if you're careful and go from stall to stall before you buy.'

Hester had truly intended to take Bridget's advice, but so far she had continued to heat up snack meals on the paraffin stove in their room and, alas, to eat out several times a week. Recently, however, she had spoken to Betsy, the other shop assistant, about her inability to manage on the money Miss Deakin paid, and Betsy had been very helpful. Older than Hester and still living at home with her mother and several younger brothers and sisters, she advised Hester, as Bridget had, to cook her own meals.

'But I don't know the first thing about cooking, apart from stuff like scrambled egg and heating up beans,' Hester had wailed. 'And the other girls dislike me as it is, they'd despise me even more if they saw I had no idea how to make pastry, or roast a chop or whatever you do to meat. Only I'm sick and tired of beans and eggs, and the food in the dining rooms is so delicious . . . But selling my things can't go on for ever . . . what would you do if you were me?'

Betsy laughed. 'If I were as pretty as you I'd find meself a nice rich husband,' she said, then shook her head as Hester's face fell. 'No, I'm only kiddin', queen. It ain't as easy as all that. But look, Hes, why don't you go to evening classes? They don't start until half past seven so you could go after work. Come to that, you're ever so much cleverer than I am, but I bet Deakin doesn't pay you what she pays me! She knows you're green – and pretty desperate, what's more. So why rely on an old skinflint like her? Why not take evening classes in shorthand and typing, or book-keeping? You'd be able to get a decent job then, and earn a good deal more money, I promise you. Tell you what, now that Denis – have I mentioned Denis? – has started taking an interest in me, I've thought about going to cookery classes meself. And I wouldn't mind havin' a go at a typewriter, either. Suppose we go together?'

Hester had jumped at the chance, but as it happened, it had been easier said than done. Evening classes, they were told severely, started each September. It was not yet February. However, if they cared to apply to join in a few weeks, when there would have been a 'settling down' in the classes which would result in some spare places . . .

Hester gathered this meant that people joined the classes with an enthusiasm which tended to flag as winter drew on, so she and Betsy agreed to apply again in a few weeks. In the meantime she continued reluctantly selling her winter clothing, eating as sparingly as possible, and of course remaining in the attic bedroom at Number 10.

The shop door opening abruptly put an end to Hester's musing and she straightened up to glance across at the woman who had entered. It was Miss Deakin, looking round her as she did each morning, all too clearly hoping to find fault. 'Good morning, Miss Deakin,' Hester said politely. 'I'm just finishing off the windows . . .'

'You've not done the outside of the windows yet, I see,' Miss Deakin interrupted rudely, 'and the curtains across the changing rooms are supposed to be drawn *back*; if I've told you once, I've told you a hundred times. And there's a smear on the looking-glass in the first cubicle – I noticed it as soon as I stepped into the shop.'

'You've always told me to clean the shop first and then the windows and to leave the changing cubicles until last,' Hester said demurely. She knew it would infuriate Miss Deakin to have her criticism parried, but she was damned if she was going to let the other woman get away with it. 'I'll fetch a chair and start on the outside of the windows now you're here, Miss Deakin. I wouldn't like to be outside, cleaning the windows, if a customer came in and there was no one to attend to her.'

Miss Deakin sniffed but made no reply and presently Hester carried a chair on to the pavement, climbed up on it and began the tedious task. When she stopped work at six o'clock, she planned to go along to Paddy's market and sell a rather nice serge jacket to the Irish woman; then she meant to buy the ingredients for a proper meal and beard the girls in the kitchen. She might even confess that she meant to take cookery lessons and possibly one of them might offer to show her how to cook some of the food she had bought. You never knew; she had thought Betsy stand-offish and look how wrong she had been there. Hester was quite intelligent enough to realise that her meals in the dining rooms and cafés on the Scotland Road were the main cause of her financial embarrassment.

Because of the advice handed out by Bridget and Betsy, she had begun to look at prices, both in shops and at the market, and was beginning to realise that if she bought chops, potatoes and vegetables she could make herself a good hot meal for a fraction of the cost that she would be charged even in the cheapest eating house.

It had been cold in the shop but it was even colder out on the pavement, perched on a chair. Hester was wearing the black skirt and white blouse which Miss Deakin had grudgingly provided and she found, to her annoyance, that the nippy little wind which came gusting along the pavement lifted her skirt from time to time, so that she was forced to hold it down with one hand while she wielded her cloth with the other. What was more, she was speedily becoming so cold that she could not feel her hands or feet, and realised that when she returned to the shop her chilblains would begin to throb and itch. I'd best fetch my coat and gloves before I do any more, Hester decided, scrambling off the chair. She had already washed the panes fairly thoroughly; now they needed a good hard rub with a soft, dry cloth.

Betsy usually came in at nine o'clock, even on a Monday, since it was always the junior assistant's job to clean through on this day, and whilst Hester was struggling into her coat she heard the shop door-bell clang and saw Betsy swinging the door closed behind her. 'Mornin', Miss Deakin, mornin' Hest . . .' Betsy was beginning, when a shriek from Miss Deakin interrupted her.

'Miss Fleming, *how* many times have I told you to take your muddy boots off before you come into this shop? I won't have you trekking mud on to me nice clean floors.'

Betsy came to a guilty halt and was beginning to tug her boots off when Miss Deakin, with an angry exclamation, rounded on Hester. 'As for you, Miss Elliott, I told you to clean the windows and look at 'em! Just how do you to intend to get them clean when they's thick with ice? You stupid, stupid girl, no one can't see a thing through that!'

Hester glanced towards the windows and was horrified by what she saw. Because she had not immediately dried the panes, the water had turned to ice, making the windows opaque. 'Oh Lord, I'm most awfully sorry, Miss Deakin,' Hester said penitently. 'The trouble was, I was getting too cold to hold the cloth, and . . .'

'I don't want to hear no excuses, I just want me windows properly cleaned so's the customers can see through 'em,' Miss Deakin said spitefully. 'Just you get out there and clear that ice and don't let me hear no excuses, you stupid, foolish . . .' The opening of the door cut the words off short and even in her distress Hester thought it downright comical how Miss Deakin's vicious and strident voice suddenly dropped to a coo as she addressed the tall, well-built woman who had entered. '. . . Good morning, madam, how may we help you?'

Relieved to find Miss Deakin's attention elsewhere, Hester jerked her head at Betsy and the two of them left the shop and stood surveying the iced-up windows with some dismay. 'What'll I do?' Hester said at last. 'If I get another wet cloth, would that work, do you think? I suppose the old devil's right and it only happened because I left the windows to fetch my coat. Oh dear, she'll probably sack me for this – or take off half my wages.'

'No she won't,' Betsy said decidedly. 'It weren't your fault, queen, it's happened to me more'n once. When you get a really cold wind, like we've got today, you shouldn't attempt to do the windows because they'll freeze up, sure as I'm standin' here in me muddy boots!'

Hester looked down at Betsy's feet and could not help smiling. The boots were on all right, but scarcely in the conventional fashion. Betsy's right foot was halfway in and her left had only descended as far as the ankle. She looked extremely uncomfortable and, following Hester's glance, grinned and bent to straighten the boots and tug them up her calves. 'Thanks, Betsy,' Hester said gratefully. 'What'll I do, though? She's right about one thing, you can't so much as get a glimpse of her window display through all this ice.'

'We'll both work on them, but first we'll have to heat up some water in the back kitchen,' Betsy informed her friend. 'We'll have to do it a little at a time – you go first with a hot cloth and just clear about a square foot and I'll come behind you with the drying duster. It'll take a while, but at least it'll clear the windows eventually. And if old Deakin tries to blame you again, I'll say as how it were her fault for making you do the windows in such freezing weather. I bet she was nagging you to get them done, weren't she?'

'Yes, she was. But that doesn't mean it won't be another black mark against me,' Hester said gloomily. 'Right, we'd better get started immediately. Oh, how I hate this icy weather! I used to grumble about the heat in India but what wouldn't I give for some bright, hot sunshine this minute!'

That evening, Hester bought a lamb chop, three potatoes and half a pound of carrots from the stalls on Great Homer Street and took them down to the shared kitchen. She had not thought about cooking utensils until she saw that there were no communal saucepans but, fortunately, Bridget was before her, cooking bacon, egg and chips on the stove, and offered to lend her a pan for her potatoes and carrots. 'You can use me frying pan to fry your chop when I've done with it,' she offered. 'No need to add dripping, 'cos there'll be plenty of fat left over from me bacon.' She grinned up at Hester. 'I'm celebratin'! Ask me why!'

'Why are you celebrating?' Hester said, busily peeling her potatoes and scraping the carrots, then popping them into Bridget's small saucepan. 'I don't feel much like celebrating myself since I hadn't bargained on having to buy pans as well as food.'

'I'm celebratin' because I've got me a really good job, a live-in job,' Bridget said exultantly. 'A pal of mine, another girl from Dublin, put me in the way of it. I'm to be housemaid at one of the big houses on Rodney Street. It's owned by a doctor and I'm to keep the surgery clean as well as working in the house. The money's ever so good and of course it's all found, even uniforms.'

Hester felt her heart sink; Bridget was the only real friend she had made in the house, though the Maskells were pleasant enough. 'Oh, Bridget, I'll miss you dreadfully!' she exclaimed. 'I wonder who will come in your place? I do try to be friendly towards the other girls but they don't really like me, do they?'

'It isn't that they don't like you, they feel you're a – a cut above the rest of us,' Bridget explained awkwardly. 'I know you aren't, you're one of us really, but you don't talk like the rest of us, and you're – you're fussy about always lookin' neat and having clean nails and that, so – so they think you despise them, not t'other way around.'

'I wouldn't keep my job if I went around with dirty nails,' Hester said, with a wry smile. 'I do try to sound the same as they do, but it's awfully hard, like learning a foreign language. Still, now that I'm cooking my own food in the kitchen, perhaps they'll be a bit friendlier. Or perhaps whoever takes your place will be as nice as you, Bridget.'

'She'll be Irish, I'm sure o' that,' Bridget said, grinning. 'I've already put the word around, amongst me pals, as there's goin' to be a bed free here. An' tell you what, Hester, you can have me pots 'n' pans! I shan't be wantin' 'em when I move to Rodney Street.'

'I'll pay you for them,' Hester said eagerly. 'You are good, Bridget, but I won't see you lose by it.'

To this, Bridget replied with a snort, assuring Hester that the pans had been bought off the second-hand stalls in Paddy's market and were not worth more than a few coppers. 'Besides, you never know, I might lose the job after a few weeks and be glad of me pans back,' she said, when Hester begged her to name a price, 'so we'll call it a loan, all right?'

Bridget's new job started the following Monday, and for the rest of the week she did her best to teach Hester some simple cookery, though marvelling that anyone could reach the age of eighteen without knowing how to boil a potato or fry a chop. Hester cut herself bread and cheese each morning for her lunch break and, following Betsy's advice, asked Miss Deakin for permission to boil a kettle and make herself a hot drink to accompany her carry-out. 'I thought you went to a dining room for your lunch,' Miss Deakin had said. 'The kitchen's crowded enough wi' me and Miss Fleming tryin' to get ourselves a bite, lerralone addin' you to the mix.' But when Hester pointed out that, on the wage Miss Deakin paid, she could no longer afford such luxuries, the manageress gave way and agreed that Hester might eat her sandwich and have a cup of tea in the back kitchen, provided she did so after Betsy had finished her own meal.

The weather continued extremely cold and on the Sunday following the ice incident Hester decided to hover around the Shaw Street house in an attempt to find out at which school Lonnie was now a pupil. It was a rainy day, the rain occasionally giving way to sleet, so Hester's only disguise was a headscarf pulled well forward over her face, and a large black umbrella. She thought that if she did not get too near the house she was unlikely to be spotted, and accordingly stood at the nearest tram stop, keeping her eyes on the ground, but still glancing furtively towards the house at any sign of life.

Presently, her vigil was rewarded; Miss Hetherington-Smith, magnificently clad in a long fur coat with a small violet toque perched on her iron-grey hair, came sweeping out of the front door. She said something over her shoulder to someone Hester could not see and erected a dark-blue umbrella before crossing the pavement and climbing into the Bentley, assisted by the chauffeur. He took the umbrella, shook it free of raindrops and placed it tenderly on the floor of the car, then climbed behind the wheel and drove off. Hester was slightly surprised to see that the big car was not facing towards St Augustine's Church, but assumed that he would turn left twice and arrive outside the church door so that his passenger might alight without having to cross the road.

It was odd that neither Lonnie nor Miss Hutchinson had accompanied Miss Hetherington-Smith, but having thought the matter over Hester imagined that either one or both of them might have a cold, or some such thing. She was surprised that Miss Hetherington-Smith had not insisted upon her companion's accompanying her and was in the very act of crossing the road to go to the house when the front door opened once more and Miss Hutchinson emerged. She was clad, as usual, in black and glanced cautiously round her before setting off in the direction of St Augustine's. On the spur of the moment, Hester decided not to approach her. Miss Hutchinson had seemed sympathetic to her plight in the past, but she was a weak woman and the weak are capable of inflicting considerable damage, albeit by accident, so Hester kept her counsel and continued to wait. Only when she was sure that both ladies would be occupied with morning service did she gingerly approach that forbidding front door. She missed Lonnie very much and even the thought of seeing the child once more gave a lift to her spirits. Ruefully, she remembered how unhappy she had been in the Shaw Street house and thought that now, if she could turn back the clock, she would appreciate a great many things which she had once taken for granted. There was Lonnie's companionship, the friendliness of the servants, the warm beds and comfortably banked up fires, and of course the three square meals a day which she had to neither prepare nor pay for.

Set against this was the spite and malevolence of Miss Hetherington-Smith herself, but Hester had scarcely escaped from such enmity since Miss Deakin showed every sign of being exactly the same.

Arriving outside the door of Number 127, Hester hesitated again. She had been forbidden to approach the house, but how was Miss Hetherington-Smith to know that she had done so? With Miss Hutchinson out of the way she felt sure that no one else would carry tales. Yet she still hesitated. She had not, after all, intended to call there when she had set out earlier in the day. She had hoped that one of the maidservants, preferably Mollie, would come out to post a letter or merely to get some air whilst the ladies were out of the way. Then she would approach the maid and ask how she could contact Miss Lonnie.

I could still continue to wait about, she told herself rather unconvincingly, even as her hand reached up and hovered over the bell-push. I need not actually ring the bell, make the whole thing official . . .

Almost of its own volition, however, her finger pressed the bell and moments later she heard footsteps approaching the door, which opened to reveal Fletcher. He started to say that he was very sorry, but Miss Hetherington-Smith was at church, then stopped short, recognising her as she smiled up at him. 'Miss Elliott! My goodness, for a moment . . . but you'd best come in, you're soaked to the skin!' He stood back. Hester took a step towards him, then hesitated.

'I was forbidden the house, you know, Mr Fletcher, and the last thing I want is to get you – or anyone else – into trouble, but I'd give a great deal to see Miss Lonnie,' she said rather breathlessly. 'I watched your mistress and her companion leaving the house a short while ago, but I didn't see Miss Lonnie. Is she not well? I've been awfully worried about her, to tell you the truth. She's an independent little person, but she is only eight, after all, and a long way from the land of her birth, and from her father, too.'

'I don't think Miss Hetherington-Smith would consider dismissing *me* for inviting a young lady into the house in such inclement weather,' Fletcher said reprovingly, a slight frown marring his brow. 'Do come in, miss . . . I can see you and meself had best have a bit of a talk, like.'

Hester obeyed and presently the two of them had descended to the basement, where Fletcher took her straight into the staff living room. It was deserted, the entire staff presumably either having a day off or helping to prepare the Sunday dinner, so Fletcher sat her down in one fireside chair by the glowing hearth and took the other himself, then gazed anxiously across at her. 'Now, miss, tell me how you've been getting along! You say you've been worried about Miss Leonora . . . well, I don't say you aren't right to worry but I can tell you, the girls and meself have been worried about *you*, and with far more reason. I was that shocked when we found out what had happened . . . but young Mollie insisted that you were bound to get a good job somewhere where you'd be treated decent, and seeing as how we'd no idea how to find you there weren't much we could do.' His eyes travelled over her thin coat, soaked headscarf and pale, anxious face. 'You look worn out, miss, and none too stout either.'

'I'm all right, really I am, Mr Fletcher,' Hester said quickly. 'I'm working in a dress shop on the Scotland Road and living in a lodging house quite near there. But what about Miss Lonnie? Is she ill? Is that why she didn't attend church with her aunt? May I go up to the schoolroom and see her for myself?'

'I fear not, Miss Elliott,' Fletcher said sorrowfully, shaking his grey head. 'I suppose you couldn't know, but Miss Hetherington-Smith has sent Miss Leonora to a boarding school and no matter how cleverly the maids or myself question her she won't give us any idea of the name of the school or even of the street.

Allsop, the chauffeur, thought he could find the place again but when he did so he discovered that it was all a trick. Miss Hetherington-Smith had made him drive the child to the home of an acquaintance of hers. After that, someone else, a taxi driver probably, took Miss Leonora the rest of the way.'

'A *boarding* school!' Hester said, aghast. 'Oh, poor little Lonnie! But I suppose she will have sent her to some first-rate place where she'll be happy once she's settled down. Only . . . well, I can't help wondering why Miss H has kept her whereabouts from yourselves.'

'So do we wonder, miss,' the butler said heavily. 'Particularly since Miss Hetherington-Smith has been behaving rather – oddly of late. I dare say you didn't notice, but Allsop has orders now, of a Sunday, to take her to the church of St Pancras, on Lidderdale Road, miles away from here, where she isn't known. And she sacked Maud because she said the girl stared at her in an accusing way, and would very likely begin to plot against her, as – well, as you had done, miss. Poor Maud was very distressed, since she wasn't aware of having so much as glanced at Miss Hetherington-Smith, but nothing anyone could say made any difference. Out Maud had to go, and then it were the kitchen maid, poor little oppressed soul, and there's talk now, below stairs, of the mistress not being – well, not being quite herself.'

'Oh my God!' Hester exclaimed. 'Miss Hetherington-Smith was always extremely mean with money so I suppose it's quite possible that she's sent Lonnie somewhere which is so cheap that she's afraid of folk finding out. Whatever can we do, Mr Fletcher?'

Fletcher sighed and shook his head wearily. 'Mollie, Mrs Ainsworth and meself have thought and thought but the truth is, miss, we don't know which way to turn. The reason she's going to a different church must be because the vicar, or one of the congregation, asked too many questions or perhaps even criticised her choice of establishment for Miss Leonora. But unless we can find out where the child is, we can't even write to her father and let him know what's going on. You see, miss, we all know he's the true master here though his sister is his deputy as you might say. And it's wrong that Miss Leonora is being treated badly by her own flesh and blood just because her father is away at sea.'

'There must be some way of finding out where Lonnie is,' Hester said thoughtfully; she was so wet that the skirts of her coat were actually steaming in the warmth from the small fire in the hearth. 'Bills have to be presented and paid . . . I seem to remember that Miss Hutchinson had access to some of the account books at least. D'you think she might help? I take it that *she* hasn't abandoned St Augustine's Church?'

'Oh no, miss, she still attends regular, same as the rest of us,' Fletcher assured her. 'Whether she knows where Miss Lonnie is, I rather doubt. Miss Hetherington-Smith seems to trust no one – I feel quite sorry for Miss Hutchinson sometimes. She's a poor creature, and being constantly criticised and blamed for every little thing that goes wrong is rapidly turning her into a nervous wreck.'

Hester thought, privately, that this would not be any great change; to her way of thinking, Miss Hutchinson had been a nervous wreck for years. However, if the woman was their only means of finding out where Lonnie was, then she decided that she herself was the best person to tackle the companion. 'Can you give me any idea, Mr Fletcher, of how I might get in touch with Miss Hutchinson without Miss Hetherington-Smith's finding out? I might persuade her to take a look at the account books when her mistress is out of the way to see if she can discover to which school Lonnie was sent. Only I'll need time alone with her; if I try to hurry things, she'll just prevaricate and end up doing nothing.'

Fletcher frowned thoughtfully. 'There's Miss Hetherington-Smith's bridge afternoon,' he said, after a moment. 'Miss Hutchinson used to play bridge as well but lately she's become so nervous that Miss Hetherington-Smith refuses to let her join the group. So she's taken to going off, on a Thursday afternoon, to the big library on William Brown Street. She changes her own books and those of her mistress and usually stays out until about six, when she comes home to change for dinner. You might try to catch her on her way to the library, miss.'

'That's a wonderful idea, Mr Fletcher,' Hester said, smiling at him. She looked down at her hands in her lap for a moment; a question had been burning on her tongue ever since she had entered the room, and now she voiced it at last. 'I wonder if you could tell me whether anyone has come to the house asking for me? I seem to have lost touch with all my friends and there was one in particular . . . We had arranged to meet a few days after Miss Hetherington-Smith dismissed me . . . I've often wondered . . .'

'Oh yes, miss, there was a young gentleman come to the house a week or so after you left. Unfortunately, Miss Hetherington-Smith came out and sent him packing before I could explain what had happened. But that Mollie, she's a good girl . . .'

Fletcher explained what happened between Dick and Mollie, ending with the words: 'So as soon as the young feller is settled across the water, he'll contact Mollie by letter, as they arranged. I hope we done right, but he were that anxious to get in touch with you, to explain . . .'

'Oh, Mr Fletcher, you've taken a great weight off my mind,' Hester said joyfully. She rose to her feet and began to put on her gloves and headscarf, which she had hung on the fender as soon as she had entered the room, and to button her coat. 'I'd best be getting along, though, or I'll meet Miss Hetherington-Smith coming back from church! I can't thank you enough, Mr Fletcher, for your help; I do hope you don't get into trouble as a result of speaking to me.'

She headed for the door as she spoke and Fletcher hurried ahead to open it for her, saying drily as he did so: 'I don't think Miss Hetherington-Smith could manage without a butler, miss, so I shan't lose any sleep on that count! Now you take care of yourself,' he added, as they walked up the hallway, 'and don't forget, this is only a temporary thing. When Mr Hetherington-Smith is back in India and can receive letters once more, I'm sure he'll take command of the situation.'

As they reached the front door, Hester held out her hand. 'I'm sure you're right, Mr Fletcher, but I doubt that even Mr Hetherington-Smith could persuade his sister to reinstate me,' she said seriously, 'nor would I wish him to do so. But Lonnie's fate is another matter. If she's happy at the school, then I'm sure both her father and myself would be glad for her to remain there. But I very much fear that her aunt will have sent her to some cheap, inferior establishment where she will be very unhappy indeed. And that, neither her father nor myself would tolerate. Goodbye, Mr Fletcher, and thank you again.'

Hester had barely crossed the pavement before she saw a tram bearing down upon her, heading in the direction that she wanted. There was a short queue of people waiting at the stop and, by dint of hurrying, she managed to get on board. It was fortunate that she did so, for as she settled herself in her seat she saw the Bentley draw up outside Number 127. As she watched, Allsop jumped out and went round to assist Miss Hetherington-Smith to alight and Hester thought, with a lurch of her heart, that she had been very lucky not to meet the older woman face to face. Had she left two minutes later . . . but it did not bear thinking about.

Next time I visit them, I shall have to keep a careful eye on the clock, she told herself, holding out her fare to the conductor. I really must see Mollie at some stage, though I'm sure if she'd received a letter from Dick, Fletcher would have known all about it. Adversity certainly brings people together, she concluded, taking the ticket the conductor held out. Because of Miss Hetherington-Smith's unpleasant behaviour, the staff at Shaw Street feel like a beleaguered family. Oh, I do hope no harm comes to anyone as a result of my visit!

The whistle for the end of his shift sounded whilst Dick was engaged in a tricky manoeuvre, so he ignored it and continued working on the bunch of grapes which decorated the front of the dining room dresser, straightening up only when he had finished carving the last leaf; then he put his tools away, picked up the little canvas haversack in which he kept his carry-out, and headed for the outside world once more. Climbing from the deck on to the yard, he saw that it was raining and turned up the collar of his jacket. It was Saturday noon and he was now at liberty for the weekend, though he thought, looking up at the lowering grey sky, that the month was well named – February fill-dyke – since it had rained without stopping for the past ten days. It did not look as though it proposed to ease, either, just because he was free of work for a couple of days.

'Hey-up, Dickie!' The shout came from a gangly youth clad in thin cotton trousers and a much darned jumper; Freddie Cox did not seem to feel the cold, Dick reflected. 'You comin' home now, feller, or is you off to see your mam and the rest o' the family?'

Dick and Freddie were lodgers in the home of a Mrs Beasdale, who lived not ten minutes from the factory gates. When the Bailey family had first moved across the water, they had all lodged with Mrs Beasdale in Priory Street whilst they searched for accommodation to rent, but it soon became apparent that this arrangement could not continue. The sanatorium to which Mr Bailey had been admitted proved to be in Bwlchgwyn, a small village in North Wales and a far cry indeed from Birkenhead. It was clear that Mrs Bailey could not possibly visit her husband daily whilst they remained with Mrs Beasdale, but soon she was fortunate enough to be able to rent a tiny cottage in Bwlchgwyn village itself. From here it was a simple matter to visit the sanatorium daily, and to his wife's joy Mr Bailey began to seem better at once, in the clear, clean air.

So now Dick and Ted were the only Baileys actually lodging with Mrs Beasdale and one or other of them went off every Saturday, when their work was finished for the week, to spend the rest of the day with the family in the cottage, to sleep there overnight and to spend Sunday at the sanatorium. Dick envied the younger Baileys their village life, for though Ben and Phyllis had grumbled at having to change schools, they soon became thoroughly at home in their new surroundings, picking up bits of the Welsh language from their fellow pupils and enjoying a good relationship both with their new playmates and with their teachers.

'Dick? Stop dreamin', old feller, and tell me what you's doin' this weekend. If you're goin' back to the 'Pool for a bit of a fling, like, I might as well come wi' you. We could see a mat'nee in the afternoon, gerrus some tea, and then go to the Grafton Dance Hall on West Derby Road and pick up a couple o' floosies, treat 'em to a fish supper if that'll make 'em . . . friendlier.' He looked hopefully at Dick, but the other was already shaking his head, though he could not help smiling at the thought of young Freddie hoping to bribe a couple of floosies with fish and chips.

'No, not this weekend, Freddie. It's Ted's turn to visit me dad, so I'm not going to Bwlchgwyn, but I'm a bit worried about a pal o' mine. She's a housemaid in one of the big houses on Shaw Street. As soon as I got settled into Mrs B's I wrote to her tellin' her my new address, but she's never written back. To tell the truth, she's workin' for a right peculiar old woman who seems to think the days of slavery aren't past, because she treats her girls as if they'd just come off the boat from Africa. I'm wonderin' if young Mollie ever received my letter, so I'll be a deal happier if I can check up with her this weekend.' He grinned at his young friend. 'Otherwise, I'd be only too pleased to tread a measure with some young floosie and buy her a fish supper afterwards,' he ended.

Freddie fell into step beside him, his eyebrows rising until they almost reached the fringe of lank hair which hung over his brow. 'And what would this Mollie have to say to that?' he asked with mock severity. 'How many young ladies do you want, Dickie?'

Dick shook his head. 'Mollie isn't my girl, though she's a nice little thing,' he told his friend. 'I don't suppose you've ever heard me mention Hester? She and me were pretty close when I lived in Elmore Street, but we lost touch. Mollie's trying to get us together again.'

'Anyone who believes that would believe anything,' Freddie said sceptically. 'Well, if you won't come wi' me, you won't. But how long will it take you to ask this Mollie whether she's been in touch with that Hester? Not the whole afternoon, surely?'

Dick admitted that it might not take all that long but pointed out that Mollie's employer would not approve of her maids' having gentleman callers, even of the most harmless kind. 'So I can't march straight up to the front door and ask to speak to Mollie,' he explained. 'I've got to hang around until either Miss Hetherington-Smith or one of her servants comes out. If the old lady is not on the premises I can go up to the front door, bold as brass, and if one of the maids – or the butler – appears then I can get them to take a message to Mollie. See?'

As he spoke, the two of them reached the jigger which ran behind the house in which they lodged. They walked along it, then opened the back gate, crossed the yard, and let themselves into Mrs Beasdale's neat little kitchen. There was a delicious smell of cooking in the air which made Dick's mouth water. Hastily hanging their caps on the pegs beside the door and discarding their coats, the two young men made for the sink where they washed the morning's dirt off their hands, faces and necks before heading for the dining room.

Mrs Beasdale was at the top of the table, presiding over an enormous shepherd's pie, whilst four elderly lodgers, already served, helped themselves to vegetables. Their landlady looked up and beamed as the two young men took their places, for she took a pride, she often informed them, in cooking good, nourishing food, and thought it their duty to be on time for meals. 'You've just made it, you two,' she said, pulling two more plates towards her. 'This here's too good a shepherd's pie for you to miss . . . there's cabbage in the white tureen, Mr Bailey, and carrots in the blue one. Help yourselves!'

When the table had been cleared of everything but the big brown teapot, a large jug of milk and seven mugs, Mrs Beasdale smiled at Freddie and Dick. 'Well, lads?' she enquired. 'And what are you up to this weekend? Not working, are you?'

'No, not this time,' Freddie said jovially, accepting a large mug of hot, sweet tea. 'We's goin' out after us dinners, and we shan't be back for tea. We'll get something out.'

Since tea on a Saturday was usually cold meat, three big white plates piled with bread and butter and an enormous fruit cake, missing the meal was no particular hardship. Certainly none of Mrs Beasdale's lodgers would have dreamed of forgoing one of her dinners if they could possibly help it, but Saturday tea was a different matter. Dick appreciated all his landlady's meals, however, and considered himself very lucky to have found such an excellent billet.

'That's all right, then. Will you be home tonight, though, Mr Bailey?' Mrs Beasdale gave him a roguish smile. 'I'd not like to lock you out!'

'He's gorra key,' Freddie pointed out, but this did not spoil the joke since Mr Brown, who was retired and had appointed himself as Mrs Beasdale's champion, pointed out that not even the most talented of keys could unlock the bolts which were shot across the doors, both front and back, once all the lodgers were in for the night. 'I expect we'll be back late, Mrs B . . . there's a dance on at the Grafton. We thought we might cross the water, see a bit o' life for once.'

This insult to her home town of Birkenhead brought a groan from the older men and a threatened box over the ears from their landlady, but Dick thought it only fair to say that he might not return to Birkenhead with his friend. 'Because I've a fancy to look up some of me old pals,' he said glibly. 'And one of 'em might well ask me to sleep over. Would that be all right, Mrs B?'

Mrs Beasdale prided herself on not interfering with her lodgers' lives, and anyway she was well used to both Dick and Ted being away at the weekend, so she said that would be fine, and would he like her to pack him some carry-out? Dick said no thanks all the same, if he stayed with a pal the pal's mam would likely feed him, and then the party broke up. Mrs Beasdale carried the used pudding plates – it had been treacle sponge and custard – through to the kitchen whilst Mr Brown took the empty mugs.

'Are you really goin' to stay overnight?' Freddie asked curiously, as the two of them set out for the ferry. 'If so, why don't you come to the Grafton first?

Only I hate goin' to dances on me tod, honest to God I do.'

'No-oo, but I thought, if I manage to talk to Mollie fairly early in the afternoon, I'll try and catch the last bus and make my way to the sanatorium anyway,' Dick confessed. 'Our dad likes to see me, as well as Ted, now and then. And I enjoy being in the village, having a bit of a crack wi' Mam and the kids. So if I'm through in time that's what I'll probably do.'

'And if you ain't?' Freddie asked eagerly. 'Aw, come on, Dickie, be a sport and come along to the Grafton wi' me! You can have the best lookin' girl, honest to God you can.'

Dick laughed and agreed that he would do so if searching out Mollie took him past a reasonable time for catching the bus, and the two lads bought their tickets and climbed aboard the ferry. Dick leaned on the rail, watching the wind-tossed water passing beneath him, and glanced up to see the familiar outline of the Liver Birds drawing ever nearer. He wondered what the afternoon would bring. If only he could at least contact Hester, make sure that she was all right! But suppose she really had gone back to India by now? He might never set eyes on her again, and one thing their enforced separation had taught him was that none of the other girls he had taken around had meant anything to him.

But Hester was different. She's in a class by herself, he dreamed, conjuring up a picture of that small, intelligent face with its wide, dark brown eyes so thickly fringed with black and curling lashes, the soft pink mouth, always trembling into laughter, and the smooth pallor of her perfect skin. If only . . .

if *only* . . . he could find her so that they might pick up their friendship where it had left off, get to know one another, perhaps establish an understanding . . .

'Come on, Bailey, we're dockin', and if you're goin' to get to see this woman of yours whiles it's still light you'd better gerra move on!'

Freddie's voice in his ear jerked Dick back to the present. He sighed deeply, then turned away from the rail and accompanied the younger boy towards the gangplank. 'All right, all right, I'm coming as fast as I can,' he grumbled. 'Nice to see the 'Pool without it actually raining, isn't it?'

Freddie looked up at the sky, still obscured by dark, fast-moving clouds. 'It won't be dry for long, so gerra wiggle on,' he advised. 'Now remember the plan! If you click early, then you'll go off to the place wi' the heathenish name an' see your folks, but if you have to hang about past bus time, then you'll meet me in the Grapes, say, on the West Derby Road. We'll have a jar, then go along to the William Brown Dining Rooms at six o'clock, so's we can have a bite before the dance.'

'OK, I shan't forget,' Dick said. He grinned at his pal. 'With a bit of luck, though, I'll be heading for Bwlchgwyn – and it's *not* a heathenish name, it's just Welsh – by six!'

Despite his hopes, Dick spent the evening with Freddie. It was well after six o'clock when he arrived at the rendezvous, for he had done his best to catch the last bus and had only failed by about ten minutes. So it was a rather gloomy young man who came panting up the West Derby Road to meet his friend.

'Well I'm blessed! Glad I waited a bit over, seein' as I thought if you'd tried to catch the bus and failed you'd be here about now,' Freddie said, rather confusedly. 'What happened then, old feller? Gal didn't show?'

'No, she didn't . . . and don't think it was anything to do with seeing me, because it weren't. The truth is, Freddie, the poor gal's been sacked! I waited and waited and then I thought "Blow this for a game of soldiers!" and went smack up to the front door and rang the bell. I were lucky, because apparently the old lady sometimes goes out on a Saturday to some friends on the Wirral, and it were one of them days. The butler – his name's Fletcher, he's a rare good old gun – came to the door and told me that Mollie was dismissed a week back because the old lady said she was pert, but Mr Fletcher said she were nothing of the sort, being a nice, respectable girl. He thinks the old gal's trying to get rid of all the servants who were there when she sent Hester and her niece off; now there's only him and the cook left of the old lot. But he give me Mollie's new address, so I can write to her there. It seems she got another job out at Crosby without any trouble, and that's made the old lady mad and all, because it were people she knew at church who told Moll there were a maid wanted in Crosby.'

'It's a queer do by the sound of it,' Freddie said thoughtfully. 'I know jobs is hard to find and probably maids are ten a penny, but even so, why sack someone who does their job well? It don't make sense.'

'No, it doesn't. Fletcher explained that Lonnie's father will be back in India soon and is sure the old man will want to know just what his sister's been up to in his absence, but . . . oh, what can he do from so far away, after all? I simply must find Hester!'

'There's other girls . . .' Freddie was beginning, but was silenced by Dick.

'Oh, other girls!' Dick said scornfully. 'Aye, I'll grant you that. But there's only one Hester Elliott, and I'm afraid she'll forget all about me at this rate. I tell you, Freddie, I've got to find her!'

Lonnie sat in the cramped confines of the punishment cupboard, and fumed. It was dark in there, though not completely, for there was a gap between door and floor through which some light came.

Not that the light made any difference, of course. For the less strong-minded, there was fear simply in the fact of being locked in. On the first occasion it had happened to Lonnie, she, too, had been afraid. Claustrophobia had threatened, so she had attacked the door with feet and fists, clamouring to get out, shrieking, threatening. In a way it had worked; a nun had come and unlocked the door, hauled her off to Sister Augustine, who had whacked away with her strap – and with evident relish – and had then locked her up again. But, since she had been returned to the basement cupboard, she was no better off for her tantrum.

That had made Lonnie think. She had remained in the cupboard, on that occasion, for about four hours. She, of course, had no idea of the length of her imprisonment, but the other girls in her dormitory had told her, in awed voices, that she had broken the record for a new girl. So she would have to either conform or grow used to the cupboard, she decided . . . and immediately set out to run away once more, though running away the first time had been the cause of her imprisonment.

She had now run away seven times in all, remaining free on the last occasion for a whole beautiful day. She had wandered down to the docks, had thought about stowing away aboard a ferry . . . had looked wistfully at the great liners, some of them undoubtedly bound for India, Australia, the Spice Islands, and imagined escaping not only from the nuns but from this cold and unfriendly land which she suddenly found she hated.

A policeman had handed her in, though she had made sure that she told him what sort of place the school was before he did so. Unfortunately, her descriptions of the nuns' behaviour had been just a trifle exaggerated – the scorpion pit had been a tactical error, she soon realised – so whilst the policeman had done so with some reluctance, he had still returned her to her prison. But even as she was cast into durance vile – the Black Hole of Calcutta, the girls called it – she had assured the nuns, in her most honeyed tones, that she would escape again, and soon, and that this time she would not be found and ignominiously returned to their wretched, evil school.

The cupboard was not large and the ceiling was sloping, so that it was impossible to stand up at the back. After a few minutes, Lonnie usually sat down on the floor, curled her arms round her knees and tried to imagine herself somewhere really nice. She often returned to India, in imagination, and saw again the large tropical garden of their bungalow, with the willow trees leaning over the river and her *ayah*'s gentle face as she told her some magical story in Hindustani, adding and elaborating as she went along.

Today, however, not even the most vivid imaginings could help to take her out of her punishment cell for long. She was cold, miserable and depressed. She had now been at the school for three months and there had been no word from her father. Well, it was not true to say that she'd not heard from him, since every couple of weeks a large envelope arrived at the school, redirected to herself. Inside it there would be pretty picture postcards, letters from her father and notes from her new stepmother. Every time she opened the envelope, Lonnie's heart filled with hope; surely this time there would be some acknowledgement from her father showing that he understood her carefully coded messages of unhappiness, her equally carefully coded pleas for his help? But there was never any indication that he had even received her letters. Of course, whilst he and his new wife had been cruising round the world, her letters – and everyone else's – would have been saved for him to read when he returned home, but surely he must be back in India by now? Surely he would notice the difference between letters penned from Shaw Street and those dispatched from the hated school? What was more, Hester too had written regularly, telling Mr Hetherington-Smith how his daughter's lessons were progressing. Surely he would realise, from the absence of such letters, that something was very wrong?

She guessed, of course, that her father had been told she was now in school, which meant that Hester was no longer in his employ. But did he have any idea how abrupt and unfair Hester's dismissal had been? The trouble with sending messages in her weekly letters was that the nuns scrutinised every word, and if they suspected that a note of unhappiness was creeping in would censor the letter and demand that it be rewritten. Lonnie still found writing a very real chore and in fact this, more than anything, had influenced her latest decision.

For the past three weeks, she had refused to write any letters at all, saying that she did not mean to tell her father lies and it seemed that any attempt to tell the truth only brought her trouble. Sister Magdalene had been furious and punishments had rained down on Lonnie's head but she had remained firm. She would not write letters to her father and nothing anyone could do would persuade her otherwise. Lonnie knew that this really worried the nuns. She imagined that Mother Superior had probably been in touch with her father, telling him not to worry about the absence of correspondence, but she could not imagine what excuse the woman would make. Illness might have her father hurrying to England to see for himself. A claim that she was too busy and happy to write would surely be disbelieved. But the nuns were used to dealing with difficult children and she supposed, gloomily, that she was not the first pupil to simply stop writing to a parent. She just hoped that the first stilted letters, followed by no letters at all, would alert her dear father and bring him to her aid.

Outside the cupboard she heard the clatter of feet descending the stairs and hurrying along the corridor in the direction of the dining room. With the footsteps came the smell of stewed meat and cabbage and Lonnie had to swallow hard and tell herself that the food here was awful and she much preferred her solitude in the cupboard to the insipid food and incessant conversation in the dining room.

She was still sitting, arms round knees, on the cold floor, when a whisper came to her ears. She recognised the voice at once as being that of her friend, Abigail. 'Lonnie? Are you still in there?'

Lonnie repressed an urge to say, Where the devil do you think I am? and put her own lips nearer the crack. 'Of course I am, you idiot! Not getting any dinner hasn't made me thin enough to slide under the door, if that's what you mean. I say, Abby, I'm terribly cold. When do you think they'll let me out?'

'In time for tea,' Abigail hissed. 'I'm pretending to tie my shoelace, but if one of the nuns comes along . . . oh, help! Here comes Sister . . .'

Her feet retreating hastily was the last sound Lonnie heard before someone wrapped sharply on the door. 'Leonora! Are you prepared to promise that you will never try to run away again?'

Lonnie remained obstinately silent. The nun's voice sounded colder than ever when she next spoke, but Lonnie thought she heard a trace of anxiety in the woman's harsh tones. 'Leonora, if you don't answer me at once . . .'

Leonora said nothing but shifted her cramped position into that of someone waiting for the starting gun to fire. If that door opened, even a crack, she would hurl herself at it, hopefully flattening Sister Magdalene's long pink nose as she did so, and would escape through the front door and simply keep running until she found somewhere to hide. She had already planned to steal some clothing from a washing line, next time she escaped, for she had soon realised that it was her uniform which singled her out as a runaway. Yes, next time she got out, she would find herself a disguise first and worry about her destination next.

She had hoped that the nun might think she had fainted and would open the door to discover whether her pupil either was prone on the floor or had somehow managed to escape. But the sounds she made as she changed her position were apparently enough to calm the nun's suspicions. The woman gave a sharp, impatient sigh and said briskly: 'Stay where you are, then!' and the click of her shoes as she made for the dining room faded quickly into silence.

Lonnie collapsed on to the floor once more and began to rub her arms as hard as she could with her cold hands. If only she had had the good sense to put on her coat! But she had been given little opportunity. The policeman had brought her in at ten o'clock the previous night and she had been sent, supperless, to bed. Hoping that a punishment deferred might merely consist of a whacking, she had gone down to breakfast in her school uniform and had been pushed into the cupboard before she had so much as raised her porridge spoon to her lips. So now she was not only cold, she was extremely hungry and actually wondered, for a brief moment, if it might be sensible to pretend compliance. After all, the nuns did not always speak the truth by a long chalk, so why should she not make a promise today and rescind it tomorrow? Since she had refused Sister Magdalene's overtures, however, this was a rhetorical question and not one on which she intended to waste any more thought. Instead, she began to think about Hester. The older girl had been her best friend, more like a sister than a paid governess, and Lonnie guessed that Hester would be searching for her. She also guessed that the staff at Shaw Street would have been kept in ignorance of her whereabouts, for Mollie's last remark to her had been: 'I'll come and visit you,

Lonnie love, on me next day off and I'll tell Miss Elliott where to find you. All right?'

At first, Lonnie had waited eagerly for Mollie or Hester to appear but later had put two and two together. Allsop had not driven her straight to the school but had dropped her and her cases – and Miss Hetherington-Smith – in a dull, grey street, flanked on either side by large houses. Miss Hetherington-Smith had waited until the car had disappeared and had then hailed a taxi cab which had taken them to their eventual destination. In retrospect, it was clear to Lonnie that Miss Hetherington-Smith had intended no one, not even the chauffeur, to know in which establishment she had placed her niece. So it was useless to wait for Mollie and Hester to find her, because they would not – could not – do any such thing. Instead, she must use her own ingenuity to find out where Hester had gone. The trouble was, the school was on the outskirts of the city and though she had tried very hard to get back to the area she knew, her escapes from the convent had not yet given her sufficient opportunity to do so. If she had only had some money, she could have caught a tram, for she saw by the destination boards that a good few of the passing vehicles were heading for the city centre, but she was penniless.

Next time I get out, I'll make my way to Heyworth Street and see Ben in Mr Madison's shop, she decided now, then stood up, head bent, and began to do vigorous exercises, trying to bring some life back into numbed hands and feet. Next time I get out, I won't just wander and peer into the shops and dodge down alleyways. I'll stand on a street corner somewhere and beg for pennies until I've got enough money for a tram fare and then I'll go to dear, kind

Mrs Bailey and ask her to tell me where Hester is, or to hide me herself until I can let my father know what has happened to me, and how unhappy I am.

Chapter Eight

'Drat the perishin' copper! Oh, it's always the same when you're in a hurry. Nothin' goes right, and now the fire's all but out, just a'cos I were in a hurry to get the kids off to school so's I could gerrup to the sannytorium in good time!'

Mabel Bailey was doing the family washing and trying to hurry so that she might visit her dear Bob and be back before the kids came out of school. At home, she told herself resentfully, she could have kept an eye both on the fire beneath the copper and on the washing whilst she did other tasks, but in this remote and lonely little cottage the wash house was not a scullery attached to the kitchen but a small, brick-built edifice halfway up the long, sloping garden. It was convenient in a way, Mabel acknowledged, as she returned to the kitchen and picked up the log basket so that she might make up the copper fire. At least, when the washing boiled over, it was just the wash house and the yard which got covered in hot, sudsy water. In Elmore Street when such an accident occurred, most of the ground floor of her home would have been awash.

Tightening her lips, Mabel made up the fire and then popped into the bubbling water the next items to be washed – half a dozen white pillowcases and the sheets off Ben's and Phyllis's beds. She waited until the linen had boiled for a sufficient length of time, then began to pull the dripping sheets out of the copper. She dropped them into the low stone sink and swished them in the rinsing water, then wrung them out as well as she could and carried them to the large mangle. Sighing, she folded them until they would fit into the mangle's wooden maw, then turned the handle, fielding them neatly on the further side and dropping them into the large wickerwork basket which awaited them. If I'd been in Elly I'd ha' nipped next door an' got Peggy Scaulby to give me a hand wi' the heavy stuff, she reminded herself. But here I've no near neighbours at all and though Mrs Hughes up the road is friendly enough, the chances are she'd start jabberin' away in Welsh, forgettin' I don't speak it . . . and that makes me feel such an outsider!

Mrs Hughes was a plump and friendly little Welsh woman whose husband worked in the nearby quarry. They had two sons, Bryn and Meirion. Meirion was in Ben's class at school and the two had speedily become good friends, though their cottages were almost a mile apart.

Since she had lived all her life in the narrow, crowded streets of Liverpool, it was only natural that Mabel found her new home both lonely and frightening. At nights, when there was no sound of traffic in the streets, no glow from the gas lamps and no comforting knowledge that there were many friends within call, Mabel felt particularly vulnerable. If it weren't for my dearest Bob I'd be on the next ferry back to me own place, so I would – but no one could deny that that there sannytorium was doin' him a power o' good. Why, he's cheerful, eats his grub, listens to the wireless . . . and how his dear old face lights up when he sees me comin' through the doors at the end of his ward! The doctors may talk cautious, say not to get excited, to remember that he's still a very sick man, but he's gettin' better with every day that passes; I can see that even if they can't.

At this point the water in the copper began to rise again and Mabel thrust in the odds and ends which always came last. Rags she used for cleaning, the thin, elderly roller towels which hung on the back door and by the sink, the boys' old work trousers which they put on for gardening, and the voluminous calico aprons she wore for scrubbing floors, cooking and other dirty work. Whilst they boiled she carried the now empty buckets into the yard and filled them at the pump, then staggered back with her burden and emptied the buckets into the sink ready for the last rinse.

By eleven o'clock the washing was all done and on the line. There was a stiffish breeze and the sky, though by no means cloudless, was calmly blue. It did not look the sort of day when sudden rain showers might undo all the good that a blow would do, so despite the fact that she was going out Mabel left the washing just where it was. She hurried indoors, checked that all was in readiness for when the youngsters came in from school, and went up to her small bedroom under the eaves. Here, she washed again, using a precious piece of scented soap which dear Bob had given her for Christmas – she did not want to smell of the strong yellow soap she used for the laundry – and put on her best white blouse with the high collar and the leg o' mutton sleeves and the long, dark-grey skirt. Bob liked her to look nice and she always made a big effort when she visited the sanatorium, brushing her mousy hair until it shone and fixing her bun in place with the gold and tortoiseshell combs which had been another Christmas present, only a long-ago one this time, dating from the year of her marriage. Then she dusted her nose with powder and rubbed her lips with geranium petals so that she would look healthy as well as clean and smart.

Repairing to the kitchen once more, she got out of the cupboard today's small gifts. A new-laid egg which Meirion's mam had given her and a two-day-old copy of the local paper, the *Wrexham Leader*, which Ted had picked up on the bus. Bob would enjoy reading the paper if he woke in the night. He never complained, though, never said he was bored, and indeed in the daytime she was fairly sure he was not, for the sanatorium was a lively place, with endless comings and goings and a good deal of harmless gossip.

He said the food was delicious, but she had seen other visitors bringing in little comforts and had decided then and there that she would do the same. She would have liked to get herself a few hens so that eggs would be an everyday occurrence, but was reluctant to do so. Her neighbour, a kindly soul, was quite willing to give her an egg now and then for 'that poor feller shut away in the sanatorium', but it would have been nice to take an egg in every day as a matter of course.

Still, if there was not always an egg, there was always something good: a piece of her homemade bread with a nobble of cheese, or a little cake, or a rosy apple. And the folk were kind to strangers in their midst – used to it, probably, with the sanatorium so close, Mabel supposed. A crossword puzzle cut from a newspaper, an article or feature which someone thought would amuse or educate, a sheet of rough drawing paper and a pencil so that the invalid might ''muse himself if he's awake in the night . . . they doesn't seem to sleep so well up there, probably because they's lyin' around all day', as one well-wisher had put it.

Carefully checking her appearance in the small piece of mirror which was propped up on the wash-stand, Mabel decided that she would do. She went downstairs, anxiously checked that all was well there, picked up her old shopping basket and placed the egg, a couple of rounds of bread and the newspaper in it, and headed for the back door. As she went she eyed the rest of the loaf rather hungrily, for doing the weekly wash was hard work and gave one an appetite. But it was no use. Though she had never confessed as much to any of her children – and had certainly not troubled Bob with the unwelcome truth – she was finding life here a real struggle. She had Bob's pension, but that had never amounted to much, and most of Dick's money – and Ted's, too – was eaten up by their lodgings and by bus fares and other living expenses. What she missed most, of course, was the money she had earned herself, and Ben's contribution. Try though she might, she could not quite feed herself and the two younger kids, take Bob little treats and pay the rent.

The neighbours guessed that things were not easy; probably things were not easy for them, either. But at least they had a wage-earner, and gardens. Mabel had never realised what wonderful things gardens were – why should she, indeed? She did not know one person in Liverpool who owned a garden and though the dwellers in the courts and indeed in Elmore Street had kept hens, they kept them in poor conditions and consequently never had the sort of egg production that was possible here. And the gardens provided so much! Vegetables were only the start. Most of the villagers had apple, pear and plum trees, currant bushes, strawberry plants or raspberry canes. But in the small cottage rented by the Baileys the garden had long gone to rack and ruin, and though there were three fruit trees at the end of the garden they were still bare of anything but leaves and blossom. Ben and Phyllis looked forward eagerly to fruiting time, but Mabel never let herself think so far ahead.

So now, as she closed the door behind her and made for the lane, Mabel only cast a glance at the food cupboard, and did not seriously think of helping herself to any food. She would eat – sparingly – when the children did. She was a healthy woman, she told herself firmly, and could perfectly well manage on one good, sustaining meal a day. Perhaps she might have some bread and marg when she got back from her visit since by then she would be extremely hungry, but for now she would tighten her belt and step out.

There was a bus from the village to the sanatorium and Mabel always gave Bob the impression that she had caught it, but in fact she almost always walked. She told herself that it was healthier, that she should take the opportunity of getting to know the countryside, but in fact it was more the tuppence she saved daily on her bus fare which influenced her.

Sometimes she met up with other visitors to the sanatorium once she reached the gates, for the drive was almost a mile long and the bus did not penetrate the grounds. But today she met no one since she was later than usual, the washing having taken up all her morning. However, she hurried on and presently was walking into the wide entrance hall. She needed no help from the staff now but made her way directly to the men's ward, with its sunny balcony overlooking the humped shoulders of the Llandegla moors. As she pushed open the swing doors she felt her smile begin. Soon, soon she would see him, touch his thin hands, drop a kiss on his white brow. Darling, darling Bob! All her self-sacrifice faded to nothing at the thought of her husband getting better, staying with her. He and she had been sweethearts at school and their love had never faltered. Her loneliness, the difficulty she had over money, the way she dreaded the night-times when she felt most lonely . . . all dimmed and vanished in the strong light of her love. I'll stay in the cottage for a lifetime if it means I can keep Bob, she told herself, crossing the room, seeing his figure in the long cane chair out on the balcony. Oh, Bob, I couldn't live without you!

It was Monday, and Monday was washing day, so Bob knew that his Mabel would be later than usual. She was always later than usual on a Monday. It was annoying that he could not picture her at her work with any accuracy since he had never set eyes on the cottage, but she had described it so minutely and so often that he had a good idea of the set-up there. She would be in her calico apron, tossing the dirty linen into the bubbling copper, rinsing it at the low stone sink, folding sheets and pillow cases and then mangling them, trotting out to the line – it was a fine day – and finally returning to the cottage kitchen and making sure that all was well there before setting out to visit him.

It was a brilliant day. The balcony was glassed in but today the windows were open, letting in the lovely, refreshing breeze as well as the warmth of the sun. Bob sighed with pleasure. He thought how sad it was that he should have come to know and appreciate the countryside so late in his life . . . when it was almost over, in fact.

For appreciate it he did. He lay on the balcony and watched the wildlife and marvelled at everything. Rabbits came each evening to graze on the sweet, well-mown grass of the sanatorium's wide lawns. Sometimes he saw a fox sneaking along beside the hedge in the early dawn or late dusk, sometimes a badger snuffled along the edge of the moor, and there were always the wild, leggy sheep and now their bouncing, happy lambs. Bob had always had the knack of stillness, but it had availed him little enough in the city. Here, however, it was different. If you stayed quiet and still you could see and note everything, from the buds on the trees as they gradually uncurled to the shy primroses on the bank, the rosettes of deep blue wild violets, the shambling run of a hedgehog and the quick, sly dart of a stoat.

He tried to tell the other men in his ward – there were five of them – that they should enjoy the life which went on beyond the glass, but they grunted and grinned at him and then turned back to their racing pages, or to the wireless, or to mending their socks or completing a jigsaw. They were not countrymen and saw no reason to watch what went on beyond the glass, though they would comment every time an aircraft passed overhead or a shepherd whistled to his dog to round up the flock.

We're all poorly, so why don't they see, as I do, that this is a wonderful opportunity to enrich the life we've got left? Bob wondered. One man, Giles, was very ill indeed. His breathing could be heard from the men's lavatories down the corridor and every time he coughed there was blood. But Giles went on backing the dogs and the horses, when he could get someone to place a bet for him, and though he was a convivial sort of fellow and sometimes padded down the corridor in his regulation dressing gown and slippers to visit a pal on another ward, he said frankly that he was not interested in rabbits or them little ginger cats or dogs or wharrever which old Bob found so entertaining.

'If we was to have a bet as to how many rabbits would be on view at once on a partic'lar evenin', now that would be worth lookin' at,' he had said in his breathy, gasping thread of a voice. 'But them other things . . . no, no, they ain't for me, ole feller.'

So Bob did not talk about his interest much, any more, except to his dear Mabs, and she was interested in everything, talked about keeping a few hens when he was well enough to join them in the cottage, never seemed to realise . . .

But no point in dwelling on that! Better to think of the pleasure he felt each weekend, when Dick and Ted would turn up with stories of Laird's. They made him laugh until he cried, sometimes. Then there was his girl, Millie, and her husband Frank, who somehow managed, despite their busy lives, to come and see him every few weeks. They did not always bring the twins because Frank's mother was willing to take care of them whilst they visited him. But once or twice, the little girls had come, filling him with grandfatherly pride as they chattered and played about his bed. Millie was expecting another baby in August and naturally they were hoping for a boy. Bob hoped so too and sometimes he and Mabel talked about the new child and Bob allowed himself to wonder whether he might hold it in his arms before . . .

Only it didn't do to think like that, particularly with

Mabs about to arrive. He glanced towards the ward and felt his heart leap with pleasure and sat himself up slowly, so as not to gasp or cough when she was actually beside him.

'Mabel!' he said as she came, beaming, on to the balcony. 'Oh, Mabs, my dearest girl, isn't it grand to see you? My, you're looking younger and prettier than ever – I can see country life suits you, queen! Now come and sit beside me so's I can feast me eyes on you whiles you tell me what's been happenin' in Bwlchgwyn!'

'Whose turn is it to make supper this evening? If it's me, I've gorra get meself some grub to cook, 'cos when I looked into the cupboard last night there were nowt but spuds 'n' onions an' half a loaf of bread.' The four girls who shared the attic room had long since decided that communal meals were both cheaper and easier to prepare. Hester looked across at the speaker; Eileen O'Farrell was the latest addition to their small company. She was a tall, well-built girl with fluffy, unmanageable light-brown hair, round, blue eyes which always looked surprised and a ready smile. She was easy-going and sweet-natured and very soon she and Hester had become firm friends. Since they both worked on the Scotland Road, they had formed the habit of setting out together and of waiting for one another in the evenings. What was more, they helped each other over domestic tasks which meant that when it was Eileen's turn to cook and market, the two girls would do the tasks together.

Now, Hester regarded her friend affectionately. 'What you mean is, you'll need a contribution from everyone or we'll none of us eat tonight,' she remarked. 'No one expects you to pay for the meals you cook – as if you didn't know! So if the cupboard's bare, we'll all put, say, sixpence into the pot; you can buy a lot of ingredients for two shillings.'

'Ye-es, but I don't know what to cook,' Eileen said plaintively. 'Wharrabout sausage and mash, girls? With a bread pudding for afterwards? Something to fill us bellies.'

'That'll suit me, though now the weather's getting so much pleasanter we shouldn't need to eat quite so much stodge,' Hester remarked.

Madge, coiling her long brown hair into a neat bun at the base of her neck, snorted. 'It may be April, but it's still pretty chilly, especially in the evenings,' she observed. 'What's more, Woolworth's don't believe in lettin' their staff sit about so I'm always on the go. By the time I get home of an evening, I swear I could eat a horse – or a load of hay – so don't you go giving us no salads, young Eileen.'

'No, I won't do that,' Eileen promised. 'Wharrabout sausage and mash, though, Madge? That suit you, and you, Ruby?'

Both girls having assented, Eileen struggled into her thin coat and began to button it whilst Hester pulled on her long leather boots. She had clung on to her boots throughout the winter and even now was glad of their warmth, though most of the rest of her good clothing had been sold in Paddy's market and replaced with cheaper, thinner stuff.

'Well? Can everyone afford sixpence at this time of the week?' she asked presently, when she was dressed and ready for the off. 'If there's any over it can go back in the pot for tomorrow, because sausages aren't expensive.'

Everyone handed over their sixpences with varying degrees of reluctance, including Hester herself, and Eileen. It was a good while since Hester had paid out for a cooked meal in a restaurant, and she was well aware of the savings she now made. She was still using Bridget's saucepans – the other girl must have kept her live-in job since she had not returned to claim the cooking pots – and she usually spent no more than a half-crown each week on food, yet she ate adequately, if not well.

And there's nothing wrong with sausage and mash, she told herself defensively five minutes later, as she and Eileen walked briskly along Scotland Road. Whoever was cooking used the kitchen, with the other inhabitants of Number 10, and thanks to her evening classes Hester herself had no objection to others watching her whilst she fried, simmered or stewed. Eileen, however, was wedded to the frying pan and did not seem able to boil herself so much as an egg without making a mess of it. She was a dreamer, Hester concluded now, as they turned into George Carr's pork butchery and took their places at the long counter. Because it was early, the shop was empty save for the staff cleaning down, so they were quickly able to buy just over a pound of his delicious pork sausages before continuing on their way.

'We can use the stale half loaf to make a bread pudding. Shall I get some currants or sultanas on the way back to the Stanny?' Hester suggested. She was all too aware that young Eileen would gaily promise to do the rest of the shopping and would then arrive home having totally forgotten all about it. 'You said there were spuds in the food cupboard – enough to make mash for all of us, would you say?'

'Yes . . . no . . . I ain't sure,' Eileen said absently.

'We could do wi' a tad more margarine, though. Mash is nicer if there's a knob o' margarine mixed in.'

'I'll get the rest of the shopping, then,' Hester said resignedly, and was rewarded by Eileen's sweet and brilliant smile. No matter how irritating the other girl was – and she could be very irritating, Hester knew – her smile simply melted all one's annoyance away. 'What time will you be finishing tonight, Eileen?'

'Oh . . . the usual,' Eileen said. 'Only thing is, Hes, I really ought to go along to Paddy's market before I starts on the cookin'. This coat . . . it only just does up and any minute there's goin' to be a 'splosion and me buttons will fire off like cannon balls.'

'You'd better have just sausages and no mash then,' Hester said heartlessly. Eileen loved her food. 'We can't have you buying a new coat every three or four weeks! Though with the summer coming I dare say we shan't need our winter clothes soon.'

They had reached Eileen's place of work, the ironmonger's, and Eileen, about to push open the door, stopped. 'Why shouldn't I buy bigger clothes?' she asked mildly. 'Don't you know nothin', Hester? Everyone needs bigger clothes, whether it's summer or winter, when they're goin' to have a baby – you gets ever so big, you know.' And before Hester could do more than gape at her, she had smiled her sweet, absent smile and disappeared into the shop.

For the rest of her working day, Hester's mind was in a whirl of conjecture. Eileen had been living in their shared room for a month and so far as Hester knew had never mentioned that she was pregnant.

Selling a dance dress in shocking pink, with black roses printed all over it, to a fat and spotty customer who was forty if she was a day, Hester wondered whether any of the other girls knew Eileen's secret; then she wondered if they all knew, and it was only she who was ignorant. The customer had to speak sharply to her to get her attention because she wanted a corsage of artificial roses to pin to the shoulder of the dress and Hester, seeing Miss Deakin's mean little eyes swivel in her direction, hastily banished Eileen, and her state of health, from her mind and tried to persuade the customer that one could have too much of roses, lovely though they might be.

It was one of those days when every customer who fell to Hester's lot was a difficult one. The nice ones wanted some shade or garment that they did not have in stock and the nasty ones demanded to see every skirt, blouse or indeed pair of gloves in the size they required and then turned the whole lot down with some flimsy excuse such as, 'I'll think it over,' or, 'It isn't *quite* what I wanted, miss. I'll have to look elsewhere.'

For the first time for many weeks, Hester scarcely gave Dick or Lonnie a thought. Indeed, she had almost stopped worrying about Lonnie since she assumed that Mr Hetherington-Smith would be back from his world cruise now and would surely have been in contact with his daughter. Hester hoped, and supposed, that Lonnie was settling down at her new school, but remembering Miss Hetherington-Smith's meanness it was impossible not to wonder whether the old woman had sent her niece to some cheap establishment, where she would be unhappy.

Normally, a good deal of Hester's thinking time was given over to planning how she would find both Lonnie and Dick, though the memory of Dick was beginning to fade. She would never forget his kindness or his humour but the picture of his handsome, good-natured face could no longer be conjured up with ease.

'Miss Elliott!' Miss Deakin's voice cut across Hester's musings. 'What on earth's gorrin to you today? I've axed you twice when you want to have your dinner and norra word have I had in reply.'

Hester had been folding cardigans and replacing them on the rack. Now, she jumped guiltily and looked around her. The shop was empty, as she might indeed have guessed, since when a customer was present Miss Deakin spoke in a squashed and prissy accent which she no doubt considered made her sound ladylike. What was more, Betsy and Hester were never invited to take their lunch break when customers were present. Hester folded the last cardigan and turned to her employer. 'I'm sorry, Miss Deakin, I'm afraid my mind was on work,' she said glibly. 'The last customer asked why manufacturers seldom made cardigans in a nice clear blue and I was wondering if it might be worth having a word with Ivy Woollens the next time you put in an order. Blue goes with most things, and . . .'

'If I want advice from you, I'll tell you,' Miss Deakin snapped. 'Most folk are quite happy with brown, grey or navy. Are you taking your dinner break now, or not?'

The girls were supposed to have an hour for their dinner but seldom managed more than thirty minutes or so, especially if they ate carry-out in the back room, where they could easily be recalled when Miss Deakin needed them. Today, however, Hester had shopping to do, so she gobbled her sandwiches and then left the shop, assuring Miss Deakin, mendaciously, that she would not be long. In fact, she intended to buy potatoes, margarine and a bag of sultanas and then to go to Williams's Hardware to see if she could have a word with Eileen. All morning she had longed for her dinner hour so that she might ask Betsy for her opinion but had belatedly realised she could do no such thing. Eileen was certainly not married, had never even hinted at the existence of a boyfriend, so her having a baby was a shameful thing which she would not want to become public knowledge. How she intended to hide her condition as time went on, Hester could not imagine. The ironmonger, a little wisp of a man, and his huge, over-blown wife would no doubt be horrified and disgusted to discover that their new assistant was pregnant. Eileen would undoubtedly lose her job as soon as they found out, and what would she do then? There were places which took in bad girls, Hester knew, but she had no idea how such places were run. She knew that they hired out the girls to do menial work such as cleaning or laundry in return for a roof over their heads, whilst they were waiting for their babies to be born, and also knew that most of the young mothers were only too happy to hand over their children for adoption. Eileen was by no means unique – girls must be having babies all over the city, otherwise such institutions would not exist – but Hester could not imagine her easy-going, fun-loving friend taking to such a regime.

As soon as her messages were done, therefore, she carried her heavy basket into the ironmonger's shop and asked for her friend. 'It's Eileen's turn to do the cooking today,' she explained to Mr Williams, 'but I got the shopping for her and just want to check I've bought everything she'll need.' She glanced around the shop, which was empty save for herself, Mr

Williams and a customer who was selecting nails and placing them, one by one, upon the counter. 'Has Miss O'Farrell left for her dinner yet?'

'No, she's in the back. I'll give her a shout,' Mr Williams said briefly. He raised his voice to yell. 'Miss O'Farrell! Shop!'

There was a short pause and then Eileen appeared in the doorway, chewing. She did not seem to see Hester but went over to the customer and began to count the nails he had selected. Mr Williams grinned. 'No, no, I'll deal wi' that, Miss O'Farrell,' he said genially. 'Your pal what's done your messages wants a word. D'you want to take her through the back? I take it Mother's gone up to the flat to get me dinner?'

'OK,' Eileen said, placidly. She jerked her head at Hester. 'Come on, then.'

Hester looked helplessly at the long counter which divided the staff from the customers. Eileen gave a snort of laughter and walked along to the end of the counter, which proved to be a flap. She swung it up, saying as she did so: 'Everything's easy when you know how! D'you want a cup o' tea? Mrs Williams put the kettle on before she went up, so the tea's only just brewed.'

Hester followed her into the little back room, admitting that a cup of tea would be most welcome. 'Isn't it snug, though?' she said appreciatively. A bright fire burned in the grate and there were three cosy armchairs with faded chintz upholstery drawn up before it. In one corner was a low sink; there was a small, square table on which Eileen's sandwiches were laid out and on a Welsh dresser against the right-hand wall hung a variety of differently patterned cups, with lots of odd plates displayed on the upper shelves. 'I wish the room at the back of our shop was like this, but Miss Deakin only lights the paraffin stove in the back if she's afraid the pipes will freeze.'

'I dunno why you stand it,' Eileen said bluntly. 'You're paid less than I am and you're ever so much cleverer than me. I bet it don't take you two minutes to count nails and work out what the feller owes in your head. I have to write it all down and even so it takes me ages. Do sit down,' she added hospitably, gesturing to the chair nearest to the fire and taking the one opposite for herself. 'What have you bought? I know about the sausages, of course, but did you get . . . ?'

'Never mind that; I got everything we agreed,' Hester said, lowering her voice. 'Eileen, did you *mean* what you told me this morning? About – about the reason for you wanting a new coat? Only you've never said a word before and I was wondering . . . were you joking, Eileen? Only it didn't sound like a joke.'

'It weren't a joke,' Eileen assured her, with a rather hunted look towards the door which led into the shop. 'I've not telled anybody yet, because when I do, horrible things will happen. Very likely the Maskells will kick me out and they won't want me here, not once I begin to show. I didn't mean to tell anyone, only it just sort of popped out. I could ha' bit me tongue out when I heard me voice tellin' you, but o' course it were too late. Oh, Hes, wharrever am I goin' to do?'

'I simply can't advise you,' Hester said slowly. 'I've only been in this country a year, so I don't really know how things work. But – forgive me, Eileen – isn't it usual to get married when you find . . . when you find . . .'

'That'd be all right for some, but the feller in question is married already. Remember I told you how I worked in a hotel when I first come to the city? Well, I were a chambermaid and he were one of the under managers. I guess he thought I were one of the perks of the job,' she added bitterly, 'and not only me, neither. One of the other chambermaids telled me . . . but never mind that. He were married anyway, wi' a couple o' kids, and I hated him. He were a horrible little man, with poppin' blue eyes and a loose, wet mouth. I promise you, Hester, I only give way once . . . oh, how I wish I hadn't!'

'If you hated him so much, wouldn't it have been possible to – to stop the baby coming?' Hester asked cautiously. The trouble was she knew so little about such things; only remembered hearing Mollie talking, in a hushed voice, about a pal of hers who had got into trouble and had gone to a back-street doctor who had, as Mollie put it, 'seen her right'.

'An abortion, you mean?' Eileen said. She both looked and sounded shocked that such a thought should have crossed her friend's mind. 'Oh, I couldn't. It'd be eternal damnation, for a start, and if me dad ever found out he'd beat me within an inch of me life.'

'I thought your mum and dad were dead?' Hester said suspiciously. 'I'm sure you told me you were an orphan.'

'Did I?' Eileen said, looking vague. 'Well, I might as well be an orphan. Me dad remarried six months after me mam died and I haven't been back home since his new wife moved in, nor I shan't go back now, norrin this state.' She pointed significantly to her stomach.

'But what'll you do, Eileen?' Hester almost wailed. 'When folk find out, you'll have to do something, you can't just live on the street. What about going to one of those places where they look after – after girls who get into trouble? Then you could have the baby adopted and no one any the wiser. That is, if you leave before folk find out.'

'They say those places are awful,' Eileen said apprehensively. She'd pulled a strand of her fluffy, light-brown hair across her mouth and began to chew it nervously. 'I don't want to go in a place like that until the very last moment, if then. Oh, Hes, I'm savin' up every penny I can spare, but I don't think it'll be enough to keep me between folk finding out and the baby bein' born. As for adoption, there's loads of people who'll arrange that for you, I'm told.' She pulled the hair out of her mouth and jumped to her feet. 'Lor' luv us, I'll forget me own head next! I promised you a cuppa and all you've had is me worries. To tell you the truth, Hester, they say there's nothin' like sharin' your troubles and we've just proved it's true. I feel as if a great weight has been lifted off me mind. Two heads is better than one, they say, so if we both think as hard as we can, mebbe we'll work somethin' out.'

Hester, sipping her tea, hoped that her friend was right and that the knotty problem would soon be solved, but secretly she doubted it. Glancing at Eileen's wide hips, however, she told herself that her friend might be one of those people who don't show that they are pregnant until the very last moment. Before she left, therefore, she put the question uppermost in her mind. 'How far gone are you, Eileen?' she asked. 'If it was only once . . . well, you should have a pretty good idea of the date the baby will come, shouldn't you?'

'Oh, I think I'm about five months gone, or maybe a

bit less, so I've another four months or so to go, which will make it towards the end of August,' Eileen said vaguely, after a moment's thought. 'An' I don't show yet, do I? I think, meself, that I've gorranother month, or mebbe two, before folk will start talkin'.'

Hester looked thoughtfully at her friend. It was true that Eileen was not showing at all yet, so far as she could see. Of course, she reasoned, I never knew her before she was in the family way so I suppose I'm no judge; but if she's careful . . . if she buys clothes that are a bit too big for her . . . why, there's no reason for anyone to suspect. Not for a while, anyway.

She said as much to Eileen, who heaved a deep sigh. 'Will you come shoppin' wi' me then, after work?' she asked hopefully. 'I put a bit o' cash aside each week, and I sell the stuff what I've growed out of, so I can afford some different skirts an' that. If you're wi' me you can tell me which blouses an' skirts an' coats look best . . . hide me belly best, I should say.'

'All right, I'll come,' Hester said. 'But better make it tomorrow evening, because we're cooking tonight. And incidentally, Eileen, if I'm to help you – and I'm happy to do so – then you must promise me one thing.'

'What's that?' Eileen asked suspiciously. 'If you mean to make me go back to me dad and that woman he's bin an' gone an' wed . . .'

'No indeed, that's no business of mine, and anyway, I'm sure you know best,' Hester said quickly. 'No, what I want you to do is to come to cookery classes with me and Betsy. You'll enjoy it, honestly you will; they sell us the ingredients extremely cheaply, and you'll learn enough cookery to be able to cope one day, when you've a home – and a husband – of your own.'

'Oh! Well, I wouldn't mind doin' that,' Eileen said at once. 'When she were alive, me mam did all the cookin', so us kids never gorra look in, but I'd like to have a try. After all, I'm that fond of me grub so learnin' how to cook nice things is right up my street! When do I start?'

'Next week,' Hester said. 'The new term starts for the cookery class next Tuesday evening. I'll tell Betsy you're going to come with us; she's awfully nice, you'll like her.'

Ten minutes later, back at Paris Modes once more, Hester found that she felt far happier about her friend. Despite her vagueness, her absent-mindedness, her woolly-headedness in fact, she thought that Eileen would probably weather the storm of pregnancy far better than some other more practical and level-headed person might have done. She realised she could not confide in Betsy but was pleasantly surprised by the other assistant's easy acceptance of a third person to accompany them to their cookery lessons.

'We're already paired up, so she won't be able to be with us for the practicals,' she reminded Hester, for the girls cooked in pairs and then took it in turns to take home the dish they had prepared. 'But there's that poor fish, Fanny Ellis, just longing for a partner and having to manage alone most of the time. She'll be right grateful that your pal's decided to come along.'

'Hey, Ben! Are you goin' to the shop?'

Ben slowed in his tracks and glanced behind him, then nodded as the other boy drew level. It was

Meirion Hughes, who was in Ben's class at his new school and who lived in the cottage nearest to the one the Baileys now rented. He was a short, stocky boy, dark-haired and dark-eyed, and he and Ben had always got along well. Usually they walked to school together in the mornings and returned home together at night, but this was Saturday so Ben, carrying a large linen bag in one hand, was off to the shops to do his mother's messages. As the weather grew warmer, Ben's initial longing for the city of his birth had begun to fade a little. There were advantages in country living. Birds-nesting was a new joy to him and fishing in streams and ponds to find tadpoles, sticklebacks and other such creatures was a novelty which did not pall.

On a Saturday morning, however, he could not help thinking, wistfully, of what his erstwhile pals would be doing in the city. There were the flicks, for a start. If you could get hold of a penny or two, you could join the crowd of youngsters outside the cinema of your choice and presently you would be in another world. Cowboys and Indians, Laurel and Hardy, the adventures of Lassie, would transport you. All your troubles would be forgotten and for two noisy, sweet-sucking hours you were just one of the crowd.

But there was no cinema in Bwlchgwyn, and you could not skip a lecky and go rattling along the road for free, bound for the delights of the Pier Head at low tide, when an adventurous lad could swing down from the floating road and become a mudlark for the afternoon. Nostalgically, Ben remembered objects which he had found in the mud, feeling for them with his bare toes: a cockle rake, an enamel mug with the ship's name printed on the side, a golf ball (what on earth was *that* doing there?) and a rather fine penny-whistle on which, when thoroughly cleaned, Ben was soon able to play many popular tunes.

There were other things he missed as well. Mr Madison's pet shop was one of them. It had been nice to earn some money to help the family and even nicer to always have a few pence in his own pocket. He had soon grown really fond of the various animals Mr Madison sold and mourned the departure of each one when its new owner bore it off. True, there were animals in plenty in the countryside, but they were not easy to see and even more difficult to stroke. Rabbits were kept in some people's back gardens, as were ferrets, and most houses had a dog or a cat, or perhaps both. But Ben acknowledged that his mother was right to refuse to keep a pet. Though no one ever talked about it openly, Ben supposed they all knew in their hearts that this country idyll would not last for ever. If his father got well enough to leave the sanatorium, then he supposed that the family would return to the city. He tried not to think of the alternatives but sometimes forced himself to do so in order that he might grow accustomed to the fact that his father was unlikely to be cured, even though he seemed more cheerful and had actually gained a little weight.

'Ben? What's on your shoppin' list? My mam wants me to go down to Wrexham on the bus. She says meat is cheaper in the butcher's market and I'm a half fare, so I'm cheaper too. If you could come an' all, we might go to the cinema. My mam give me tuppence. D'you have any money?'

'I could probably manage tuppence,' Ben said cautiously. His heart had lifted at the mention of a visit to the pictures. 'What's on? Is it a cowboy?'

'Dunno,' Meirion said briefly. 'Come on, Ben, tell me what's on your list! If your mam wants a joint for Sunday, you might as well come with me into the town. My mam says meat is half the price down Wrexham.'

Ben sighed. If only Meirion had said something the previous day, he could have asked his mother to let him go into town with his friend. As it was, if he simply disappeared for three or four hours, she would not only be worried, she would be without the food which she had told him to buy. As they entered the long, winding village street, Ben began to explain that Meirion's idea, though a good one, was impossible this week. 'I dare say your mam would be real upset if you bobbied off to town wi'out a word to her,' he observed. 'Why didn't you say something yesterday, Meirion? I do love two penn'orth of dark, but it just ain't possible.'

Ahead of them, a bus drew to a halt and people began to climb down. Ben gave them a cursory glance, then looked more closely. 'Dick! It's our Dick! He must have got off work early! If he'll do my messages and explain to our mam, then I'll come wi' you, Meirion. I'll buy the joint in town because Mam won't be wantin' it till tomorrer.' He grinned widely as his brother came rapidly towards them. 'Hey up, Dickie! Why's you here so early? Cammell Laird's give you a day off, did they? Will you do me a favour?'

'What a greeting!' Dick said, rumpling his young brother's hair. 'I worked late three evenings this week to finish a fancy bureau for the captain's cabin, so they give me time off in lieu. And why can't you do your own messages, you idle young blighter?'

Ben explained briefly and Dick took the list and

read it through. 'Mam wants all this lot for the weekend?' he asked incredulously. 'Where's the shop, then?'

'You'll get it all from Mr Evans; I'm goin' to get the meat, so you needn't go on to the butcher,' Ben said. 'Me pal, Meirion – oh, I forgot to interdooce you – Meirion, this is me brother, Dick, Dick, this is me pal, Meirion.' The two grinned at each other and Ben continued: 'Meat's a deal cheaper in Wrexham town, there's a butcher's market. So Meirion and I mean to buy the meat there and then go to the Majestic, to see their Saturday show.'

'If you're goin' to get into town in time to see even the second half of the Saturday show, you'd best gerron the next bus,' Dick said. He took the bag from his brother. 'You'll have to ask the butcher to wrap the joint up well 'cos I'll need the bag to carry the rest of the messages.' He fished around in his pocket and withdrew a sixpence. 'Here, this is for you and your pal. Don't go spendin' it all in one shop. Where's the messages money?'

Ben grinned and dug in his pockets, then handed over an assortment of small coins wrapped in what had once, no doubt, been a clean handkerchief. 'That's what our mam gave me for the whole lot,' he explained. 'I think she said a decent joint would cost the most, the rest is for veggies, flour, margarine . . . well, all the other things on the list.' He felt it would be niggardly to point out that tuppence of the money had been his payment for getting the messages, particularly as Dick had stumped up so generously.

Dick sorted out a florin and a shilling and handed the money back to his brother. 'That should see you right . . .' he was beginning, when they all heard the roar of an approaching engine. 'Hey up, lads, that sounds like the bus. You'd better gerra move on, you don't want to miss it. Oh, I'd better give you a few pence for your fare.' Dick thrust some pennies into Ben's hand and then the two boys were hustling themselves aboard the bus. Ben was gleeful. After weeks and weeks of country living, this trip to the local town, with a promise of a cinema thrown in, seemed the height of adventure. He and Meirion slid into an empty seat and Ben's happiness was complete when his friend produced two licorice sticks and handed him one of them.

'If we get the meat cheap, then mebbe we'll have enough money over to buy ourselves some dinner,' he observed. 'There's eatin' houses in Wrexham what'll do a big bowl o' vegetable soup and a thick slice of bread for a few pennies. Mam said I could get me some dinner if the money stretched.'

Ben supposed that this would be all right, then concentrated on the view from the window. It was a wide and splendid one, for Bwlchgwyn was perched on the side of a mountain and below them came first the forestry of Nant-y-Ffrith, then the plain, spread out like a map, with Wrexham looking like a toy beneath the haze of light-blue smoke arising from house and factory chimneys. The town was surrounded by coal mines which probably added their own dirt to the blue-grey cloud hovering above it and Ben guessed that later in the day Wrexham would be hidden from view beneath a thick smoke-screen. Now, however, in the early morning, it looked a pleasant place and Ben wondered why he had never been tempted to visit it before. He should have guessed that it would have a cinema – it had several, according to Meirion – and probably other forms of entertainment as well.

The shops, too, would be crowded and busy because Wrexham was a market town and according to the teacher at school attracted people from near and far, particularly on market day.

It was not going to be anything like Liverpool though, Ben realised. Wistfully, he imagined himself walking along the Scottie, shouting greetings to his pal, going into a shop to beg a length of orange box rope or to ask if there were any spare crates which he could chop up for firewood and subsequently sell. Mrs Evans had looked at him as though he had run mad when he had asked her a similar question. 'Chop up my good boxes?' she had said incredulously. 'Why would you want to do that, cariad? There's many a child has begged a box off me so's he can make a rabbit hutch or a little house for play, like, but to chop up good wood . . .'

Ben had explained that he meant to sell the wood for kindling and the elderly lady had laughed and shaken her head. 'Why should anyone pay for kindling when the forest is full of fallen twigs and branches?' she enquired. 'Us country folk don't have money to burn and it would be like burning money to buy kindling when it's free for anyone who cares to pick it up. No, no, cariad, you'll have to find some other way of making money while you live in Bwlchgwyn.'

Ben had been disappointed but not despairing; surely there must be someone willing to pay for a service which he could render? But when questioned on the point, Meirion had not been very helpful. 'In the summer we helps on the farms, cut cabbage, dig spuds, do a bit of harvestin' come hay-makin', but right now things is quiet. You can't help wi' the lambing 'cos they need fellers wi' experience, and anyway most of them sort o' jobs is took by farm workers' kids. But later . . .'

Ben had thought grumpily that back home it did not matter what season it was, if you were willing to work there was usually some way to earn the odd penny. However, Meirion told him that on market days he could take a bus down into Wrexham and earn some cash helping farmers drive their beasts home from the market there, and though so far he had done nothing about it, it was a possibility, he supposed.

'It were good of your brother to do your . . . your errands,' Meirion said presently, as the bus began to trundle through the suburbs of the market town. 'Is he wed? I've seen him gettin' off the bus in the village several times, but he's always alone. Does he have a girlfriend? I suppose he must, 'cos he's quite a lot older than you, isn't he?'

'He is,' Ben said briefly. 'He were never one for the gals . . . that is, he liked 'em all right, but he didn't like one of 'em more'n the others. Then, last summer . . .' And Ben found himself telling Meirion all about Hester and Lonnie, about the horrible old aunt, the sacking of Hester herself, followed by that of various servants, and the incarceration of Lonnie in a boarding school somewhere, but no one knew where.

'And our Dick's been real miserable because he says he's lost touch wi' Hester and may never find her again; he thinks she'll go back to India as soon as maybe, if she's not gone already,' he concluded with some melodrama. 'It's awful, ain't it? That wicked ole woman won't tell anyone where the kid is, and *I* think that if we could find Lonnie, she'd know where to look for Hester. But there ain't no way of discovering where she stuck the kid, and of course I ain't in Liverpool no more, else I'd search every girls' boarding school in the place, honest to God I would. But y'see, Dick's workin' at Laird's – that's Cammell Laird's, the ship builders – and so he doesn't have time to comb the streets. He's been over to the house in Shaw Street – where Hester used to live – but they can't tell him what they don't know themselves. So it seems hopeless.' He turned to his friend as the bus drew to a halt. 'Is this our stop? Where's the picture-house? I say, it's busy; the street is fair black wi' folk.'

'Yes, we've arrived,' Meirion said laconically. 'I'm sorry for your brother, but I'm sure there must be a way to find out where them gals have gone. You've just got to hit on the right scheme.'

'And what would you do, clever-clogs?' Ben asked sarcastically, as they stepped down on to the pavement. 'Why, there's nowt we've not thought of, and much good it's done us so far!'

'I'd write a letter to the little gal,' Meirion said placidly, 'because from what you've said, her father will be writin' to her often. Who's to say that the letter you send ain't from her dad, or from this woman he's married? I bet the old woman has got fed up wi' openin' harmless letters by now, and will just bundle it up wi' the others.'

Ben stopped in the middle of the pavement and stared at his friend, open-mouthed. 'We-ell, yes,' he said slowly at last. 'But it can't be that simple. There must be a snag somewhere, else we'd ha' thought of it ourselves.'

'Ah, but you're not a wily Welshman,' Meirion said, grinning. 'The English have suppressed us and mistreated us for so many generations that we've had to learn to get around obstacles instead of blunderin' straight into 'em.'

Later, as he'd said goodbye to his friend and agreed with him that they had had a splendid day, Ben's thoughts returned to Meirion's suggestion; the more he considered, the more he was beginning to think that it was the scheme likeliest to succeed out of the various ploys which Dick had come up with. Walking along under the stars – for the boys had stayed in Wrexham to see a proper showing of a two-feature film in the afternoon – he began to plan a strategy for getting the letter delivered. If it was meant to come from foreign parts, then there would be a problem over the stamp. He was wondering whether he could get over this by pushing the envelope through the door himself when he remembered Topper Jones in his class. Topper was a keen philatelist, which meant he collected stamps, and he often swapped stamps he already possessed for ones that he did not. Ben knew that letters and postcards from Lonnie's father would come from a variety of different countries. All he had to do was to stick one of Topper's unwanted stamps on to the envelope and hope that it would get delivered with the rest of the post. Then there was the letter itself. We can't rely on the old girl not to open the envelope and have a snoopy read, so whatever we say will have to be kind of coded, Ben reminded himself. He was longing to see Dick's face when he put the idea to him and broke into a trot as he grew closer to the cottage. This is more exciting than the film we saw this afternoon, he thought, because this is real life and not just a story.

He reached the cottage, opened the small gate and closed it carefully behind him, then went down the side of the dwelling and round the back. The front of the cottage had been in darkness but light streamed out through the long low kitchen window and Ben stood in the small porch to remove his dirty boots and then opened the back door and entered the kitchen. Dick, his mother and Phyllis were seated round the table with plates of scouse before them and mugs of tea at their elbows. All three of them looked up as Ben came in and Mrs Bailey got to her feet at once, picked up an empty plate and went over to the fire. 'You're awful late, Benny,' she said, ladling food on to the plate. 'Where have you been? No, don't say Wrexham, 'cos I know that, but I thought you told Dick you were goin' to the butcher's market and the afternoon picture show. Where's my joint for tomorrow? I hope it's a good 'un.'

'It's a prime shoulder of mutton, and it were dead cheap,' Ben said proudly, putting the huge joint down on the kitchen table. 'Meirion said if we waited till the market was about to close we'd get a real bargain, so that's why I'm late. I reckon it were worth it, 'cos I didn't pay half what it would have cost me in the village and I reckon this is a meatier joint an' all.'

'It's a grand piece of meat all right,' Dick observed, smiling at his brother's evident pride. 'I'm glad I did your messages for you, young Ben, since there's nowt I enjoy more than a shoulder of mutton with some nice mint sauce and a big helping of new potatoes. And since I bought a bunch of mint and the potatoes from the village shop earlier, I guess I'm in for a treat.'

Mrs Bailey put the plate of blind scouse in front of Ben and sat down in her place once more. 'You're lookin' awfully pleased wi' yourself, son,' she said shrewdly. 'What else happened in Wrexham today, eh? Lose a sixpence and find a sovereign?'

'Better'n that,' Ben said, beaming round at his family. 'Meirion an' I were talkin' on the bus and I telled him how we'd lost touch wi' Hester and Lonnie and he said . . .'

At the end of the recital, Dick, Mrs Bailey and even young Phyllis were all beaming, though Dick's smile, Ben thought, was easily the widest. 'Your pal's brilliant – I can't think why we didn't think of it ourselves,' Dick said admiringly. 'I'm sure Hester will get in touch with Lonnie somehow, so if we can get in touch with Lonnie too, our problems should be over. Ben, tell your pal he's a bleedin' genius. We'll start work on the letter tomorrow!'

'Well, my darling? How does it feel to be back in India once more?' Leonard Hetherington-Smith took his wife's hand and squeezed her fingers. They were in a taxi cab, heading for the home they had left, and despite the heat, the noise and the all-pervading odour of the streets, Leonard found himself glad to be home. 'I was planning a party so that all my friends could meet my new wife, but after nearly seven months of cruising round the world together we seem more like an old married couple than newly-weds!'

Rosalind Hetherington-Smith returned the pressure of his fingers and smiled her brilliant, three-cornered smile. 'I've had a wonderful time, darling, and I'm going to find it hard to settle down to an ordinary life again,' she admitted. 'Of course, I'd love to meet your friends, Leonard, but the person I most want to meet isn't in India. I know you've left your business in other hands for an awfully long time, but wouldn't it be possible for us to travel to England fairly soon? I know you say Lonnie is very happy living with her aunt and the young governess, but

I'm afraid she may feel I have caused you to neglect her.' She turned impulsively towards him. 'Leonard, I do want her to love me! The relationship between a little girl and her stepmother is always difficult; I don't want to make it even more so by putting off our meeting. I know you say that India is no place for a child, but I've never truly understood why parents keep young children with them and send them Home just when they are beginning to be more self-reliant and self-confident.'

'That's the reason, my foolish one,' Leonard said, grinning at her. 'It wouldn't be fair to send a very young child Home, because a young child needs its parents. But once a child is seven or eight, a life of being constantly waited upon and spoiled to death by Indian servants saps their strength and does not improve their characters. The ideal thing would be for the children to have six months in India with their parents and six months in Britain attending a good school. But this is rarely possible for reasons which I don't have to explain to you.'

'No, I understand. I know what you mean. It's the school holidays, and missing half a year would scarcely help a child's education,' Rosalind agreed. 'But Leonard, she's such a little girl and you've said yourself that your sister is a difficult woman, and seven months is an awfully long time. I'd be far happier, truly I would, if we could at least plan an early trip to England.'

'I don't see why we shouldn't, if it would please you,' Leonard said. 'But remember, we've seven months' post waiting for us when we get home. After reading her letters, you may well feel reassured that there is no need for such a trip. As you say, I've left the business in other hands for longer than I should have done and there may be a great deal of work for me to do before I can even consider yet another trip abroad.'

He had not meant to sound reproachful, but he saw by Rosalind's flush and downcast eyes that his remark had upset her. He had made it sound as though she were wanting another pleasure trip, whereas, in fact, the journey to England was scarcely that. He realised that most women in her position would have pushed Lonnie and her possible plight into the background and would have been eager that he should do likewise. Lonnie, he reflected, was going to be a very lucky little girl; she was going to have a truly loving stepmother who was already fond of his child and did not consider her a rival for his affections. Impulsively, he put his arm round Rosalind's shoulders, turned her to face him, and kissed her still trembling mouth. 'Darling Rosalind, I didn't mean that the way it sounded. You are quite right and we should make visiting England – and Lonnie – a priority. When I decided to ask you to be my wife I thought you were an angel, but now I know you are.'

Rosalind was eagerly returning his kiss when the taxi jolted to a stop. Leonard sighed and straightened. 'I wonder what sort of mess the house will be in,' he said, not believing for one moment that it would be anything but perfect. He got out of the taxi, then turned to help her down. 'Best foot forward, darling! Whatever else we may have to face, we know there will be a great deal of post.'

The pile of post had, indeed, been daunting, but Leonard agreed with Rosalind that they must read through everything – and do so in date order – before they stopped for lunch. They were only halfway through, however, when Rosalind put a hand on his arm. 'Leonard, I don't like it! Why on earth has your sister sent Lonnie to boarding school when you had distinctly told her you wanted her to remain in the care of her governess until such time as you thought she needed to broaden her education? And have you noticed how the tone of Lonnie's letters has changed? She no longer chatters on the way she did, telling you of the little everyday occurrences in her life. Why, one would think that the letters before and after the New Year were written by two entirely different people! And Miss Elliott's letter is the strangest of all. Your sister says the governess left because Lonnie was so rude and overbearing and she felt the child needed the discipline of a boarding school. But Miss Elliott says she was dismissed and is very worried that she had no opportunity to explain her sudden departure to Lonnie.'

Leonard frowned down at the letter he was holding. 'Perhaps she gets less time to write letters now that she's at boarding school,' he said doubtfully. 'She makes no complaint about either the school or the teachers and seems to like her fellow pupils, which may mean that she truly did need to mix more with other girls and now feels no necessity to pour out all her doings in her letters. Look, my dear, I think we ought to take a break after all. Luncheon has been set out in the dining room, so we can have a light meal before we begin to work our way through the rest of the correspondence.'

Rosalind agreed and the two of them went through to the dining room where a meal consisting of bowls of saffron-flavoured rice, little dishes of vegetable curry and tall glasses of creamy makhania lassi awaited them. Leonard began to eat with a good deal of enthusiasm, for despite the heat he found he was very hungry, but Rosalind picked at her food, though she drank a great deal of lemonade. He could see by her expression that she was still deeply worried. After glancing thoughtfully at her, he ordered a servant to bring coffee to the study. 'You would rather go back to the letters at once, would you not?' he said gently. 'I'm sure you are worrying for no reason but I find myself beginning to feel uneasy too.' He sighed deeply. 'And when we've read through that little lot I shall have to go into the office, where I've no doubt an equally massive pile is awaiting my attention.'

It took another hour and a half to finish the letters and at the end of it Leonard felt reassured, for his daughter had not voiced any sort of complaint over her school or teachers. But when he said as much to Rosalind, she shook her head. 'You're wrong, Leonard. You say everything must be all right because the child has not complained, but children are very much at the mercy of their teachers when they are in boarding school with no parents to take their part. I spent eight years separated from mine, as you know, and they were not happy years. But I don't believe I ever complained because it would have brought down the wrath of my teachers on my head. What is more, have you not noticed that there is no word of her spending the Easter holiday with her aunt? Neither does she mention her governess, though her earlier letters, before she went to school, were all Hester this and Hester that.'

'Perhaps she's so happy in her new school that she has forgotten all about Miss Elliott,' Leonard said, but even to his own ears the remark did not ring true. 'I wonder, should I send a telegram to my sister asking her for Hester Elliott's address? I'm sure Hester will have kept in touch with Lonnie if possible.'

'I've just noticed something else,' Rosalind said, ignoring his last remark. 'Lonnie writes every week, does she not? Well, her last letter is dated a month ago. Why is that, do you think?'

'I don't know; dear God, I hope she isn't ill,' Leonard said worriedly. 'Wait! Here's a letter from the school, from a Sister Magdalene.' He read it, then handed it to his wife. 'It's an explanation of sorts, I suppose.'

Leonard watched his wife's face as she read the letter and saw the trouble deepening upon it. Sister Magdalene said that Lonnie was doing project work with several other girls and the whole group had been spared the task of letter writing whilst the project continued. She had assured Mr Hetherington-Smith that the letters would recommence as soon as the girls' task was done.

Rosalind threw the letter down on the table. Her face was flushed and her eyes very bright. 'Sister Magdalene is telling *lies*, Leonard,' she said fiercely. 'Your daughter adores you; she would have made time to write you a letter even if she had to sit up half the night to do it! I promise you, Leonard my love, there's something wrong. It wouldn't surprise me to know that St Catherine's Convent School is one of those awful places where the poorer Indian civil servants send their children. From what you've told me, it would be just like your sister to choose the cheapest school available, regardless of its merits or non-merits. Leonard, we must *do* something. Is there no one in England whom you trust? Surely you must know someone apart from your sister?'

Almost as worried as his wife by now, Leonard tried desperately to think but could bring no one immediately to mind. 'I've been Home so rarely,' he said wretchedly. 'My whole life has been spent in India, but people go Home when their service here is ended . . . let me think, let me think!'

Rosalind put her arms around him and kissed the side of his face. 'Of course you may think, my love,' she said remorsefully. 'I'm sorry if I sound as though I'm trying to bully you into taking action, for I know you are as worried as I am. But Leonard, if you can't think of someone you can trust, then we must book our passage on the first steamer leaving for England!'

Chapter Nine

Dick got off the bus at the end of the lane which led to his mother's cottage. It was a fine day in early May, with the birds shouting their heads off and the hedges heavy with blossom. Dick strode along, going over in his head the words he would presently say to his mother and enjoying the thought of the day ahead, for he had found Lonnie at last. He was no nearer finding Hester, but felt that with the little girl's efforts, and his own, they were bound to come across her soon.

It had not even been necessary to write the letter which young Meirion Hughes had suggested, because it had been sheer luck which had brought Dick and Lonnie face to face. Dick had been visiting his sister, Millie, in her small house in Handel Street. When it was Ted's turn to go to Bwlchgwyn, Dick liked to pop round to Millie's place so that brother and sister could catch up on each other's news. He and Millie had been close before Millie's marriage – only eighteen months separated them in age – and Dick wanted their happy relationship to continue, so the visits were important to him. He usually caught the ferry as soon as work finished and was in Millie's house and sitting down to a good dinner by one o'clock. On this occasion, however, Millie had met him on the doorstep with a frown creasing her usually placid brow.

'Oh, Dick, it's grand to see you and your dinner's

on the table but I wonder if you'd mind very much takin' the kids off me hands for the afternoon? Frank's mam came round an hour ago and said could we go over to her place this afternoon and give a hand with movin' furniture. It seems Frank's gran has decided to move in with her daughter after all and she's bringin' a good deal of her stuff with her. They want me to clean their back bedroom out – Frank's brother, Gilbert, is goin' to have the furniture that's in there now – and make the room ready for Gran's stuff, when it arrives. I hate to ask you, Dick, but I don't want the twins underfoot when there's heavy furniture bein' carted, so if you could keep them amused I'd be real grateful, honest I would.'

Dick, sitting down to a large plateful of boiled salt beef, carrots, onions and potatoes, had been glad to be able to help his sister. He was fond of the twins, Rosie and Ruth, and saw no difficulty in being responsible for them for an afternoon. At three years old, they were delightful company and very fond of their Uncle Dick. 'I'll take 'em to the park. If you've got some spare bread, we'll feed the ducks,' he had suggested between mouthfuls. 'And I'll buy their tea out – sticky buns and an ice-cream will probably fill the bill, I reckon.'

Millie had been very grateful and had promptly given him an old shopping bag with odds and ends of bread in it, and presently Dick and his nieces had set off, the little girls travelling in an ancient black perambulator and squabbling amicably over the breaking up of the bread.

At first, all had gone swimmingly. Rosie and Ruth had fed the ducks whilst their Uncle Dick had hung on to their little woolly jackets since he had no desire to see them plunge into three feet of water. Then they had run races, played catch with the ball their mother had provided and fed a number of stout pigeons with the remains of their ice-cream cones, for Uncle Dick had spotted a 'Stop me and buy one' and had generously purchased ices for all.

It was when they were sitting on a bench and recovering from their exertions that Dick had spotted the crocodile of small, brown-clad girls coming towards them. 'See the schoolgirls, children?' he had said brightly, for Rosie had taken a swipe at her sister for no apparent reason and Ruth was beginning to bawl. 'Look at the little girls in their brown print frocks; don't you wish you had frocks like that?'

Rosie gave the approaching crocodile a disdainful glance. 'We often sees 'em,' she said aggressively. 'We doesn't like them ugly dresses, does us, Ruthie? And we don't like them nun ladies what swishes along in black, 'cos they's cross an' angry and they says shush all the time.'

'Oh, they can't be *that* bad,' Dick said tolerantly, glad to see that Ruth had decided not to cry after all. 'I expect it's quite a nice school really – a school!' for he had remembered his quest as soon as he said the word school. Hastily, he stood up and began to stroll towards the crocodile, which was headed by a tall, heavily built woman in a nun's flowing habit.

The girls were an innocuous-looking group, he thought, with hair tugged back from their small, pale faces and large straw hats crammed down over their brows. This made it more difficult to see their features but Dick remembered Lonnie too well to mistake her and was speedily certain that the child was not in the crocodile. Disappointed, he returned to the bench to find Rosie and Ruth having a fight over the shopping bag. 'I want it!' Rosie squeaked whilst Ruth, red-faced and tearful, said that it was her turn and her sister was 'A norrible beast!'

'It would serve you right if your mammy sent you to that school and made you both wear hats like puddin' basins, and ugly brown dresses,' Dick said wrathfully, pulling them apart. 'What does it matter who carries the bag? Most children would be glad to share the job. Now how about if we go to the café and I buy you your tea? Would you like that?'

Both small girls had abandoned the bag and admitted that tea would be nice. 'We want ice-creams,' Rosie had said at once. 'Pink ones and fizzy lemonade, not 'orrible milk.'

Dick had been about to reply when a commotion broke out from the direction of the schoolchildren. He turned round to see the nun from the head of the line walking rapidly along it, counting heads, and presently he heard her harsh voice announcing that someone was missing. 'I brought out twenty children and there are only nineteen of you here,' she said. 'Whose partner is absent?'

After a long pause, one of the girls put up her hand. 'Please, Sister, I think it's me,' she muttered. 'But I never noticed until you said, honestly I didn't.'

The nun gave her a withering glare. 'Nonsense!' she said briskly. 'Who was your partner?'

'It was Leonora,' the child said wretchedly. 'We were almost the last pair . . . she can't be far away, Sister. She was here two minutes ago when we passed by the boys playing footie.'

The nun heaved an exasperated sigh and motioned to the children to turn about. 'No doubt she stayed behind when we stopped to look at the palms in the Palm House,' she said resignedly. As she re-passed Dick, he heard her mutter almost below her breath:

'For even Miss High and Mighty Leonora wouldn't be such a fool as to run away in full uniform in the middle of the afternoon!'

Dick felt his heart give a leap. He told himself exultantly that there was no doubt the Miss Leonora who had gone missing was Hester's Lonnie, and now that he knew to which school she had been sent he would make a point of visiting her there. Around the crown of the straw hats was a brown ribbon with the name of the school emblazoned upon it – St Catherine's Convent – so Dick knew now how to find Lonnie.

Dick took a hand of each twin and turned to follow the crocodile, but Rosie and Ruth squealed indignantly at this betrayal and tried to tug him in the opposite direction. 'The café's *this* way,' Rosie squeaked. 'You *said* tea now, Uncle Dick!'

'You did said,' Ruth corroborated. 'You did said tea next.'

'Ye-es, but I want to see whether they find the little girl who's gone missing,' Dick mumbled. 'Wouldn't you like to know if she's safe?'

''Course she's safe,' Rosie said scornfully. 'She's hidin' behind that big bush with the yellow flowers all over it.'

'That's right, she's behind the scrambled egg tree,' Ruth said positively. 'We see'd her, didn't we, Rosie? If you want to see her, Uncle Dick, to make sure she's all right, it's that way to the café.'

Dick turned and stared at the forsythia bush which his nieces had indicated and thirty seconds later he and the little girls were greeting Lonnie in its shelter. She grinned at them mischievously, her hat on the back of her head and leaves on the shoulders of her brown blazer, where she had pushed through the bushes. 'I saw you sitting on the bench and decided to make a break for it. I knew old Maggie – that's Sister Magdalene, the nun in charge – would go back and search rather than forward, so I ducked into the bushes and set off in the opposite direction to the one I knew she'd take. Oh, Dick, where is Hester? I've tried and tried to get in touch with her, but each time I run away I'm caught quite quickly because of the uniform and I have no money, not even enough for a tram fare, or I'd have gone to Elmore Street and asked your mother if she'd heard. Quick, quick, tell me how to find Hester!'

'I can't, queen,' Dick said regretfully. 'I only wish I could! The fact is, I've no idea where Hester went when she left Shaw Street. I've been searching for her too, without any success, so when I saw you I hoped to get some news myself. But it's no use us standing here talking.' He dug into his pocket and produced a handful of loose change. He was about to give it to her when a thought struck him. 'Will the nuns find this if I give it to you? I don't want you getting into more trouble on my account.'

'If you could give me two sixpences – they're small enough, I think – I'll slip them into my shoes; they'll never find them there,' Lonnie said. 'Oh, Dick, I'm so glad we've met up again. I have a plan for getting away from the school and I mean to come to Elmore Street. Your mother was so kind to Hester and me, I'm sure she'd help me to get away from the convent. Dick, it's a dreadful place! If my father knew what his sister had done he would come and rescue me right away, but the nuns read our letters and if there is even the suspicion of a grumble we are made to re-write them. And I miss Hester most horribly. She's the best person in the world after my daddy, and not knowing where she is or what's happened to her has been the worst thing of all.'

'We aren't living in Elmore Street at present,' Dick said quickly. 'Oh, Lonnie, I've got so much to tell you. Look, can we walk towards the café? These kids are desperate for their tea, and once we're inside it perhaps we can have a proper talk without you fearing to be seen. You can take off the hat and blazer and shove them into me shopping bag, and if you unplait your hair . . .'

Ten minutes later, the four of them were sitting at a table in the darkest corner of the café. Whilst they ate sugar buns and sausage rolls and drank fizzy lemonade, Dick told Lonnie everything: about his father's health, the sanatorium and the rented cottage in Bwylchgwyn. 'The cottage is very remote, in wild and lonely country. No one ever comes there, apart from Ted and myself and the odd gypsy selling clothes pegs. But of course, we shall come back to Elmore Street just as soon as my father is well enough to be moved,' he added. He even made her memorise Mrs Beasdale's address in Birkenhead so that she might drop him a line if she was desperate. 'I'll give you a stamp; you can shove that in your shoe as well.'

'When you're living in Elmore Street again, do you think I might stay with your mam for a short while, just until Daddy knows what's happening, and then he'll come for me, I know he will.'

'I think that's a very good idea,' Dick said approvingly. 'Tell you what, Lonnie, as soon as we move back to Liverpool I'll get a message to you. I'll either write a letter or I might get Ben to hang around by the convent until he sees you come out on one of your walks. Do you always visit the park at the same time?'

'Yes, on a Saturday and on a Wednesday. It's about the only decent thing we do, though we go out whether it's snowing or hailing, which isn't always much fun.'

'That's fine. At any rate, you'll be told just as soon as we cross the water again, I promise. But Lonnie, isn't your father back in India by now? I thought someone said they were cruising for six months.'

'I think so, but I haven't heard from him yet,' Lonnie said dolefully. She glanced around her, a trifle apprehensively. 'Oh, Dick, it's been grand seeing you but I'd better be getting back. I'll be in awful trouble anyway, but it would be worse if they knew I'd enjoyed myself.'

Dick laughed, but fished her clothes out of his shopping bag and held them out. 'Don't put them on until you're well clear of the café,' he advised. 'Tell you what, Lonnie, why not pretend you stopped for a moment to look in a window, or to watch a game of footie, and then couldn't find your schoolmates? You could pretend to be crying and accuse the nun of deliberately leaving you behind.'

'Don't worry, Dick, I'll think of something,' Lonnie said airily. 'I say, can you plait my hair again? It's impossible to do it myself and I don't want *them* to know I've been in disguise.'

Dick obliged, though rather clumsily, and then they said goodbye and Lonnie slipped unobtrusively out of the café and mingled with the strollers outside on the gravel paths. The last they saw of her was a small, hatted and blazered figure making off at a trot in the direction of the Palm House.

Thinking over the events of the previous day had

made the walk to the cottage seem very short and Dick found himself heading up the garden path and swerving round the side of the cottage in next to no time. He was delighted to be able to tell the family that he knew where Lonnie was and burst in through the back door, words already on his lips. 'Guess what, our Mam? I told you I was going to visit Millie yesterday . . .'

He stopped short. His mother was sitting at the kitchen table, her shoulders slumped in an attitude of such defeat that it was almost palpable. She raised swollen, red-rimmed eyes to his and the expression in them was so unutterably sad that Dick scarcely needed to whisper: 'Mam! Whatever's happened?' before he was hurrying across the room to take his mother's frail body in his arms. Over the top of her head, Dick looked wildly at Ben, who was sitting on the sofa with an arm round Phyllis's small shoulders. It was clear that both children had been crying and now Ben knuckled his eyes and spoke up, his voice gruff. 'It's our dad, Dick. We – we went up to the sanatorium as soon as we'd had us breakfasts and the sister, the one we like the best, Sister Hart, met us at the door to the ward and wouldn't let us go in. Dick, she – she said our dad were – were . . .'

Mabel Bailey had been sobbing into Dick's jacket, but now she pushed herself erect, wiped her eyes on an already sodden handkerchief and sat down heavily on the couch beside the two children. 'Sister said it were a grand way to go – he went in his sleep, like – so he didn't have no pain. She said as he'd been getting weaker, but he was so quiet and good, none of 'em realised the end was near. They – they wouldn't let us see him, but we's to go back after dinner. We can all see him then, even the kids, though Sister Hart said she weren't no believer in taking kids to see someone they loved, once his spirit had fled.' She held out a trembling hand and gripped Dick's fingers convulsively. 'I don't know how I shall go on wi'out my Bob,' she said in a low, trembling voice. 'I've fallen into a kind o' routine these past weeks, wi' the bright part of every day me visits to the sannytorium. I know I've got you kids – and you're all grand, so you are – but Bob and I have been sweethearts since we were in school. I don't know how I'll go on wi'out him.'

'I think the only way to tackle it is to live each day as it comes, Mam,' Dick said gently. 'Later on, you and I will go up to the sanatorium because there'll be a great deal to arrange, you know, but right now I'll help you to get the dinner.'

'I shan't be able to eat a thing,' his mother said feebly, but Dick told her that she must keep her strength up and when the meal was on the table, she managed to eat her share.

As soon as dinner was over, Dick took Ben and Phyllis down the lane to the Hughes' cottage. He explained briefly what had happened and Mrs Hughes agreed at once to keep Ben and Phyllis with her until Dick called for them later in the day. 'I won't go into work tomorrow because Mam needs all the support she can get at present,' Dick told Mrs Hughes. 'I'll telephone the offices tomorrow morning and I'm sure they'll give me compassionate leave – until after the funeral, at any rate.'

Mrs Hughes assured him that she would do everything she could to help, including looking after the children when necessary, and Dick trudged the long mile back to their cottage, feeling that his mam had a good friend in the other woman. He and his mother made up the fire and tidied round the place before setting off for the sanatorium.

They had reached the long ward where Dick's father had been a patient before Mabel Bailey began to clutch Dick's arm. 'I don't think I can go through with it, chuck,' she said tremulously. 'Isn't it better to remember Bob as he was, rather than as he is now?'

As she spoke, Sister Hart emerged from the ward and smiled at them. 'We've moved Bob down to the Chapel of Rest,' she said gently. 'He looks very peaceful and not at all frightening, but if you would prefer not to see him, we'll quite understand.'

The three of them walked slowly down the long corridor and Sister Hart drew them to a halt outside the Chapel of Rest. Mabel Bailey gave Dick an appealing glance. 'You'd best tek a look, our Dick,' she said tremulously. 'I'd sooner remember him as he was, always so cheery and bright.' Dick patted her arm and sat her down on one of the upholstered chairs which stood in the corridor. He and Sister Hart went into the Chapel, emerging again after a very short space of time. Dick was glad that his mother had chosen to remain outside, for at the sight of his father's waxen face and closed eyes he had known positively that this was just a shell and that the grim expression on his father's down-turned mouth meant nothing.

His mother looked up anxiously as Dick and the nurse emerged. 'Is it all right? Can we go now?' she asked. 'Dick says there'll be a great deal to do, though I'm sure I don't know what, but can we get on with it as soon as possible? You see, I want to go home.'

Sister Hart, misunderstanding, said soothingly that

of course Mrs Bailey could go home just as soon as they had filled in some forms and signed some papers, but Dick knew at once what his mother meant. 'Mam means she wants to go home to Liverpool,' he told the nurse. 'The family have been living in a rented cottage up on the fringe of the Llandegla moors, but there's no need for us to stay there any longer. We've kept our own place in Elmore Street on; a neighbour's daughter had it until ten days ago, but it's empty now, since she's took a place of her own, so we can move back there just as soon as we can arrange for a van to take our furniture home.'

Beside him, his mother tugged timidly at his arm. 'Not just us; I want Bob to come back with us as well,' she said urgently. 'I want him buried in Anfield Cemetery, where I can visit him every week. Then there's the funeral; this is a tedious long way for folk to come, but if we have the funeral in Liverpool, then all his pals can say goodbye – an' all his relatives, too.' She turned from Dick to the nurse. 'Will it be all right for me to take my Bob home?'

Sister Hart assured Dick and his mother that it would be quite in order for them to arrange to transport the body back to Liverpool and presently, when all the forms were filled in and the papers signed, mother and son set off once more on the long walk back to their rented cottage.

'We'll go just as soon as maybe, won't we, Dick?' his mother said as they walked along. The sun still shone from a clear blue sky and the breeze was gentle on Dick's cheek. He glanced around him as he walked, remembering how his father had loved this countryside and glad that the day had been fine. Once the pain of loss had eased, he hoped his mother would remember Bwlchgwyn and its surroundings with something very like affection, for it had given his father many weeks of peaceful contentment, even of happiness. He thought now that his father had known that his stay in the sanatorium would not be a long one – had known in fact that he would never leave it alive – but that knowledge had not stolen any of the enjoyment he had felt over being so close to nature for the first time in his life.

'Will you be able to manage if I go back to the city on the last bus tonight?' Dick asked presently. 'You see, Millie doesn't know yet, nor Ted, and I know they'll want to be with you at such a sad time. What's more, Mam, we ought to put a notice in the *Echo* giving the time and date of the funeral, so's friends and family can come. I'm awful sorry, Mam, but someone's got to see Father O'Donnell, and I think it had better be me.'

'Very well, son,' Mabel Bailey said, as they turned into the cottage garden. 'If there's one thing your father's illness has taught me, it's how to cope on me own. Ben and Phyllis is good kids, they'll do whatever they can to help me, and I know you'll come back just as soon as you can, to see to things this end.'

'I'll do that,' Dick said heartily, as they entered the kitchen. 'Put the kettle on, Mam, and we'll have a cup of tea and a sandwich, because I doubt I'll have time for a meal at Mrs Beasdale's this evening.'

Mrs Bailey's eyes flashed and she hurried across to the food cupboard. 'You will not make do wi' tea and a sandwich, you'll have a good hot meal,' she said roundly. 'I've a pastie here and it don't take two minutes to boil up a few veg, so sit yourself down and we'll talk while I work. Come to think of it, when you arrived this afternoon you were full of something, some news, only you never got a chance to tell me what it was.'

'I'd forgotten all about it,' Dick admitted, sitting down by the table. 'The fact is, Mam, I've found Lonnie! She doesn't know where Hester is but she's a bright kid and between us I'm sure we'll track Hester down.'

He told his mother all about his chance meeting and by the time the narrative was finished the meal was ready and the two of them sat down on opposite sides of the table and even managed to enjoy the food, despite the sad events of the day.

When the meal was finished, Dick went down to the Hughes' cottage and fetched his young brother and sister back in the gathering twilight. He talked seriously to them on the way, explaining why he himself could not remain at the cottage and impressing upon them – particularly Ben – that they must be very brave and do everything they could to help their mother.

'I'll come back as soon as I can,' he promised them. 'And I'm sure Ted and Millie will come over on the first bus they can catch tomorrow. But I don't think any of us will be here for very long because Mam wants our dad back home in Liverpool, where she can visit the grave whenever she feels the need. I don't think you'll be going back to the village school, but you must pop in before you go home to Liverpool and thank your teachers and your pals and say your goodbyes.' He squeezed Phyllis's small hand and gave Ben's shoulders a brief, hard hug. 'I know I'm leaving our mam in good hands,' he said. 'No one ever had a nicer brother and sister. Just remember to keep cheerful and we'll all get through it somehow.'

* * *

All through the winter Hester had been glad enough to eat her carry-out in the chilly little room behind the shop, but with the advent of fine weather she and Betsy ventured farther afield, though they were rarely able to eat their sandwiches together. Miss Deakin was neither an easy nor a pleasant person to work for, but both girls understood that it was necessary for them to leave the shop separately so that customers did not have to wait too long for attention.

Since Eileen worked in a different shop, however, she and Hester often took their lunch down to the Leeds and Liverpool canal, where they sat on the bank and watched the passing traffic, chatting as they did so. Eileen's employer was a pleasant, easy-going man, and she usually got off a few minutes early and walked up to meet her friend. Then the two of them dived down Hornby Street, crossed Lime Kiln Lane and Vauxhall Road and emerged opposite the factories and warehouses which lined the canal. The walk, generally taken at a smart run, took no more than ten minutes, thus leaving them time to get their breath back and eat their carry-out before they had to return to work.

Today the weather was splendid, following two days of rain, and when Eileen's cheerful face appeared round the door of Paris Modes Hester was already struggling into her light jacket. She greeted her friend cheerily and the two of them set off, arriving by the canal and beginning to eat their sandwiches immediately. Other people had had the same idea, including a group of young men working at the nearby railway station. They were armed with bottles of beer and packets of sandwiches and as soon as they had settled themselves a dozen feet further along the bank began nudging each other and calling across to Hester and Eileen. 'If they knew I were in the family way, they'd think twice before tryin' to date me,' Eileen said gloomily. 'It just shows though, folks still can't tell, can they, Hester?'

'No, not yet,' Hester agreed. 'Are you sure Mr Williams – or more likely Mrs Williams – has noticed nothing?'

'No one's said a word,' Eileen said placidly, between mouthfuls of Marmite sandwich. 'The fact is, I've always been kind o' bulgy, so I suppose folk will just think I've got . . . kind of bulgier,' she ended triumphantly.

Hester giggled. It seemed to her that once Eileen had confided her secret, it had completely ceased to bother her. She no longer worried about discovery, what she should do with the baby when it came, or how bad giving birth might prove to be. She simply sailed through each day with her customary good humour and trusted to Providence to see her right.

'Want to swap a Marmite sandwich for a honey one?' Eileen said presently. 'If them fellers don't stop callin' across to us, I'll give 'em a mouthful – and I don't mean a mouthful of sandwich,' she added darkly. The group of young railway workers had moved along the bank and were now only a few feet away. One of the lads, round-faced and cheerful, was making a real play for Eileen, calling out to her that he'd always fancied a gal wi' fly-away hair and pink cheeks and why didn't she offer him a sandwich while she was about it?

Eileen gave him an indignant glare and turned her back on him, but she grinned at Hester. 'Are my cheeks very red?' she said anxiously. 'I know

I blush something awful and somehow the wind always seems to unravel my hair, though yours stays smooth enough. Why is mine so slippery and soft?' she added plaintively. 'I couldn't look elegant wi' this hair, could I, Hes?'

There was a chuckle from behind them. The boy with the round face had come even nearer and had obviously heard the last remark. 'I'd rather have a gel what's cuddly and pink in the cheeks than one of them there fashion plates, all cold and neat,' he said boldly. He held out his bottle of beer. 'Would you care for a pull, miss?'

It was said with so much good humour that both Hester and Eileen smiled, though Eileen, with as much gravity as she could muster, said that they neither of them drank beer and were, in any case, about to return to work.

'Where do you work?' the lad said eagerly. Hester, deciding that he was serious, turned and took a good look at him. He had a pleasant, freckled face, curly reddish hair and the hazel-green eyes which go with such colouring. He was sturdily built and was clearly a porter at nearby Waterloo Station, since he held a peaked cap in one hand with the letters L.M.S.R. emblazoned upon it.

'We work on the Scotland Road,' Hester said. She smiled at him. 'It's no secret where you work,' she added, jerking her head towards his cap.

The boy grinned. 'Aye, that's right, queen,' he said, 'we all work at Waterloo. Porterin' ain't the height of me ambitions, but it'll do for now, I reckon. The pay ain't bad and there's all sorts of perks.' He stood his beer bottle on the ground and delved in his jacket pocket, producing a creased but clean copy of the previous day's *Echo*. 'Free newspapers, for instance,' he added. 'And sometimes real good magazines and books. Folk in the first-class compartments leave 'em in their seats when they gerroff the train; sometimes they ain't even opened.' He held out the newspaper enticingly. 'Want this one? You're welcome, ladies.'

Hester, who could seldom afford to buy the *Echo*, glanced enquiringly at Eileen, who shrugged. 'I wouldn't mind a bit of a read later,' Eileen admitted. 'Tell you what, Hes, we're usually quietish round tea-time, so if I take it first, you can read it this evening while our dinner's cookin'.'

She held out her hand for the newspaper and the young man handed it over, saying as he did so: 'I'd best tell you me name, else you won't know who to thank when you've read the paper! I'm Tommy Liddell. I'm a most respectable person an' I lives wi' me mam and dad, a sister and two brothers, in a court just off the Scotland Road.' He smiled beguilingly at Eileen. 'An' who might you be, miss, if I may make so bold? Do you know, I believe I've seen you somewhere before . . .'

'That's the oldest come-on in the book,' Eileen said scoffingly, but she did not object when he fell into step beside them. 'At least, I'd think it was a come-on if it weren't for the fact that I've seen *you* before as well.' She screwed up her eyes as though with intense mental effort, then opened them and smiled. 'You come into Williams's ironmongery last week. You was after half a pound of two-inch ovals and a battery for your pocket torch,' she ended triumphantly.

The young man beamed. 'Wharra memory!' he said admiringly. 'You're a real little wonder, Miss . . . Miss . . .'

'Eileen O'Farrell,' Eileen said absently, then shot

a guilty look at Hester. 'I didn't mean to be forward and give me name, only it seemed rude not to,' she said anxiously, as though Tom Liddell had already left them. 'Still an' all, I guess he's harmless, eh, Hester?'

Hester could not help laughing, though she shook her head reprovingly at her friend, before turning to the young man. 'I'm Hester Elliott,' she said, holding out her hand. 'How do you do, Mr Liddell? We seem to have skipped most of the usual preliminaries, don't we? But we don't want to get you into trouble – hadn't you better be making your way back to Waterloo Station?'

The young man gasped, then crammed his hat down over his reddish curls. 'You're right, miss, I'll be in dead trouble if I'm late,' he agreed. He turned to Eileen: 'What time did you say you finished tonight?'

This made Eileen laugh outright but again she shot a questioning look at Hester before replying: 'I finish at six o'clock, Mr Liddell. Now off with you before you make us all late.'

Tom Liddell set off, running towards the station as hard as he could pelt, and the two girls turned their steps towards Scotland Road once more. When they reached the ironmonger's, however, Eileen thrust the paper into her friend's hand. 'You like readin' much more'n I do,' she observed. 'Besides, if you bring it back to the Stanny, I can tek a look later. Will you come along to Williams's at six? Only I don't want no young feller gettin' ideas.'

Hester agreed to this and went on her way chuckling to herself. She thought that it would do Eileen a lot of good to have a young man, even though her situation made an intimate relationship difficult.

But soon enough, she told herself, Eileen would be leaving the area to have her baby and provided she had it adopted, then Hester saw no reason why her friend should not become better acquainted with young Mr Thomas Liddell.

Later that evening, Hester sat on her bed, leafing through Mr Liddell's copy of the *Echo*. She was flicking over the pages to try to find an advertisement she had spotted earlier when something caught her eye and presently she jumped to her feet. Eileen, also lying on her bed, looked up enquiringly. 'What's up?'

'Oh . . . someone I know has died,' Hester said, putting her hands up to her hot cheeks. 'The funeral's tomorrow . . . I must send my condolences. Or – or I might call round since the family is back in Elmore Street.'

'Elmore Street? Ain't that where you went a while back, only there were new people in the house?' Eileen said. 'Who's died, queen? Not that feller you seemed keen on?'

'Oh no, it's not Dick, thank God,' Hester said fervently. 'It's his father. I knew Mr Bailey was a very sick man – he hasn't worked for years – but I hadn't realised the end was so near. His wife will be heartbroken – the children will, too, because they're a very loving and united family.' She picked up the paper and read it again. 'The funeral's at three o'clock tomorrow afternoon. I shall have to get Miss Deakin to give me the afternoon off. Oh dear, she won't like it.'

'Why not tell her you're sick?' Eileen said. 'I'll pop in first thing if you like, and tell her you've been throwing your heart up all night. If we do that, she can't say much, 'cos you've never had a day off since you started with her, have you?'

'Oh, I'm sure that won't be necessary,' Hester said, handing the newspaper to her friend. 'After all, Miss Deakin isn't a monster. I'm sure she won't refuse permission to go to a funeral, particularly as I can offer to work through my lunch hour. I'll have to leave the shop at around half two, but I'll go in early and re-do her window for her. That'll put her in a good mood for a start.'

On one occasion, Miss Deakin had been too busy buying in new stock to dress the window and had told Hester she might have a go at it. The result had been a good deal better than Miss Deakin's own efforts, since Hester had an excellent eye for colour and sufficient artistic flair to enjoy what she was doing and to make the gowns and accessories she chose look very attractive. Ever since then, Miss Deakin had made some excuse when the window needed re-dressing; though she always took the credit for it herself, Hester ended up doing most of the work. Since she thoroughly enjoyed the task, Hester had never complained, and now she saw a chance to make use of her natural talent. She would go in early next day and make an especially good job of the window, so that Miss Deakin would find it impossible to refuse her request for a couple of hours off.

Next morning, despite the fact that it was a grey and rainy day, Hester was in the shop by seven o'clock, carefully choosing the garments for her display. She worked hard and by the time Miss Deakin arrived – ahead of Betsy for once – the window was a dream of palest pink and dark rose. Hester had even managed to find a couple of hats which went admirably with her display and when Miss Deakin bustled into the shop, shaking her umbrella and cursing the rain, not saying a word about the window, she felt quite hurt.

'Good morning, Miss Deakin,' she said, as her employer stood down her shopping basket and began to take off her coat. 'Did you notice I'd done the window? I came in especially early because my friend's father died a few days ago and I'd like your permission to attend the funeral at three o'clock this afternoon.'

Miss Deakin gave her a long, suspicious stare. 'Is he a relation of yours?' she asked bluntly. 'I allow my staff to attend the funerals of relatives but not those of chance-met acquaintances. As for the window, I've got a deal of summer stock in the back room which hasn't been shown yet. I meant to use that in the window this week.'

'I used the stock from the back room,' Hester said mildly, though inwardly she was seething. Why couldn't the woman be pleasant for a change, pretend to like the window even if she did not? 'And though Mr Bailey is no relative of mine, his wife is a dear friend and I feel I must give her what support I can at this sad time.'

'Well, I'm afraid Mrs Bailey will have to manage without your support,' Miss Deakin said with grim – and obvious – satisfaction. 'I suppose you have failed to notice that Miss Fleming has not yet arrived, Miss Elliott? No doubt you have been far too wrapped up in your little scheme for getting the afternoon off to realise that it is a quarter past nine and she was due in some time ago. As it happens, her mother came round to my flat earlier to say that Miss Fleming had a stomach upset and would not be able to work today. So you see, even if I believed in this – this grief-stricken friend of yours, I should be unable to grant your request.'

Hester stared at her, sick with disbelief. 'But, Miss Deakin, I *must* go,' she said. 'I can't possibly let my friends down. I promise you I won't go back to the house afterwards, or anything like that. I'll work right through my dinner hour, of course, though I'm afraid I can't possibly get back much before closing time. I've already worked two hours over this morning, and I'm quite willing to do so for the rest of the week, but attend Mr Bailey's funeral I must and will.'

Miss Deakin's narrow, weasely little face became blotched with red and her eyes gleamed with spite. 'If you take one step outside this shop before six o'clock tonight, then you can kiss your job goodbye,' she hissed. 'I'll not be defied by a bit of a girl, nor I won't have you tryin' to teach me my business. Coming in early to do the window, indeed! I've done that window for years and never a complaint! It weren't as if I'd *asked* you to give me a hand wi' dressin' it, yet you turn round and ask me for time off when it ain't convenient. So do you hear me, Miss Elliott? If you take time off today, you can take your cards an' all.'

'I see, Miss Deakin,' Hester said quietly. She was filled with an icy calm and an equally icy resolution. She would go to the funeral, even if Miss Deakin did dismiss her as a result. It wasn't as if the job was a particularly good one. She reckoned she could do better in almost any other shop along the Scottie, but she did not believe that Miss Deakin would really dismiss her as she had threatened. Who else would do as much as she did for a paltry twelve bob a week? And Miss Deakin had grumbled more than once about Hester's predecessor, Annie, who had never got on with Betsy. She had said that Annie was a lazy slut who refused to do her share of the cleaning work necessary in a busy dress shop and hung back when customers appeared.

Accordingly, Hester said no more but went about her work and very soon a number of customers, attracted, Hester was sure, by the bright and summery window display, came into the shop. Both she and Miss Deakin were busily occupied, but Hester kept an eye on the time. When two o'clock struck, she finished with her customer and turned towards the back room to fetch her mackintosh, only to hear Miss Deakin's raised voice: 'Miss Elliott! This customer would like to try the dress in the middle of the window display, the one with the pleats and the chiffon scarf. Get it out of the window, please.'

Poor Hester felt she had no choice. It was she, after all, who had chosen that dress for the window display. And when the customer tried it on and called to her for assistance in doing up the row of little buttons on the back she felt she had no option but to obey. Half an hour later, she was about to head for the back room to pick up her outdoor clothing when another customer approached her. Hester decided that the time had come to be firm.

'I'm sorry, madam,' she said pleasantly, 'but I have to go to the funeral of a very dear friend. However, Miss Deakin will attend to your needs.' She rushed into the back room and grabbed her mackintosh, and as she passed her employer she said in a lowered tone: 'I'll be back as soon as I can, Miss Deakin.'

Miss Deakin turned away from the customer she was serving, her face reddening as it had done earlier. 'You'd best take your things off my premises then,' she said angrily. 'How dare you leave me when you can see I've no one to take your place, no one to help me. Get your cards!'

Hester ignored this diatribe and continued on her way out of the door. She would have to hurry. She realised she was far too late to attend the church service at St Benedict's, but decided to go straight to Anfield Cemetery for the committal.

She had asked a friendly customer which tram she should catch to reach Anfield and had been advised to wait for a Number 44, since this would take her right to the cemetery gates. To her relief, a Number 44 drew up at the stop as she reached it, and several people piled aboard.

Settling on a seat, Hester glanced at her watch and saw that she was in good time. Relaxing, she watched as the city passed by, first Kirkdale Road, then right into Everton Valley and at last into Walton Lane. I should have taken Eileen's advice, she told herself ruefully. I should have pretended I was ill. She may be only young but she knows a thing or too, does Eileen. She's been brought up in a hard school, and I suppose I was rather over-indulged. My parents could afford to teach me to tell the truth, but poor Eileen knows very well that the truth sometimes works against you. Miss Deakin would have quite understood if Eileen had popped in with a message to say I was sick. She would have thought that Betsy and I had caught an upset stomach from one another and would have asked that sister of hers, who Betsy says is just as hateful as Miss Deakin, to stand in for us. As it is, she'll have to stay in the shop, serving customers, until I get back from the funeral, unless she decides to close a couple of hours early and I can't see the old skinflint doing that! Still, it's taught me a lesson. I shall always tell the truth to decent, upright people, but when someone is unpleasant and devious, then it sometimes pays to bend the truth a little.

'Priory Road – Anfield Cemetery!' the conductor shouted and Hester, along with several others, alighted and turned towards the cemetery entrance.

As she made her way along the path, she realised that quite a few of the people were known to her, at least by sight. One of them, a woman in her fifties, with a round red face, tiny twinkling grey eyes and thinning grey hair tied back in a bun, grinned cheerfully at her. 'Mornin', miss,' she said genially. 'Come to say your farewells to poor old Bob, have you?' She tutted vigorously, shaking her head. 'He were a grand bloke, so he was, and little Mabel Bailey's the salt of the earth; you wouldn't find a better if you travelled a hundred mile. Still an' all, poor Bob hasn't had an easy time of it these past ten years so I reckon he'll have his reward now he's reached the other side. That's what the vicar says, any road.'

Hester fell into step beside her, thinking that the woman's cheeks were hard and red as apples and with the thought came recollection. This was Mrs Tebbitt, whose husband owned the best greengrocery shop on Heyworth Street. When she had lived in the area, Hester had often popped in for apples, oranges or bananas to make Lonnie's diet more interesting and remembered Mrs Tebbitt well, having frequently been served by her.

'Well, Mrs Tebbitt, it's nice to see you again and looking so healthy, too, despite the rain,' Hester said, rather confusedly. 'I'll be glad of your company since

I don't know a great many of the other mourners. I had no idea so many people would attend. Mr Bailey was indeed well loved!'

Mrs Tebbitt agreed heartily, adding that the whole family were well liked. 'St Benedict's were crammed, wi' folks standin' in the aisle,' she said impressively. 'Of course, there were a good few traders – me husband came to the service and me son George – but they can't all come to the committal. It's a good distance from Heyworth Street to the cemetery and would ha' meant closin' the shop for the rest o' the day, just about. But as you can see, those that could be spared have come along to pay our last respects.'

They made their way, along with the rest of the mourners, towards the newly dug grave where Mr Bailey would be laid to rest, and both Hester and her companion fell silent as the vicar motioned to the pall bearers to get the coffin into position. Hester's heart gave a painful little bound; Dick was at the head of the coffin, his brother Ted was opposite him and the four other men, though strangers to her, must be Dick's brother-in-law and other relatives.

The vicar began the committal and the coffin was lowered slowly into place. As the men stepped back from the grave, Hester saw Mrs Bailey for the first time. The poor woman's face was white and strained, though her eyes were swollen and red from weeping. Ben stood very close to her, his own face showing traces of the tears he had shed, and Mrs Bailey's hand clutched Phyllis convulsively. Phyllis must have been crying too, but now she simply looked exhausted, staring into the grave as though she could not believe what was happening.

'Man that is born of a woman hath but a short

time to live, and is full of misery . . .' As the familiar words rang out, Hester felt her own eyes grow wet. Her mind went back to her father's funeral, scarcely more than a year ago, and then to her mother's, though that was more difficult to recollect, for she had only been a child at the time and her father had spared her as much as he could. But the memory of the deep sense of loss and bewilderment which had accompanied each tragic occasion almost overcame her and she had to concentrate very hard on what was happening now. Sad though it was, she reminded herself that it was not her tragedy and, biting her lip, she managed to stem the tears.

'. . . earth to earth, ashes to ashes, dust to dust . . .' The vicar's voice and the rattle of soil as it fell on the coffin brought Hester abruptly back to the present. She saw that Dick, as the eldest son, was stepping forward, scooping up a handful of soil from beneath the canvas cover and tossing it gently into the grave, his face working as he did so. Ted followed him, then Dick drew Mrs Bailey forward and Hester watched whilst the small woman unpinned a bunch of white violets from inside her coat and threw it down on to the coffin. The family had evidently provided both Ben and Phyllis with a few little white flowers, and they followed their mother's example, Phyllis beginning to sob convulsively as she did so. 'I want my daddy!' the child wailed. 'I don't like it here. I want to go back to the sanatorium.'

The sextant and his helpers came forward to fill in the grave and the mourners began to move slowly away. Hester hesitated for a moment, then turned to follow them.

Dick went and put his arm round his mother as the

men began to work on the mounds of earth. 'You all right, Mam?' he said gently; he gestured to Ted to take her arm and picked Phyllis up, lodging her comfortably on his hip. 'Only the car's waiting by the main gate and we want to get home so's we can put the kettle on and get the food laid out before everyone else arrives.'

Mrs Bailey gave him a watery smile. 'I'll be fine now,' she said. 'As for puttin' the kettle on an' gettin' out the sandwiches and cakes, Mrs Burridge couldn't come to the funeral 'cos her Peggy's in bed wi' an attack of the croup. But she said she'd pop up an' do the necessary so's everything would be ready when we got back.'

'That's grand . . .' Dick was beginning, when a movement caught his eye. He saw a slim girl in a navy raincoat, her gleaming dark head bare, turning away from him. Dick gasped. 'Mam, there's Hester!' He stood Phyllis down. 'Ted, take Mam and Phyllis to the main gate for me, would you? I shan't be a mo', I must just . . .'

Afterwards, he assumed he must have flown over the intervening space between them for suddenly he was at Hester's side, swinging her round to face him, saying agitatedly: 'Hester! Where have you *been*, queen? We'd almost give you up. I searched and searched, but there were no sign of you. I even visited the Shaw Street house, but no one knew anything and now the old lady has sacked most of the original staff, so it was no manner of use calling there again. To tell you the truth, I thought you must have gone back to India, especially when we couldn't find Lonnie either, only . . .'

'Oh, Dick!' Hester said tremulously. 'I was so sorry to read of your sad loss in the paper. He was one of the best, was Mr Bailey. But you aren't the only one who's been searching. I went round to your old house twice – the first time a young girl answered and virtually slammed the door in my face. The second time, it was a friendly young woman, but she was only able to tell me the family had moved to some little Welsh village, up on the Llandegla moors, or somewhere up in the Welsh hills, which wasn't much help. Oh, Dick, I've missed you so badly – the whole family, I mean,' she added hastily.

Dick groaned. 'I left my Birkenhead address with them, but I suppose it were only their mam who realised it was important to pass it on,' he said, taking both Hester's hands in his and giving them a gentle squeeze. 'But look, we can't talk here. You'll come back to the house? The Evans family had already moved out before me dad died, so as soon as we'd settled everything in Bwlchgwyn we moved our stuff straight home. As for you missing us, that's nothing to how we missed you! But Hester, how did you get here? And where are you living now? I don't mean to lose touch with you again, so just you give me your address, queen.'

Hester laughed. 'I came by tram and I'll go back to work the same way,' she told him. 'I'm working on the Scotland Road in a dress shop called Paris Modes and I'm lodging a bit further along the Scottie, at Number 10, Stansfield Court, but now that I know you're back in Elmore Street you may be sure I'll visit you there.'

Dick could have kicked himself because he could not offer her a lift. The car would be crammed to capacity, with the children sitting on adult laps, unable to squeeze even one more soul aboard. He would have liked to say that he, too, would catch the tram, but could not go against the convention that families stuck together at such times. 'I wish you could come in the car with us, but I'm afraid it's jam packed, what with Millie's twins and our kids. But you will come back to the house, won't you? Our mam's laid on a really good cold meal back in Elmore Street. Do say you'll come, Hester!'

Hester hesitated. 'The trouble is, the woman I work for didn't want to give me time off, even for the funeral. If I go back with you to the house she'll be closed by the time I'm back on the Scottie . . .' She glanced up at him, smiling with her eyes the way he remembered, then seemed to make up her mind. 'Thank you, Dick, I'll be glad to come back to the house,' she said decisively. 'After all, what can Miss Deakin do but sack me, and I don't really think she'll do that. I may not be the best shop assistant in the world, but she pays me very little and I seem to please the customers.'

Dick took her arm, thinking that the customer who was not pleased by this charming and attractive young woman would be hard to please indeed. 'Good,' he said. 'I'll walk you as far as the gates, but then I must join the family. Our mam will be that delighted to know we've found each other again . . . nearly as delighted as I am,' he finished, highly daring, but Hester only smiled and tucked her hand into the crook of his elbow.

'You can't be more pleased than I am, though,' she assured him. 'I've done my best to be self-sufficient and independent, but it's been hard. And I've not caught so much as a glimpse of Lonnie, so I just hope . . .' She stopped speaking to look up at Dick. 'Do you know, when I said that, something like an electric shock ran up my arm! Don't say you know where she is!'

'I do,' Dick said, not mincing words. 'It's rather a long story, but I'll tell you just what happened when we get home. No, on second thoughts, I'll settle Mam and the kids in the house, then come back and meet you off the tram. We can have a talk as we walk home. Oh, look, there's a tram now. You won't have to run; there's a good few waiting at the stop.'

Hester sat on the tram in a daze of happiness. Despite all the difficulties which had beset them, Dick had not forgotten her, any more than she had forgotten him. Just to see that firm, humorous face, to feel the touch of his hand on hers, had been wonderful enough, but to see the tender look in his eyes as they met hers was best of all. Because of the months which had passed since their last meeting she had honestly begun to wonder whether she had imagined his interest and concern for her. She wondered no longer. It was writ large in his expression; very much, she suspected, as it was in hers.

The journey was both long and rather tedious for she was not so lucky in her trams as she had been on the way to the cemetery. She had a wait of almost fifteen minutes when changing at Everton Valley and the rain began to blow sideways so that her neat little umbrella, which had kept her nicely dry earlier, was pretty helpless against the gusts. Consequently, it was a damp and dripping Hester who descended from the tram in Heyworth Street, straight into Dick Bailey's arms.

'Hold up there, you don't want to slip on these wet flagstones,' he said cheerfully, a strong arm round her waist. 'I had hard work to stop Ben from accompanying me, incidentally. He's longing to have a good old talk about what's been happening to us. To tell you the truth, your turning up again has been downright miraculous. Mam's scarce spoke above a whisper since our dad died, but when I told her you were coming on to the house for a bite of tea and a bit of a chat, she was that pleased . . . even little Phyllis smiled.'

'It's a dreadful time for everyone, but probably worse, in a way, for the kids,' Hester said. 'It's so hard for children to understand that someone they love can leave them. I remember how dreadfully hurt and upset I was when my mother died . . . I was ten.'

'I guessed you'd understand,' Dick said and began to explain about the sanatorium, the rented cottage and everything that had happened to the family since he had seen Hester last.

Hester's eyes filled with tears as she heard how happy Bob Bailey had been in the sanatorium and how sudden and shocking his death had seemed.

'But the sister on the ward told us that Dad had known right from the beginning that he wouldn't have long with us,' Dick told her. 'And the point is that he put himself out to enjoy every minute of the time he had left and he couldn't have done that if Mam or the kids had known his days were to be so few. I always admired my dad and now I think he was almost a saint. Well, no, not a saint,' he amended, ''cos saints aren't much fun to live with, and me dad was great fun. He was a good man, good all through, and we shall all miss him horribly, but we've got a deal of happiness to look back on, and that's really important.'

Hester carried his hand to her face and rubbed it

gently against her cheek. 'I wish I'd known your dad better,' she murmured. 'He and your mam really loved one another and had a wonderful marriage, and though it ended sooner than it should have, nobody can take that away from them.'

'That's true,' Dick said. He heaved a deep sigh, then smiled down at her. 'Now I'll tell you about finding Lonnie from the very beginning, when I took my sister Millie's twins to the park so that she could give her mother-in-law a hand with some changes she was making, to the moment when Lonnie and meself came face to face.'

He told the story well, Hester thought, making it both interesting and amusing. He told her about feeding the ducks, the crocodile of school children . . . and at last came to the meeting, the tea eaten in the café, and Lonnie's plan for escape.

'So you see, we're all well on the way to sorting things out,' he said triumphantly as he finished his recital. 'The only thing is, why hasn't Lonnie's pa turned up already to rescue her? It does seem odd, don't you think? It's May now and high time, if you ask me, that they were told what's been going on.'

'In a way, I'm glad I didn't know,' Hester said ruefully. 'I'd have worried myself sick wondering how I could help. We'll have to talk over our plan of action, though, Dick, because I mean to write to Lonnie's father and tell him that he must make arrangements to get Lonnie out of that school just as soon as may be. I know that he's a very important businessman and may not be able to come dashing over to England as soon as he would like. But there should be nothing to stop him getting someone he trusts to act as his agent over Lonnie and her education.'

'If it were a kid of mine, I'd let me business go hang,' Dick said frankly. 'Why, if little Phyllis were in trouble I'd journey to – to India, yes and back again, to see her right.'

'That sounds grand, I'll grant you that, but remember, a great many people in India – and elsewhere for all I know – are totally dependent upon Mr Hetherington-Smith's business to keep their own children fed and to pay their rent and so on,' Hester pointed out. 'So we mustn't judge him, Dick.'

Dick nodded his understanding. 'I know what you mean; India's a very poor country, isn't it? So if Lonnie does get away, she'll come to us just as soon as she's able, I'm sure. As I told you, I gave her some money, so unless the nuns discovered it at least she can catch a tram to Elmore Street and won't have to trek all that way on foot.'

'I think it would be best if I went straight round to the convent after work tonight and had a word with Lonnie. I don't believe even the most narrow-minded of nuns would object to a child seeing her old governess when her parent is unable to visit. Even if they remain in the room with us whilst we're talking – and I suppose that is quite on the cards – I will be able to reassure her that her father will soon know the truth. She would do far better to stay right where she is until we can arrange for him, or his representative, to deal with the situation officially. If she was to run away, there could be all sorts of complications. Why, if your mother takes her in, the police might accuse her of kidnapping, or some such thing.'

Dick whistled softly beneath his breath. 'I never thought of that; you've got a clever head on your pretty shoulders, young Hester! Right then, you go round there after work and tomorrow, when I've finished at the yard, I'll hang about outside Paris Modes until you're free, then you can tell me how Lonnie is and then perhaps the two of us can go to a café, get ourselves a meal and write the letter to Lonnie's father together.'

'That sounds lovely, Dick,' Hester said gratefully.

'Well, goodbye for now, Hester love. It was so good of you to come to the funeral! Dick telled me that your boss wasn't too willing for you to have the time off, but it's meant so much to me and the kids to have you here. It were the first time you've met our Millie and Frank, and the twins, weren't it? Well, it won't be the last, because us Baileys stick to our pals and I hopes as how you'll be a frequent visitor in Elmore Street now we's home.'

Mrs Bailey stood on the doorstep clasping Hester's hand in hers, and Hester leaned forward and kissed the older woman's pale cheek. 'Goodbye, Mrs Bailey,' she said gently. 'And thank you so much for making me feel welcome. Millie is a dear and the twins are charming and of course I'll visit you just as often as I can. I've given Dick my address and told him the name of the shop where I work, so hopefully we shan't lose touch again.' She erected her umbrella, having quite a struggle to do so against the fierce wind and rain. 'Goodbye, Mrs Bailey, and thanks again.'

Battling her way to the tram stop, Hester reflected that she and Dick had already made up for the time they had missed. Dick had ushered her into the front parlour and introduced her to the multitude of friends and relatives there and had then taken her into the kitchen where Millie, Ted's girlfriend

Ruby and a couple of neighbours were frantically pouring cups of tea and cutting fresh sandwiches. Dick had cleared a space at the table and the two of them had joined in the work, slicing loaves, buttering bread and chatting quietly as they did so. Ruby took the place beside Hester, staring at her curiously out of a pair of heavy-lidded, rather sly eyes. Hester did not much like the tone of Ruby's conversation, since the other girl had a vulgar streak. But as she was Ted's girlfriend – at least for the moment – Hester did her best not to appear shocked. Nevertheless she thought Ruby's remarks were rather unsuitable for a funeral tea and was glad when Millie, Dick's sister, gave Dick a significant look and sent Ruby to join the others in the parlour.

'She's got no sense of what's right or wrong, that Ruby, if you ask me,' Millie said quietly to Hester. 'But no doubt she'll improve if she stays with our Ted.'

Millie was a pretty, self-confident young woman in her mid-twenties and clearly very fond of her brothers. Hester thought her both kind and sensible and hoped that the two of them might become friends.

Despite the sadness of the occasion it had been a happy afternoon, but now, glancing at the clock over the chemist's shop, she saw that time had indeed flown. She would get back to the shop in time to help Miss Deakin to clean down, though she was sure the older woman would have closed the premises to customers by now. Thanks to the vile weather, she doubted very much if Miss Deakin would have missed her and knew, in any event, that the older woman would dock her a day's pay. And it will be no use reminding her that I worked from seven right through till half-past two, she told herself, because it will only make her angrier. Better to simply accept the unfairness philosophically.

Hester had guessed right; she reached the shop at half-past six, in no state to start work immediately. Her wretched umbrella had blown inside out, snapping its ribs as it did so, and had had to be abandoned in the nearest litter bin. Wondering whether she would ever be able to afford another one, Hester had had to turn up the collar of her mackintosh and battle on without it. Now, soaked to the skin and with her hair blown into a mass of tangles, she slid into the shop and faced Miss Deakin across the floor. Miss Deakin did not look up and Hester decided to brazen it out. 'I'm sorry I'm late, Miss Deakin, but I felt I could not abandon my friends immediately after the committal, so I returned to the house with the family and helped Mrs Bailey with the funeral tea. I'll work overtime tomorrow, if that will . . .'

Miss Deakin looked up. 'I telled you you was finished if you left the shop and I meant it,' she said icily. 'Get your things out of here and don't bother to come back, because me sister Aida's gal leaves school next month and I've already gived her your job.'

'Very well,' Hester said quietly. She reminded herself that she was underpaid and overworked and that Miss Deakin had always had it in for her, but this did not stop her heart from sinking. Searching for another job would not be easy. She did not doubt that she would find work eventually, but knew she might be unemployed for several days, perhaps even for several weeks, and the thought was a frightening one. Whatever happens, she must pay her rent and buy food. However, she put the thought resolutely from her and went past Miss Deakin into the back room with her head held high. Gathering up her small possessions, she pushed them into her bag and returned to the shop. 'Can I trouble you for my wages, Miss Deakin? I shall need some money to keep me going until I find another job.' She hesitated, then, with some difficulty, swallowed her pride. 'I – I believe it is customary to be given a week's warning. If you intend to dismiss me at once, then surely I'm entitled to a week's wages in lieu of notice?'

Hester walked slowly along the Scotland Road, so immersed in her own thoughts that she never even bothered to avoid the large puddles spreading across the flagstones. Her instinct was first to go back to the Stanny and get herself some decent dry clothes. It would not do to go job hunting looking like a drowned rat without even an umbrella to shelter her from the rain. But then she reasoned that only the desperate job hunted after six o'clock in the evening and in such appalling weather. Besides, she had promised Dick that she would visit the convent and try to see Lonnie. Accordingly, she set out for Stansfield Court, deciding as she walked that she would defer her job hunt until the following day. Reaching Number 10, she went into the hall and set off up the stairs, aware that she was dripping water at every step, but unable to do anything about it. Once in her shared room, she removed every stitch of clothing, rubbed her chilly body dry with a rough towel, and pulled her suitcase out from under the bed. Despite the fact that May had been a mild month, she felt thoroughly cold, so dressed herself from the skin up in what warm clothing she still possessed. Glancing towards the window, she saw that the rain continued to fall steadily, occasionally gusting sideways as the wind caught it.

Once she was respectable, she gathered up her wet things and carried them down to the kitchen where she hung them over a clothes horse which she pulled as close to the range as she dared. Then, returning to her room for a dry jacket, as she had no second coat, she noticed that Eileen's umbrella was still in its customary place. Clearly, the other girl had forgotten it that morning. I'm sure Eileen won't mind if I borrow it, Hester told herself; my mackintosh is simply drenched. She knew it was not usually done to borrow umbrellas without first asking the owner's permission, but she was desperate. She felt she must get in touch with Lonnie today because tomorrow she would be too busy job hunting to risk a protracted visit to the convent. Accordingly, she picked up the umbrella and made for the door and was halfway down the stairs when she was hailed by Roy Maskell.

'Is that you, Miss Elliott? Wharra day, eh? It's easin' off now, mind, so if you're goin' to take a bolt out to the cinema or something, now's the time to do it.'

Hester slowed as she reached the bottom of the flight and smiled at her landlord's son. He was a pleasant youth, always friendly, but she really had no time to chat to him now, since she hoped to be safely sheltered at the convent before the rain started once more. 'I'm not thinking of going to the cinema. I'm going to visit a friend . . . well, not exactly a friend, a child I knew rather well when I was in India. She's at a boarding school in Liverpool, in the Prince's Park area, and very lonely. I thought I'd go over there and perhaps offer to take her out for some tea . . . something like that, anyway.'

Roy, who had just come in, took off his waterproof and hung it on the newel post at the bottom of the stairs. 'Which school would that be?' he asked, running both hands over his dark hair to flatten it. 'There's a grosh of schools in that area.'

'St Catherine's Convent. Know anything about it?' Hester asked, pausing at the foot of the stairs.

Roy shook his head. 'No, but I know a great deal about the film that's on at the Commodore on the Stanley Road and it just happens I'm in the money this week; how about comin' along to the picture house with me? I'll mug you to fish and chips after.'

Hester sighed inwardly. This was not the first time that Roy had suggested she might like to go out with him and it was becoming increasingly difficult to turn him down without giving offence. However, on this occasion, she had a really good excuse. 'Thank you very much, Roy, but I couldn't possibly disappoint my young friend,' she said primly. 'Has the rain really stopped, or is it just a pause between showers, do you suppose?'

She walked towards the front door and swung it open. Roy, beside her, examined the sky with a critical eye. 'I think the worst is over, at any rate,' he was beginning, when someone shouted from further up the street.

Hester peered, then smiled delightedly; it was Eileen. Roy heaved a deep sigh and turned to go back indoors. 'I see your mate's here,' he said resignedly. 'So if you goes off with anyone, it'll be with her. I were goin' to offer to go up to the convent with you.' He grinned ruefully at her. 'Another time, eh?'

'I'm awfully sorry, Roy,' Hester called after his retreating back, then turned to face Eileen as the other girl arrived outside the house. 'Oh, Eileen, am I glad to see you! So much has happened, you wouldn't believe. I met up with Dick Bailey and his family at his father's funeral. It meant taking time off, of course, and when I got back to the shop, old Deakin fired me. Then I got drenched coming home and my umbrella blew inside out and broke and of course my mackintosh was soaked . . . I'm afraid I was about to borrow your umbrella, but it looks as though the rain is over for now, so if you need it . . .'

'Ole Deakin *sacked* you?' Eileen said incredulously. 'She's that spiteful, the acid in her must have turned her brain. Heaven knows, she pays you little enough and you work all the hours God sends! Wharrever were she thinkin' of? What'll you do, chuck? Even if you marry that Dick, I guess you'll both need to work for a bit.' She tried to turn Hester back into the house. 'I've bought some minced beef and a mound of spuds and onions to make a nice supper for us. Come and talk to me while I work.'

Hester pulled away. 'I can't. I promised Dick I'd visit Lonnie and I really must. As for marrying, you're jumping the gun a bit, aren't you? We've met for the first time after months apart so we're going to have to get to know one another all over again. Don't worry, I'll tell you everything – we'll have a good talk when I get back.'

Eileen shook her head. 'No we won't, because if you're going out, I'm comin' with you. A poor sort of friend I'd be if I let me mate, what's just been sacked, go off by herself on such a miserable evenin'. Where did you say the kid was livin'?'

'She's at St Catherine's Convent school on the Belvedere Road,' Hester said diffidently. 'It's a fair distance from here. Dick said it was near Prince's Park, so we'll be able to catch a tram. Oh, I'm ever so grateful that you're coming with me, Eileen, because I'm sure I'll go to pieces if they try to stop me seeing Lonnie.'

Chapter Ten

An hour later, the two girls, both crestfallen and mystified, were making their way back along Belvedere Road in the direction of the tram stop. 'Well, that were a wasted journey,' Eileen said. 'D'you think it were true, what that nun told us? That your Lonnie was bein' punished for writing something rude on the flyleaf of her prayer book?'

'Oh, I think so,' Hester said, after some thought. 'I don't believe a nun would tell a deliberate lie, do you? And we know Lonnie ran away in the park so that she could speak to Dick privately, because he told me so. They've promised I can see her at four o'clock tomorrow, though.'

'If you ain't in work by then,' Eileen pointed out. 'If you gerra job, then you'll likely be workin' till six, or even later, same as wi' Miss Deakin. Mind you, as they keep tellin' us, we're in a Depression, so mebbe it won't be quite that easy to gerranother job.'

'I'm sure it will,' Hester said stoutly. 'After all, I've had a good deal of experience of shop work now, and that was what stopped me from getting a better position the last time I was job hunting. Come to think of it, though, I'm supposed to be meeting Dick tomorrow evening, outside the shop. If I'm not in work, I'll go up to the convent first, but if I am . . . oh, goodness, however shall I get in touch with Dick?'

* * *

Lonnie waited until all the children in her dormitory were asleep and then sat up and quietly reviewed the past dozen hours or so. She had been in the punishment cupboard for what had felt like a lifetime though, in fact, the nuns had released her shortly after the other children had finished their tea. Lonnie, who had missed all three meals that day, had been absolutely furious when the nuns ordered her to bed without so much as a piece of bread or a drink of water to satisfy what was now a considerable degree of hunger. But think of their faces tomorrow morning when they find me gone, she had told herself. Oh, they will be mad as fire – and worried too, I shouldn't wonder – because they won't catch up with me in a hurry now, not with a bit of money in my pocket and somewhere to hide myself away from them!

Having made up her mind to go, she slid quietly out of bed and began to dress. It was not a particularly cold night but the wind was still gusty, though the rain had ceased and the moon rode high in an almost cloudless sky. So better to wrap up as warmly as she could since clear skies could mean a frost before morning and for the time being at least she would have to manage without a coat or hat. The downstairs cloakroom was far too dangerous, what with having to descend the stairs, the creaking boards of which might easily give her away, plus the fear of meeting a nun coming away from or going towards one of the night offices. No, when she made up her mind to run away by night, it was simply because she had noticed the fire escape.

If it had been near her own dormitory window she might have made use of it before tonight, but it was not. However, to punish her for some sin, Abigail had recently been moved to another attic room and it was when visiting her there (illegally of course) that Lonnie had first set eyes on the fire escape. It wound down from the attics to ground level and was a rather wobbly-looking edifice, but Lonnie thought it a good deal safer than the stairs. No one would dream that a child would risk an escape which meant descending its fragile-looking metal steps, especially at night, she was sure, so she set off, silent as a moth, along the corridor to Abigail's room.

She inched the door open, suddenly full of a nervous fear that one of the girls within might be wakeful, but it seemed safe enough. Six little iron bedsteads with six little sleepers therein, she saw with satisfaction. Oh, and joy of joys, the sash window was slightly open, with wedges of newspaper holding it. Abigail had told her how those wedges fell out when the window was rattled by the breeze, so that the girls were forced to sleep through the constant creaking.

Lonnie crept forward and pulled out the newspaper wedges, then eased the window gently up. No one woke, or even stirred, and it was the work of a moment to slide out of the gap she had created and step on to the fire escape.

It was, as she had thought, somewhat wobbly. In fact, had she not been so desperate to escape, she might have judged it too unsafe. But though wobbly, it was not noisy. She began to descend the steps, gaining confidence with every moment, and presently was actually standing on the ground, breathing a little hard and considering her next move.

First, she decided, she must get as far away from the convent as she could, and she realised of course that she must stay out of sight. A child in convent uniform in this area would be instantly recognised for what she was, a runaway. But a mile away . . .

or two . . . it might simply be assumed that she was about her normal business. Though what normal business a child of her age might have on the streets after midnight she did not pause to consider.

If she had had time, she had meant to pinpoint a line with some clothing on it which she could take. Well, steal. Only it wouldn't have been stealing but merely borrowing, since she fully intended to take it back just as soon as her father came for her. Unfortunately, however, she had jumped the gun and done her midnight flit without any real preparation. So she would either have to get far enough away from the convent for the uniform to mean nothing, or have to go amongst the smaller streets where there might be washing left on the line. The nuns sometimes walked their pupils through very poor areas and more than once Lonnie had eyed the lines of damp, greying washing and longed for the opportunity to 'borrow' something as a disguise.

As she considered these things she had moved away from the convent, flitting along in the shadows, glad for once of the dull brown of the uniform since it was far less conspicuous than blue, red or even green would have been. And presently she had a piece of luck. An ancient pram was propped up against a wall, the tramp who owned it being sprawled out asleep in a doorway with a bottle clasped to his chest. The tramp smelt and so did his pram but nevertheless Lonnie peered inside, half expecting to find a baby within. Instead, she saw newspapers, some split kindling, and a moth-eaten woollen shawl.

Lonnie's fingers itched to grab the horrid garment but this really would be stealing, since no matter how you looked at it she would be unable to return it to the tramp when she no longer needed it. Then she thought that he had probably prigged it in the first place, and then a little voice in her head said sagely: 'Exchange is no robbery,' and before you could say 'knife' – or even 'thief' – she was wrenching off her limp brown cardigan, pushing it into the pram, and extracting the shawl.

It was a long one, and very ragged, but it covered Lonnie completely, from her shoulders to the soles of her feet, and when she pulled it higher and draped it round her head she was pretty sure she was unrecognisable, not only as a convent girl but as . . . well, as a girl. Not even the hated Sister Magdalene would have recognised her in that shawl.

Lonnie was still draping the garment around her, wrinkling her nose against the smell, but realising that she would soon grow accustomed, when some movement or the slight scrape of her shoes on the pavement must have alerted the tramp to her presence. He lurched to his feet, muttering imprecations in a slurred voice, and reached out a hand to grab hold of her; it was so black that it almost blended with the night, save for his fingernails, which looked white in the gaslight. Lonnie, however, was too quick for him. Fear lent wings to her feet and she fairly flew along the pavement, twisting and turning along the narrow streets, determined not to be caught by the nightmarish figure of the filthy old man. The trouble was by the time she realised that the pursuit had faded into silence, she was thoroughly lost. With her heart still hammering and her breath coming short, Lonnie stopped and considered the situation. There was no need to fear the tramp any longer – she had got clean away – but the streets were empty and should a scuffer come along she would stand out like a snowflake in a coal shed.

The thing to do was to take shelter in some convenient passage or doorway, to curl up beneath her shawl and to sleep until morning. Accordingly, Lonnie dived down the nearest jigger and began cautiously to investigate the small courtyards behind the houses. It was not long before she discovered a tiny shed with a pile of potatoes in one corner and some sacks in another. The owner had locked the shed but had neglected to remove the key so Lonnie slid inside and made herself a nest on the sacks. For a little while she lay wakeful, thinking what a nice surprise the tramp would get when he looked into the pram and found her neat cardigan. Poor old man, he'd probably be able to sell it for – oh, a shilling – and then he could buy himself a nice meal. She had considered leaving him one of her precious sixpences, but prudence forbade it.

The thought of a nice meal reminded her of her own hungry and hollow state. She picked up one of the potatoes and rubbed the dirt off it, then took a large bite and was surprised to find it quite tasty after her long fast. She had noticed a tap in the yard but suddenly realised she was far too tired to go in search of a drink and snuggled down, promising herself that she would wake as soon as it was light and get some water then.

She did not truly believe she would sleep, but the long, uncomfortable day in the cupboard, followed by the extreme activity of her escape, proved too much for her, and very soon she did.

Lonnie awoke to broad daylight and movement. For a moment she could not imagine where she was, then she remembered and cast a terrified glance around the shed. Where should she hide? She jumped to her feet and hurried across to the door, dragging the shawl around her as she did so, but even as she reached it, the door opened outwards and a large man, wearing a flat cap and very dirty overalls, came in. Lonnie supposed, afterwards, that his eyes were not accustomed to the dark, for he did not seem to see her but walked straight over to the potatoes, picked up a sack, and began loading the one into the other. He was whistling a tune beneath his breath and Lonnie slid out of the shed and was tiptoeing across the yard towards the back gate when a woman's voice said loudly: 'Who the devil do you think you are? Bert, there's some thievin' little bugger been shut in our shed all night. Here, you! I bet you're laded down with spuds, ready to sell 'em to anyone for a few pence. Stop, thief!'

The last words were spoken as Lonnie shot through the gate and belted along the jigger, her heart once more thundering out its message of fear and pursuit. As she had the previous evening, Lonnie continued to run until she felt safe, then slowed to a walk. I'm making a real mess of this, she told herself severely, clutching the shawl around her and trying to look inconspicuous. I wonder where I am? It's no use going to Elmore Street because there's nobody there I know. I dare not go back to Shaw Street, though I'm sure Mollie would shelter me if she could, but that's the first place they'll look. I don't know where Hester is – nor did Dick – so it's no use expecting help from that quarter. If Dick hasn't left for work I suppose I could go to his lodging in Priory Street, only I don't know where it is and anyway, Mrs Beasdale might turn me away and I haven't got enough money to go traipsing round the country if she sends me off. No, definitely the best thing for me to do is to go straight to Wales, to that village Dick spoke of – Bwlchgwyn – find the cottage and cast myself on Mrs Bailey. I know she'll help me because she's a mother and mothers always help children, my *ayah* told me so.

Lonnie was a practical child with a keen, retentive memory. In the halcyon days before Hester had been wrested from her, she and her governess had often taken the tram down to the Pier Head and watched the ferries leaving for Woodside, so she was in no doubt as to her next move. First she must catch a ferry to cross the water, and when she reached Birkenhead she would search for the bus station. Dick had described the journey which he had intended to take on the morrow whilst they ate their tea in the café in Prince's Park. Even then, she had realised that Mrs Bailey and the cottage would be a far safer refuge than the best of landladies. Besides, Birkenhead was only just across the water from Liverpool. If the police were informed of her defection, they might easily pass the word to Birkenhead that a convent child had gone missing. But Wales was a different place – they even spoke a different language – and Dick had said the cottage was remote, with few neighbours. From there, she could write to her father freely and tell him the awful truth about St Catherine's Convent School for Girls. Rescue, she did not doubt, would swiftly follow.

It could not be said that Lonnie walked swiftly up the long lane which led to the cottage. It would be truer to say she limped slowly, for it had taken her a good twenty-four hours from the time of her escape from the convent to reach this particular point in her journey. She had made her way to the landing stage and had caught the ferry to Birkenhead Woodside where she had asked a passer-by the way to the bus station.

This had been only a short walk, but when she got there she realised that yet another choice awaited her. She could either catch a bus at least part of the way into Wales, or she could buy herself one more meal.

She hung around the bus station for a little while, meaning to cup her hand and whine for money, for she realised she would be exceedingly hungry by the time she reached the cottage, but found her pride would not let her do so. She had grown to hate the shawl but realised that folk would more willingly help a pathetic little down and out than a child dressed neatly in brown gingham and sandals. So she had remained wrapped in the shawl and presently she was proved right when a plump young woman, emerging from the chip shop, saw the wistful way Lonnie was eyeing the portion she had just bought and gave her a generous handful.

Munching her chips, she remembered that Dick had said there was no bus which would take her all the way to Bwlchgwyn and she might have to change buses in Chester and again at Wrexham. Resigning herself to a tedious journey, she climbed aboard the first bus. She rather enjoyed the ride despite being told, when the conductor asked for her money, that she had insufficient cash to take her all the way to Wrexham. 'But there's no reason why we shouldn't take a chance on turning a blind eye to a littl'un like you, especially since I had an inspector aboard less than an hour ago,' he told her.

'Thank you ever so much,' Lonnie said gratefully. 'I'm afraid I hadn't realised I should need quite so much money to reach my friend's house. But when

I get there, they'll see that I have my fare back to Birkenhead, I'm sure.'

The conductor looked at her sharply. Plainly, he had not expected a dirty child in a shabby shawl to speak in the clear-cut accents of the upper class, but Lonnie gave him her most appealing smile and he grinned back before continuing to collect the fares.

Presently the bus reached its destination and Lonnie climbed down. She would have liked to look round this bustling market town, but decided she must head straight for Bwlchgwyn. The day was already advanced, the sun sinking towards the west, and she had no desire to sleep under a hedge.

She had to ask directions several times since she was not used to the strong North Wales accent, though she thought it vaguely similar to that of her dear *ayah* back in India. The last person she asked, a fat farmer's wife carrying a large basket covered with a chequered cloth, looked at her shrewdly, then set her basket down on the pavement and addressed Lonnie in a motherly tone. 'Where have you come from, cariad?' she asked. 'Wasn't you the little lass that got on the bus at Birkenhead? If so, you'll be wanting a drink and a bite to eat before you set off for Bwlchgwyn. There's a good café in Hope Street, opposite the Horse and Jockey pub. It's called Stevenson's and they do a grand steak 'n' kidney puddin' for tenpence.'

'I'm afraid I don't have tenpence,' Lonnie said regretfully. 'In fact, I don't have any money at all just at present, but I'm going to friends, so that's all right.'

The woman bent down and pulled back the chequered cloth, revealing a great deal of food. Lonnie's mouth watered as she looked at the tempting display and when her new friend delved into the basket and produced two large slices of bread and a wedge of cheese, her hand shot out involuntarily, even as she thanked the farmer's wife. 'It's most awfully kind of you,' she said through a mouthful. 'I hadn't realised that it would take all of my money just to get this far, but once I reach my friends I shall be all right.' She glanced hopefully at the older woman. 'Is it *very* far to Bwlchgwyn?'

'It isn't the distance, but you're going up into the mountains,' the farmer's wife explained. 'I live on the plain myself, but of course I've been through Bwlchgwyn many a time, when we go for a day's pleasuring to Rhyl or Colwyn Bay on the coast. It don't seem far when you're in a charabanc, but on foot I dare say it will take you an hour or two. Still, there's a village on the way where you can sit yourself down for half an hour or so and get your breath. I wonder who you're going to visit? In these parts, most of us know each other.'

'I don't think you'd know the Baileys,' Lonnie admitted. 'You see, Mr Bailey is a patient in the sanatorium on the Llandegla moors, so Mrs Bailey has only rented the cottage until he's well enough to go home. I'm going to visit him and then stay with the Baileys for a couple of days,' she added.

The woman fished in her basket and produced a hard green pear which she handed to Lonnie before covering the basket over once more. 'You gnaw on that,' she said kindly. 'I know the sanatorium, we all do in these parts. I hope as your friend's husband gets well soon.' She picked up her basket and turned away. 'Good luck, cariad.'

Before she had gone more than a mile, Lonnie realised that the farmer's wife had been right. The distance was bad enough – that woman had said it was seven or eight miles – but it was the gradient which soon began to defeat her. She reached the promised village and sat down for a while on a convenient seat. Then, glancing at the setting sun, for it had been quite a pleasant day, she decided that she must press on.

By the time she reached the village of Bwlchgwyn, the sky had clouded over and heavy drops of drain had begun to fall. Tired out but still filled with icy determination, Lonnie continued on through the village, but when she reached the lane of which Dick had spoken it was full dark and she was so tired and hungry that she sat herself down on the grass verge and indulged in a hearty bout of tears. However, resolution had always been Lonnie's main characteristic and she very soon wiped her eyes, blew her nose on the shawl and set off once more.

She passed the cottage which she guessed belonged to the Hughes family and noted, wistfully, that the lamps were lit and that a good smell of cooking warmed the night air, but no doubt Mrs Bailey, too, would be preparing a meal – her mouth watered once more at the thought – and she quickened her lagging steps a little so that the final mile along the lane seemed to go a little faster than the previous one.

At last, the cottage loomed, black against the sky. With a sob of relief, Lonnie opened the gate, walked down the garden path and turned left alongside the wall of the house, so that she might approach it from the rear. She remembered Hester telling her that front doors were seldom used in Britain and that friends and family – and even tradesmen – usually went round the back, so naturally she must do likewise.

She turned the corner and stared towards the windows, then stopped short, her heart giving a loud, unnatural thump. She could see at a glance that the curtains were drawn back and that the interior of the cottage was black as night.

For the first time since she had left St Catherine's, Lonnie's resolution failed her. She simply did not know what to do. Her entire escape plan had revolved around the finding of Mrs Bailey in the cottage. Her fertile imagination had painted the happy picture of her arrival at the cottage so convincingly that at first she could not believe it was not about to happen. Perhaps they were all in bed, having had a busy day. Perhaps they were visiting the Hughes and had not yet returned. Presently she forced herself to go and peer in through the kitchen window. She expected to see the glow of a fire in the grate or perhaps the table set for breakfast next morning because, although she had no very accurate idea of the time, she knew it must be late.

Cupping both hands around her face, she stared into the darkness of the cottage and her heart faltered. Dick had told her that the family had moved a good deal of their belongings into the cottage since it was let unfurnished and now, her despair deepening with every moment, she was forced to face the truth. All the comfortable clutter which she remembered from the Bailey's house in Elmore Street was missing. There was no fire in the grate, no rug on the hearth, no dresser filled with the cheap but cheerful china that she remembered. Indeed, there could be no breakfast set since there was no table, nor any chairs. No matter how hard she tried to persuade herself that it was otherwise, the cottage was clearly deserted. No one was living here and she was a very long way from friends of any description. She had no money and had eaten all the food the farmer's wife had given her. What was more, she was totally worn out, freezing cold, and her shawl clung damply round her shoulders.

Lonnie sat down on the flagstoned path with a thump. She told herself wildly that she must pull herself together, stop being so silly and decide what to do next. But for several moments she could think of nothing. The rain, which had eased, began to come down again in earnest and this galvanised her into action once more. She jumped to her feet and tried the back door but it failed to give to her endeavours so she surveyed her surroundings carefully. The Baileys had told Lonnie and Hester that every household kept a spare back door key tucked away in some spot which the family knew all about but a burglar was unlikely to discover. One hiding place which Lonnie particularly admired was only possible if there was a letter-box in the door and this door was thick, old-fashioned wood, without so much as a crack. So a key, dangling on a piece of string and popped through the letter-box, was an impossibility. Lonnie looked round for another hiding place. Close against the back door was an iron foot-scraper of quite elaborate design with a revolving brush at the back, so that one might remove not only the chunks of mud but also the dirt which gathers around the toecap of one's boots. Lonnie went down upon her knees and ran her hand around the foot-scraper, then gave a tiny crow of triumph. Hanging on the wrought ironwork was a large key.

It was the work of a moment to insert the key in the lock and though Lonnie had some difficulty in turning it, for her fingers were icy cold, she managed it at last and let herself into the kitchen. The room seemed large and bare in the small amount of light which filtered in through the low windows but it was a good deal warmer than the garden had been and Lonnie took off her shawl and spread it right across the old-fashioned range. Then she looked round for something – anything – in which she could wrap herself, for she was still extremely cold. I'll find something somewhere, she vowed, heading across the kitchen for the little parlour which Dick had told her about, and then, tomorrow morning, I'll decide what to do next.

Hester's anxiety for Lonnie had grown overnight. She went round to Elmore Street and told Mrs Bailey that she had not been able to see the child the day before but intended to visit the school that afternoon.

Mrs Bailey nodded understandingly but reminded Hester that Lonnie had never been exactly an angel. Though the nuns were undoubtedly strict, she was sure they would let Hester see her young charge as they had promised. 'And there's a job goin' down at the bakery on Heyworth Street,' she added, almost as an afterthought. 'Mr Briggs, he's a very pertickler man, so his staff – the younger ones that is – don't usually stay long. You have to wear a white cloth over your hair so that not a strand shows, almost like being a nun, and he won't have no make-up worn, nor no perfume, and the girls wear real ugly white wraparound overalls, flat shoes, and gloves to handle the bakery products. But the pay ain't bad and if you don't mind washing your hands four hundred times a day, you'll probably stick it for a week or two.'

The two women were standing in the kitchen, Mrs Bailey rolling out pastry whilst her guest watched. Upon hearing her hostess's words, Hester flew across the room and planted a kiss upon Mrs Bailey's floury cheek. 'That sounds wonderful, Mrs Bailey,' she said enthusiastically. 'Will it be all right if I go round there straight away?'

'Aye, you do that,' Mrs Bailey said. 'I didn't mention the hours; them's the big drawback really. You see, when you're on bakery shift, you'll start work at twelve midnight and work till eight the following mornin', so you'll be sleeping when other folks is going off to their jobs. But if a baker's going to serve fresh bread and cakes, and so on, the fellers have to bake through the night.'

'I see,' Hester said, rather faintly. 'Is that why Mr Briggs's staff don't stay long?'

Mrs Bailey grinned. 'Mebbe,' she admitted. 'But jobs is hard to come by, queen, and I know you've not got fambly behind you, so if I were you I'd gerroff there right away.'

'I will,' Hester said, bending to pick up her bag which she had dropped on the kitchen floor, 'and many thanks, Mrs B; you're a pal.'

'Aye, I'm worth me weight in gold,' Mrs Bailey agreed. 'When you've finished wi' Mr Briggs, you come round here for your tea, then I dare say our Dick will want a word.'

'I'd love to,' Hester said happily. 'By then I'll have seen Lonnie and we'll have a better idea of what to do next. 'Bye for now.'

Hester remembered, as soon as she saw the shop, that she and Lonnie had been regular customers here when they had lived in Shaw Street. Lonnie had always declared that Briggs's Bakery made the most delicious doughnuts and the best sugar buns to be found in the area. What was more, Mrs Briggs was a dab hand at such confections as coconut ice, peppermint creams and stick-jaw toffee, so a good deal of Lonnie's pocket money had found its way into Mr Briggs's till.

The interview with the master baker was brief but thorough and at the end of half an hour Hester found herself once more in gainful employment. 'You'll start with the day shift, first thing on Monday morning,' Mr Briggs said, smiling at her. He was short and fat and as pale as his own bread, with the shy and confiding smile of a baby and about as many teeth. Hester had always liked him and felt sure that they would get along famously. She was issued with two vast wraparound aprons, four hair tidies and four sets of boot covers, though Mr Briggs advised her to leave these items in the back room, since he was responsible for the laundering of all the staff garments.

By four o'clock, Hester was on the doorstep of St Catherine's Convent. She rang the bell, and after a long delay the door was opened by a small and trembling nun who took one look at her and slammed the door in her face. Hester, who had been stepping forward, recoiled, but seconds later the door was opened again by another nun. 'I'm sorry if Sister Francis was rude, but I'm afraid the convent is in an uproar,' she explained, ushering Hester inside. 'One of our pupils . . . my goodness, are you the young lady who was coming to see Leonora Hetherington-Smith at four this afternoon? I'm to take you straight to the Mother Superior's office.'

I wonder what she's done now, Hester was thinking as she was ushered into the office. I do hope she isn't in trouble of some sort!

* * *

'She's run away,' Hester said tearfully, facing Mrs Bailey across the kitchen table. 'The police were there and they asked me if I knew where Lonnie might have gone. I thought of you at once, Mrs Bailey, but the awful thing is, the nuns weren't at all sure when she had left. Apparently, it is their dreadful practice to lock wrongdoers in a cupboard, often for hours and hours at a time. It appears that Lonnie was shut into the cupboard for a few hours yesterday, released to go to her dormitory for a night's sleep and was then to be re-imprisoned this morning. Apparently, two particular nuns are responsible for the punishment cupboard and both assumed that the other one had re-imprisoned Lonnie when in fact no one has seen her at all today. I was totally shocked at the nuns' behaviour and so was the policeman. He spoke very severely to the Mother Superior and said he would be forced to report her actions to his senior officer. But that doesn't help Lonnie, of course.'

'I wonder she didn't come here,' Mrs Bailey said. 'Philly, don't sit there with your mouth open, catching flies! Go and fetch a cup off the dresser and Miss Elliott and meself will sit down and talk this thing over.'

'Do call me Hester, please,' Hester said, accepting the cup of tea gratefully. 'I'm certain Lonnie will come here, Mrs Bailey, just as soon as she is able. Dick gave her some money for the tram fare but she may well have decided to walk so that she could spend the money on food. One of the nuns – a shy little thing, I didn't catch her name – told me that Lonnie had not been fed the whole of yesterday, so hunger may have forced her to buy food. But she doesn't know where I live and Dick told her to come to you, I know he did.'

When Dick arrived home, he congratulated Hester on her new job, making this an excuse to give her a hug and a kiss on the cheek, but as soon as he heard of Lonnie's escapade, he suggested that the child might have gone to Birkenhead and waited outside Laird's for him to appear. 'Or she might have gone to Mrs Beasdale, I suppose, if she's not realised I've moved back home,' he finished. 'Where's young Ben, by the way?'

'Gone off to help Mr Madison, I expect. If there's a deal of work to do, Mr M will give him some tea and they'll work on until really late,' Mrs Bailey said. 'Funny thing, though. He and Philly were sitting at the kitchen table mucking around wi' some toy or other when Hester was telling me about Lonnie, an' all of a sudden he jumped up to his feet and shot out of the kitchen, not even stopping to pick up his jacket.'

'He'll have remembered he ought to ha' been at Madisons's,' Dick said. He pulled out a chair and gestured to it. 'Sit down, Hester, my dear, and we'll talk this thing through, but I'd lay a pound to a penny that young Lonnie turns up here in the next couple of hours. Now, Mam, how about that tea you spoke of?'

Ben had listened to Hester's story and, unlike the rest of his family, had immediately realised what must have happened. Girls shut up in convent schools were very unlikely to set eyes on a newspaper, so Lonnie would have no idea that Mr Bailey had died, far less that the family were back in Elmore Street. So what would she do? Why, she would make her way to the cottage in Bwlchgwyn . . . and find it empty. At the horrid suspicion, Ben had leapt from his seat and rushed out of the room, hoping against hope that if he reached the Pier Head in time, he might catch her before she boarded the ferry.

He was unlucky. Though he hung around at the ferry terminal for some time, he saw neither hide nor hair of Lonnie and eventually decided that he must have missed her. He reasoned that if she had left the convent early that day, she would have had ample opportunity to catch the ferry before he had even heard of her escape. He was turning away, meaning to go back to Elmore Street, when he suddenly realised the plight in which his young friend might find herself. He had no doubt that she would make her way to the cottage and, upon finding it empty, would be panic-stricken. She would be totally alone and probably without money in a strange place, and having gone all that way she would be unlikely to try to retrace her steps that night. It had been a cool and rainy day and he guessed that a night up on the Llandegla moors would be an uncomfortable experience for anyone. Sighing, he dug his hands into his trouser pockets and fished out his loose change. He had been saving the coins his mam would not take from his wages, and there was sufficient money to take him up to Bwlchgwyn; sufficient to pay for the return fares for himself and Lonnie as well.

The ferry for Woodside was about to depart. Ben hesitated for a moment, worried that he could get no word back to Elmore Street. Then he decided he would pop in on Mrs Beasdale as soon as he crossed the water and ask her to get a message back to Dick. Considerably cheered by the thought that he could prevent his mother from worrying, he joined the jostling crowd headed for the ferry.

* * *

By the time Ben reached the cottage the stars were paling in the night sky and he guessed dawn was not far off. As he walked round to the back it occurred to him, for the first time, that he had no idea at all where Lonnie might have hidden herself. When the Baileys had moved out they had taken all their furniture, traipsing back and forth with a big old-fashioned van until the cottage was empty. Then Mrs Bailey and Millie had scrubbed the place from top to bottom, despite the fact that the landlord had told them he had no tenant waiting to move in.

When they had first arrived at the cottage, there had been curtains at the windows because the landlord had said this discouraged tramps from breaking in. There had also been, Ben remembered, a lantern in the *ty bach* at the end of the garden. The landlord had explained that this was provided for the convenience of those wishing to use the lavatory during the hours of darkness, so now Ben set off down the garden path, thinking that at least, if he had the lantern, he was less likely to tread on Lonnie and scare her out of her wits.

He opened the door of the *ty bach*, which gave a horribly ominous creak, and took down the lantern from its nail on the wall. Like most boys', his pockets were stuffed with odds and ends – bits of string, a ball of chewed chewing gum, a couple of matches and a rusty old penknife. The only trouble was that his mother had neglected to fill the lamp before she left so he had lit his two matches in vain. Cursing his own stupidity, for if he had thought, he could have searched around for something else inflammable, Ben stumbled back to the cottage. He was beginning to suspect that Lonnie had never even got this far until he investigated the foot-scraper beside the back door and found the key was missing.

Ben felt a grin spread across his face and tried the back door, which opened to his touch. As silently as he could, he slipped into the kitchen, and glanced at the window behind him. For a moment he wondered what was different about it, then realised that the curtains were missing. Strange! But before he had done more than take two steps into the room, he was frozen to the spot by the most blood-curdling shriek he had ever heard, and then he found himself staggering back beneath the onslaught of a small but furious person, who flew at him, fists and feet flailing. Trying to get out of the way, to explain, Ben somehow managed to fall backwards, clouting his head hard on the still open back door as he did so. This made him feel both dizzy and furious and he tried to restrain his attacker, who had fallen on top of him and was cursing him – he assumed it was curses – in a foreign tongue. For a moment he thought that some small, but mad, Welsh tramp must have gained entry to the cottage, but then a fold of dark material fell away from his attacker's white face and he recognised Lonnie.

'Lonnie! It's me, Ben! Do stop . . . aargh!'

Lonnie, far from desisting, seemed to be actually fighting herself and Ben suddenly realised that she had wrapped herself in the kitchen curtains, presumably for warmth, and was now not so much struggling with him as endeavouring to get free from the enveloping material. Ben, sitting up, for they had both landed on the quarry tiles of the kitchen floor, tried to help her, only to be rudely repulsed.

'Get away, you nasty, interfering boy!' Lonnie squeaked. 'How dare you come in, frightening the life out of me! I thought you were a *thuggi* or a bandit! Oh, how you scared me, Ben Bailey.'

Ben scrambled to his feet, not sure whether to laugh or cry. His head was still ringing; one elbow had met the quarry tiles with enough force, he was sure, to shatter it to bits, and despite her wrappings Lonnie had landed a number of punches and kicks on his person. What was more, it appeared to have escaped her notice that he was her rescuer and that in fact it was she who had attacked him and not vice versa.

'Stop wriggling, Lonnie, and let me get you out of that,' he said, therefore. He grabbed the curtains and began to pull them from her shoulders, then dropped them in a heap at her feet. He noticed she was still clinging to some shabby and pungent garment but had no chance to ask her what on earth it was before she had bent and snatched up the curtains once more.

'What on earth do you think you're doing, Ben Bailey? These curtains are my bed. I was nearly freezing to death before I thought of the curtains and I'd just dropped off to sleep when I heard someone scratching around in that little shed thing at the end of the garden. I remembered then that I'd not locked the door – the key was too big and stiff – so I came and stood behind it, ready to frighten off anyone who tried to get in. And it was you! And – and I hate you and I'll never forgive you for giving me such a terrible fright.'

Ben stood quite silent for a moment. He was fighting an urge to grab Lonnie and give her a good shake, tell her she was an ungrateful little beast, and then to turn round and walk out of the cottage – and her life – for ever. But his mother had brought him up to respect girls and his father had often told him that women were illogical creatures but that mostly they meant well. So he swallowed his anger and said in as gentle a tone as he could manage: 'Don't be cross, Lonnie. You gave me just as much of a fright as I gave you. That shriek near stopped my heart, so I reckon we're quits. I came to tell you that we've moved back to Elmore Street and I've brung some money wi' me so's we can both go home. What about that, eh?'

Lonnie sniffed. 'Well, all right, I suppose you didn't mean to scare me,' she said grudgingly. 'Is it nearly morning? Can we go home soon?'

'I don't know what the time is,' Ben said, peering out at the starlit sky through the kitchen door and then closing it firmly. 'Look, you kip down on them curtains and I'll go and fetch the ones from the parlour. That way, we'll be snug enough till morning.'

He suited action to his words and presently the two children curled up in their respective curtains on either side of the cold and empty fireplace. After a few moments, Ben said sleepily: 'What's a *thuggi* when it's at home? I know what a bandit is, of course.'

Lonnie heaved a sigh and sat up on one elbow. 'There are *thuggis* in India; my *ayah* told me all about them,' she said. 'They sneak up to travellers with a thin cord, one end held in either hand, and they whisk it round the traveller's neck and then throttle him to death.' She glared angrily across at Ben. 'I wish you hadn't made me tell you that. Now I'll be too scared to sleep.'

Ben sighed; it seemed that no matter what he did, he would be wrong. So he shuffled across the intervening space and put an arm around Lonnie's skinny shoulders. 'We'll be warmer if we share our curtains,' he said gruffly. 'An' I'll make sure no one sneaks up on you while you're asleep. Besides, it'll soon be morning and then we can start on our journey home.'

To his secret surprise, Lonnie did not attempt to push him away but settled down once more, and presently he could tell by her even breathing that she slept.

Rosalind Hetherington-Smith would have enjoyed the voyage from India had it not been for her very real worries over the fate of her brand new stepdaughter. She was deeply in love with her husband and thought him the kindest and best of men, but she had soon realised that his business was tremendously important to him and in all conscience could not be easily cast aside, particularly after a six-month absence, even for the sake of his beloved daughter.

He had not wanted his bride to leave him, to go off to England by herself, but when he had been brought to realise that his little Lonnie was almost certainly suffering great unhappiness he had booked his new wife a first-class berth on the *Florealis* and waved her off, telling her to bring Lonnie back with her if she must, but otherwise to settle the child in some pleasant and friendly house with good, kind people and place her in a first-rate day school. After hearing about Rosalind's own experiences at a poor quality English boarding school some years before, he had decided that this was not for his little girl. He knew that India could not provide the sort of education she needed, however, and feared for her health if she returned there, for children did not thrive in the tremendous heat of the plains.

As soon as the ship docked, Rosalind booked herself into the Adelphi Hotel and called a cab to take her to Shaw Street. Her interview there was not a long one but she came out with her eyes flashing and her cheeks very bright pink. Miss Hetherington-Smith had been downright obstructive over her reasons for ignoring her brother's wishes and putting Leonora into a boarding school. When Rosalind had queried the whereabouts of the governess, she had shrugged her shoulders and tried to change the subject, but when Rosalind persisted she had simply said, snappishly: 'I have no idea what has happened to that dreadful young woman, neither am I at all interested. I dismissed her for insufferable behaviour and do not wish to discuss the matter further.'

'I thought you said Miss Elliott could not control Leonora when you wrote to my husband,' Rosalind said craftily. 'You made it clear that it was Leonora's behaviour which had caused you to send her away from her father's house, yet now you are blaming the governess.'

That had ended the interview. Miss Hetherington-Smith had gazed at her blankly for a moment and had then said, in a strange, sing-song voice: 'God works in a mysterious way and I am only His mouthpiece. Kindly leave me.'

Rosalind thought Miss Hetherington-Smith was a little mad and this impression was heightened when a tall, thin woman, who introduced herself as Miss Hutchinson, stopped her in the hallway as the butler was leading her back to the front door.

'Miss Hetherington-Smith has not been quite herself for several months,' the woman hissed, glancing nervously about her as she did so. 'I have spoken to the doctor and he says my employer is suffering from delusions and should be treated with great care. Both he and I feel that the child is a good deal safer away from this house. I should have written to Mr Hetherington-Smith myself, but . . .'

'Hutchinson!' The voice, high yet harsh, came from the room which Rosalind had just left and the companion hurried off towards the sound without another glance in Rosalind's direction.

Now, hailing a second cab to take her to the convent school, Rosalind reflected that whatever she might find there, it could not be worse than what she had seen in Shaw Street. The house itself was rather a grand one, but the state of it! The butler, whose name was Dawson, was so old and doddery that it was all he could do to swing the heavy front door open, and it was plain to Rosalind that the dust and dirt she saw all about her was the result of many weeks of neglect.

I suppose it's none of my business, Rosalind told herself, settling into the worn leather seat. Yes it is, though; I remember Leonard telling me that the house was his property and that he paid his sister generously to be chatelaine there in his absence. Rosalind heaved a deep and weary sigh. Once I have dealt with Lonnie and her situation, I suppose I will have to do something about Leonard's house, she thought ruefully. That old sister of his isn't completely sane, I'm sure of it. But if I explain to Leonard how things are, he will feel he has to come over himself and deal with it. Oh, my dear love! How I do miss you!

'Missing?' Rosalind clapped her hand to her heart and stared incredulously at the Mother Superior across the wide, leather-topped desk. 'How can you possibly have lost a child? Are you sure she's not somewhere in the building or in the grounds?'

The Mother Superior was a tall, gaunt woman with the sort of face normally seen in Italian Renaissance paintings. Now her expression became grave as well as worried at Rosalind's words. 'I'm deeply ashamed to have to tell you, Mrs Hetherington-Smith, that we are not sure exactly when Leonora left the building. She was sent to the punishment cupboard for – for breaking the rules, but naturally was released to her dormitory at bedtime. Next morning, she was to return to the punishment cupboard since she refused to apologise for her bad behaviour. Sister Magdalene assumed that Sister Enda had dealt with her incarceration and Sister Enda assumed that Sister Magdalene had done the deed. In fact, neither of them had seen the child and we have to assume that she slipped away during the night.'

Rosalind stared at the older woman. 'Are you telling me that you actually shut my stepdaughter in a cupboard, a horrible, dark cupboard, for hours at a time, as a punishment?' she asked incredulously. 'We are talking about a child not yet ten years of age. No wonder Leonora ran away.' She stared challengingly at the older woman. 'I would have run away myself,' she ended.

The Mother Superior's long, olive-skinned face reddened slightly above the cheekbones, but she said haughtily: 'Leonora is a very difficult child, Mrs Hetherington-Smith, as you will no doubt discover when she is found. We have done our best to turn a wild, ill-educated little savage into a meek and biddable schoolchild. If we are to be allowed to continue with our work . . .'

'Continue with your work!' Rosalind jumped to her feet, feeling the tide of blood rise within her own cheeks. 'Just as soon as Lonnie is found, she will become a pupil in a decent school, where the teachers care for their children and bring them up with love. I pray she has not come to any harm, for this most certainly will be laid at your door. And if she is not found . . .'

Mother Superior's icy voice cut across Rosalind's hot and impetuous speech. 'The matter has been placed in the hands of the police,' she said coldly. 'I understand your anxiety and forgive your rash and heedless words, since I am sure, after a little cogitation, you will regret what you have said. It is, after all, a worrying time for you.'

Rosalind bit back the angry retort on the tip of her tongue and turned towards the door. 'If you find Leonora, I trust that you will inform me immediately. I am staying at the Adelphi Hotel,' she said coolly. 'I shall go straight to the police station from here. Good morning!'

Rosalind had actually left the convent and was walking briskly along the flagstones when she heard the swift patter of feet behind her. She stopped when a small hand clutched at her elbow and looked down into the face of a tiny, wrinkled nun, whose pale-blue eyes were blinking rapidly. 'Mrs Hetherington-Smith, the Mother Superior sent me after you. She thought it might assist you to know that Leonora's governess called at the convent earlier and left us her address, so that we might tell her if . . . when her former pupil was found. Her name is Miss Hester Elliott and she is at present residing in a lodging house just off the Scotland Road. Her address is Number 10, Stansfield Court.'

Rosalind felt as though a great weight had been lifted off her shoulders. It had been clear from the first moment she had set eyes on her sister-in-law that she would get no help from that quarter. The nuns had not been obstructive, but they had not been helpful either. Rosalind was in awe of the police force and did not feel capable of dealing with them should they take Lonnie's disappearance lightly. But Leonard had thought a great deal of Hester Elliott, considering her both likeable and extremely competent; if she could just get hold of Hester, she was sure that between them they could find Lonnie.

Ben awoke. For a moment he wondered where on earth he was, for though he shared a bedroom with Dick and Ted he had his own little truckle bed, yet now he could feel someone curled up within the circle of his arms, someone who was snuffling heavily as he stirred.

Ben glanced around him and realised, all in a moment, that he was in the cottage on the Llandegla moors and that he had found Lonnie. He even remembered – particularly when he wincingly moved – her attack on him and his subsequent fall on to the hard quarry tiles. Groaning slightly beneath his breath, he sat up and gingerly felt the back of his head. There was an awesome lump the size of a hen's egg on the back of his skull which hurt to touch, and his elbow must be black and blue, for when he bent his arm pains shot from his wrist to his shoulder.

Trying not to disturb Lonnie, Ben unwound the thick curtains and scrambled to his feet. Bright sunlight was pouring in through the window and when he went over and looked out he saw that the sky was a brilliant blue, without a cloud in sight. Lonnie was still curled up, so he decided to pay a quick visit to the *ty bach*. He meant to beg some breakfast from the Hughes family but thought he ought to wake Lonnie first. He could imagine the panic she would feel if she awoke to find herself alone once more.

He was returning from the *ty bach* when he heard someone whistling. He hurried round the corner of the cottage and saw Meirion Hughes's dad, his cap on the back of his head, striding past the gate. Ben broke into a run and was greeted with astonishment by his erstwhile neighbour.

'Thought you'd gone, we did, mun,' Mr Hughes said genially. 'Forget something, did you? You're up wi' the lark, I'll say that for you. Our Meirion is still abed, I'll be bound.'

'Oh, Mr Hughes, what *is* the time?' Ben said eagerly. 'I'm in a bit o' trouble, to tell the truth. A friend of – of my sister didn't realise we'd gone back to Liverpool and she come a-visiting last night. Me – me mam sent me up to make sure she were all right – she's only a kid – but of course there isn't a crumb of food in the house and we're really hungry, the pair of us. I wondered if – if Mrs Hughes could give us breakfast? A cup o' tea and a bite o' bread would be just fine.'

'First things first, bach,' Mr Hughes said. He fished a large old-fashioned turnip watch out of his waistcoat pocket and consulted it. 'Not yet seven, it is, but my good lady had the porridge cooking over the stove an hour ago and there's always bread in the crock and butter on the slate shelf, to say nothin' of tea in the pot. You and your pal go along there as soon as you're able – say I sent you – and Mrs Hughes will give you something to line your stummicks.'

'Thanks ever so much, Mr Hughes,' Ben said

gratefully. 'Can you tell me what time there's a bus from the village?

Mr Hughes sucked his teeth thoughtfully, cocking his head on one side and frowning with the effort of remembering the timetable. 'There's one at eight,' he said at last. 'You and your pal had best get going as soon as may be, though, 'cos your mam's had enough trouble without worrying over a young *cnaf* like yourself.'

Ben was happy to obey and quite soon he and Lonnie, having had a brisk splash under the pump in the yard, locked the cottage behind them and set off for the Hughes' place. Ben had explained to Lonnie as they tidied themselves up that his father had died and the family had returned to Elmore Street. 'None of them thought that you'd not know about me dad's death,' he had said, rather proudly. 'Dick and Hester and me mam were all waiting for you in Elmore Street, certain that you'd go there. But I nipped down to the ferry, hoping to catch you before you left, and when I realised you must have already gone, I followed you.'

'I hope your mam won't be very cross with me,' Lonnie said, rather apprehensively. 'But she's so kind that if I beg very hard, perhaps she'll let me stay with her until my daddy comes for me. I'm sure he will come when he hears what's been happening to me,' she finished.

Mrs Hughes greeted them cheerfully, fed them porridge, boiled eggs and bread and butter, and sent them on their way feeling well satisfied, though in Ben's case at least, still a little anxious. I hope to God Mam hasn't called the scuffers in to find me, he thought, as he ushered his companion aboard the first bus, but I dare say when she knows I've found

Lonnie she won't scold too much – especially if Mrs Beasdale managed to get a message to her, telling her I'm all right.

When they eventually arrived at Elmore Street, Ben and Lonnie's return was in the nature of a Triumph. Ben entered the kitchen rather cautiously, fearing to find the Law there before him, or his mother torn between hysterics and rage, but instead Mrs Bailey hugged them both indiscriminately, with tears running down her face, for though Mrs Beasdale had sent a neighbour's lad over on the ferry to explain where Ben had gone she had worried about him all night, far from convinced that he would find Lonnie safe and sound.

'But all's well that ends well,' she said, sitting the pair of them down at her kitchen table and feeding them with weak tea and new-baked bread spread with margarine and gooseberry jam. It had taken them a good while to get back to Liverpool and they had been glad to tuck in to the bread and jam since the family's main meal was saved for when the workers returned in the evening. 'I suppose it's our duty to tell the scuffers, though I'm mortal afraid that if we do they'll take young Lonnie back to that convent school, and Miss Elliott said as how Mr Hetherington-Smith would be furious if he knew his daughter had been sent to such a place.' She clasped her head with a thin hand. 'What would be best to do?' she said worriedly, more to herself than to the children. 'It's times like this that I really miss my dear Bob. He'd have known what I ought to do.'

'It's all right, Mam,' Ben said comfortingly. 'Dick will be home this evenin', and you know wharra steady feller he is. He'll tell us what to do near on as good as our dad would have done.'

'Aye . . . but Dick's never back here much before half-past six, even if he's nigh on finished a job when the hooter goes,' Mrs Bailey said worriedly.

'I could wrap my shawl well round me and go and see Hester,' Lonnie suggested. 'After all, my daddy left me in her charge, I'm sure he did. And she's not frightened of policemen or Miss Hetherington-Smith or the nuns or anyone. At least, I don't think she is. Then you wouldn't have to worry,' she finished.

Mrs Bailey laughed but shook her head. 'No, it wouldn't be right to send you off. You stay right here until Dick comes home,' she decided. 'As for you, young Ben, hadn't you better go along to Madison's and tell him as you're real sorry you didn't turn up yesterday? I dare say he were relyin' on you to help him clean down and that.'

'I wish I could come with you,' Lonnie said wistfully as Ben pulled on his jacket and crossed to the back door. 'It would be lovely to see Mr Madison and all his animals, but perhaps it would only make me miss Kitty more. Do you suppose that my aunt will let me have Kitty back once my father comes to rescue me?'

'I'm sure your aunt will be only too glad to get rid of the cat,' Ben said. 'And if your father takes you back to India and Kitty can't go with you, I'm pretty sure our mam would let her live here.'

'That would be lovely; your mam is *so* good,' Lonnie said gratefully. 'And now I'm going to help her to get the supper so when you and Dick come home there'll be something nice waiting for you.'

'Grand,' Ben said, hoping devoutly that his mam would make sure Lonnie didn't have too much of a hand in the preparation of the meal, 'See you later, then.'

'It's almost unbelievable how much has been done in one short week,' Hester said. 'Mind you, Mrs Hetherington-Smith – only she told me I might call her Rosalind – is tremendously efficient and very sure of herself. Why, she gave notice to the convent that Lonnie would not be returning there, settled the child into a room at the Adelphi, booked passages for both of them to return to India in just over two weeks, and even chose a new school for Lonnie so that when she returns in September it will be to a thoroughly respectable establishment where there will be no corporal punishment or censoring of letters, or anything of that sort.'

'Aye, but you're pretty efficient yourself, Hes,' Eileen said. The two girls were sitting in their room, preparing to go out for the evening. Eileen was brushing her long, toffee-coloured hair and trying to persuade it to curl under in a fashionable page-boy style whilst Hester did her best to press the creases out of her pink blouse. In order to do this, she had to balance a small flat iron on top of the paraffin stove and now, frowning with concentration, she applied the iron to the frills around the neck, then stood the iron on the floor and waved the garment at her friend.

'If I was really efficient, I'd move to a better lodging where I could plug in my electric iron and wouldn't have to fiddle around with a flat,' she remarked. 'Oh well, I'm not really earning enough to want to double my rent so I shouldn't grumble.'

Eileen grinned a trifle ruefully and Hester, smiling back, knew that her friend was well aware that

Hester stayed in their present room solely for Eileen's sake. When she had got the job with Mr Briggs, with higher wages than the dress shop had paid, due to the shift work, she had suggested to Eileen that the two of them might move to more salubrious surroundings. Eileen had always been better paid than she and could have afforded such a move but had explained to Hester her reasons for wishing to remain where she was.

'No one stays here long; the minute they gets a halfway decent job, they moves on,' she had explained. 'That way, no one gets to know us real well, do they? Because the girls change every two or three weeks – apart from you and me that is – it don't occur to them that I don't eat that much but I seem to get fatter. And when they see me knittin' a little jacket or some such an' I say it's for a pal, they aren't around long enough to wonder why I'm gettin' such a deal o' stuff just for a pal. See?'

Hester had seen and understood. Not that she thought Eileen's argument was really necessary. After all, they shared the kitchen with a number of girls who had been at Number 10 as long as they, and no one had ever remarked on Eileen's burgeoning figure. Indeed, thanks to the care we've taken, making sure she wears loose floppy dresses and jackets, Eileen still doesn't really look pregnant, just a bit overweight, Hester consoled herself. Come to think of it, if she's happier staying here it will save us a double move, because she won't want to return to the same lodging after the baby's born.

Now, Hester shook out the blouse and began to put it on, fastening the tiny buttons with nimble fingers. They were alone in the room since the occupants of the other two beds were down in the kitchen, preparing an evening meal. 'This will be the first time I've been to a dance since I came to Liverpool,' Hester said. 'Dick is so nice that I shan't worry if I can't do all the dances because he says he'll teach me the steps as we go round the dance floor. Is Tom a good dancer, Eileen?'

'I dunno. We've not been dancing yet,' Eileen said briefly. 'I'd rather go to a flick meself but when I said as you and Dick were off to the Grafton, he said he'd like to go along as well.'

'You're seeing quite a bit of Tom, aren't you?' Hester said, stepping into her skirt. It was a black taffeta patterned with pink roses and swirled satisfactorily when she made a sharp movement. 'D'you think it's wise, Eileen dear? If you go on seeing him then I suppose you'll have to tell him about the . . .'

'Shush,' Eileen said automatically. 'Least said, soonest mended. And I'm not tellin' him nothin', an' nor are you. Don't forget the promise you made, Hester Elliott, 'cos I'll never forgive you if it gets about.'

'I wish you'd let me tell Mrs Bailey, or even Dick,' Hester said worriedly. 'I've never seen a baby born or had anything to do with babies, come to that. I won't be any use when you need me most. Mrs Bailey's had six babies of her own and even Dick has been around when his brothers and sisters were tiny. I'm worried that you might begin to have the baby before you're in the home and then what'll I do?'

'Well, *you* may know nothing about having babies, but I know a great deal,' Eileen said briskly. 'I've seen me mam at it and they pops out like peas from a pod, no trouble. Me mam's like me, broad in the beam, so I 'spec I'll be like her and the kid'll be born before you can say Jack Robinson. An' don't you dare tell nobody, hear me?'

'All right, all right, I hear you,' Hester said. She had recently bought a cream-coloured jacket from Paddy's market and now she slipped into this garment. She was helping Eileen into the loose-fitting coat when the door shot open and their two sleeping companions came in, both carefully carrying a laden plate.

'Evening, Miss O'Farrell, Miss Elliott,' the newcomers chorused; the shorter of the two adding inquisitively: 'Off out, are you? Where's you a-goin', if I may make so bold?'

'Dancin' wi' our fellers,' Eileen said briefly.

'What? Ain't you havin' no supper first?' the second girl asked curiously, sitting down on her own bed with a thump and eyeing the plateful of food on her lap lovingly. 'We've got sausage and mash, baked beans and a fried egg. We'd ha' done you the same if you'd asked.'

The planned sharing of the cooking had tended to lapse since, as Eileen had already said, the other occupants of the room rarely stayed long. Now it was usually just Eileen and Hester who put money in the pot and took turns to make their meals, leaving the remaining girls to join in or arrange a similar scheme for themselves.

'We're having a meal out before we go to the Grafton,' Hester explained, picking up her handbag. 'Probably only eggs or cheese on toast. Come on, Eileen, we don't want to be late.'

Hester, floating round the ballroom in Dick's arms, thought she had never been happier. She felt so safe and secure when she was with him. When she had emerged from the ladies' cloakroom where she had left her jacket and had seen the admiring look in Dick's eyes, it had made her evening complete, or so she had thought. Now, waltzing dreamily around the floor, she scarcely remembered to look for Eileen and Tom when the music stopped. Dick put a proprietorial arm round her waist and led her over to the door where a man was rubber stamping the backs of the hands of those who wished to go outside and get some fresh air. Hester had been much amused when Dick had explained to her that the rubber stamp stopped people who had not paid for admittance sneaking in during the interval.

Outside, a balmy little breeze lifted Hester's hair gently from her forehead and in the gas lamp's glow she saw Dick looking down at her very tenderly. He drew her round the corner and along a small passageway until they emerged in a quiet street which no other couples seemed to have discovered. He led her over to a low wall, brushed the top of it and spread a clean white hanky and then sat her down, taking his place beside her.

'Look, Hester, I know it's early days but I honestly think I fell in love with you the very first time I set eyes on you, when you came callin' for Lonnie. Remember? I've been longing to ask you to marry me ever since we met up again, but – but I wasn't really sure how you felt. Only this evening I thought that if I didn't chance me arm, I might lose you. Don't think I haven't seen how other fellers stare, 'cos I have. I'd never have thought meself a jealous bloke but when that smart naval rating tapped me on the shoulder in the "Paul Jones" and took you in his arms . . . well, I were ripe for murder. That made me realise I'd got to speak out or risk losing you to someone wi' a bit more courage and – and a better future. Hester, it may not be fair to ask you to marry me because I'm a good deal older and much more experienced than you and I know you've not had many fellers. What's more, we both know I've got responsibilities now me dad's gone, but – but we can buy a little ring and if we both save like the devil we could mebbe marry in a year.' He put his arm round her shoulders and hugged her convulsively. 'I thought this evening that – that you weren't indifferent. Hester, could you . . . would you . . . ?'

'Oh, Dick, I haven't had any boyfriends, apart from you,' Hester admitted, tucking her head into the hollow of his shoulder. 'But I know my own mind – and my own heart. I love you ever so much. I was so miserable when we were parted! I kept imagining you with some other girl and it made me so unhappy . . . yes of course I'll marry you! Oh, how happy I am. I never thought I'd be so happy again. As for a ring, it's up to you, of course, but all I really want is to be with you for always – a ring doesn't really matter.'

'You're going to have a ring, but if you don't mind waiting till Christmas it'll be a really nice one,' Dick promised. He turned her in his arms so that their faces were only inches apart. 'Oh, God, you're the most beautiful thing and I'm the luckiest feller alive. Kiss me!'

They kissed, at first tenderly and then with so much passion that Hester was shaken by it. Drawing away from him, she said: 'That – that was wonderful, but I think we'd better go back to the dance before Eileen and Tom begin to wonder where we are. Oh, Dick, I'm so happy!'

* * *

Lonnie, sitting opposite her stepmother in the Adelphi's magnificent dining room, wondered what her dear Hester was doing at this very moment. She and Rosalind – for her new stepmother had told her to use her first name – had seen Hester several times since their own meeting a week earlier and Rosalind had confided to Lonnie that she did not intend to let such a lovely person slip through their fingers.

'I have a plan for when you return to England in the autumn,' she had said mysteriously, her big blue eyes twinkling, 'but I don't intend to say anything until I've talked it over with your father. As things stand at present, Hester is happy working at the bakery and earning sufficient money to keep herself until our return. Your father wanted me to pay her an allowance but when I suggested it she got quite cross. She said she was doing very well and was proud of her ability to manage her own affairs.'

Rosalind had gone on to say that she would not be at all surprised if Hester and Dick made a match of it, and although Lonnie secretly thought this a very soppy thing to say she was forced to agree that Mrs Bailey's eldest and her ex-governess did seem to get on remarkably well and to enjoy each other's company. However, that seemed to her a long way from 'making a match of it', as Rosalind had put it.

'Only another week or so in England, and then we'll be embarking on the SS *La Sagrita*. As soon as we dock in Bombay, your father has arranged a first-class sleeping compartment for us on the train which will take us home. We shan't be in Delhi long since we will be arriving in the middle of the hot weather, but will make our way to Simla and from there to your bungalow in the hills. Your father means to take a little time off because he feels so guilty at having abandoned you whilst we were on our honeymoon.' Rosalind's gentle face grew anxious. 'You don't hold it against him, Lonnie, do you? He thought he had settled you so comfortably, was sure his sister would not dare to flout his wishes . . . he has been deeply unhappy and has suffered the most terrible guilt, my dear. Do say you'll forgive him!'

At this moment, the waiter arrived with roast pheasant for Rosalind and roast chicken for Lonnie, along with two large silver tureens of vegetables and a jug brimming with delicious gravy. Lonnie waited until they had both been served and then said decidedly: 'None of it was my daddy's fault, nor yours, Rosalind. I know you think Aunt Emmeline has gone a little mad, so in a way we should not even blame her. There is a saying I heard once in India: *whom the gods wish to destroy, they first make mad*. So I think we should feel sorry for Aunt Emmeline but make sure that she is not able to do any more damage. She didn't only sack Hester, you know, she sacked all the maids, including my dear Mollie, and at the last even Mr Fletcher, her butler. As for forgiving, I never blamed either of you for what happened because I knew it wasn't your fault. Mrs Bailey says you turn over life's pages each day and begin on a fresh sheet and that's what I mean to do.'

'What a sensible little girl you are,' Rosalind said, beginning to help herself to vegetables. 'Will you miss your good friends while you're in India, dear?'

Lonnie smiled, but shook her head. 'No, because I know I'll be coming back to Liverpool quite soon.'

She heaved a deep, contented sigh. 'Only this time you will be with me, making sure that everything's all right so I can see my friends whenever I want to.'

'And you may be sure that for the rest of your school days either we shall come to you in England every year, or you will come to us in India,' her stepmother remarked. 'I think everything will go swimmingly.'

Chapter Eleven

It was the end of August and extremely hot. Hester and Eileen had eaten salads every night for a week and Eileen had just remarked that if she had any more lettuce she would turn into a rabbit. 'I ain't suggesting hot food, 'cos heaven knows that kitchen is like the halls of hell when everyone's in there making their evening meal,' she said now, as the two girls headed for Stansfield Court. 'But what about getting some fish and chips and goin' down to St Martin's Rec so that we can eat them in the fresh air? If we were a bit younger, we could go and bathe in the Scaldy – it's near enough – but by the time we've had our snap it'll be time to think about going to bed. Oh, how I hate that boiling hot bedroom, right up under the eaves. No air seems to get in at all, not even when we leave all the windows and doors open.'

'Fish and chips is a good idea,' Hester said. 'I know the weather's hot, but I don't suffer from it like you do. I suppose it's because I was born and bred in India and often spent the hot season on the plains if my father was unable to get away to the hills. Imagine, we're probably suffering more from the heat now than Lonnie is, because her father meant to take her straight up to Simla. Simla's in the foothills and beautifully cool compared to Delhi, which was where we spent a good deal of our lives. And the Hetherington-Smiths have a beautiful bungalow in the hills above Simla, surrounded by pine forests, lakes and rivers.'

'Lucky old Lonnie,' Eileen said absently. 'When are you seeing Dick again?'

'Tomorrow evening,' Hester told her. She had confided in Eileen, telling her that Dick had proposed marriage to her and was saving up to buy her an engagement ring for Christmas. 'He works most awfully hard, you know, but we like to go out a couple of times a week. He says when a chap's going steady he ought to be able to see his girl more than just on a Saturday night.' She eyed her friend with a mixture of amusement and curiosity. 'And talking of boyfriends, have you told Tommy yet?'

'No, an' nor I aren't goin' to,' Eileen said, ungrammatically but forcibly. 'I've telled you all along, our Hester, that I don't mean to tell nobody about the baby. I've gorraway with it so far and you must admit, no one's so much as mentioned that I look suspicious. It's one advantage of bein' on the big side; folk take it for granted that you're simply gettin' bigger, they don't think as you're hidin' a little secret.'

'It is amazing,' Hester agreed. 'You still don't show and you can't have more than a week or so to go, can you? You really should start making arrangements for the confinement, you know. Why, you've not even seen a doctor, let alone booked yourself in anywhere for the birth.'

'I'm not doing anything until I have to,' Eileen said obstinately, as they neared the fish and chip shop. 'Give it a rest, Hes, there's a dear. Anyway, I reckon I were out on me countin'. I reckon me time won't come on me for two or three weeks, mebbe more.' The two girls turned into the fish and chip shop and joined the short queue at the counter. Presently, they emerged on to the Scotland Road once more and headed for the recreation ground. As they walked, Eileen began to tell Hester, for the umpteenth time, that her friendship with Tom was the nicest thing that had happened to her since she had left home and she did not intend to jeopardise it by telling him she was pregnant. 'He need never know,' she pointed out, 'since I'm havin' the kid adopted. I reckon I'll stay in one of them home places a day, or mebbe two, an' tell folk I were visitin' me fambly. If I get some warnin' then I'm lookin' to you, as me best pal, to tell the Williamses I'd had an urgent message to say me mam were took bad and I've gone home to look after her.'

'Well, I'll do my best and you might even get away with it,' Hester said, rather dubiously. 'If only you'd let me tell Dick . . . I told you that we're getting engaged at Christmas, after all, and not even Dick's mam knows that, and Dick wouldn't tell a soul, you know he wouldn't.'

Eileen sighed. 'How you do keep on,' she said plaintively. 'This is our secret, yours and mine, an' if I'm not worried about it, why should you be? We'll brush through and no one any the wiser, just you wait and see.'

The next evening, Hester, who had been on an early shift, finished work at four o'clock. She returned to the Court, changed into a clean, pale-green cotton dress, and set out for Elmore Street. Ever since Dick had asked her to marry him, it had become a pleasant habit to go to the Baileys' on a Tuesday evening after work. She would help Mrs Bailey to get the evening meal, learning a good deal about the art of feeding a family on a small income, for Mrs Bailey knew very well how best to spend whatever money came her way and was very willing to share this knowledge with Hester.

It was a fine evening and Hester strolled along the sunny, dusty street, wondering how soon she and Dick would be able to marry. Dick had told her that because of his family responsibilities they would not be able to marry immediately. 'Mam depends very heavily upon me,' he had explained. 'But Ted's doing well at work now and in a year or so, when his apprenticeship finishes, he'll be bringing in a real good wage. When that happens I reckon we can start looking around for a place of our own and planning a wedding.'

Hester had been glad to agree with this scheme, though having to wait for as long as a year or so seemed hard. Still, she supposed that it was better to take a bit of time and to save as hard as they could rather than jumping in at the deep end and spending the rest of their lives scrimping and going short.

She had known for weeks that she loved Dick and that he loved her. When he held her in his arms, she felt the first stirrings of desire and wondered how they would get through another year of holding themselves back, but supposed they would manage it somehow. After all, there were dozens of young couples in the same position: wanting to marry but being unable to do so for financial reasons. Ted and Ruby would doubtless want to marry one day – unless they found other partners, for they were always quarrelling – but they had obviously learned to wait as she and Dick must.

Reaching Elmore Street, Hester went round by the jigger and in through the back door to find Mrs Bailey placidly preparing vegetables. She greeted Hester with her usual friendly warmth and very soon the two of them, with a cup of tea apiece, were working side by side and chatting comfortably as they did so. By the time Dick arrived home from work, the meal was on the table and Ben and Phyllis were seated and watching the preparations for the meal hungrily. Dick crossed the room and dropped a kiss on Hester's forehead, then gave his mother a quick hug. 'You dish up while I have a wash.' He eyed the large saucepan standing in the middle of the table hopefully. 'Is that ox-tail stew? Well, aren't we the lucky ones! Ox-tail stew is almost me favourite food.'

Once the family were seated, with the exception of Ted who had not yet arrived, Mrs Bailey gestured to Phyllis. Everyone took a turn to say grace and Phyllis was well used to doing so when her turn came round. She bent her head, clasped her hands and chanted the familiar words, and then they began to eat.

There was little conversation during this part of the meal but later, when stewed apple and custard was put before them, conversation became livelier. Phyllis talked about her friend Annie; Dick described the carving he was doing in the captain's cabin of the SS *Aurora*; Hester told them a funny story about a batch of buns which had failed to rise and had been sold to the staff as currant biscuits; and even Ben chimed in to describe the sad-faced little monkey which was Mr Madison's latest acquisition.

They were clearing the plates away and Hester was about to start the washing up when the back door burst open and Ted came into the room, pulling Ruby after him. Hester took one look at their faces and decided that they had been quarrelling again. Ruby's eyes were red-rimmed and her mouth quivered convulsively.

'Oh, Ted, I'm awful sorry, we thought you was either working late or had taken Ruby out for a meal or something,' Mrs Bailey said apologetically. 'But it won't take a minute to warm through the stew I saved for you and there's plenty of spuds left. Where have you been?'

'We – we've been to see Ruby's mam and dad,' Ted mumbled. 'We – we thought we oughta see them first. The thing is, Mam, me an' Ruby is gettin' wed.'

Mrs Bailey stared at the young couple in silence for a moment. Then she said coldly: 'This is rather sudden, ain't it? What do Ruby's mam and dad say? Why, Ted, you've not worked out your apprenticeship yet and Ruby's job pays peanuts, she's said so many a time. Wharrever are you thinkin' of? You *can't* get married. You're far too young.'

'It's Ruby's mam an' dad who say we've got to get married,' Ted said sulkily. 'There's a baby on the way. I said I weren't out of me apprenticeship yet, I telled 'em we couldn't afford a place of our own, but Ruby's mam said they weren't having their good name dragged through the mud by us. They said we could live with them till we got somewhere of our own. I telled 'em there weren't enough room there and that they lived too far from the ferry but it didn't make no manner o' difference. Mrs Hudson said I'd – I'd done the damage an' I must pay for it.'

'You've both acted in a stupid, greedy way; you've probably ruined the rest of your lives because marryin' at your age, living with in-laws, never havin' no spare money, will just make you hate one another in the end,' Mrs Bailey said frankly. 'Ted, there's never been no mention of marriage before; you've talked of lighting out for America, making your fortune there, once you're out of your apprenticeship.' She took hold of her son by both shoulders, staring into his ashamed eyes. 'Are you in love with Ruby, son? Is marriage what you truly want? Because you're under age so no one can force you to marry, I'm pretty sure of that.'

Ted looked sulkier than ever. 'Of course I don't want to marry . . .' he was beginning, when Ruby gave a shriek and rushed at him, her face contorted with fury.

'You swine!' she shouted, her face only inches from his and her clawed fingers endeavouring to grab at his mop of hair. 'You were keen enough to get me knickers off . . .'

'That's enough of that sort of talk,' Mrs Bailey said sharply. She moved forward and took Ruby by the wrists but the girl twisted free, though she dropped her hands to her sides. Ben had left the house as soon as the meal was over, but Phyllis sat, round-eyed, on a fireside chair, drinking it all in. 'How dare you talk like that before a child of five! Your mam should have washed your mouth out with soap, young lady. Now let's sit down and discuss this sensibly. We'll share the blame betwixt the two of you, but there's no doubt you're in a real mess. Look, Ruby, there's places you can go to give birth to a baby without anyone knowin', then you can have the kid adopted. That way, if you and Ted really love one another, you can wed in a couple of years, when he's earning real money. As for the child, no one will be the wiser. You can give it out as you've took a live-in job somewhere on the Wirral so as you can save up to marry our Ted. How about that, eh?'

Ted's face brightened and he tried to put an arm

round Ruby's shoulders but she shrugged him pettishly away. 'I want to get married,' she muttered sulkily. 'Me mam says we can get wed in St Thomas's and I'm to have a white dress and a veil and me cousins Beattie and Marge can be bridesmaids. Me mam says she'll give an eye to the baby so's I can go on workin'. I don't want to be hid away somewhere, I want to get wed. I *will* get wed. Me dad says he'll horsewhip Ted if he don't make an honest woman of me.'

Hester and Dick, silent observers of the scene, took their places at the table when Mrs Bailey gestured them to do so. Hester was appalled by the whole situation and thought that Ruby needed a damned good spanking far more than Ted wanted horsewhipping. Ruby was clearly determined to marry and Hester was pretty sure that neither love nor even affection came into it. Mrs Bailey's attitude was the sensible one in view of the extreme youth of both parties, but clearly it was not a view shared by Mrs Hudson. Dick had told Hester that Ruby was an only child, for though Mrs Hudson had borne half a dozen babies since her daughter's birth sixteen years ago, none of them had lived. She wondered now if Mrs Hudson had encouraged Ruby to get pregnant so that she might, at long last, have a baby to care for. If so, she felt deeply sorry for the older woman but thought it an irresponsible and selfish way to behave.

Whilst Hester's thoughts had wandered, the battle had continued to rage. In vain did Mrs Bailey point out the disadvantages of marrying too young. Neither Ted nor Ruby had ever had a girl or boyfriend before, she said, so how could they know that they might not meet someone else within a twelvemonth, someone more suited to them? Hester saw Ruby give one of her quick sly glances round the table at the mention of previous boyfriends and suspected that the girl was nowhere near as innocent as poor Ted. However, it clearly made no difference; the young couple would marry, Ted would move out and just where would she and Dick be?

When the party finally broke up, nothing whatever had been resolved. Dick walked Hester home and for the first part of the journey said very little, until Hester decided that the problem must be aired. 'Dick, if Ted and Ruby get married, it's going to make things very difficult for us, isn't it?' she said. 'I remember you saying that the situation at home would be much easier for your mother once Ted was earning a proper wage. But if he's going to move out and live with the Hudsons, then I don't see how anyone could expect him to contribute to the Bailey household. Every penny he earns will be swallowed up by the baby and Ruby and her family.'

Dick sighed deeply and drew her to a halt. He put both arms round her and kissed her very tenderly before admitting: 'I'm afraid you're right, sweetheart. But I'm a good cabinet maker, so mebbe I could get extra work in the evenings and at weekends. It's a blow, I grant you, but what can I do? God knows, Mam did her best to make them see reason, but that nasty little trollop is hell bent on marryin' and I don't see as anyone can stop her catching our Ted. Poor lad, I feel downright sorry for him.'

'Well, I don't,' Hester said roundly. 'If you and I had wanted to kick over the traces – and I'm sure we have both wanted to from time to time, if we're honest – then we could easily have been in the same position. But we've got a bit of control over our – our urges, which is what Ted and Ruby should have had. I think it's very wrong to go making a baby when you can't afford to support it and have no home for it.' Abruptly, she remembered Eileen. 'I've got a friend who's in the family way,' she said slowly. 'But she hasn't tried to blackmail the father into marriage, and she's taken it upon herself to have the baby adopted when it's born. I think her attitude is both responsible and sensible and I could shake that nasty little Ruby until her head fell off, because you can see she doesn't think of the baby at all, just of herself.'

'And her bleedin' white dress,' Dick said gloomily. 'And her perishin' bridesmaids and her white veil! Oh, Hester, I am sorry, but you know I'll have to support Ted, don't you?'

This time it was Hester who drew him to a halt. 'You aren't trying to tell me that you'll give him money out of your savings so that he can marry that horrible little creature, are you?' she asked incredulously. 'If the Hudsons are so keen on the marriage, let them bear the cost.'

'We'll have to contribute towards the wedding breakfast . . .' Dick was beginning, but Hester had had enough.

They were on the Scotland Road now, fast approaching Stansfield Court, and she pulled herself free from his arm and set off along the pavement as fast as she could go. When he caught her up she ignored him, too angry to consider whether she was being fair or not. 'I'm tired out and don't want to talk about it any more,' she told him, climbing the three steps to Number 10.

'But, darling, be sensible. None of this is my fault, so why should you blame me for it?' Dick said pleadingly. 'Look, I know you're tired now but if we think hard we might be able to find a way out. Shall I call for you as usual after work on Saturday? What shift are you on?'

'I'm on earlies,' Hester said briefly, opening the front door. 'All right. I'll come down to the Pier Head and meet the ferry but I'm warning you, Dick, you'd better think of something, because if we have to wait until Ben's earning a decent wage, then we'll both be drawing our pensions before we walk up the aisle.'

Dick laughed and assured her that it would not come to that, but when he tried to follow her into the house she gave him quite a sharp shove in the chest. 'I told you I was tired,' she said crossly. 'See you on Saturday.' And with that, she slammed the front door and trailed miserably up to bed.

When Dick and Hester met the following Saturday, nothing had been resolved save that Ted's reluctance to become a bridegroom and breadwinner had grown a trifle stronger. Dick told Hester that the two of them had had a very frank discussion as they walked home from the Pier Head the previous evening, and from what his brother had said Dick was pretty sure that Ruby had had her mind set on marriage from the very first moment Ted had asked her out to the pictures. It had been at her suggestion that Ted had returned to her parents' house and had been lured upstairs to her bedroom. When Dick had questioned him, he had admitted that Ruby was three years older than himself and had quite a reputation for being 'keen on the fellers'. He had known he was not her first boyfriend whatever she might like to pretend.

'Then why is he going through with it?' Hester had asked. She was still angry with Dick because he would not put up a fight to protect their own relationship but she did see that he was awkwardly placed. 'As your mother said, Ted's still a minor, which must mean that he could refuse to marry. Your mother is his guardian, I suppose, and goodness knows she isn't keen on the match, so why not make a real effort to nip it in the bud?'

'If Ted asked me to do so, then I suppose I might try to make things difficult for them,' Dick said reluctantly. 'But when my dad died, he asked me to look after Mam and the kids. He'd think it was pretty shabby if I let Ted down.'

'But you wouldn't be letting him down, not if he really doesn't want to marry the girl,' Hester reminded him. 'You'd be doing him a good turn, truly you would.'

'Ye-es, but the truth is, Ted's terrified of Mr Hudson,' Dick disclosed. 'Not just Mr Hudson either. Ruby's old feller is one of a family of five brothers. They all live around the same area and Ruby told Ted that if he meant to cry off and let her down her dad and her uncles would beat him to a pulp. It's probably true, too,' he added thoughtfully. 'They've got a bad reputation, have the Hudson fellers. They wouldn't think twice about doing our Ted over, even if we informed on them afterwards. It's a difficult thing to prove an' Ted would be too scared to stand up in court and accuse them. He says if he did, they might start in on Mam, or Ben, and he couldn't bear that.'

Hester shuddered. 'I couldn't bear it either,' she said resignedly, giving Dick's arm a squeeze. 'Oh well, we'd best wait and see what happens.'

They did not have long to wait. On the following Tuesday, when she and Dick met for tea at Elmore Street, Mrs Bailey scarcely let them get into the kitchen before bursting into speech. 'Ted's gone,' she said, without preamble. 'I thought he might; that's why I reminded him how he'd always wanted to see America. I can't pretend I'm sorry he took the hint because that little hussy had caught him good and proper. If you ask me the whole thing were planned and her mam and dad . . . well, least said soonest mended, I dare say. Anyway, our Ted went round to her place last evening, mumbled something about talking things over quiet-like. I don't know what was said but he came home late and in a mood to kick the cat, if you understand me. Then this mornin', when I come down to make meself a drink o' tea, for sleep after four o'clock I could not, I found a note on the kitchen table. I opened it wi' me heart in me mouth, in case . . . but never mind that. It were from Ted, o' course, not sayin' much save that he'd took a berth in a liner and would be gone awhile. I think he hopes that young madam will marry someone else as soon as he's out of reach, an' I can't say I'm sorry. I never said nothin', but since Ted broke the news to us I've asked around and he ain't the only young feller as she's played cat's cradle with, not by a long chalk.'

'I reckon our Ted's had a lucky escape,' Dick said, looking vastly relieved. 'Though to go givin' up an apprenticeship when it only had another year to run . . . and where he'll get a job when he comes home I don't know. Still, the important thing is he'll not be tied to Ruby and to a babby who may not even be of his get for all we know.'

'That's a bit unfair,' Hester said, speaking for the first time. 'Ted didn't try to deny he'd . . . he'd carried on with Ruby, did he? And they've been going out together for several months. I expect he'll have to pay something towards the baby's keep, and Ruby, won't he?'

'Aye, if he ever comes back to Liverpool to live,' Dick said rather grimly. 'There's nowt wrong wi' young Ted that time and a bit more commonsense won't put right and I reckon he'll send money home for Ruby until she marries someone else, if she does. But if she's gorra grain of sense she'll do what Mam suggested and have the kid adopted as soon as it's born.'

'Oh, the Hudsons will work something out,' Mrs Bailey said airily, fetching the cutlery out of the dresser and beginning to lay the table. 'I'm that relieved our Ted had the sense to scarper, though.' She turned to Hester. 'You must think we're a bad lot, queen,' she said apologetically. 'But quite apart from not wanting our Ted to get involved wi' a girl like Ruby, there's you and Dick to consider. You've not said much, but it's plain as the nose on my face that the pair of you will make a match of it as soon as finances permit. Young Ted gettin' wed could have purra stop to that for a good while, so that's another reason I ain't sorry Ted's gone. Yes, I reckon it's all for the best.'

Dick had gone over to the sink and was beginning to wash, soaping his face, neck and arms with great thoroughness whilst his mother and Hester bustled about, getting the tea. 'Hester and meself had hoped to get engaged at Christmas. I'm saving up for a ring and Hester's started putting money away and buying bits and pieces for her bottom drawer,' Dick said. He turned to grin at Hester, then switched his attention back to his mother once more. 'It were goin' to be a surprise but I reckon we'll go ahead anyway. Ted'll send money home as soon as he can afford it and even if some has to go to Ruby and the child I'm sure he'll put something aside for the family.'

Mabel Bailey gave a little squeak of pleasure and seizing Hester in her arms kissed her cheek soundly, then rushed over to the sink and kissed Dick as well. 'I'm so glad, because the pair of you is just like Bob and me. We had a bit of a struggle at first 'cos Bob's mam had eleven children – Bob were the eldest – so she needed all the help her sons could give. But we hung on and saved our money and as soon as we could we rented a couple o' rooms, got ourselves wed and moved in.' Her eyes misted with reminiscent pleasure. 'Eh, they were happy days! An' you'll be just the same, you too. Bein' in love makes the whole world rosy, somehow, and even the hardships of life aren't so bad when there's a couple o' you to tackle 'em. So you go ahead and get wed just as soon as you can afford it an' don't worry about me and the kids, 'cos we'll manage just fine. As for that Ruby, she's an only child with a mam and dad to watch out for her, so don't let her condition affect what you do.'

'Oh, Mrs Bailey, how very kind you are,' Hester said fervently. 'Dick and I know we must wait and not try to rush things, but when it seemed as though we would have to wait years and years, I felt terribly miserable. If we could just set a definite date, that would be wonderful.'

Dick finished drying himself on the roller towel which hung by the sink and Hester, used to the routine by now, went to the back door and shouted Phyllis and Ben. Phyllis came tumbling in almost at once, barefoot, the ribbon which had once tied her hair neatly back from her face dangling on the extreme end of one fair curl. 'Ben's at Madison's,' she said breathlessly. 'What's for tea, Hester?'

That evening, Dick and Hester had a long and serious

talk as they walked along the waterfront, gazing at the shipping moving up and down the Mersey. Hester would have liked a spring wedding but told Dick that, in the circumstances, she would understand if he preferred to put it off for a year. 'Your mother is a lovely person, brave and self-reliant,' she told him. 'But with Phyllis only just in school, it wouldn't be fair for you to leave home next spring. After all, Mrs Bailey is still getting used to being a widow and having all the responsibility for the family on her shoulders. I know Ted's situation isn't as bad as we'd expected it to be, but she's going to worry about him, Dick. He didn't tell her the name of his ship or its destination. He didn't even say whether Liverpool was her home port. Why, for all we know, he may stay in the States, which might mean your mother wouldn't see him for years.'

'I know what you're sayin', queen,' Dick said thoughtfully. 'He's a good worker is Ted and if he writes to his manager at Laird's and explains the situation it's possible that he might get a good reference, which would enable him to find a job in the States. It's not as though he was given the DCM, or the OBE for that matter,' Dick added with a chuckle.

'The OBE? Isn't that the Order of the British Empire?' Hester said with a frown. 'Why should Laird's give him a medal?'

Dick laughed again and squeezed her hand. 'It's just Laird's talk for being give the sack,' he explained. 'The OBE stands for the "old brown envelope" and the DCM for "don't come Monday". Sorry, love, I'd forgotten you weren't a born and bred scouser.'

Hester chuckled in her turn. 'Scousers make a joke of everything, even dismissal,' she said. 'It's far better than weeping and wailing, anyhow. And for

Ted's sake, it might be as well to stay away for a little while, all things considered.'

'Aye. If I were Ted I'd steer clear of Liverpool until I knew what was happening with Ruby,' Dick agreed.

'Surely he'll send your mother an address as soon as he can, won't he?' Hester asked. 'Once she can correspond with him, it won't be nearly so bad. And what do you think about our wedding, darling? I know next spring would be too soon, but how about this time next year? Do you think we might manage that?'

Dick shrugged rather helplessly. 'What we'd better do is save every penny we can spare and see how we're situated,' he said. 'If I take an evening job and work weekends we'll get the money together sooner, but we won't see so much of each other. It's up to you, queen. We can either go all out for an autumn wedding next year and not see a lot of each other until we actually wed, or we can take it a bit slower, go on seeing each other two or three times a week and plan a wedding in '37.'

Hester stared at him incredulously; she could not believe what he was saying! Was he truly suggesting that they should wait even longer than they had planned? It was now almost September, 1935, so waiting until March 1937 was one and a half long years. Hester thought about her work in the bakery, which was hard and messy, with unsocial hours. When she came off a night shift, she found it difficult to sleep during the day and ended up feeling stale and dispirited. The wages were better than those paid by Miss Deakin in the dress shop, but the work was not nearly so congenial. It might be easier in winter when the warmth of the bakery would be welcome, but Hester had sweltered and sweated through the summer, checking the loaves in the enormous ovens, carting trays of confectionery out to the delivery vans and, when she was in the shop, serving customers who were always in a hurry.

When she returned home, it was to the cramped and crowded lodging house in Stansfield Court. The girls were not quarrelsome by nature, but the conditions made them so. The kitchen was always crowded with lodgers trying to cook a meal or queuing to fill their jugs at the tap. It was all very well to tell herself that when Eileen's confinement was over they would move to more spacious surroundings, but if she were to continue scrimping and saving so that she and Dick might marry, there was little chance of that.

Dick had his arm around her; now he turned her a little towards him and kissed her gently on the cheek. 'You're very quiet, queen,' he said. 'A lot's happened today and you don't want to go making up your mind in a hurry. We'll talk about it on Saturday, after the pictures. Or would you rather go dancing?'

'I don't know,' Hester said glumly. 'Can we afford to go to the pictures, or dancing for that matter?'

She expected Dick to laugh, to assure her that they would do one or the other, and received an unpleasant shock when he said thoughtfully: 'Perhaps we'd best take a walk in the park since the weather's still nice. When winter comes, we'll have to be indoors. Will you meet me off the ferry? Or are you on a late shift Saturday?'

'I'm on earlies,' Hester said briefly. She felt crushed and defeated by Dick's obvious acceptance that their marriage could not be planned in the foreseeable future and for the rest of the evening she was very quiet, immersed in her own thoughts.

'Letter for you, chuck!'

It was Monday morning and Hester was getting breakfast. She was dressed and ready for work and about to carry two bowls of porridge from the kitchen up to their attic when Eileen hailed her. 'A letter? Oh, that's lovely; I expect it's from Lonnie,' she said, handing Eileen her porridge and taking the long blue envelope from her friend. 'I'll read it when we get upstairs.'

As soon as the two girls were settled on their beds and rapidly spooning porridge, Hester opened the envelope, which proved to be from Rosalind Hetherington-Smith. It was a lovely letter, chatty and full of information, and when Rosalind talked of her and Lonnie riding their ponies through the tall forests and fishing in the rivers which came foaming down from the mountains, Hester felt a real stab of regret that it was not she who had gone to the hills. Having perused the letter carefully and with great enjoyment, she came to a postscript which made her exclaim aloud. 'Goodness! Oh, how very generous they are!'

'What is it?' Eileen asked curiously. She was still waiting for some sign that her baby was on the way, but nothing had happened yet. 'Are they going to give you a hundred pound?'

Hester laughed. 'Not exactly, but Mr Hetherington-Smith was horrified to hear how I had been treated and Rosalind has written to suggest that they pay my passage to India for me – first-class too – and then employ me for three months as Lonnie's governess. She even mentions a salary which is at least double what I could earn in England. The original plan was that Lonnie should come back to England immediately and go to a good day school, but they're a bit worried about where she would live. Do you know, I'm quite tempted! Dick wants to put off our wedding until the spring of '37 and not meet as often so that we can save every penny, so I might as well be in India earning a small fortune – and enjoying myself because I'll be doing work I love.'

'But could you bear to be separated from Dick?' Eileen asked dubiously. 'I know I couldn't bear to be separated from Tom for long.'

'I don't know,' Hester said slowly. 'Tell you what, Eileen, I'll put it to Dick this very evening. In fact I'll tell him that if we aren't to marry until 1937, then I'm going to accept Rosalind's generous offer. That would put the ball firmly back in his court. If he really cares about me and wants us to marry, then I think he should agree that eighteen months is too long to wait.'

'Aye, I reckon you're right,' Eileen said. She finished her porridge and stood up, then sat down again abruptly. 'Ooh! My bleedin' little passenger kicked me right in the porridge. Made me feel queer for a moment. You've got to be in by eight, ain't you? You'd best gerra move on. I'll take the plates down to the kitchen and wash 'em up since I'm not due in till later. See you this evenin', queen.'

When Hester had gone, Eileen lay back on her bed and gazed thoughtfully up at the low ceiling above her. The baby had not kicked her, either in the porridge or elsewhere, but she had been aware for some time of a very odd sensation indeed in her lower back. It wasn't much; a low, growling sort of pain, which made her want to hold her breath, but it was soon over and could, she supposed, be put down to sleeping in an unusual position. Nevertheless, she waited until it had gone before carrying the porridge plates down to the kitchen and washing them up.

She was upstairs once more and wondering whether to make herself a sandwich for her midday break when the pain struck again – if you could call it a pain. It isn't the baby, Eileen comforted herself, sitting down heavily on the bed. Me mam's told me over and over that the pains is like your stomick bein' ate up by a tiger, and this pain's in me back. No, it ain't the baby, but I'll just have a bit of a rest on me bed before I gets ready for work.

By three in the afternoon, Eileen could no longer deny that the baby was on its way. Yet still she hesitated, suddenly aware that she did not fancy climbing down the two long flights of stairs in order to fetch help. She thought briefly about calling out, persuading someone to fetch an ambulance, or simply getting a taxi to the nearest home for unmarried mothers, but simply could not face the effort involved, for by now her whole body was racked with pain.

After another half hour, she decided that she was going to have to fend for herself. It took her ages to get out of her shop clothes and back into her nightie but as soon as she had done so she felt a good deal more comfortable. Indeed, the pains actually seemed to have eased and for ten blissful minutes she thought thankfully that the baby had decided not to come after all. Relaxing, she climbed into bed and pulled the covers up to her chin.

Some time later – she could not have said how long – the pain developed an urgency which she could not deny. *Push*, it demanded. *Push for all you're worth or I shall make you regret it. Hold on to the bedstead like they do in all the films and push and push or you'll die alone up here with no one to help you and the poor little baby will die too.*

Groaning, Eileen squatted on the bed, almost glad to be told what she must do, if only by a mysterious voice in her head. She began to push and the pain reminded her that she must only push at its command; that when it left her she must stay quiet and breathe deeply, restoring her strength for the next effort.

In between the pains, Eileen looked wildly around the room, trying to remember everything she had ever heard her mother say about childbirth. She covered her eyes with her hands and prayed for motherly advice to descend upon her and presently heard her mother's voice, as she had heard it so often when Mrs O'Farrell's time was upon her. *Plenty of clean rags, a drawer to put the baby in and heaps and heaps of boiling water*, her mother had said. *A bit of warm blanket to line the drawer, a pair of scissors and some string for the cord – and don't forget that boiling water!*

Obediently, Eileen heaved herself off the bed. She poured water from the blue and white enamel jug into the kettle and set it on the small paraffin stove, which she lit. Then she heaved a box out from under her bed, tipping the contents higgledy-piggledy on the floor, save for one piece of blanket. She found her nail scissors in her handbag and, failing string, removed the laces from her best boots and draped them across her pillow. Just as she completed this last task, another pain hit her, a pain stronger and more demanding than all the rest. Eileen crouched on her haunches, put her forehead down on to her knees and gave one enormous heave. She felt as though she was splitting in two but suddenly there was easement and glancing incredulously down she was just in time to grab the baby as it was born.

It was weird how astonished she was, almost as though she had never truly believed that there was a child within her, or that she would ever successfully give birth. But after that one blank and breathless moment, Eileen became practical once more. She seized the baby by its tiny feet, dangled it upside down and smacked its small pink bottom. Had she not done so when her younger brothers and sisters had been born? The baby gave an astonishingly loud squall and Eileen reached for the laces. She had cut the cord for her mother and knew the importance of tying it in two places and cutting between them and presently, her task done, she laid the wet and slippery baby on the piece of blanket in the box and pushed it under her bed. She turned to survey the room.

It was a shambles. It looked as though a bloody battle had been fought – as indeed it had – and Eileen remembered why her mother had demanded boiling water. Normally, someone would clear up now, get rid of the things which were no longer needed and bring her a hot cup of tea whilst tucking her and the baby back into bed.

But it ain't the mum that does things like that, Eileen reminded herself. Anyway, I'm tired to death, I can't do another thing – it'll have to wait until one of the girls comes home. And burying her face in the pillow, she fell fast asleep.

As she had said to Eileen, Hester met Dick off the ferry and almost immediately told him about Rosalind's offer, reading the letter aloud to him as they walked along. One glance at his face was enough to convince her that he was thunderstruck and appalled. 'But you can't even consider it, queen,' he gasped as soon as he realised that this could mean a long separation. 'What does the money matter, after all? I want to be with you, not to have you miles and miles away! Why, you'd be bound to meet other fellers and – and who knows what might happen if I weren't around to keep you on the straight and narrow?'

He probably meant it as a joke but Hester did not find it amusing. 'How dare you insinuate that I'm the sort of girl to promise to marry one man and then play fast and loose with another,' she said, feeling the heat rise to her cheeks. 'If you know so little of me that you believe I would behave like that, perhaps we shouldn't get engaged even, let alone married!'

'It was a joke; don't you know a joke when you hear one?' Dick said. 'Anyway, you can't be serious. When folk love one another, they don't go off to the opposite end of the earth.'

'You said we might have to see less of each other and you didn't seem particularly disturbed by the thought,' Hester reminded him. 'It's all right for you to go off and earn extra money, evenings and weekends, but it's obviously not all right for me. What's more, if I go to India, I'll be earning a great deal of money, much more than I could ever earn in Liverpool. I wouldn't need to spend much because I'd be living in, so I'd be able to save really hard. That means we could easily marry next year – if you still want to, that is.'

'Of course I still want to, but if I work evenings and weekends . . .' Dick was beginning, but Hester would not allow him to start that again.

'Dick, although Mr Briggs is a very nice man, the

job I'm doing at the moment is terribly hard work and – and not at all the sort of thing I'm used to. I live in a cheap, overcrowded lodging house so that I can begin to build up a bottom drawer for when we're married and I almost never go out. You said things would be even harder if we meant to try for an earlier wedding, but can't you see, there's no need? If I go to India then I'd be having a very good sort of life and *you* wouldn't need to work every hour that God sends. Don't you see the advantages?'

'No I do not,' Dick shouted, his colour rising. Hester had never seen him so angry. His eyes flashed and his hair seemed to bristle like a dog's hackles. 'I'm the feller and it's the feller who earns the money so's a couple can get wed! Change your job if you don't like the bakery, but don't you go haring off to India. I'm telling you, it's my duty to earn the money to keep my family and to finance our marriage. If you earn a bit extra that's fine, but . . .'

Hester, however, had heard enough. She turned blindly away from Dick just as a tram slowed to a stop beside her. Before she had even thought, she had jumped aboard, the conductor had rung the bell, and they were off, leaving Dick standing, open-mouthed, on the edge of the pavement, gazing after her.

It was sheer luck that the tram on to which Hester had leapt was heading for the Scotland Road and home. Having taken a seat, Hester simply sat there and fumed. How dare Dick refuse to even consider her going back to India in order to earn more money so that they might marry earlier! How dare he insinuate that if she left England she was no longer to be trusted to remain true to him! By insisting that he'd be the main wage earner, he was putting off their marriage for an indefinite period. Whilst he lived at home, Mrs Bailey could manage well enough. If she and Dick had a nice little savings account which they could use to furnish their home and dip into for any extras, then Dick would still be able to give his mother a good deal of financial support.

Hester glared out of the window at the crowded pavements. She had thought Dick such a generous and understanding man, yet it seemed that his pride would not allow him to let her earn more than he could. Rosalind's offer had been very generous; she knew she would be able to save ninety-five per cent of it. Hester pressed her burning forehead against the cool window glass and tried to banish the anger and pain she had felt so that she could consider the matter more coolly. Dick worked extremely hard and was a first-rate craftsman. It was not his fault that the Depression in England meant that wages had gone down rather than up. In her heart, she was sure he loved her, knew he wanted to marry her as soon as possible, but realised that in the society in which he lived, men were almost invariably the main earners.

If only he had not made that fatal remark about meeting other fellows! It was natural, she supposed, that he might feel jealous, since the social life in India for young women was known to be very much more exciting than that in England during the Depression. Balls, picnics, expeditions to famous beauty spots, rides, boating trips . . . she remembered telling the Bailey family when she had first visited them of the innumerable entertainments enjoyed by the British in India. Perhaps she had been wrong to condemn Dick for his feelings. If the boot had been on the other foot . . .

The tram jerking to a halt brought Hester's mind

back to the present. This was her stop and she had best get down and continue to consider what she should do as she made her way to Number 10. She was sorry now that she had let her temper get the better of her and decided that she would go up to her room, get herself a sandwich and a cup of tea, and then seek Dick out to make up the quarrel.

She rounded the corner, walking slowly, head bent, thoughts a million miles away, crossed the Court and entered Number 10. She headed for the kitchen then stopped short, sniffing. There was a decided smell of burning in the air and judging from the clatter, and the sound of voices, the kitchen was already occupied; it would be quicker, and easier, if she went up to the attic room and boiled the kettle up there.

Hester climbed the first flight of stairs and began on the second, realising with a slight frisson of alarm that the smell of burning was growing stronger. As she began to ascend the last flight of stairs, she glanced up and saw thick smoke billowing out of the door of their attic room even as a figure emerged and began to descend the stairs towards her. It was Eileen, clad in a bloodstained night-dress, with her hair hanging across her face and her whole demeanour that of someone more asleep than awake.

'Eileen! What on earth's happened?' Even as Hester spoke, a fresh gush of acrid smoke came pouring out of the room her friend had just vacated, and to Hester's horror it was closely followed by a tongue of flame. She seized her friend by the shoulders and began to hustle her down the stairs, saying as she did so: 'You're covered in blood, queen! Better get out of this smoke before you pass out. There's girls in the kitchen; we'll get one of them to fetch the fire brigade before the whole house goes up. Do you know how the fire started?'

Eileen had been stumbling down the stairs, clearly scarcely conscious of what she was doing, but suddenly she stopped short and gave a terrified wail. She turned and began to try to retrace her steps. 'I must ha' kicked over the paraffin stove after I'd used the hot water, and . . . me baby, me baby! Oh, Gawd, I've gorra go back, queen. Me baby's still in there. I purrit in a box under the bed and fell asleep. Oh, Hester, me baby's goin' to die!'

'I'll go back. You're in no state . . .' Hester was beginning, when a figure came charging up the stairs towards them. It was Dick, and Hester had never felt so glad to see anyone in her whole life. She thrust her friend into Dick's arms. 'Take her into the fresh air and find a nurse or someone.' And scarcely waiting to see whether or not she was obeyed, she raced up the stairs once more.

The wind had blown the door to the bedroom closed again, or at least so Hester supposed. But as soon as she opened the door, she realised that it was not going to be easy to reach Eileen's bed. A good deal of the bedding was already smouldering and when she put out a hand to clutch the bedstead it was red hot and agonising pains shot up the palms of her hands. Wrenching herself free, she crouched lower yet, pushing herself beneath the bed, and saw the box. Hester thought wildly that the baby might already be dead from smoke inhalation, but even so, she reached into the box for the blanket-wrapped bundle within, backed out from under the bed and at last stood up, the child in her arms. For a moment, she was so confused by the choking smoke that she did not know which way escape lay, then she saw the outline of the window and ran away from it towards the door. The heat was appalling and the pain in her chest as she sucked desperately at the burning air made her double up. She saw, as she neared it, that the door frame was alight but knew she must pass through it in order to escape from certain death. Staggering and weaving with weakness, she regained the landing and realised that her hair and one side of her jacket were actually burning, but with the baby in her arms her one thought now was to get as far away from the conflagration as possible before putting the child down to see to herself.

As she crossed the small landing, she saw the stairs and the banister rail begin to waver before her. There was someone climbing the stairs, calling her name, his voice shocked and faint. She said: 'Take the baby, take the . . .' And then the stairs seemed to rush towards her and she plunged into darkness.

'Well, my dear? Isn't that an improvement on how you looked a week ago, when you were brought in here? I declare, I never knew you had such curly locks, but that young nurse had a real flair for cutting hair. A professional hairdresser couldn't have made a better job of it.'

Sister Partridge was holding a mirror in front of Hester so that she could admire her new appearance. For the first few days in hospital she had been far too poorly to worry about her looks. Because of the burns to her hands and arms, she had been swathed in bandages and had not, at first, realised that a great deal of her long black hair had burned off. Indeed, she had scarcely thought of anything but the pain she was suffering and had simply lain between the sheets, accepting the pain-killing draughts which were given her by the nurses at four-hourly intervals.

Dick had been a constant and loving visitor and her one contact with the outside world. Hester had told him, as soon as she was able to speak coherently, that she had been wrong even to consider going back to India. 'I couldn't bear to leave you for three minutes, let alone for three months,' she had said tiredly. 'Why, you saved my life, Dick.'

Dick had pooh-poohed this remark, but had been delighted that she no longer considered the trip to India an option. 'We'll marry just as soon as we may,' he promised her fervently. 'Oh, Hester, I do love you!'

After that, he had told her that Eileen and her baby were in a small side ward. Miraculously, the baby had suffered less than any of them. Dick had snatched the baby from Hester's arms even as she fell, had beaten out the flames smouldering in her hair and on the shoulders of her jacket, and had somehow contrived to carry both Hester and the child down the stairs and out into the fresh air. The fire brigade and an ambulance had arrived by then and soon Hester, Eileen and the new baby were on their way to hospital.

Naturally, Dick had followed them to the hospital as soon as he could and they had confirmed that the child was fit and well, despite its dreadful experience. Eileen, it appeared, had fallen deeply asleep after the birth struggle and had awoken in a daze to find the paraffin stove on its side, the room on fire, and choking smoke filling the air. She had stumbled out of the room to give the alarm, initially forgetting about her new baby in her panic, and because Hester had acted so quickly was hardly the worse for her experience.

'Eileen wants to call the baby James,' Dick had told her, 'and Tommy thinks it's a grand name.'

'So Tommy knows,' Hester had said in a weak, wondering voice. 'I thought she'd never tell him. She didn't mean to, you know. She meant to have the baby adopted.'

'Many a mother says that before they set eyes on their child,' Dick had said wisely. 'She wasn't nearly as badly hurt as you, so she's been up and about, doting on that little feller, for a couple o' days. As for Tommy, he came rushing to the hospital as soon as he heard what had happened. He said it were a shame the baby weren't his, but Eileen told him the whole story and he says he's happy to take young Jim on.'

'Take Jim on?' Hester had said feebly. 'Why should he take Jim on?'

'Because he's going to marry Eileen, you daft ha'p'orth,' Dick had said fondly, gently stroking one finger down the side of her face. 'They're only young, the pair of 'em, but I think they've got the right idea. They aren't goin' to wait till they can afford it, they're goin' to dive straight in the deep end. Good for them, I say!'

Hester had agreed, rather listlessly, that this seemed sensible. She had then drifted off into a sort of uncomfortable half sleep; the result of all the pain-killing drugs, she supposed.

Now, however, she looked at herself critically in the mirror. 'Don't forget, Sister, that I can't compare the way I look now with the way I looked when I was brought in, because none of you would let me have a mirror,' she reminded the older woman. 'I was lucky, wasn't I, that the flames only got at the back of my head? Though my eyelashes look a bit frizzled,' she added.

'Oh, eyelashes will grow in no time,' Sister assured her. 'And tomorrow your bandages should come right off at last. And the day after, or perhaps the day after that, you'll be able to go home!'

'But I haven't got a home,' Hester said dolefully. 'Oh, I know Mr and Mrs Maskell said they'd fit us into one of their other houses, but that was a week ago. By now they're probably full up again.'

Sister was about to reply when another voice interrupted her. 'Don't talk daft, Hester Elliott. You're moving in with us Baileys just as soon as the hospital will let you go. You can share with young Phyllis until – until we've sorted out something else for you.' It was Dick, a bunch of bronze chrysanthemums in one hand and a box of chocolates in the other. He took Sister's place by the bed and watched the little woman bustle off, then bent and kissed Hester's cheek. 'You're looking a lot more like my own little Hester,' he said, smiling down at her. 'How pretty your hair is, cut short like a boy's and all curly! You should always wear it like that!'

He went to pull up a chair but Hester shook her head at him and patted the bed. 'Sit here,' she commanded. 'This is the first day I've felt really well, not a bit muddled or stupid, the way I have been feeling. The pain was so much easier yesterday that I stopped taking the pain-killing medicine and now I feel livelier and more like myself. Tell me what's been happening, Dick.'

Dick settled himself comfortably on the bed. 'Well, I've been interferin' in your life in a way which will probably make you want to clack my head,' he said genially. 'For a start, I got the letter from Mrs Hetherington-Smith – the one you read to me – out of your handbag, so that I could write to her myself and tell her what's been happening. I remembered she had said she would appreciate a quick reply, as she would be bringing Lonnie back to England if you decided not to take up her offer of some time in India, so I thought it only right to explain about the fire an' all.'

'Oh, thank you, Dick,' Hester said gratefully. 'I'm so sorry I lost my temper and said awful things but you did rather ask for it, you know! Saying I'd go off the rails if you weren't there to keep me on the straight and narrow, indeed!'

'I was a fool to even think such a thing – not that I did think it, of course, it were just the old demon jealousy making itself felt,' Dick said ruefully. 'Honest to God, I think me mam must have dropped me on me head when I were a baby, 'cos only an addle-brain would imagine anything so impossible. No, what was really eating away at me was the thought of being separated for so long. Why, when I hopped on the next tram and followed you into Number 10 and saw the smoke billowing down the stairs and you disappearing into it, I thought I'd lost you for good . . . My heart nearly stopped and I knew then that I'd rather live with you in a hovel than with anyone else in a palace. Oh, Hester, I . . .'

The bell for the end of visiting interrupted them. All around them people were saying their farewells. Men were giving their wives self-conscious pecks, mothers were giving last-minute advice, nurses were coming down the ward to see the visitors off the premises, or so it seemed. Dick stood up with the others but did not immediately leave. He said quietly: 'Do you understand what I'm saying, Hes? I wanted the best for you, but when it comes down to it, perhaps to be together is the best thing for both of us. You don't know how much I've missed you, nor how wonderful it will be when we can talk, take a walk, make plans . . . oh, Hes!'

He leaned over and cupped Hester's face in his hands. He was bending closer with the obvious intention of kissing her on the mouth, when a voice from the next bed said: 'Hey up, gals! There's monkey business afoot over there – that young feller will be climbin' into kip wi' her any minute! D'you think we ought to call Sister and tell 'er what's goin' on?'

The speaker was a fat, fair-haired woman in the bed opposite Hester's and she laughed loudly when Hester, crimson-faced, pushed Dick away. 'Don't you go a-shovin' of the young feller like that,' the woman continued breezily, giving Dick a broad wink. 'We don't gerra lot of entertainment round here; a nice little love story would cheer us all up no end. Go on, young feller, show us what you're made of, give the girl somethin' to remember you by!'

Dick laughed but contented himself with the lightest of kisses on Hester's brow before he moved away from the bed. 'Now you've spoiled everything,' he told the woman. 'I can't make love to me fiancée with a couple of dozen lovely ladies – in nightgowns – lookin' on. But Sister says you're comin' home tomorrow, Hester, so I won't have to keep me kisses to meself for too long. Oh, and by the way.' He fished around in his pocket and produced a tiny box. 'Want to take a look? I meant to save it till your bandages came off but I dare say you can wear it round your neck on a bit of string till then.'

With her hands still swathed in dressings, Hester could not possibly have opened the box so Dick did it for her, revealing the tiny gold and pearl ring within. 'It didn't cost much,' he muttered, 'and I'd rather you chose for yourself, but it'll do until you're up and about.' And before Hester could do more than exclaim with pleasure, he had turned and left the ward.

As soon as he had gone Hester got carefully out of bed and went round the other beds, showing off the tiny ring. It was much admired, and most of her fellow-patients told her that Dick was 'a grand young feller, so handsome' . . . and if they were ten years younger she'd have to watch out.

'I know it,' Hester assured them. 'And it's not just that he's nice-looking, he's kind and – well, and *good,* somehow. We want to marry in the spring,' she concluded.

It was not encouraged for the patients to wander in and out of the ward, particularly in the evening after visiting, when the hot drinks trolley and the last medication round would soon appear, but Hester nipped out and along to Eileen's side ward, where she found her friend nursing her little boy and reading *Peg's Paper* over the top of his mossy head. Hester slipped into the tiny room, holding out the box in one white-swathed hand. 'Dick's bought me a ring; he says I can wear it round my neck until the bandages come off,' she said. 'So I suppose you might say we're officially engaged, though he wants me to choose a ring for myself as soon as I'm up and about. Not that I shall,' she added, before Eileen had done more than smile at her, 'since this little ring – the one *he* chose for me – is simply the loveliest, prettiest thing I could possibly imagine. Has Tom visited you this evening?'

'He has. They almost had to chuck him out when the bell went,' Eileen said, with evident pride. 'He were holdin' young Jimmy here . . . he dotes on the kid, honest to God he does, Hes. He likes it that everyone thinks the baby's his as well as mine and as I said to your Dick when he came callin' yesterday, there's no reason why anyone need know different. We won't be goin' back to the Stanny when we leave here, because apart from the fact that Number 10 was pretty well burnt out – our floor, I mean – Tom's purrin for a transfer to Crewe. He went and saw some lodgings, says the cottage were nice an' clean and the landlady the same. He says Crewe's a right nice place, very countrified, but that'll suit yours truly fine. So we shan't be here long,' she ended.

'I'll miss you,' Hester said ruefully, but presently, making her way back to the main ward, she thought that the loss of Eileen's companionship would be less painful because she would be with Dick and the other Baileys. They were a grand family, and Mrs Bailey had told Hester that she might stay as long as she liked, though she had also said that she thought Hester and Dick ought to marry as soon as they could find somewhere to live.

'We'll manage, me an' Ben an' young Phyllis,' she had said stoutly, though she could not prevent a little worry crease from appearing between her brows. 'When Ted's settled he'll send money – did Dick tell you, Ruby's suddenly discovered she ain't expectin' after all? Well, truth to tell' – she had lowered her voice – 'her father come round, he an' Dick gorrin a huddle, then there were money changin' hands and next thing we knew . . . but there, least said soonest mended, I always say. But our Ted's safe.'

Hester had had no idea what Mrs Bailey had been talking about but Eileen, far worldlier in some ways than her friend, had enlightened her. 'That Ruby had an abortion,' she had said airily. 'Her dad must 'ave asked Dick for the money to pay for the operation, or perhaps they went halves, you never know. Gals like Ruby always take the easy way out if the feller lets 'em down. An' they make lousy mams, so it's a good thing, by an' large.'

So now Hester, returning to her own ward, realised that she was looking forward to the future once more. Things always turned out for the best, she told herself as she climbed between the sheets.

Chapter Twelve

Several weeks had passed since Hester had left the hospital and now, outside, a wind almost strong enough to be described as a gale was whipping the brightly coloured leaves from the trees, piling them up in drifts around the bases of statues and in the gutters. Hester had not yet returned to the bakery, since the hospital doctor had said the scars on her hands must heal completely before she did any heavy work, but presently she meant to go up to the clinic on Brougham Terrace to see the doctor there. She usually saw Dr Merchison, and was pretty sure that he would clear her for work since her hands now bore only faint traces of the original burns.

She had been polishing Mrs Bailey's collection of brass animals. Sitting at the kitchen table with the brass spread out around her, she surveyed her work with some satisfaction. The brass was kept in the front room, and because they had not yet started lighting the fire in there of an evening the ornaments had not been particularly dirty. However, they had yellowed, as brass will, and now they were gleaming white-gold. They would look delightful when taken back into the room and grouped on the long slate mantelpiece.

'Ah, you've done 'em!' Mrs Bailey stood in the doorway for a moment, her arms full of clean linen, then closed the door hastily as the wind swirled some dead leaves in after her. 'Don't they look grand when they's newly cleaned! I were goin' to keep you company, ironing this lot, but I see I'm too late. Still, if you're in a polishin' mood, you might like to give me cutlery the once over.'

'Of course I will, but I'll make us both a cup of tea first,' Hester said readily, getting to her feet. She was halfway across the kitchen when someone knocked on the front door. Hester pulled the kettle over the fire and then went up the short corridor. Friends and neighbours automatically came to the back, but council officials and insurance salesmen found it easier to knock on your front door, so she assumed the caller to be someone like that.

It was a sunny day and when she first opened the door she was blinded by a shaft of sunlight falling directly upon her face. She stepped back, about to ask the caller their business, when a small figure hurtled into the hallway and two arms were flung round her waist. 'Hester, oh, Hester! It's me, Lonnie, and Rosalind! We've come to call on you. We were so sorry about the fire and your being hurt. It must have been awful. Oh, Hester, it's *so* good to see you!'

'Lonnie! Rosalind!' Hester gasped, returning Lonnie's hug. 'This is wonderful! I didn't expect you so soon. Oh, but we can't stand here talking in the hall. Come through to the kitchen. I was just about to make a cup of tea.'

Mrs Bailey was as delighted as Hester to see their guests, and the four of them settled themselves comfortably round the table as Rosalind began her story. 'After Dick's letter came, explaining about the fire, we realised that you would not be able to join us in India, Hester. Since school term starts in September and Lonnie was keen to get back to Liverpool, my husband booked us both on the next liner to sail from

Bombay and here we are. We wrote to the school, of course, telling them when we would be arriving, but Lonnie wanted to surprise you. I hope it hasn't been an unpleasant surprise?

'Then, soon after we had Dick's letter, we had a letter from Miss Hutchinson. Apparently, Miss Hetherington-Smith had had a fall. She had been coming downstairs with a candle in her hand, since she had had the electricity cut off. A few stairs from the top, she slipped in a puddle of candle grease and descended the flight a good deal faster than she intended. She broke her collar-bone and the bone in her upper arm, as well as dislocating her shoulder, and was taken to hospital at once. Miss Hutchinson gave it as her opinion that when she came out she would be a great deal better off in a residential Home for the Elderly since she herself – Miss Hutchinson, that is – is no longer capable of curbing her employer's sudden whims and strange fancies.'

'Oh, poor Miss Hetherington-Smith,' Hester cried involuntarily. 'But I'm sure Hutch – Miss Hutchinson – is right; Miss Hetherington-Smith will be properly cared for in a good residential home.'

Lonnie, who had listened to the story in silence, piped up at this point. 'I told Daddy how horrible his sister had been to you and me, Hester, and he was very angry with her. But even so, he said she's family, so we couldn't just desert her, even if she deserved it. So Ros and I are going to see the old misery in hospital and then Rosalind will settle her into this residential home and arrange the sale of the house in Shaw Street.'

'That's very kind of you,' Hester said, trying to suppress a smile, 'but what will Miss Hutchinson do, I wonder?'

'My husband is going to pay her a pension and she intends to move into a small terraced house on the outskirts of the city,' Rosalind said.

Mrs Bailey, who had been listening intently as the others spoke, nodded sagely. 'And he'll get a right good price for that house in Shaw Street, because it's a fashionable district and Hester tells me it's a grand house with a lovely garden,' she said. 'But, Lonnie, wasn't you tempted to stay in India with your stepmother and father?'

Rosalind started to speak but Lonnie cut in. 'India's lovely in lots of ways but I'd forgotten how dreadful the heat can be,' she said. 'And though I was very unhappy at St Catherine's, I really enjoyed being with other girls and working in classes of twenty or so. I wanted to come back to Liverpool and go to that lovely school which Rosalind and I visited when we were here last, but I dreaded living with someone I didn't know, someone who might turn out to be as bad as Aunt Emmeline. And then Rosalind had another letter from Dick, explaining that he and Hester were engaged to be married, and Ros had her bright idea.'

'Well, it was an idea, but whether it was a bright one or not is for you to say,' Rosalind said, looking directly at Hester. 'I thought that if Mr Hetherington-Smith bought a small house not too far from the school, you and Dick might move into it and take this terrible child as a sort of permanent boarder. You wouldn't have to teach her, you would only have to see that she did her homework and that she did not step out of line. You were like a mother to her in Shaw Street and that is what Leonard and I want for her now. We would pay you a proper salary, of course,' she added hastily, 'because Leonard would not want you to go out to work. Is there – is there any chance of your agreeing to this plan, Hester? What would Dick think, do you suppose?'

Hester could feel a broad smile spreading across her face. She looked at Mrs Bailey, who was beaming, and at Lonnie, who was hopping up and down on her chair. 'I'll ask Dick as soon as he comes in, but I'm sure he'll be as delighted as I am with the idea,' she said breathlessly. 'It's extremely generous of you and Mr Hetherington-Smith. Oh, Rosalind, it all sounds like a dream come true!'

It was December and outside Madison's pet shop the snow whirled steadily down from a darkening sky, turning Heyworth Street into a fairyland. The shop windows were bright with coloured lights and Christmas displays but in the pet shop all was quiet, for the weather had sent most shoppers home early.

'I reckon we might as well clean down and start packin' up, young feller,' Mr Madison said, rather gloomily, peering out through the glass panel in the door. 'We shan't do much trade for the next four or five days – 'cept for youngsters and their mams and dads comin' in to reserve the animals they'll buy on Christmas Eve – so we might as well get the place ship-shape.' He glanced across at Ben, who was cleaning out the big rabbit cage and spreading a thick layer of sawdust on the floor. 'It's your brother's wedding tomorrer, ain't it? I bet you're excited, ain't you? Though I dare say the house is upside down, what wi' Miss Elliott and Lonnie crammed in wi' the rest of you. I tek it the house hunting went all right in the end?'

'Oh aye, they've got a real nice house on Devonshire Road,' Ben admitted. 'Nobbut I thought they'd never find anything which would please Lonnie; I tell you, Mr Madison, that gal's enough to drive anyone crazy! It weren't the house itself so much as the garden. She wanted a lawn to play games on, apple and pear trees to climb, a Wendy house, wharrever that may be, enough room for a run so's she could keep hens and rabbits . . . there were no pleasing her.'

'But you said they'd found somewhere,' Mr Madison reminded him, filling water bowls and inserting them delicately into his bird cages. 'Has the house in Devonshire Road met wi' Lonnie's approval then?'

'Oh aye. It's gorra nice garden with fruit trees down the bottom end and room for a hen run and a couple of rabbit hutches. There ain't much of a lawn, but Hester told the young madam she can play games in Prince's Park, because it's only just down the road. It's a grand house,' he continued enthusiastically. 'They've got three big bedrooms and an indoor lavvy, as well as a proper bathroom. Wharrabout that, eh?'

'That sounds real nice,' Mr Madison said appreciatively. 'They won't know what to do wi' theirselves in all that space, after Elmore Street.'

Ben sniffed. 'I don't say we ain't been a bit crowded,' he admitted grudgingly. 'But Dick moved into our Millie's spare room so he and Hester weren't livin' under the same roof before they got wed. That's meant I've had the boys' room to meself. Still an' all, I know what you mean. Hester's a grand person, an' she's been a great help to me mam, but it'll be nice to have the house to ourselves again.'

'I reckon you'll miss Lonnie, wharrever you may say,' Mr Madison observed. 'How's she gettin' on at the new school? I know she hated St Catherine's, but this new place is a different kettle o' fish, ain't it?'

'Oh aye, she's real happy at the new school,' Ben

agreed. 'And though I grumble, she's norra bad kid, not really. Well, if I didn't like her quite a lot, I wouldn't be buyin' her the white kitten for Christmas.' He jerked his thumb at the cage full of kittens, smiling delightedly as the white one, almost as though it knew it was being talked of, came prancing over to the wire and miaowed hopefully at him. 'She's goin' to be tickled pink with Whitie,' he finished triumphantly.

Mr Madison straightened up and turned to look at the kittens. 'It's the best of the bunch, easily the prettiest of the litter,' he agreed. 'But how will it get on wi' the growed cat, what she bought last year? I suppose she gorrit back from the old lady when the house was sold?'

'No, 'cos the maid, Mollie, took Kitty with her when she was sacked and went to work in Crosby. It turned out to be a grand little mouser, and the new people have got real fond of it and didn't want to lerrit go, so Lonnie has let them keep it. That's why Hester agreed that I might buy the kid another kitten for a Christmas box.'

'Cats does grow attached to places as well as to people, so I guess young Lonnie's done the right thing in letting the new folk keep the cat,' Mr Madison observed. He pushed the last water pot into the last cage and walked over to the door to peer out. 'It's still snowing quite fast, though I doubt it will lay unless we have a sharp frost overnight,' he said. 'D'you want to help me close down, or are you eager to gerroff home in case the storm grows worse?'

'I'll stay,' Ben said. The women of the house had been cooking and baking for days and since they had strictly forbidden either Phyllis or himself to so much as touch the goodies, which would not be eaten until the wedding reception, he rarely went home until he was sure that the evening meal would be on the table. Not that it was much of an evening meal at present. Bread and scrape and a mug of tea, or possibly fish and chips from the shop up the road, was all that Mrs Bailey could manage. If he got home early, Ben knew that the chances were he would be dispatched to Briggs's Bakery with a tray of uncooked rolls or cakes. Later, he would be sent out once more to fetch the finished goods home again, so he might as well stay at Madison's until the work was finished.

He said as much to Mr Madison, who laughed but said, philosophically, that he must remember it was all in a good cause. 'You'll be feedin' your face with all the good things tomorrer,' he reminded his young friend. 'I think the snow's easin' off a bit, too, so you'll mebbe get home drier if you wait for a bit.'

The following morning was cold but clear, with pale sunshine melting the last of the previous day's snow. Lonnie and Phyllis, in their scarlet velvet bridesmaids' dresses and little white fur shoulder capes, were hovering nervously outside the church, waiting for the bride to appear. They had travelled from Elmore Street in a beautiful black car, which had impressed Phyllis so much that she had not opened her mouth once on the journey. Lonnie, of course, used to cars, taxi cabs and other vehicles, was not so overawed, but now that they had actually reached the church she was beginning to feel a little uneasy. Mrs Bailey had travelled in the car with the two girls and now began fussing over the stiff little posies of white violets they held.

'Don't forget to pick up the bride's train as she goes past you into the church,' Mrs Bailey reminded them. 'It's a great shame that Hester has no relatives of her own in England, but Millie's Frank is a kind, steady sort of chap and he'll do the givin' away bit beautifully, I'm sure. Hey up, kids, here comes the bridal car.'

The car swooped to a halt beside them and Frank jumped out, then helped Hester to alight. Lonnie thought she had never seen her governess look so breathtakingly beautiful. Hester's short dark curls were caught up on the top of her head by a wreath of artificial white roses. Despite the white veil, Lonnie could see that her dark eyes were brilliant with excitement and the soft pink lips curled into a smile as she saw the girls come forward to pick up her train. 'Good thing it isn't actually snowing,' she whispered as Phyllis and Lonnie pounced on the ruched satin, lifting it carefully clear of the paving stones. The bridesmaids' dresses and Hester's bridal gown had been a gift from Rosalind before she had left for India once more. 'Oh, Mrs Bailey, when you think how it snowed yesterday, Dick and I are very lucky that it didn't lay underfoot. I'm shaking anyway, though with nerves not with cold.'

Mrs Bailey bustled forward and began to arrange the veil about Hester's shoulders. 'You look like a film star, queen, so you've no cause to feel nervous,' she said gently. 'This is *your* day, the most important day of your life, very like, and you've got to remember every moment of it with pleasure.' She ran a critical eye over her son-in-law's suit, then brushed an imaginary speck of dust from his shoulder. 'In you go, the pair of you!' she said briskly. 'Lonnie, Phyllis, try to walk at the same rate as Hester does so everyone can see that beautiful train. Off we go!'

* * *

Inside the church, Dick was every bit as nervous, though he didn't intend to show it. He would have been happier had Ted been able to be his best man, but Joey Frost, his foreman, was a very good substitute. Now Joey turned his head a fraction, then checked his pockets, clearly making sure that he had not lost the ring. 'She's comin',' he breathed hoarsely. 'I've seen many a bride in me time, but your Hester knocks spots off all of 'em. Dick Bailey, you're the luckiest feller alive!'

'Wilt thou have this man to thy wedded husband, to live together after God's ordinance in the holy estate of Matrimony? Wilt thou obey him, and serve him, love, honour, and keep him in sickness and in health; and, forsaking all other, keep thee only unto him, so long as ye both shall live?' The priest's sonorous voice rolled around the church and Hester spoke out, soft but clear.

'I will.'

'Who giveth this woman to be married to this man?' Frank stepped forward, then released Hester's arm and stepped back. The service continued on its solemn yet joyful course. Hester did her part almost in a dream, and when Dick slipped the ring on her finger and she smiled up into his eyes she felt the heat rise in her cheeks. We're married, she thought wonderingly. I never really thought this would happen but now it has and I'm Mrs Richard Bailey. I've got a beautiful home, a little girl I'm fond of to share our lives, but best of all I've got the most wonderful husband in the world.

The triumphant music swelled from the organ and Dick swung her round towards the congregation. Every face wore a broad smile. As they processed towards the west door, Hester saw Eileen, Tom and young Jimmy, various friends from the bakery, Millie and the terrible twins, and then other members of the Bailey family, as well as what seemed to be half the employees of Cammell Laird's.

'Phew! Now the serious bit is over, we can begin to enjoy ourselves,' Dick whispered in her ear. He put his arm round her waist as they emerged from the porch and even as they did so a tall figure ran towards them, hurling confetti as he came. Hester ducked, laughing, but to her astonishment Dick released her and rushed over to the man in seaman's clothing who was standing grinning at them.

'Ted!' Dick shouted. 'Oh, Ted, you made it after all. I'm that glad, old feller, and Mam will be pleased as punch.'

The reception was held in the church hall and Hester soon lost the last trace of nerves and began to enjoy herself. She was introduced to a good many of Dick's friends whom she had not previously met, as well as to their wives and girlfriends, and chatted happily with neighbours from Elmore Street. Everyone had contributed to the wedding feast, though Mrs Bailey, Hester herself, and Millie had spent days preparing it. There was cold ham, tongue, cold beef and sausage rolls, as well as quantities of sandwiches, hard-boiled eggs, pickled onions and a number of huge bowls of trifle. Mr Briggs at the bakery had iced and decorated the wedding cake, which Mrs Bailey had made, and the hall was gay with holly and ivy which the children had collected from the surrounding area.

Dick and Hester, seated at the head of the table, had their first opportunity for a quiet word. 'I left a message for Ted at the shipping office, telling him about the wedding on the off chance that he might be back in Liverpool for Christmas,' Dick told her. 'It were the best wedding present I could have had, to see me brother grinning like an ape and chucking confetti all over us. Mam's so thrilled, she's scarcely took her eyes off him. As for Ruby, Ted's learned a thing or two since he left and isn't worried about reprisals, or anything like that.'

'It'll be a wonderful Christmas with Ted back,' Hester agreed. 'Nothing can make up for the loss of your dad, but at least your mam won't be missing two of her men. We'll be home from our honeymoon in plenty of time to hang up our stockings on Christmas Eve, and we'll go straight round to Elmore Street on Christmas morning. Your mam wants a family Christmas, same as always.'

'Mam's right; we'll all have to do our best to make it a good Christmas, but there isn't one of us that won't be missing Dad sorely,' Dick agreed. 'But Dad wouldn't want us to be miserable, you know. He loved Christmas and was always at his happiest on that day, no matter how hard up we were.' He squeezed Hester's hand. 'You an' me's lucky, queen. I've a good trade and what with the help we're having from the Hetherington-Smiths, and Ted contributing to Mam's expenses, we'll never know the hardships Mam and Dad suffered.'

'Yes, we are lucky,' Hester agreed. 'There aren't many people who are able to have even a couple of days' honeymoon, let alone a whole week. But in a way, I wish we weren't going away at all. We've got our own beautiful home waiting for us and I do so want to start being a proper housewife. Your mam has given me lots of advice and lots of help and it will be such fun to cook and bake and dust and sweep in my own home.'

Dick chuckled. 'You'll be spending the rest of your life cooking and cleaning, so just be grateful that we're having a bit of a holiday first,' he advised her. 'We don't have to worry about Lonnie, since she'll be with Mam, so we might as well enjoy ourselves while we can.'

'You're right. Your mam says Llandudno and the surrounding countryside is beautiful,' Hester said.

Dick gave her a wicked grin. 'I don't think honeymooners spend much time admiring the scenery,' he told her. 'I think they spend most of their time admiring one another. But you're right, of course. I loved the mountains and the moors around Bwlchgwyn. We'll have a grand time, just you wait and see.'

It was the day before Christmas Eve and the last full day of their honeymoon, for Dick and Hester would be returning to Liverpool on the 11.50 train next morning. Right now, however, well wrapped up against the cold, they were having a last walk along the promenade in the windy darkness. To their left, the white-tipped breakers crashed against the shore, and the long roar of the pebbles being dragged back into the ocean as the waves ebbed made conversation difficult. Dick shouted something and Hester dug him in the ribs and yelled that he would have to speak up.

'I asked if you were happy,' Dick bawled. 'Hasn't it been a grand week, queen? I shall miss our walks along the shore each night when we're back in Liverpool.'

'So will I,' Hester shrieked. 'But there are compensations . . .'

'What?' Dick shouted. 'I can't hear you for the wind and the waves.'

Hester laughed and pulled him round so that they were facing back the way they had come. Together, arms round each other, they battled their way along the promenade under the frosty stars. As they turned into their boarding house, Hester glanced back at the humped shoulders of the Great Orme. 'What I was trying to say,' she said, as they entered the warm little hallway, 'was that, much though I've enjoyed this wonderful week, what is ahead of us will be even better. Ordinary married life, when you have the perfect partner, is bound to be wonderful.'

She went to mount the stairs to their room, but Dick caught her round the waist and turned her to face him. 'Tomorrow, real life starts,' he said huskily. 'Things won't always go right, because nothing is perfect, but we'll make it a good life, Hester, troubles an' all. Oh, Mrs Hester Bailey, I *do* love you!'

To find out more about Katie Flynn why not join the Katie Flynn Readers' Club and receive a twice-yearly newsletter.

To join our mailing list to receive the newsletter and other information* write with your name and address to:

Katie Flynn Readers' Club
The Marketing Department
Arrow Books
20 Vauxhall Bridge Road
London
SW1V 2SA

Please state whether or not you would like to receive information about other Arrow saga authors.

*Your details will be held on a database so we can send you the newsletter(s) and information on other Arrow authors that you have indicated you wish to receive. Your details will not be passed to any third party. If you would like to receive information on other Random House authors please do let us know. If at any stage you wish to be deleted from our Katie Flynn Readers' Club mailing list please let us know.

arrow books

ALSO AVAILABLE IN ARROW

Orphans of the Storm

Katie Flynn

Jess and Nancy, girls from very different backgrounds, are nursing in France during the Great War. They have much in common for both have lost their lovers in the trenches, so when the war is over and they return to nurse in Liverpool, their future seems bleak.

Very soon, however, their paths diverge. Nancy marries an Australian stockman and goes to live on a cattle station in the Outback, while Jess marries a Liverpudlian. Both have children; Nancy's eldest is Pete, and Jess has a daughter, Debbie, yet their lives couldn't be more different.

When the Second World War is declared, Pete joins the Royal Air Force and comes to England, promising his mother that he will visit her old friend. In the thick of the May blitz, with half of Liverpool demolished and thousands dead, Pete arrives in the city to find Jess's home destroyed and her daughter missing. Pete decides that whatever the cost, he must find her . . .

From the rigours of the Australian Outback to war-ravaged Liverpool, Debbie and Pete are drawn together . . . and torn apart . . .

arrow books

ALSO AVAILABLE IN ARROW

Darkest Before Dawn

Katie Flynn

The Todd family are strangers to city life when they move into a flat on the Scotland Road; their previous home was a canal barge. Harry gets a job as a warehouse manager and his wife, Martha, works in a grocer's shop, whilst Seraphina trains as a teacher, Angela works in Bunney's Department Store and young Evie starts at regular school.

Then circumatsnces change and Seraphina takes a job as a nippy in Lyon's Corner House. Customers vie for her favours, including an old friend, Toby.

When war is declared the older girls join up, leaving Evie and Martha to cope with rationing, shortages, and the terrible raids on Liverpool which devastate the city. Meanwhile, Toby is a Japanese POW, working on the infamous Burma railway and dreaming of Seraphina . . .

arrow books